PRAISE FOR

The Darling

"Russell Banks's work presents without falsehood and with tough affection the uncompromising moral voice of our time. You find the craziness of false dreams, the political inequalities, and somehow the sliver of redemption. I trust his portraits of America more than any other—the burden of it, the need for it, the hell of it."

—MICHAEL ONDAATJE

"Russell Banks's twentieth-century Liberia is as hellish a place as Joseph Conrad's nineteenth-century Congo. The only creatures that behave with humanity are the apes. A dark and disturbing book."

—J. M. COETZEE

"Hannah [the narrator of *The Darling*] is a descendant of Joan Didion's alienated, terminally detached women . . . and she is a relative, too, of Graham Greene's quiet but not so innocent Americans and V. S. Naipaul's Western war tourists, who somehow imagine they are exempt from the chaos and violence they witness in their wanderings abroad."

—*New York Times*

ALSO BY RUSSELL BANKS

The *Darling*

RUSSELL BANKS

HARPER ● PERENNIAL

NEW YORK ● LONDON ● TORONTO ● SYDNEY

To C. T., the beloved

and in memory of Anne Trachtenberg Hughes (d. 2004)
and Charles Pratt Twichell (d. 2004)

HARPER ⬤ PERENNIAL

FIRST HARPER PERENNIAL EDITION PUBLISHED 2005.

Designed by Elliott Beard

The Library of Congress has catalogued the hardcover edition as follows:
   Banks, Russell.
      The darling / Russell Banks.
         p. cm.
      ISBN 0-06-019735-8
      1. Americans—Liberia—Fiction. 2. Human-animal relationships—
Fiction. 3. Animals—Treatment—Fiction. 4. Endangered species—Fiction.
5. Women—Liberia—Fiction. 6. Chimpanzees—Fiction. 7. Liberia—
Fiction. I. Title.
PS3552.A49D37   2004
813'.54—dc22   2004047431

ISBN-10: 0-06-095735-2 (pbk.)
ISBN-13: 978-0-06-095735-3 (pbk.)

05 06 07 08 09 ❖/RRD 10 9 8 7 6 5 4 3 2 1

I

AFTER MANY YEARS of believing that I never dream of anything, I dreamed of Africa. It happened on a late-August night here at the farm in Keene Valley, about as far from Africa as I have been able to situate myself. I couldn't recall the dream's story, although I knew that it was in Africa, the country of Liberia, and my home in Monrovia, and that somehow the chimps had played a role, for there were round, brown, masklike faces still afloat in my mind when I awoke, safe in my bed in this old house in the middle of the Adirondack Mountains, and found myself overflowing with the knowledge that I would soon return there.

It wasn't a conscious decision to return. More a presentiment is all it was, a foreboding perhaps, advancing from the blackest part of my mind at the same rate as the images of Liberia drifted there and broke and dissolved in those dark waters where I've stored most of my memories of Africa. Memories of Africa and of the terrible years before. When you have kept as many secrets as I have for as long as I have, you end up keeping them from yourself as well. So, yes, into my cache of forgotten memories of Liberia and the years that led me there—that's where the dream went. As if it were someone else's secret and were meant to be kept from me, especially.

And in its place was this knowledge that I would soon be going back—foreknowledge, really, because I didn't make the decision until later that day, when Anthea and I had finished killing the chickens and were wrapping them in paper and plastic bags for delivery and pickup.

It was at the end of summer, the beginning of an early autumn, and though barely a year ago, it feels like a decade, so much was altered in that year. The decade here: now, *that* seems like a few days and nights is all, because nothing except the same thing has happened here day after day, season after season, year after year. No new or old returning lovers, no marriages or divorces, no births or deaths, at least among the humans. Just the farm and the world that nourishes and sustains it. Timeless, it has seemed.

The farm is a commercial operation, inasmuch as I sell most of what I grow, but in truth it's more like an old-fashioned family farm, and to run it I've had to give over my personal clock. I've had to abandon all my urban ways of measuring time and replace them with the farm's clock, which is marked off by the needs and demands of livestock and the crops, by the requirements of soil and the surge and flux of weather. It's no wonder that farmers in the old days were obsessed with the motions of the planets and the waxing and waning of the moon, as if their farms were the bodies of women. I sometimes think it's because I *am* a woman—or maybe it's merely because I lived all those years in Liberia, adapted to African time—that I was able to adapt so easily to the pace and patterns and rhythmic repetitions of nature's clock and calendar.

It was *as usual*, then, on that August morning, with the darkness just beginning to pull back from the broad river valley to the forests and the mountains looming behind the house, that I woke at five-thirty and came downstairs wearing my flannel nightgown and slippers against the pre-dawn chill, with the dogs clattering behind me, checked the temperature by the moon-faced thermometer outside the kitchen window (still no frost, which was good, because we'd neglected to cover the tomatoes), and put the dogs out.

I made coffee for Anthea, who comes in at six and says she can't do a thing until after her second cup, and the other girls, who come in at seven. I lingered for a few moments in the kitchen while the coffee brewed, enjoying the dark smell of it. I never drink coffee, having been raised on tea, a habit I took from my father as soon as he'd let me, but I do love the smell of it when it's brewing and buy organic Colombian beans from a mail-order catalogue and grind them freshly for each pot, just for the aroma.

For a few moments, as I always do, I stood by the window and watched the dogs. They are Border collies, father and daughter, Baylor and Winnie, and when they have done their business, the first thing they do every morning is patrol the property, reclaiming their territory and making sure that during the night nothing untoward has happened. Usually I watch them work and think of them as working for me. But this morning they looked weirdly different to me, as if during the night one of us, they or I, had changed allegiances. They looked like ghost dogs, moving swiftly across the side yard in the gray pre-dawn light, disappearing into shadows cast by the house and oak trees, darting low to the ground into the garage, then reappearing and moving on. Today they worked for no one but themselves; that's how I saw them. Their gait was halfway between a trot and a run—fast, effortless, smooth, and silent, their ears cocked forward, plumed tails straight back—and they seemed more like small wolves than carefully trained and utterly domesticated herding animals.

For a moment they scared me. I saw the primeval wildness in them, their radical independence and selfishness, the ferocity of their strictly canine needs. Perhaps it was the thin, silvery half-light and that I viewed them mostly in silhouette as they zigged and zagged across the yard, and when they'd checked the garage, an open shed, actually, where I park the pickup truck and my Honda, they moved on to the barn and from there to the henhouse, where the rooster crowed, and then loped all the way to the pond in the front field, where they woke the ducks and geese, never stopping, running in tandem, a pair of single-minded predators sifting their territory at peak efficiency.

In their mix of wildness and control, they were beautiful. In their silence and indistinct, shape-changing fluidity, they frightened me. Five minutes ago they had been under my control, curled in my bed, crowding me to one side of it like a pair of human children. And now they were wild dogs, the kind of beasts the ancient people glimpsed slipping through the brush at dawn between the campsite and the forest.

They had not changed overnight, of course. But maybe, because of my dream of Africa and the chimps, I had, and the dogs were sensing it, as if I had somehow betrayed them. Then when Anthea drove in along the lane from the road, headlights bobbing like heavy fruit on a tree as her beat-up Jimmie pickup passed along the ruts, the dogs ran to her truck as they do every day, and when she stepped out they greeted her with their usual yipping commotion and followed her to the side porch. But when they entered the kitchen behind her, they slipped quickly into the living room, then furtively circled through the dining room to the kitchen again and made for the door and scratched at it to be let back out.

Anthea yanked off her cap and ruffled her auburn curls with one hand and watched the dogs. She screwed up her face and said, "What's with them doggies?"

"I don't know," I said. "Maybe something spooked them."

She opened the door, and the dogs bolted across the yard and out of sight. "Must be you that's spooking them, Hannah." She laughed and filled her mug with coffee, sighed heavily, and sat down at the table.

"Maybe it's the moon. I had strange dreams all night. You?"

"Nope. Slept like a hibernated bear. Full moon's not for another three days anyhow." Anthea is impish and winking, a large woman, strong; if she were a man you'd call her burly. She has a broad, flat face the shape and color of a raspberry, a peasant face, some might say, and probably a lot of the summer people have. But if you look, you can tell at once that she's good humored and hard working and possesses an abundance of mother wit. Everything about her expresses intelligent energy.

She's a local, and I, of course, am not. When I first bought the place from her aunt and uncle and learned at the closing that Anthea had run the farm by herself for years, I knew that I would need her at least as much as her invalided uncle and bedridden aunt had, and I hired her on the spot to be my manager. Besides, I felt sorry for her and angry on her behalf. Her aunt and uncle, having elected to move to the village and live at the Neighborhood House, an assisted-living home for elderlies, had put the farm up for sale without consulting her. She told me that she drove home one afternoon from picking up their weekly groceries at the Stop & Shop in Lake Placid and saw a For Sale sign posted where the lane left the road, and another stuck in the middle of the front yard.

Anthea should have inherited the farm. Or her uncle should have somehow arranged for her to buy it from them. Her parents died when she was a child, and her uncle and aunt had raised her as their own. But she was an unmarried woman in love with a married woman from the next town, and the affair was widely known, probably known even by the woman's alcoholic husband, a house painter who rarely worked but was liked and looked after in the town because of his sweet nature and their three small children.

Her aunt and uncle went straight from the closing at the realtor's office to the Neighborhood House. When they are dead, whatever's left, if anything, of the nearly one hundred thirty thousand dollars I gave them for the farm will likely go to Anthea. But it won't let her buy the place. Not even if I were willing to sell it. The farm is worth three times now what it went for in 1991. I may feel sorry for Anthea and angry on her behalf, but I wouldn't sell her the farm at a discount. The truth is, I'm not very generous and don't mind saying so.

The other girls, Frieda, Nan, and Cat, arrived at their usual times, Frieda and Nan together at seven roaring up on Nan's motorcycle, and Cat, drifting in ten minutes later like a petal falling from a daisy, strolling blithely down the lane as if wondering what to do with this lovely, end-of-summer day opening up ahead of her, when she knew very well that

Anthea and I had her day all laid out for her. Cat's a third-generation hippie, in her late teens, a dreamy throwback to the sixties, her grand-parents' era. My era. Catalonia's her real name, given to her at birth by her parents, Raven and Rain, who got their names in adulthood from a Bengali guru on a New Mexico commune, Cat told me. Her woozy, laid-back affect and language are the same as her parents' and grandparents', but she's replaced their form of soft, open-ended rebellion with a post-hippie, puritanical adherence to abstinence. She's a drug-free, home-schooled, vegan virgin from Vermont, childlike and winsome on the surface, but inside tight as a fist. Cat's the type of girl thirty years ago I would have tried to recruit for Weatherman. Cat is a girl you can picture nowadays becoming a born-again Christian fundamentalist, dark and judgmental. She's the kind of girl I once was.

But Anthea and I and the other girls love Cat and can't help pro-tecting her—mostly from ourselves, as it turns out, and our rough edges and indulgences. None of us is drug free, virginal, or even a part-time vegetarian. We smoke, drink beer after work and stronger stuff often till bedtime, and eat meat whenever possible.

I hadn't meant to hire an all-female workforce and don't hold to it on principle. It evolved naturally, first with Anthea, who knew who in town was looking for work—which turned out to be pretty exclusively women and girls. It was early summer when I moved in, and all the men and boys who wanted to work already had jobs, most of them seasonal, and weren't interested in organic gardening or raising free-range chick-ens or renovating long-neglected apple orchards—women's work. And they certainly weren't eager to take orders from two women, one of them a skinny, white-haired, rich bitch *from away*, as they say here, who didn't know what she was doing anyhow, the other a tough-mouthed lesbian from town who knew all their dirty little secrets. So we hired local high-school girls, out-of-work nurses, college dropouts living temporarily with their parents, young mothers whose husbands had left them and weren't paying child support, and sometimes off-season winter athletes, like

Frieda and Nan, ski bums and ice climbers who spend the six snow-and-ice-free months up here in the mountains.

The place is called Shadowbrook Farm, a name I'd never have given it myself—a little too poetic or, if taken another way, morbid, almost gothic—but it came with the property. And since it was still known locally as Shadowbrook Farm and reflected the physical fact of the wide, year-round brook meandering through the fluttery shadows cast by the groves of birches and other hardwoods at the far end of the broad front meadow, I saw no reason to change the name. The brook—it's really a river, the Ausable River—is the most picturesque aspect of the old farm, which is otherwise a simple, nineteenth-century colonial house with a wide front porch; the three tipped outbuildings we use for storing vehicles, farm machinery, hay, and feed; a tool shed; and the henhouse and sheepfold that Anthea and I built ourselves that first summer.

Strangely, more than anything else about the farm, more than the land or the buildings or the animals and crops, I feel the river is mine. My permanent, personal property. Yet, unlike everything else here, the river continuously changes. It talks to me: I've heard voices coming from it. The voices of children, usually. I hear them from the porch, from the kitchen, and from my bedroom upstairs at the front of the house, at all times of day and night in all seasons, even with the windows closed— long conversations and sometimes songs whose words I can almost make out, as if there were a playground out there on the far side of the field and the children were calling to one another or to me in a language other than English or were singing another country's nursery rhymes and songs.

I don't know if it's because it's all women, but over the years everyone I've hired has seemed to enjoy working here. It's hard work, and I can be demanding, I know, and edgy, moody, and not all that communicative or personal, although I like to think I'm democratic and fair-minded and, when it comes to expectations, reasonable. But I'm not easily intimate, haven't been for years. Maybe never. And while I think of Anthea, for instance, as a close friend, perhaps the closest friend I have in this town or anywhere, a woman who tells me everything she knows about herself, the truth is I don't really return the confidence or offer her much information about myself, especially my past. I've given her only the bits and pieces that I've given everyone else in this town since the day I first arrived here eleven years ago, a suddenly wealthy woman who had inherited from her recently deceased mother, the widow of her famous father, an estate worth half a million dollars after taxes and the copyrights to the famous father's five best-selling books. No one locally knows the details, of course, although it was obvious from the beginning to everyone that I was a woman of means.

Keene Valley is a small town, a village, and because I couldn't really keep it a secret and didn't want to anyhow, everyone knew or soon learned from my lawyer, from the realtor who handled my purchase of the farm, or from Anthea—to whom I had to confide a few things, after all, or I'd look like I had something dangerous to hide—that before coming here to the Northcountry I had lived for many years in West Africa, in a country called the Republic of Liberia.

Wherever *that* is. Someplace out there in the jungle was close enough.

TEN DAYS LATER, I rode overland in the dark, traveling northwest from Côte d'Ivoire into Liberia and down to the coast from the Nimba highlands, most of the time hidden under a tarpaulin in the back of a truckload of milled boards. At first and for several hours, I rode up front beside the trucker. I had crossed the border illegally, but with no more difficulty than if I'd been a crate of Chinese rifles or a case of Johnny Walker whiskey. In West Africa, if you're carrying enough U.S. cash, nearly any legal technicality can be erased. It had been a quick, hundred-dollar arrangement made with the driver of the truck, a slim, middle-aged Lebanese from Monrovia, a man with yellow eyes who licked his lips a lot and smiled like a lizard. His name was Mamoud.

He owned the truck and was able to buy gas for it and bribe the guards at the borders—obviously an intelligent man thriving in evil times, and was dangerous therefore. I'd been passed on to Mamoud by the driver of the bush taxi I'd hired at the Abidjan airport to take me as far as Danane, a few kilometers east of the Liberian border. I hadn't known it, but they were a team, the taxi driver and the trucker. Everyone in West Africa eventually turns out to be a member of a team.

At this particular crossing I was only smuggled goods, contraband, but at Robertsfield Airport in Monrovia or at one of the more carefully patrolled crossings, I'd have been a potential enemy of the state, stopped for certain and turned around and sent back to Côte d'Ivoire or possibly arrested and jailed. Which is why I had flown from JFK into Abidjan, on a Côte d'Ivoire tourist visa with no entry visa for Liberia. There had been no point in my even applying for one, and no reason to fly directly from Abidjan to Monrovia—quite the opposite, if I wanted to get into Liberia at all. Although the war was officially long over, the man who'd begun it, Charles Taylor—with whom I had once enjoyed a long-time personal relationship, let me say that much, and I will eventually tell you about that, too—was now president, elected by people who had voted for him to stop him from killing them. His enemies, the few who had come out of the war alive, had scattered into the jungles and across the borders into Sierra Leone or Guinea and had regrouped or, like me, had made their way to North America and Europe, where they plotted the death of the president and their own eventual return.

We had no problems at the border crossing, where Mamoud was evidently known and liked and must have had outstanding favors owed him. The soldiers simply waved him through, even with an unknown white woman sitting beside him. *Mamoud's French girlfren', prob'ly. Dem Lebaneses got a taste for dem skinny ol' white ladies.* Laughter all around.

And then I was back in Liberia once again, passing darkened daub-and-wattle huts with conical thatched roofs and clusters of small cinder-block houses with roofs of corrugated tin and bare front porches and swept dirt yards and, alongside the road, a barefoot man or boy walking, suddenly splashed by the glare of the headlights, refusing to show his face or turn, just stepping off the road a foot or two, then disappearing into the blackness behind. Inside the roadside huts and houses I saw now and then a candle burning or the low, orange glow of a kerosene lantern, and here and there, close to the door, the red coals of a charcoal fire pit, and I caught for a second the smell of roasted meat and a glimpse of the ghostly figure of a woman tending the fire, her back to the road. It was all immediately familiar to me and comforting, and yet at the same time new and exotic, as if this were my first sight of the place and people and I had not lived here among them for many years. It was as if I had only read about them in novels and from that had vividly imagined them, and now they were actually before me, fitting that imagined template exactly, but with a sharpness and clarity that subtly altered everything and made it fresh and new.

It was the same anxious, edgy mingling of the known and unknown that greeted me when I made my first journey into the American South nearly forty years ago, when I was a college girl using her summer vacation to register black voters in Mississippi and Louisiana. I was an innocent, idealistic, Yankee girl whose vision of the South had arisen dripping with magnolia-scented decay and the thrill of racial violence from deep readings of William Faulkner and Flannery O'Connor. A newly minted rebel, fresh faced and romantic, I rode the bus south that summer with hundreds like me into Mississippi, confident that we were about to cleanse our parents' racist, oppressive world by means of idealism and simple hard work.

Up to that point, my most radical act had been to attend Brandeis instead of Smith, and I had done that solely to please my father and to avoid granting my mother's unspoken wish that I follow her example. I'd never been out of New England, except for a high-school civics class trip to Washington, D.C., and a flight to Philadelphia for an admissions interview at Swarthmore, my second choice for college after Brandeis and my father's first choice. But I had gazed overlong into those Southern novels and stories, and for many weeks that first summer in the South they provided the reflecting pool in which I saw where I was and the black and white people who lived there. Eventually, of course, literature got displaced by reality, as it invariably does, but for a while my everyday life had the clarity, intensity, and certitude of fiction.

A FEW MILES WEST of the town of Ganta, the road bends perilously close to the Guinea border, where, as I knew from the newspapers at home, there had been sporadic fighting in the last year between small bands of regular and irregular soldiers from the two neighboring countries—the usual jockeying for control of the Nimba diamond traffic. Even the *New York Times* seemed to know about that, which had surprised me. It was here, in the middle of a long stretch between rural villages, that Mamoud abruptly pulled over and parked the truck by the side of the road.

He told me to get out and bring my backpack, and I thought, *Damn him! Damn the man. He knows who I am, or he's just figured it out and he's got evil on his mind.* Back at the border, just as we crossed, he had insisted on learning my last name. When I said it, Sundiata, Woodrow's well-known last name, he didn't react. But I knew at once that I should have said only what it read on my passport, Musgrave, my father's last name. Mamoud had merely smiled and then said nothing for the entire two hours after.

The old, all-too-familiar, Liberian paranoia came rushing over me. It's in the air you breathe here. It's like a virus. You can't escape or defeat it. It hits you suddenly, like when you've had a close call. At first you feel foolish for not having been more frightened and warily suspicious, and you promise yourself that it won't happen again, it had better not, because next time you may not be so lucky. From then on, you assume that everyone is lying, everyone wants to hurt you, to steal from you, and may even want to kill you.

I got slowly down from the truck, slung my pack onto my back, and made ready to bolt. On the near side the jungle came up tight to the road, but on the far side of the road I saw a field of high sawtooth grass and knew that if I got there before him, he'd have trouble catching me in the dark. I had no idea what I'd do after he gave up the chase and drove on. *If he gave up and drove on.* I was three hundred kilometers from the city of Monrovia, a white American woman afoot and alone. Never mind that there was probably a standing warrant for my arrest and the U.S. embassy would do nothing to protect me. All my chits with the Americans had been spent a decade ago. And never mind that there would probably be rumors of a reward offered by Charles Taylor personally, making me a target of opportunity for any Liberian with a knife or machete to slice my throat or take off my head. Liberia is a small country, and in any village, even out here in Nimba, my corpse could be exchanged for a boom box or maybe a motorbike and passed along in a farther exchange and then another, the price going up with each transaction, until finally what was left of my body, maybe just my head with its telltale hair, got dropped at the gate of the Executive Mansion in Monrovia.

Beyond all that, even if I was just being paranoid in that Liberian way, and none of it were true, and there was no warrant, no reward, and in the passage of time and the blur of alcohol and drugs and the intoxication of having ruled his tiny country with absolute power for so many years, Charles had forgotten me altogether, I was nonetheless a white woman alone, a sexual curiosity, spoilage, perhaps, at my advanced age, but with a little use still left to the madmen and crazed boys here in the madhouse.

For the first time since leaving my farm in the Adirondacks, I wondered if somewhere along the way—going back to those early days in Mississippi and Louisiana and coming forward to the afternoon at the farm when I suddenly announced to Anthea that I was returning to Liberia to learn what had happened to my sons—I wondered if I had lost my mind. Not figuratively, but literally. I thought, *I could be a madwoman.* And I wondered if I was standing there in the dark by the side of a narrow, unpaved road in the eastern hills of Liberia because somewhere back there, without knowing it, I'd lost touch with reality. Lost it in small bits, a single molecule of sanity at a time in a slow, invisible, irreversible process of erosion, and couldn't notice it while it was happening, couldn't take its measure, until now, when it was too late.

On the driver's side of the truck, Mamoud was hurriedly unfolding a stiff, old tarpaulin and spreading it over the lumber and tying it down at the corners. He worked his way around to my side, and I darted four or five steps away from him, ready to make my escape. I looked toward the front of the truck, searching for a rock, a brick, something to injure him with.

Mamoud said, "Checkpoints be comin' up now, missy. Dem won't bother me none, but mebbe best f' you t' hide back here." He held up the corner of the tarp and indicated with a nod a hollowed-out area the size of a coffin in the middle of the cargo.

"Oh! You want to hide me," I said, relieved. "You don't think that's the first place they'll look, under the tarp?"

They wouldn't look there, he explained, because they knew that that was where he carried the stuff he didn't want them to see. Perfect Liberian logic. Surprised at the turnaround and a little shaky, for I had gone into fight or flight and my adrenalin was running high, I climbed onto the stacked lumber. When I had lain myself down in the hiding place, Mamoud drew the tarp over me and finished tying it at the corners, leaving a flap loose so I could peek out and breathe fresh air. A moment later, the truck was chugging along the rutted road and then trundling steadily downhill from the highlands towards the towns of the savannah and the cities of the coast.

ALL THROUGH THE NIGHT I rode back there, stretched out between the boards, sweltering from the heat, jostled, pitched, and bumped, and every now and then I peeked out from under the tarpaulin, and when I did I felt more borne down by the wet air than by the stiff canvas. A decade in the hills and valleys of upstate New York and I'd almost forgotten the moist weight, even at night, of the tropical air against my body, its nearly tangible density, as if, between the tarpaulin and the freshly planed planks that I lay upon, a large animal were holding me down. And the odor of the bleeding green lumber and of the canvas that hid me, old, patched, and smelling of rotten fruit and urine and wood smoke, made me nauseated and dizzy.

My discomfort disappointed the puritan in me. I wondered if in those few years away I'd turned delicate and, traveling again in Africa, would have to hold a scented hanky to my nose. For that's all this was, the same old smell of Africa and its sense-surrounding, watery heat and its sounds—the blat of a battered, out-of-tune diesel truck and, whenever the truck passed through a village or town or came to a crossing and slowed and the clatter of the engine eased, the yips of a small dog, the clack of dominoes against a masonite lapboard, or a transistor radio playing its lonely juju song to no one at a village crossroads cookshop. Once, I heard the call of a desperate boy from the side of the road as the truck rumbled past him, *Take me wit' you, take me to Monrovia, to the city, an' from there, m'am, carry me to the Great World beyond, where is plenty of jollof rice an' tinned meats an' good water, where no one sick, no one hungry, no one 'fraid!* All of it, his whole, long, hapless plea compressed into one repeated, fading cry, "Hoy, hoy, hoy!" as the truck picked up speed and roared down the red-dirt road into the African night.

Several times the truck was stopped at checkpoints—gates, we used to call them—at Ganta and where the road crosses the St. John River. Without looking, I could tell where we were, because the map of Liberia and its few roads were still clear in my mind's eye, and I knew people in these towns, or once had known them, and was even related to some of them by marriage, for we were not far now from Fuama, my husband's tribal village. But surely most of those people, all Liberians, were gone by now, dead or swept away like dry leaves by the fierce wind that had blown across the country in the civil war and burned by the fires of chaos that had followed. Even if they had somehow survived and still lived in their old homes and villages, they would have been of little help to me anyhow. Not now. Not back then either, when we were all running for our individual lives.

The truck wheezed and slowed and downshifted, then crept along for a few moments at a walking pace, and I knew that we were approaching another checkpoint. Then the truck stopped, and I heard men's low voices, speaking first in a Krahn dialect, then switching quickly to Liberian English for Mamoud, the Monrovian Lebanese, with light, conspiratorial, male-bonding laughter interjected—he was a regular on this route, obviously, and he paid the soldiers on time and gave them good dash. *Yeah, Mamoud, him a* good *Arab guy.* A loud hand slap on the front fender of the truck, like a slap on a horse's flank, granting permission to leave, and the truck moved ahead again, soon picking up speed.

I was wrapped in my thoughts in the darkness like an animal hiding in its burrow. I had a plan. I wasn't so out of touch with reality, I wasn't so far gone that I had come out here without some sort of blueprint. Lord knows it wasn't much of a plan. It couldn't be; there was so little here that I could predict or control. I had in my mind merely a vaguely worded, partially completed outline whose blanks I would fill in as I passed from moment to moment: I would get into the country somehow; I would make my way to Monrovia; I would ask after my sons in a way that would not put me or them in danger, although I had no idea yet whom I would be able to ask; and I would either go to my sons, wherever they were, and try to bring them home with me or, if no one could tell me where they were, I would leave the country and return to my farm. That was it. That was as far in advance of my actions as I was able to think.

I was carrying enough U.S. currency around my waist and in my backpack to buy my way through these few steps and probably enough to let me take advantage of any exigencies or opportunities that arose. Unless, of course, I were attacked, stripped, robbed, or worse. Mostly, though, I counted on buying my safety. The comforting and most useful thing about total corruption is that it's total. It's systemic, top to bottom, and therefore predictable and more or less rational. So I wasn't being especially brave or even reckless.

I don't travel in fear anyhow; I never have. When I am afraid, I don't travel at all; I stay put. Years ago, when I was in my early thirties and living underground in the States, moving from safe house to safe house, I was taught by comrades more experienced at flight than I that if a person, especially a woman, travels in fear, she is never safe. So if you're afraid, don't move. Freeze. Disappear into the scenery. You'll only attract attention to yourself by running.

Despite my plan, however—which was like a long-faded path through the jungle, nearly overgrown now, with only a few landmarks still recognizable—and despite there being an ostensible goal, a consciously chosen destination that I'd imagined lying at the end of the path, it felt as if I were being mysteriously drawn towards that goal by a magnet, and that the pull was generated out there, in Liberia. Not here, inside me. I was being reeled in. I could say, and had, that I was going out to Liberia to learn what happened to my sons after I left the country those many long years ago and, if possible, to bring them back with me to the States; I could say, and had, that I was going out there to honor my husband's memory somehow, a private, solitary thing I had to do. I could say that I was going to try to learn what happened to my friends and my husband's family. I had said these things any number of times— to Anthea, to the other girls at the farm, to the few good citizens of Keene Valley whom I counted as friends. And to myself. I said them especially to myself. All the way across the Atlantic to Abidjan, then in the bush taxi to the border between Côte d'Ivoire and Liberia, and down to the coast from Nimba in the back of the truck, I kept naming my reasons for coming there.

And I will tell you something that at the time made me ashamed, although now it makes a kind of sense. Not moral sense, but psychological, emotional sense. From the beginning, from the day that I decided to leave my farm and return there, I did not once picture my husband Woodrow's dark, perpetually somber face in my mind; nor did I see the faces of the boys, little Dillon, my crackling smart, hyperactive one, or angelic Paul, my peacemaker, or William, as somber as his father. They were my family—the only husband I have ever had and probably ever will, and my missing sons, my only children, for I know that I will never bear another. I am too old. Old and dried up, a husk of a woman. So they are not just the family of my past; they are the family of my future as well. But it was as if they had become names only. I have their photographs in frames on the sideboard in my living room at the farm, all four faces gazing at me, and another set is on my bedroom dresser. Yet once I had actually departed from the farm and driven in my Honda along the lane to the road and headed down the Northway from the Adirondacks to New York City, once I was on my way to Africa again, I did not, I could not, I *would* not see their faces. No, the truth is I saw only the faces of my chimpanzees.

On a deep—perhaps the most basic—level, my chimpanzees were drawing me back. Not my husband's memory, not my sons. My chimpanzees. And during that long night coming down the half-destroyed road from Nimba to Monrovia, enduring the pronged heat under the canvas tarp as if I were inside a covered, black, cast-iron pot baking in an oven, I lay there and remembered the creatures that I had abandoned, my chimpanzees. I did not remember my husband or my sons or our life together. I remembered only those poor, confused creatures whom I had nurtured and protected for so long, the innocents for whom I had been willing to give my life—or so I had believed.

In the early days, when I first set up the sanctuary, I cared mainly for the babies, newborns and infants. I had two helpers more experienced with chimps than I. They took care of the older, more demanding and sometimes dangerous chimps, who often arrived at the sanctuary traumatized by abuse and from afar, found stuffed into packing crates at JFK or LAX or in birdcages or cat carriers on their way to an even more abused life and a mercifully early death in a pharmaceutical laboratory in Vienna or New Jersey. To help them, one needed much more experience and knowledge of animals than I had then. So at first I worked in the nursery, as we called it, and from the appearance and actions of the babies in my care, from the quality of their gazes and the intensity of their attention, I thought it was in their nature to dream, even when awake. From the start I tried to penetrate their consciousness, for it was obvious that they possessed consciousness, and to me its particular quality was the same as what the Australian Aborigines meant by dreamtime—not drifting or soporifically sliding through life, their attention always askew or elsewhere, like ours, but behaving as if they were free to look at every single thing as if it had never been seen before, as if everything, a leaf, an ant, a human ear, were of terrible and wondrous significance. As it is in a dream. Or as it must be for someone suffering from dementia. For them, it seemed there was no consciousness of past or future, only the immediate present, from which nothing could distract them. For us it's almost the opposite. They are nonhuman animals imprisoned on the far side of speech, but they share nearly ninety-nine percent of our genes and more closely resemble humans than a bluebird from the East Coast of the United States resembles a bluebird from the West. But because they're mute, from birth to death locked out of spoken language, their powers of concentration appear to exceed ours—except when we dream, when we, too, are mute.

And so I began to call them dreamers. Mornings, when I headed from the house for the lab or later on for the sanctuary, I might say to Woodrow, "I've got a new dreamer coming in today, a baby. They found him in a market in Buchanan with a chain around his neck." At first Woodrow would smile tolerantly in his usual manner, maybe slightly amused by my, to him, eccentric insistence on referring to them as dreamers. But before long he, too, gave up relying on the word chimpanzee or chimp. The boys, even sooner than their father, took to calling them dreamers, especially Dillon, for whom the word seemed to have a special resonance, as if he thought that he himself might be a dreamer. "How were the dreamers today, Mammi? What's happening with the dreamer that came down from Nimba last week, the one whose mother you said got eaten by the soldiers? Why do they even *want* to eat dreamers, Mammi? You'd have to be kind of crazy, right?"

Early on in the work at the lab and later at the sanctuary, before it had become my obsession and, in a way, my salvation, I wondered where the word *chimpanzee* had come from. It was a peculiar word, I thought. Whenever I said it aloud, I heard a combination of sounds that were slightly comical to me. Their name was a little bit ridiculous and thus ridiculing. Once, shortly after I started the sanctuary, I looked the word up in Woodrow's battered old *Webster's Collegiate*, because I hated calling them that, *chimpanzees* and *chimps*. Their name seemed to make subtle fun of them, to diminish and demean them, and was not at all a word like *human* or even like the names we give to other mammals putatively lower on the evolutionary ladder than chimps, like dogs and lions and horses.

It's a bantu word from the Congo, meaning "mock-man"—a name derived, not from the creature's own nature, but from its relation to us, to humans, as if its essential nature were a lesser version or a negation of ours. It's the only species named in such a purposefully distancing way. It's the not-human. The not-us. The un-man.

Maybe its scientific name would be better, I thought, more democratic somehow, since chimpanzees and humans belong to the same genus, *Anthropopithicus*. But, no, the zoologists had long ago named the creature *Anthropopithicus troglodyte*, and every mother's child knows what a troglodyte is.

Nonetheless, I looked that word up, too, hoping, I suppose, that it would turn out actually to mean something like "a highly intelligent and sociable animal found in sharply decreasing numbers in the jungles of West Africa." But a troglodyte is "one of various races or tribes of men (chiefly ancient or prehistoric) inhabiting caves or dens."

It was circular and kept coming back to us—to *not-us*.

I KNEW THAT the truck had come to a stop beside the sea, for I smelled salt in the air, even from beneath the heavy tarp, and heard the waves breaking on the reef and sandbars beyond. I pushed my way out and inhaled the cool, fresh air of dawn. I grabbed my backpack, rolled off the bed of the truck, and swung down to the gravel roadway. The sky was milky in the east. Half hidden in the mists a few kilometers south, beyond the all-but-abandoned Freeport, was the humped back of Cape Mesurado, and sprawled across the cape like a rumpled, drunken sleeper was the city, Monrovia.

Mamoud leaned from the cab and said, "This where you tol' me to put you, missy. Still got a ways to get to town, y' know."

I said no, this was fine, which puzzled him. He slowly rolled a cigarette and lighted it and studied me for a moment. "Don' make no sense, missy," he said. He studied me some more, as if for the first time considering my use to him and not his to me, and said, "Gimme some dash, missy."

"I paid you already. We're even."

He shook his head no and licked his thin lips, took a deep drag on his cigarette. "Gimme dash," he repeated, and when he reached for the handle to open the door and come out of the truck, I bolted—scrambling from the road down the crumbly landfill through the thorn bushes into the dark, gloomy gully below. I shoved my way through the brush down there for half a hundred yards or so, stumbling over garbage and old tires and broken bottles, sea wrack and road tossings, and then stopped, scratched on the face and bare arms by the puckerbushes, and waited there, crouched close to the wet ground, breathing hard, listening. Finally, I heard the door of the truck slam shut, and heard the truck chunk into gear and slowly move on down the road.

A light, cooling breeze drifted through the underbrush from the sea to land. I stood up and heard the waves lap the shore on the farther side of the gully and break on the reef a quarter mile out and smelled the stink of dead fish and wet sand. Then suddenly the yellow African sun was in the glowing sky, and dawn had been here and gone almost without my seeing it. There are no gray shades this close to the equator, no evening's gloom or dawn's early light. There's night, and then there's day, and night again. The wind shifted slightly, and I smelled wet, charred wood and rotting citrus and fresh human feces. I was alone.

No, I wasn't alone. A dark brown young man, shirtless, scrawny, and wearing only a pair of pale blue nylon running shorts, stared at me from a few feet away. He backed off, eyes wide open, as if frightened of me—but why, I wondered, frightened of what? It should have been the other way around. But I was not afraid of him; he was exactly whom I should have expected to see there. It must have been my long, white hair, straight and undone—surely peculiar to him—my pale skin, the inexplicable presence of such a strange creature in what was probably *his* gully, his personal territory. All of that, I supposed. But there was something more than my oddity reflected off his wide-eyed gaze—it was as if he thought I was a jumby, a ghost.

He waggled a finger at me, *no-no-no*, turned, and scrambled back up the side of the gully to the road, and then away, in the same direction the truck had gone, towards the city.

A madman, I thought. He'll never return now to this place, which had been his field, his little garden, where, like an insect, a dung beetle, he had learned to scavenge his daily food and safely hide himself at night. I had contaminated his place, put a ghost into it. I slung my pack onto my back and made my careful way along the garbage- and trash-strewn incline out of the gully and over the low ridge to the narrow beach below, away from the road, where I turned toward the city, the harbor, the mouth of the river, and the island in the river where, ten years earlier, I had abandoned my dreamers.

AT THE FARM in Keene Valley and throughout the village, I was thought to have gone out to Liberia as a Peace Corps volunteer and somewhere along the way had married an African man and had borne him three brown children. I had framed photographs of them in the house. "That's me with my husband, Woodrow. And those are my sons when they were little boys, Dillon and the twins, Paul and William." And then the photographs of my parents: "That's my father. Yes, *the* Doctor Musgrave. And my mother. Both dead." And no one else.

I volunteered as little as possible. In a partial and carefully reticent way, which people understood once they heard what I had to say, I let on that in the late 1980s, when Liberia erupted in civil war, my husband and sons had been caught up in the violence. "It's one of those wars that never seem to end."

I related this in a way that did not invite further questions, told my story in a low, flattened voice that deflected both inquiry and suspicion that I might be lying or had something to hide. "It was a terrible time . . . People were being brutally murdered. . . . There was chaos every-where. . . . There still is." And so on. It's easy to construct a believable false story from a miscellany of partial truths.

People felt sorry for me and admired my reticence. In my neighbors' and workers' minds, even Anthea's, Africa generally and the Republic of Liberia in particular were places from which any sane American woman would flee anyhow, whatever the cost. Everything I had told them, everything they heard in the post office, at church, at the Noon-mark Diner, convinced my fellow citizens that I had suffered enough already. It was as if I had endured and miraculously survived a terrible disease, and no one wished to cause me unnecessary additional pain by asking for details.

THE DAY IN LATE AUGUST when I decided to return to Liberia arrived and passed in a normal enough manner. Frieda and Nan drove the pickup out to the northside orchard and were filling it with late McIn-tosh apples, and Cat was in the greenhouse seeding the last crop of let-tuce for the season. The dogs slumbered in a circle of sunshine on the grass in front of the house. It was warm, in the high fifties by noon, and sunny—a golden day. The leaves of the maple trees, oaks, and birches in the cool spots along the river had begun turning, tinting the air with pale shades of reflected red and yellow and orange light. Occasionally the first Vs of Canada geese crossed the cloudless sky from north to south, their harsh calls and cries rousing the dogs, who looked at the sky and considered for a few seconds the idea of giving chase, if only to keep up appearances, then gave it up, yawned, and went back to sleep.

Soon there was something far more interesting for them. With the dogs' help, Anthea and I herded the chickens together so we could pack them four to a crate. Though the dogs, Baylor and Winnie, easily kept the hens clustered in one corner of the large, fenced-in pen, the birds were hysterical—there's no other word for it—making the job absurdly difficult and therefore slightly humiliating. Finally, however, we managed to crate enough to fill our standing orders, four dozen of them, all plump broilers, Rhode Island reds, and lugged the crated chickens to the shed that we call the butcher shop, an old tool shop with a cement floor, a double laundry sink, a hose, and a floor drain.

We waited till after lunch before beginning the nasty work of killing the chickens, which we do the old-fashioned way, with a machete and a wooden chopping block. The chopping usually falls to me, as if it were my responsibility, or perhaps my privilege, though I'm sure Anthea would do it if I asked her. I don't really mind; Lord knows, I've seen worse. But it wouldn't be nearly as unpleasant if, when you decapitated the chickens, they didn't bleed the way they do—profusely and in spurts that last longer than you think they should—and their headless bodies didn't scramble wildly around the shed as if in crazed search of eyes and mouths and tiny brains. It's strange, I don't really like poultry or birds generally. They don't quite register with me as animals. They seem more like complicated plants or higher-order insects, and that's more or less how I treat them, providing them from the moment they hatch with the same carefully calculated food, water, space, and shelter as I do the vegetables. Until it comes time to kill them, when they seem suddenly to possess all the familiar mammalian emotions—fear and sadness and love of life. Consequently, whenever I have to decapitate thirty or forty or fifty of the squawking, wild-eyed creatures in a row, it's a stressful, wrenching time for me.

Yet I wouldn't for a minute think of fobbing the job off onto Anthea or anyone else. It feels somehow just and necessary that I do it myself, that I let Anthea lay the puffed-up, panting body of the chicken against the block, that I slap my left hand around the creature's small head as if covering a child's coin purse, stretch out the neck, and with my right hand lift the machete over head and bring it swiftly down, as if driving a nail with a hammer, cutting cleanly through the neck with one stroke. I drop the head into the bucket beside the block, and Anthea tosses the body aside, to let it pump out as much of its blood as it can before the heart stops, and its body staggers in smaller and smaller circles, and finally flops over onto the concrete floor, quivers, shudders, and is dead. The dogs, who know what is happening now, are locked outside the butcher shop, barking wildly, almost joyfully, to be let in.

Forty-eight times I do this. Then we fill the double sinks with water that's hot enough nearly to scald our gloved hands and gather up the still-warm bodies and dip them, and working in a kind of mindless fury, we yank the feathers out by the handful, tossing them in the air, hurrying, pulling feathers with both hands, before the skin of the hens cools and the feathers set and can't be pulled out without tearing the flesh. We cover ourselves, each other, the entire room with feathers— making a bloody, gruesome mess of everything inside those four walls. We stack the naked, headless bodies of the chickens on a counter top, one on top of the other, until we have them arranged in a neat pile, a pink, squared mound of flesh, and all that's left now is the removal of the innards, evisceration, which we do together, standing at the counter side by side with our slender knives, enlarging the anus, reaching into the body cavity and pulling out the organs, separating the liver, gizzard, heart, and kidneys, which we stuff into small plastic bags, and when we have washed the body in cold water, we shove the bag of organs back inside the cavity. Our long, white aprons and knitted wool caps and our faces, hands, and rubber boots are splashed with blood. Feathers and guts are stuck to us everywhere, as if we have been tarred and feathered by an angry mob. We are breathing hard. We have been at this for hours and are nearly done.

We wrap each body in plastic and again in paper, and now it is simply meat, food, protein and fat, ready to be delivered to the little Keene Valley Supermarket or picked up later today by our special-order customers—forty-eight organically fed, free-range chickens, a luxury item here in the Northcountry, hundreds of miles from any gourmet restaurant or store, sold at a price that's competitive with mass-produced, chemically fed, chain-store chickens. I pity those poor sick creatures that, unlike our more fortunate hens, are dosed with antibiotics and spend their entire lives packed in tiny boxes under bright lights in food factories somewhere in Maryland or Arkansas, birds from start to finish raised, fed, watered, killed, plucked, and packaged entirely by shiny machines, never touched by human hands. Our creatures, we believe, have been provided with lives worth living, and they repay us with their healthy, clean bodies.

This, I have convinced myself, is our little battle won. It's me and Anthea and the girls against Tyson's and Frank Perdue and the industrialization of the food chain, and for us it justifies the carnage and the stress and high feelings that the bimonthly killing arouses in us. There's still something of the ideologue inside me, I guess. All these years later. It explains why we find ourselves at the end of the day standing there, bloody and feathered and smelling of gore and guts; it tells us why we are near tears, panting, our chests heaving and our legs weak; and why we look at each other like suddenly estranged lovers. We're doing it, by God, for a *reason*. It's *political*.

"I never get used to this," Anthea said and lighted a cigarette and with a shaking hand passed it to me and lighted another for herself.

I smoked and said nothing. There was still work to do, the cleanup. The dogs, sensing the fun was over, had drifted off, so I swung open the door of the butcher shop and let fresh air and late-afternoon sunlight into the room to dispel the smell of wet rust and motor oil, the odor of spilled blood and opened bodies—the stink of fresh death.

But there was something else, it was the residue of my dream of Africa, a stream of vague, almost erotic feelings that had been released in my sleep and then got left behind when I awoke and the dream dissipated and I could no longer call the generative images and story back to mind—a range of forgotten emotions that the killing of the hens today had summoned and now had suddenly brought forward and that unexpectedly and against my will had taken on the hard focus of a specific desire. I said to Anthea, "If I had to be gone a while, do you think you could run the farm? Could you handle it okay?"

"Well, yeah, I guess. Sure, I could. For how long?"

"I don't know. Maybe a few weeks, maybe longer. Maybe less. Depends on what I find out there."

"Where?"

"Liberia. Africa."

Anthea stared at me in disbelief. "Geez, Hannah, you sure? I mean, *Africa*. How old are they now, your sons? I mean, if they're . . ." She stopped herself mid-sentence. "What're their names? You told me once, but I forget."

Their names, yes. "Dillon and William and Paul." When I left Liberia the names of my sons were Fly, Worse-than-Death, and Demonology. I didn't tell that to Anthea. I added the numbers, the years since I had left Africa, and said, "Twenty-four for William, the twins are twenty-three," and finished her sentence for her, ". . . if they're still alive." But I did not tell her that when I left our home in Monrovia they were fourteen and thirteen. Little boys. She could work out the numbers if she wanted to, but I knew that she wouldn't, because she's a kind woman and loves me.

"All right. Go ahead, and don't you fret the farm, honey. Me and the girls can keep the place running like clockwork. Stay out there in Africa as long as you need to."

"Let's get cleaned up," I said. "You pack the chickens in the cooler, and I'll hose this place down. Then let's take a swim. You up for it?"

"Too damned cold! You got to to belong to one of them whatcha-callits, polar bear clubs, to swim this time of year," she said, and peeled off her bloody apron and cap.

BUT IT WASN'T too cold after all. Nan and Frieda drove in from the orchard, and a little later Cat joined us on the porch, where by then we were drinking beer and yacking in our usual way—I think Frieda was trying to convince Nan to join her on a climb in the Ecuadorean Andes in November, while Anthea and I teased the two, saying there was no way they could handle altitude with their kind of drug use. I sent Cat for the towels, and when she returned, we tossed our empty beer cans in the trash, and the five of us walked arm in arm across the lawn and cut through the field in front of the house, making our way gaily down to the river.

I felt strangely liberated that afternoon, almost like singing, not faking my comradery, as I normally did on these occasions. Up ahead the dogs bounded through the tall grass, scaring up small flocks of slow-moving, chilled grasshoppers, snapping the insects out of the air as they ran.

On the near bank the grove of tall, spreading, fifty-year-old oak trees cast its long shadow out to midstream. Beyond the shadow, all the way to the far bank, the river was in sunlight, glittering and warm. We stripped off our clothes and entered the cool, shaded water, Frieda and Nan first, plunging ahead, showing off their tanned, athletic bodies and their reckless abandon, followed by Anthea, who shoved her way into the water and hollered as she got waist deep, swearing at the cold and at us for talking her into doing a thing this dumb, and behind her came Cat, slender and childlike, holding her arms over her small, tight breasts, until she was up to her chin, when she finally let go of her fragile protection and swam like the others for the sun-warmed water on the farther side.

Finally I entered the stream, more timidly than they, for I am a little shy, actually, and because I am the old one among these women: my breasts are no longer perked, and my thighs and belly are loose, my pubic hair has thinned and is turning gray. But once I was entirely in the water and swimming—my feet free of the ground, my back arched and arms sweeping ahead of me, my legs scissoring easily, powering me into deeper and deeper waters—none of that mattered. My long white hair, still a point of vanity for me, swirled behind me like a bride's veil, and my body felt strong and taut and young again, so that there was no perceptible difference between my body and the bodies of the other women. We were, all five of us, a school of porpoises dipping, diving under, surfacing, rolling over on our backs, and swimming out of the fast-running, shaded half of the stream into the sunlit pool beyond. Once there, we floated in place, and when we spoke our voices were softened and low, as if each of us had entered her own mind alone and when she spoke it was only to let the others know that she was still there, still close by, still their friend.

I leaned back in the water, my arms behind my head, and peered up at the cloudless, drum-tight, pale blue sky, and brought my gaze slowly down to the mountain ridges that surround the valley, where the foliage from halfway up the mountains was already glowing with early-autumn reds and yellows. Turning from the bright striations of the higher altitudes, I looked lower and lower, down through the evergreens to the near bank. And there were the dogs, my black-and-white Border collies, Baylor and Winnie, standing on the shore, watching us. They weren't prancing up and down the bank as they always do, yelping excitedly and after a few moments leaping into the water themselves and paddling out to join us. Instead, today they both stood stock still, tails and ears lowered.

I swam a few yards downstream, separating myself from the others, and when I looked towards shore again, I saw that the dogs' gazes had followed me. I was the one they were watching. Not the others.

"Really, Hannah, what's up with the doggies today?" Anthea called.

"I . . . I don't know."

Nan laughed and said it was because they were too smart to swim in water this cold, and Frieda agreed.

Cat said, "This is so awesome," and disappeared beneath the surface, and when she reappeared a minute later and ten yards downstream from me, the dogs didn't react. They kept their gaze fixed only on me, and their expression was both accusatory and sorrowful, as if I had committed a crime, and only they and I knew about it. But at that moment I could think of nothing bad that I had done.

I suddenly felt heavy, gravity bound, and old again. "I'm going in," I said, and started swimming slowly for shore. When my feet felt the smooth rocks on the bottom, I stood, my shoulders and breasts exposed, and stared back at the dogs. They both cocked their wedge-shaped heads and looked as if they were capable of speech but were waiting for me to speak first.

"What?" I said to them. "What do you know?" I asked. "What do you want to know?"

They turned their heads away, and I nervously laughed and cupping my hands tossed water at them, and they grinned and leapt and yelped. Then, as if suddenly remembering why they were there, the dogs jumped from the bank into the water and, mouths closed, breathing sharply through their nostrils, paddled happily out to join the girls, and I clambered from the river onto the grassy bank and covered my body with a towel and gathered up my blood-stained clothes.

MY STORY IN all its versions is only a tale of too-late. Maybe at best it's a cautionary tale. To my sons I used to say, "Be careful what you wish for. Know what you love best. Beware the things that catch your eye." And this, which I tell to you as well: "Never love someone who can't love you back." The truth is, most of the time, even now, I don't want to tell my story. Not to you, not to anyone. It's almost as if I'm beyond all stories and have been for years. You want to see me in light, but I'm visible only in darkness. I'm obliterated by light, and can't cast it, either. I'm like a white shadow. And at night, when I'm visible, wherever I am, even here on the farm in the heat of summer, I lock all the doors and windows and pull down the shades, draw the curtains, and keep the dogs shut inside my bedroom with me and the bedroom door latched and bolted. I'm as afraid of the dark in upstate New York as the bush people are in Liberia, who sleep with their huts closed tight against the thousands of evil spirits that come in the night to steal people's souls—leopard-devils that bite your throat first and eat you before you die, and two-step snakes that bite you and you take two steps and die, and bad white men and black men from the coast remembered in tales of slave catchers passed down by the elders.

I'm an elder myself now. Fifty-nine this year, in late middle-age, but old enough to have watched other people, my parents, for example, find themselves suddenly elderly and soon dead. Old age is a slow surprise. And at a certain point one's personal history, one's *story*, simply stops unfolding. Change just ends, and one's history is not completed, not ended, but stilled—for a moment, for a month, maybe even for a year. And then it reverses direction and begins spooling backwards. One learns these things at a certain age. It happened to my parents. It happens to everyone who lives long enough. And now it's happened to me. It's as if the whole purpose of an organism's life—of my life, anyhow—were merely for it to reach the farthest extension of its potential with the sole purpose of returning to its single-cell start. As if one's fate were to drop back into the river of life and dissolve there like a salt. And if anything counts for something, it's the return, and not the journey out.

When I returned to Liberia from my little farm in upstate New York that last time and saw at once that I had come back too late, I wondered if it had been, from the very beginning, too late. It was my question way back then; it's my question now. Should I instead have stayed in Liberia a decade ago when the war was still raging and somehow lived there for as long afterwards as possible and shared my husband's known fate and the unknown fates of my sons? Lord knows, it's a simple enough question. But the simple questions are the hardest to answer. They always seem to carry with them a hundred prior questions, all unanswered, and probably in the end unanswerable now anyhow. They had to be answered at the moment they were first asked. Intentionality may be all that matters, but who knows a woman's true intentions? Who knows what she truly wished for? Or what she loved best? Or even what caught her eye? Not Hannah Musgrave Sundiata. Not I. Especially not back then, over a decade ago, when I fled Liberia and left that endless war behind, turned away from the savagery and the madness of it, and abandoned to its flames my home, my husband's body, my lost boys, and left to be shot and eaten by the soldiers my innocent, frightened, beloved dreamers, the eleven apes that had been placed in my charge.

My poor animals; they were mine to protect, the creatures I loved nearly as much as I loved my husband and sons and whom I tried, vain and proud and deluded, to save by placing them onto an island. Which I suppose was only what I wished someone would do for me. Place me onto an island.

A fantasy, that's all it was. Just another fantasy of self-sanctification. It was futile then, and probably futile now, all of it. Even here on this little island.

And yet, that day in the midst of the war, when I boarded that final flight out of Monrovia, if I'd known my true motives for leaving, if I'd examined them closely enough at the time, they might have seemed puny to me, puny and unworthy, and I would not have left at all. I wouldn't have made it to this enchanted isle, my farm—in the good, cheerful company of Anthea and the girls and my faithful collie dogs, all of us caring for sheep and hens and my beautiful gardens—with its inhabitants, me included, sanctified and blessed. And I wouldn't have been obliged to return to Africa one more time as I did last year.

Mainly, we return to a place in order to learn why we left. Nothing else. That's what all those nostalgic novels of return are really about. Had I known at the time my true reasons for leaving in the first place, I probably wouldn't have ended up doing what women have done for eons: I wouldn't have become one of those wives and mothers walking mournfully through the wreckage and desolation made by men and boys trying to kill one another. I wouldn't have become one of those howling widows searching like some ancient Greek woman for her slain husband's body, so that he can be properly buried, would not have become a doleful mother asking for the whereabouts of her lost sons, so that her sons' rage can be calmed, their fears assuaged, and their wounds cleansed and dressed. I would not have gone out to the river island where I had so cleverly placed my dreamers, my charges, and when I got to the island found only their hacked, burnt bones and broken skulls.

In vain. All of it in vain. It's always been that way, yet we keep on doing it. For tens of thousands of years, since before Biblical times, since the species first learned to make weapons and tame fire, women have fled carnage and returned later to gaze at the wreckage of their plundered homes, stunned by the violence of the destruction and its force, and tried to understand why we came back to it, if this is all we can come back to, and why we fled in the first place, since we have no choice but to return, and nothing but loss and permanent grief await us there.

SOMEHOW THE CHIMPANZEES are central to my story, and I can't tell it without them. My heart stops when I picture them in my mind. And I can't think of my husband or my sons at all, beyond naming them. Not this early in the story. And so I'll tell you instead of what happened to the dreamers.

Before I fled the war, for a few days I had help in transporting them to the island from the Toby sanctuary, help I needed, especially with the adults and the adolescent males. We took them out in Kuyo's borrowed motorboat. Kuyo was the man who had worked at the house for us for years, a cousin of Woodrow's, and for a long time he had shown no more interest in non-human animals than most Americans do. Less, actually. To a poor Liberian, an animal that can't be eaten and can't be put to work or serve as trade goods is a liability and deserves only to be punished for it. But somehow the dreamers had begun to invade Kuyo's imagination. Or maybe it was merely my love for them that lit up his sympathies, for he had always regarded me with genuine interest and apparent affection.

I remember sitting on the back steps bottle-feeding a wide-eyed baby girl named Gilly. Kuyo, a tall, dark brown, almost black man, flat chested with wide, bony shoulders, stopped in the patchwork shade of the cotton tree, leaned on his rake, and asked me, "Why you wanna take care of them monkeys alla time, ma'm?"

I tried explaining to him that soon, if we don't take care of the chimps, they'll be gone from the planet forever, and Kuyo's grandchildren and mine will live and die without having seen one. Our grandchildren's grandchildren won't even know that such a creature ever existed, except in legends.

He pushed his lips out and asked me, "Was there, long time before now, way way long time, some kinds of animals, d'you think, that we don't know about? Strange animals to us that we be scairt of in our dreams, but not so strange an' scary-scary to the ancestors? Animals we got no names for no more?" He chewed on his lower lip and studied Gilly for a long moment.

As if the tiny chimp knew the man was watching her and for the first time in his life was contemplating the fate of her species, Gilly rolled her head slightly towards him and returned his look. Kuyo said, "Mebbe one day soon I come out to Toby wit' you an' view these monkeys for myself. See if mebbe I can give 'em a little care now an' then. Just to check what they really like close up an' all."

"That's a fine idea," I said. "Why don't you go over on your way home? I'll be there then feeding them, and you can help me."

Which he did, and soon he was a regular visitor at the sanctuary, and within the year he'd forsaken his job as our yard man and had become one of the caretakers at the sanctuary. And that was where he was killed, later, after he'd helped me move our clan of dreamers away to Boniface Island, where we hoped to hide them until the war was over.

What an absurd pair we made, Kuyo and I, carrying the babies and leading the adolescents by the hand, as if they were frightened schoolchildren and we humans were their teachers, shuttling the older dreamers in the wheeled cage along the winding pathway to the dock on the river where the boat was hidden, ferrying our terrified charges in twos and threes under the shroud of darkness across the broad, moonlit estuary, putting them carefully ashore, and returning to the sanctuary on the west side of the city for more. A couple of confused, frightened, latter-day Noahs we were. What naiveté and vanity on my part, faithfulness and belief on Kuyo's, and trust on the part of the dreamers, who squatted on the island among the mangroves and out on the muddy landing and watched the humans head back towards Monrovia, knowing somehow that we would return with the others, until finally all eleven had been moved there.

We left them food enough for a few days—bananas, rose apples, squashes, and several baskets of leafy greens—promised we would soon return, and departed for what turned out to be the last time. The dreamers did not know that we were not saving them, we were abandoning them. Nor did we. The dreamers did not know that Kuyo and I, as if in cahoots with the soldiers, had trapped and imprisoned them on the island.

I walked alone to my silent, empty house on Duport Road, in town. The streets were deserted, and everyone who had not fled the city had barred his door and shuttered the windows. I heard the occasional stutter of distant gunfire from Waterside and the rumble of military trucks and jeeps entering and departing from the Barclay Barracks, where the remnant of the president's special Anti-Terrorist Force was encamped. In darkness I sat out on the patio, exhausted, utterly unsure of what to do next, now that I had done what seemed to me the only and the last thing I actually could do. Half a bottle of gin was sitting on the patio table with a filthy glass next to it, inadvertently left behind, no doubt, when the servants fled. I filled the glass and drank it down slowly, bit by bit, and filled it again, until I had drunk half a quart of gin with no tonic and no ice, a thing I'd never done before. Then I went inside and lay down on the sofa, and with all the windows and doors of the house wide open and the gate to the street unlocked, slept for twelve hours, till evening the next day.

Kuyo had gone back to the deserted sanctuary in Toby southeast of town to gather up the record books, the ledgers and data we'd accumulated over the years, to carry them to me for safekeeping. He'd wanted instead to flee the city for his family's village in the back country of Lofa and hide there and had argued against going back to the sanctuary. "Them's only papers, Miz Sundiata, ain't no point to gettin' 'em now wit' all them soldiers about." But I had insisted. This was the last time that I still believed I could somehow protect valuable documents for the duration of the war—for who, I wondered, would want to destroy numbers, calculations, the birth, death, and kinship records of chimpanzees? Despite everything that had already happened, I'd still not imagined the discovery by men and boys of the pleasures of pointless destruction. Back then, at least until that night, murder, rape, pillage, and the butchery and roasting of animals, even chimpanzees, when it occurred, still had to have a political point—the sad but necessary consequences of warfare.

At the sanctuary, Kuyo came out of the office lugging a plastic milk carton overflowing with the papers and was met in the yard by three men with guns. I never saw them myself but can all too easily imagine them. You've seen magazine photographs of them, I'm sure. Americans, especially white Americans, like to scare themselves with those photos. Most of the fighters in that war wore parts of cast-off nylon exercise suits and torn and filthy tee shirts with American college and sports team logos and oversize high-top basketball sneakers, do-rags and baseball caps turned backwards—hip-hop leftovers looted from the stores and shops and scavenged from the street markets of the villages and towns they had rampaged through on their way to Monrovia. Some of them, especially the young boys, wore women's clothes— nightgowns and skirts and bonnets—and they flashed fresh tattoos on their arms and bare chests and juju amulets around their necks and white paste on their faces. These were the soldiers I had been seeing for weeks on the streets of Monrovia. The officers in their armies—for there were three armies of Liberians fighting one another at that time, President Doe's, Charles Taylor's, and Prince Johnson's—had put these boys in charge of the checkpoints in and out of town and all across the country, and their actions had been generating tales of random drug- and alcohol-fueled murders and rapes and always robbery, looting, and pillaging. Here in town, when off duty, they were seizing houses, painting their names on the walls—Rambo, Quick-to-Kill, Flashdancer— to claim ownership for their planned return when the fighting was over. So far, no one had claimed our house.

The soldiers had come to the sanctuary for the dreamers. Bush meat. There was a sixteen-year-old girl, also a cousin of Woodrow's, Estelle, who lived on the grounds and had not yet left for her village. She didn't know which army the men belonged to, Prince Johnson's or Charles Taylor's or the army of the man who was still the president of Liberia, Samuel Doe. She had climbed into a cotton tree to hide from the fighters, and the following day, when she finally dared to come to me, Estelle told me that the men had cut off Kuyo's penis and made him eat it and then had shot him many times in the mouth. They threw his body into the river, she said, and drove away. She said, "Mebbe they be Prince Johnson men, them was in so big a hurry-hurry to get away from town before Charles Taylor's men come get them an' kill them dead. Or mebbe them be President Doe's men who mus' be scairt of everybody now, even the peoples."

My journals, years of meticulous records and data, were still at the sanctuary, scattered across the sandy, blood-spattered yard where Kuyo had dropped them, wet from rain and driven into the dirt by the fighters' jeep and feet as if they were old newspapers. For hours, Estelle and I gathered up the soaked books and loose sheets of paper, until finally we had them all collected in the plastic milk carton.

I held the carton and looked at the contents for a long moment.

Then, halfway through that moment, something inside me cracked and split, and there the dark entered in. Weeping, I dumped the contents of the carton onto the ground at my feet. Without thinking, mindless, as if merely following orders, I doused the pile with kerosene from a lamp, lit a match, and tossed it onto the papers. An auto-da-fé it was. The heap burst into yellow flames and sour-smelling smoke and began to burn. I felt the light inside me, what little of it still shone, dwindle and die, smothered by the dark.

Grabbing my arm, Estelle yelled at me, "Why you doin' that, Miz' Sundiata! After we work so hard to collect 'em!"

I shook my head and said slowly, "I don't know, Estelle. I don't know why I'm burning the papers. I just don't." It was the simple, perplexing truth. I told her that I was sorry not to know, and instructed her then to run home to her village and stay with her family and not to come back to the sanctuary ever again. "There is no sanctuary here now, Estelle," I said. "It's gone. Like Woodrow. Like my sons. Like Kuyo. Like the chimps. Gone. And if you don't go home and stay there, you'll be gone, too."

As if before her eyes I had turned into a ghost, the girl simply turned and ran, and I never saw her again. Estelle is probably dead now, if she was lucky. Or a ghost herself. She was a pretty little young woman, from Samuel Doe's mother's tribe, the Gio. During the months and years that followed, until the people elected Charles Taylor president to stop him from killing them, most of those women, especially the younger ones and the girls, were lucky to have been killed.

TEN YEARS AND A LIFETIME later, I walked in painfully bright sunlight along the narrow beach outside Monrovia towards the harbor and the town, passing the spot on the beach where, nearly twenty years and two lifetimes ago, Master Sergeant Samuel Doe and his men erected thirteen telephone poles in the sand. I knew the story. I was there. Everyone in Liberia knew the story. Drunk and high on drugs, blood-lust ramping through their veins, Samuel Doe's men had eviscerated their president, William Tolbert, in his office and carried his ministers, fifteen baggy old men stripped naked, to the beach, where they lashed them to the poles and shot them dead in front of television and home-movie cameras and a crowd of wildly jeering citizens and left their bodies tied to the poles to feed the vultures and the dogs. The poles lie buried in the sand now, and the bones of the corrupt old men have long ago washed out to sea.

At the far end of the beach, where the land elbows into the harbor, I saw the same man in nylon shorts who had fled from me at the gully after the Lebanese truck driver, Mamoud, had let me off. The man stood beside a beached, dark red pirogue, with both hands on the bow in a proprietary way, as if he were about to launch the boat, and watched me approach. So he was a fisherman, then, not a mad scav-enger, as I'd first thought, and I must have interrupted him at his morn-ing toilet. He had merely been embarrassed by me, but not frightened. With West Africans, the two sometimes look the same.

A pair of osprey swooped past, dipped close to the glittering surface of the sea, and methodically cruised the length of the beach a hundred yards from shore, searching for breakfast. Now that the man and I could see each other's faces clearly, I covered my teeth with my lips and smiled, and he smiled back. *How strange*, I thought, *and how nice*—a relief, in fact, that a Liberian man and I were greeting each other with friendly curiosity. I hadn't thought that possible anymore.

I wished the man good morning, and he said the same, and soon we were talking about how bad the fishing had been in the last few months, since the end of the rains, he said. He was named Curtis. He was a young man who looked to be in his early twenties, with a wife, he said, "An' five pick'nies. But wit' no fish to catch me can't feed them, an' so the wife gone on the streets now, sellin' pens an' Bic lighters an' other suchlike t'ings but ain't nobody can buy t'ings in dis country no more, so what a man t' do?" He spoke rapidly, anxiously, as if afraid I'd cut him off. "Can you help me out wit' a little somethin', Miz?" He held out his hand. "Can you gimme dash?"

"Do you know Boniface Island?" I asked him. He did, though he'd never been there. I asked if I could hire him to take me there in his boat. "I'll pay you twenty American dollars," I said. "To go out and back. And to wait for me for an hour or so. I won't need to stay long."

He wondered why I needed to go to Boniface. "Nothin' t' see on those little bitty river islands but birds an' crocodiles an' mangroves. Turtles sometimes though," he added.

"I was there long ago," I said. "During the war. Some of my friends were killed there. And I need to pray for them."

He nodded, understanding. From Cape Mount to Maryland County, all over this land, "people's friends an' family needs prayin' for," he pronounced. "The war not over yet, mebbe never will be over," he said and held out his hand again for money. I placed a folded twenty-dollar bill into it.

AT BONIFACE ISLAND, the long pirogue, shaped like a plantain, slid onto the dark landing. It was a short, sloped, brown beach with a small clearing surrounded by low bushes a short ways beyond and, on both sides, a mass of tangled, head-high mangroves half in the water and half out. Though it was the largest of the river islands in the broad estuary of the St. John River, it was barely the size of a schoolyard. Standing barefoot in the bow, my sneakers stashed in my backpack, I stepped from the boat and went ashore.

Behind me, squatting in the stern, Curtis held the boat tight to the beach with his single long paddle. He was looking in my direction, but his face was expressionless, as if I weren't there. Then, without warning, he moved his oar up to the bow, placed the end of it into the mud, and shoved the boat away from shore. It floated past the mangroves, where it caught the river current and slowly spun stern to bow towards the wide, gray waters of the estuary. Standing, he took his long oar in hand and like a Venetian gondolier worked the handle back and forth, driving the boat still farther from the island and into the river.

"Wait a minute! What are you doing?" I cried. "Curtis! Where are you going?"

He was a hundred yards or more from the island now, and he said nothing, did not look back, kept rowing.

I screamed, "Don't leave me here! Please, Curtis! Don't leave me here!"

Then he was gone to the far side of the island, heading rapidly on a line towards the city of Monrovia, in the distance downstream. In moments, he was out of my sight altogether, twenty American dollars richer than this morning, when he found me, but with no more money coming to him again for a long, long time—unless he was willing to hit me with a rock and leave me on the island for dead. He must have been too timid a man to do that, I thought, and turned away from the disappearing boat. Afraid that if he'd killed me he'd end up sleepless at night with my spirit haunting his hut, he had done the next Liberian thing, he'd merely taken the twenty dollars and abandoned me.

I looked around at the drooping mangroves, their roots like limp snakes dangling their heads into the water, and stepped away from the shore in search of shade against the glare of the sun. But there was none, unless I were willing to crawl on hands and knees into the tepid water and huddle beneath the mangroves leaves. But the water looked filthy enough to make me sick on contact, and I remembered the crocodiles that Curtis had mentioned and was afraid to leave the clearing in spite of the sun's beating on my head.

Though I was alone on the tiny island, from the instant I stepped ashore I knew that I was alone with the ghosts of my dreamers. I could almost see them shuffling side to side in the heat-crinkled air. I sensed their presence all around me. There was a rustling from the bushes as if a cool breeze had blown over, but everything was dead and heavy. Then I heard a familiar huffing sound, the low woofs of a pair of adult male chimpanzees, as different from one another as two human voices, and as recognizable, and I knew at once that it was Ginko and Mano. And then came the distinctive pant hoot of the leader of the clan, Doc, the first of the apes that I had dared to name, followed by the chuckling close by of mothers Deena and Wassail and Ellie, nursing their babies and scolding their older children, and the squawks and high-pitched screeches from the adolescents vying for rank and dominance—they were all over this tiny, brush-covered islet! I looked for them in the low, leafless, prickly bushes at the edge of the clearing, tramped from one side of the island to the other, and peered under the mangroves, but could not see them.

But they were here, I knew, still waiting after all these years for me to come back and save them. Or, no, they were waiting for me to step forward, to bow my head, and receive their judgment. Yes, that was it. I suddenly realized that I'd come solely for this. It was the possibility and the necessity of receiving their strict, final judgment that had driven me from my farm and drawn me across the ocean to this tiny island. And I hadn't known it until now. I hadn't allowed myself to know it, until, like the dreamers, I myself was trapped on this island, and it was suddenly all too clear why, after years of safe retreat, I'd taken it upon myself to leave my quiet Adirondack valley one autumn afternoon and fly away to Africa.

The dreamers gradually went silent, as if they had seen me standing in the center of the small clearing and knew that I was alone. Emerging slowly from the dense scrub brush, one by one they came forward, all eleven of them, the entire clan, as if they had never been abandoned, slain, eaten. Bent over slightly, looking ready to spring, they hitched themselves cautiously towards me, closer and closer, until they had surrounded me. Their eyes were wide open, with heavy brows lifted in mild surmise, lips sucked tightly together, and when they stared up at me it was in sad puzzlement, not in accusation—which I expected and could have endured and may even have welcomed. After having first made them trust me to provide for their safekeeping, in spite of my weakness and fearful self-interest, and to know what was good for them, in spite of their own best knowledge, I had treated them shamefully. Unforgivably. And now, in consequence, though calm, almost placid, they had been transformed from my charges into furies. Their gaze showed me—as if I needed fresh reminding—that the themes of my life were betrayal and abandonment.

It came to me then that where I now stood in the clearing was the exact spot in which my dreamers had been slain, their corpses butchered and eaten. Their skulls and bones and the charred remains of the fires in which their flesh had been roasted lay like midden deep in the silt beneath my feet. It had been ten rainy seasons since Kuyo and I last stood here, and many flood tides had washed over the island, leaving behind each time a thick carpet of fresh mud floated down from the eastern highlands, sinking the remains of my dreamers deeper and deeper into the body of the island. They were buried far beneath me, and yet it seemed, nonetheless, that I had placed myself in the midst of those old bones as if at the center of a charnel house. The bones were piled up to my knees, a rough pyramid of leg and arm bones, of spines with hooped ribs still attached, skulls large and small, the bones of fingers and toes, yellowed teeth, and thatches of brown and black hair.

The large, yellow, equatorial sun lay pasted against the pale gray sky directly overhead. I knew that my blood and brain were dangerously overheated. I was dizzy and could not see clearly anymore. The faces and shapes of the ghosts of the dreamers had grown fuzzy and indistinct, and they resembled now a cluster of hooded medieval priests at prayer, kneeling in a circle around me. My legs were weak and began to tremble. Everything was spinning. I had not brought water from the mainland—there was no fresh water on the island, none at least that I could have located myself, and the river was brackish and filthy with sewage and rotted corpses—and I had not eaten since the previous night, when Mamoud had stopped briefly at the cook shop outside of Gbanga and the boy had run after us begging for a ride away.

I know now, of course, what was happening to me, but I didn't realize it at the time. I had thought I was on a secret guilt trip, a return visit to the scene of my crime. One of my crimes. It was sunstroke and dehydration and hunger, but to me it was a vision. And here it came, a huge wave rising in front of me and then breaking and falling over me, shoving me to my knees, bending my body into an *A*, a wave replaced by a second, still bigger wave, and a third and a fourth, rolling me over, their enormous weight and force pummeling my body to the ground.

I lay on my back and looked up at the silhouette of a black, featureless head blocking out the sun. It was the large, gray-splotched face of Doc—who had been both the fiercest and the gentlest of the dreamers and the most intelligent—staring down at me in rage, a monstrous Caliban. He opened his mouth wide and bared his large canine teeth. The others, male and female alike, adults and offspring, all the dreamers, gathered beside and behind Doc and watched him intently, as if waiting for him to give the signal that would free them. Free them to do what? To rend and disembowel me and devour my raw flesh? It's what I expected. It's what I thought I deserved.

I crouched against the muddy ground and extended my hands in a pathetic gesture, as if to fend them off. They had come forward from the spirit world with no other purpose than to avenge themselves on my stringy, old lady's body, to tear my hair from my scalp and toss bloody handfuls of it like gobbets into the air, to scream bloody murder and spit into my face. These were my imaginings. It's what I must have desired. For years, since my youth, hadn't I been seeking exactly this? The freeing of the slave, the resurrection of the slain, the revenge of the betrayed and abandoned human and not-human. I'd not been able to become any one of them, and had grown angry and then had slain them, the not-us. Now the not-us had come back to claim blood kinship by returning blow for blow, curse for curse.

And Doc spoke. I heard him *speak* to me! His voice was low and dark, his accent and intonation West African. He called me by name, *Hannah-oh, Hannah-oh, Hannah-oh*, he moaned, as if making a mysterious, final, despairing benediction for humankind, for my kind in particular, and he said that I had once made much of him and his clan, and I had fed them and had taught them the names and uses of things that they had never seen before. And when I had let them believe that I and they were kin, I had imprisoned them on this island and had delivered them into the hands of the soldiers, who saw them only as food and viewed the babies of their clan as toys to be sold on the streets.

His large, powerful hand descended towards my face as if he meant to tear my pale mask from the bone beneath. Blackness interceded. And that is the last of my memories of the vision.

UNTIL I FOUND MYSELF with my head lying against the brown thigh of a man who was trickling fresh cool water into my mouth. He must have seen that I was now aware of him, for he tipped my head forward slightly and smiled and brought the plastic jug closer to my lips so that I could drink more easily. There were broad, green mangrove leaves overhead, shading us from the sun. The man was the boatman, Curtis, who had carried me to the island and left me there—permanently, I had thought. But no, there he was, pushing my wet hair away from my face, helping me drink, and speaking softly to me, "You gonna be fine now, Miz, don' you worry none, you gonna be jus' fine. Good t'ing I come back f' you an' bring water, or by now you in the belly of the crocodiles for certain, Miz."

He helped me sit up and let me hold the jug myself and drink from it. Then he held his hand out to me. "Gimme more dash now, Miz. The water not come free, y' know. Nothin' come free in this country anymore. Not for me, an' not for you neither," he said.

WHEN A YEAR AGO I went back to Liberia, I thought it was in search of my lost sons, and found something very different instead. Twenty-seven years ago, however, the first time I went to Africa, it was to Ghana, to avoid arrest and imprisonment or possibly simple assassination in the United States. It was 1975, and I was living with Carol—poor, large-hearted Carol—in New Bedford, as part of a tiny Weather Underground cell made up, as far as I knew, of just me and a man named Zachary Procter.

Zack was actually a mainline Cincinnati aristocrat whom I'd known in the Movement back at Brandeis. He was tall—six-and-a-half feet at least—and slim, with ginger-colored hair, freckles, pale blue eyes with crinkly, premature laugh lines at the corners, and teeth like Chiclets. Zack and I had marched arm in arm at various peace protests at the university, but otherwise we had avoided each other. Perhaps because we sensed that we were too much alike. We could see behind each other's mask of idealism and ideology the face of the privileged, angry kid who, in the name of peace, justice, and racial harmony, had declared war against the state, the university, and, before long, his parents' entire generation. The face behind the mask was not a pretty sight. Later, the mask absorbed the face and became it, and for a while at least we weren't ashamed of what we were looking at. Then, eventually, I guess the mask got peeled away, and we saw our true faces again.

Zack's major was anthropology; I was pre-med. It was the mid-1960s. In our dorm rooms we listened to folk music, Negro blues, and jazz; smoked dope; drank cheap red wine from basket-wrapped bottles; and wore black turtlenecks, jeans, and peasant sandals to class, even in winter. We were conventionally ambitious students, however, and worried about our grades and calibrated our final class standing two and three years before graduation. But on our own, outside of class, we read Nietzsche, Heidegger, and Sartre in Anchor paperbacks, loved Godard and Bergman movies and called them "films," and cultivated what we regarded as morally meaningful alienation from bourgeois society and values. Our forms of rebellion had been handed down to us from the fifties, after all, by the Beat Generation and famous European café existentialists.

It was a sweet, almost innocent interlude, especially compared to what came later. Zack and I slept together for the first and last time the same night we organized the SANE chapter at Brandeis. At that age, sex is usually part of one's family drama, and at college Zack had a hankering for middle-class black and Jewish girls, anyone not like Mom, and I was attracted only to middle-class black and Jewish boys, anyone not like Dad. As a result, sex between me and Zack was too close to incest to give us anything but anxiety. The next morning we somberly agreed not to do it again, and we didn't, ever. We insisted that it was nothing personal, and the truth is, it wasn't.

After graduation, Zack went to Ghana with the Peace Corps, and I went to Mississippi and Louisiana for the first time with the Southern Christian Leadership Conference. That September I returned to Massachusetts to attend Harvard Medical School, where I helped form the SDS chapter, got myself arrested twice by the Cambridge police for disturbing the peace—committing acts of civil disobedience, we called it, blocking entry to the provost's office and disrupting military recruiters on campus. *Making* peace by disturbing it. We hadn't yet brought the war home. But in 1966, as the Civil Rights and antiwar movements blossomed and exfoliated left, right, and center, I dropped out of school six months before finishing and became a full-time political activist. A year later I was living in a commune in Cleveland, organizing and then running a day-care center for working mothers by day and printing pamphlets and broadsides and the occasional phony ID by night. I wasn't ever a leader; I was a worker, and it was my point of pride. SDS, and before long Weatherman, had become my university, my employer, my church, my family.

THERE'S MUCH ABOUT that period that you don't need to know, or perhaps much that I don't care to remember right now. Or *can't* remember. I was a different person then. After the Chicago Days of Rage in 1969 and my federal indictment in 1970, I came back to New England and went underground. My name was Dawn Carrington. Carol, who was my lover and roommate, thought of me not as a Marxist and certainly not as a terrorist but as an intellectual, some kind of college-educated, deep-thinking, liberal Democrat was all.

A trusting, utterly honest woman, Carol was small, almost child size, with urchin eyes, wide, round, and dark. Stubborn like a child and willful, she was always exactly who she seemed and claimed to be, my extreme opposite, in a way. To her, I was the distant, gruff, skeptical woman a few years older than she whose presence in her life kept her from falling in love again with the kind of man who would beat her and cheat on her, a man like her daughter Bettina's father. Though she had been on the streets for years, I was more worldly than she, skeptical and sharp edged. "You make me stronger than I am," she used to whisper to me, and I would say, "Cut the shit, Carol. You're as strong as you want to be." And it was not "Dawn" that she called me, but "Don." Sometimes she wrote it in little love notes left on the kitchen table for me to find when I left the house early for work, while she slept till Bettina woke her for breakfast. *Good morning, Don. I wanted to wake you up when I got in but it was too late and you looked too peaceful asleep. I'm off tonight so let's go have a cookout at the beach when you get home. XXX*

Neither Carol nor I was a bona fide lesbian. We were just sick of men, and lonely. We'd both gotten to the same place, but by rather different and class-specific routes. A mill-town bad girl, Carol was homeless and hooked on speed by fourteen; married, pregnant, and abandoned by sixteen; turning tricks for rent and food money by eighteen. I was a veteran communard by the time we met, someone whose bourgeois sexual conditioning and power structure had been attacked and revamped by months of group critique, group sex, and recreational drugs. Carol and I both, in our own way, just wanted to be alone for a while, and that's what we provided for each other, a comforting solitude.

For the first year and a half that we were together, I was only marginally a Weatherman, filling coded mail orders for phony IDs and passports, a specialty I'd developed in Cleveland and was able to practice easily in Boston, thanks to my job at the hospital, which provided opportunistic access to the IDs of the dead and dying, and a flirty friendship with the teenaged kid who ran the hospital print shop. I was able to think of myself as a revolutionary, but didn't have to put myself at high risk.

Then one night, after I'd put Bettina to bed. Carol was working at the bar, and I was as usual flopped on the mattress on the floor of my room in the apartment, a book-cluttered sanctuary from which I had barred both Bettina and Carol. "This is where I *work*," I told Carol. "It's where I read and write and *think*, and those are things you do alone, in private. It's like going to the bathroom, taking a shit. You understand?" She understood. I was reading—who knows what, probably Franz Fanon or Régis Debray—and listening to music on my portable stereo, classical, I'm sure, because Carol hated classical. It made her insecure, she said, and I only played it when she was at work, because I couldn't stand her insecurity sometimes.

I remember at one point, very late, I dimly heard the door buzzer from down the hall, a steady, unbroken, irritated noise made by someone kept waiting too long. This was more than unusual. We never had uninvited nighttime visitors. *The police*, I thought, *the FBI, U.S. marshals—oh, Jesus, the pigs!*

I panicked and looked around my room, suddenly seeing it with a cop's eye. In a shoe box under the bed: *aha!* a batch of unfinished phony IDs and half a dozen stolen Massachusetts driver's licenses. And in the dresser drawer: an ounce and a half of marijuana. And over there on the table: a spiral notebook with the names and addresses of four or five people who'll find themselves being interviewed by the FBI tomorrow. Stupid! Stupid!

There was someone banging on the door now, and a man hollering my name, my *real* name, "Hannah! Hey, Hannah, open up!"

So it wasn't the cops. I tiptoed down the hall to the door and listened. Silence. Then a man's voice, "Shit," and an audible sigh.

"Who's there?"

"Hannah? Hey, it's me, babe. Zack."

"Who?"

"Zack Procter, for Christ's sake."

"Jesus! Shut up. Are you alone?"

He laughed. "Yeah, I'm alone. Lemme in."

I jerked the door open, grabbed his sleeve, pulled him inside, and shut and locked the door. "Asshole!"

"You're hard to find, babe, but not that hard." He talked as he walked ahead of me down the hall to the kitchen, dragging a large army-surplus duffel and carrying a paper bag that he set onto the table. "Dawn Carrington, eh? Where'd you get that one? Sounds like a character from a TV soap opera. Want a beer?" He pulled a six-pack from the bag, opened a bottle for himself, and sat down at the table. He studied me, a mocking smile on his face, took a long, slurping pull from his beer and wiped his mouth with his sleeve. "Oh, man, I needed that!"

I watched him from the door, my arms crossed at my waist. Zack was even thinner than he'd been in college, and his face had turned craggy, wearing a new set of vertical lines on either side of his mouth, as if he'd actually done a little suffering in the intervening years. But it was only a fresh mask, I decided; he still looked like a gleefully defiant boy.

"You shouldn't have called me Hannah," I said evenly. "I'm glad my roommate isn't here and her kid's asleep."

He apologized in that easy way of a man who knows he's quickly forgiven, and asked if I'd like to know how he'd found me, which in fact I did, but hadn't wanted to ask. He explained that he'd bumped into a couple of old Brandeis SDS contacts who'd stayed more or less out of trouble but were still politically active in the Boston area, and they'd put him in touch with New York Weatherman, people who, he said, took him in and really turned his head around on what's going down here in the States. From them he heard about my having been busted during the Days of Rage pillage and riot three years earlier and that I'd gone underground, was still more or less Weather, and camped out here in New Bedford. He said word had come down from the Weather Bureau that he should come here and crank up a functioning cell with me, generate a little more action than manufacturing phony IDs. "So I went to Detroit for a crash course in bomb-making, which was cool, and caught the Greyhound for New Bedford," he said. "They told me about the Dawn Carrington bit; it's not that big a secret, babe, which is why I figured if I called you Dawn you'd freak and think it was the pigs or something, but if I called you Hannah you'd definitely open the door for me. Maybe you oughta change your name again, babe," he said and drained the bottle. "Sure you don't want a beer?"

"Yeah, okay, give me one," I said and sat down across from him, believing about half his story.

Gradually, Zack brought me up to date on his life. "Changes, man, big changes." After his tour as a Peace Corps volunteer in Ghana, he'd taken our generation's version of the Grand Tour. Though he didn't say it, I knew he'd been financed by his trust fund as he drifted through most of the Third World, with extended stops in Tangier, Calcutta, Nepal, and Thailand for drugs and enlightenment, shorter visits to Saigon, Mexico City, and Havana for politics, and had ended back in the States, convinced that a worldwide revolution was inevitable and imminent. For Zack, the introductory music for the Revolution had already been struck up, and the theme song was "Street Fighting Man."

"The past is prelude, man, and the prelude has passed. We're in it now!"

Around two in the morning, Carol came home, and I introduced Zack as my cousin. From his extreme height, he splashed kindly attention onto her, and she responded with surprised pleasure and quick affection, and when he asked if he could crash at our apartment until he found a job and a place of his own, she readily agreed, without so much as a sideways glance in my direction.

"Where's he gonna stay, Carol?" I asked.

"Your workroom," she said. "It's only temporary. Right, Zack?"

And to his credit, it was. A few days later, he rented a room in a downtown flophouse and took a part-time job driving a local cab.

It was hard not to like Zack, and especially hard for me not to take some of his voltage and use it to charge my own depleted batteries. Until he showed up, I had been moving slower and slower with every passing week. For the first time in my life, I depended more on habit and routine than on political commitment to get me though my days and nights, and no matter how much comfort I took in Carol's and Bettina's familial presence, I was lonely and sad and aimless most of the time. For years, since adolescence, I'd lived with the sense that soon, very soon, something life changing, maybe world changing was going to happen, that a political Second Coming was locked into the calendar, into my personal calendar. That belief had made my life seem exciting to me and purposeful. But in the past year, especially in the last few months, as the Vietnam War chewed up Southeast Asia and ate away at the American economy, and the body count kept rising, and Lyndon Johnson's America got replaced by Nixon's and Kissinger's, and as I found myself growing older, in my thirties now, gray hairs showing up in the tub drain, it had started to seem that all I had to help me explain the content of my present life was the form of my past life.

There is a crucial transition from radical activist to revolutionary, and when you've made that crossing, you no longer question why you have no profession, no husband, no children, why you have no contact with your parents, and why you have no true friends—only comrades and people who think they're your true friend but don't know your real name. Until Zack showed up, even though I was paying the price of being a revolutionary, I hadn't really made that crossing yet, and consequently my life had come to feel shriveled and gray, boring and pointless. I had the effects, but no cause.

Zack changed that. Almost immediately, as if we were a couple of pimple-faced kids starting a fan club for a rock star, he and I formed an independent Weather cell together—which was how it was generally done in those days, as there was no central authority or headquarters that kept track of us or passed out membership cards and a handbook. We were expected to work independently and generate and carry out actions against the War Machine ourselves. Within weeks, in the dingy, damp basement of the three-storey wooden tenement building on Phillips Street, while in the apartment upstairs, Carol and I and her daughter, Bettina, still pretended that we were a family, Zack and I were in the basement, two or three nights a week and on weekends, trying to make pipe bombs and Molotov cocktails. Cousin Zack, as the little family half-jokingly called him, and I hinted to Carol that what we were making was cool and secret, which she assumed was a present for Bettina's upcoming birthday, a dollhouse, maybe.

The rest of the time I sleepwalked through what passed in those days, the early and mid-1970s, for a normal, if quasi-bohemian, life. Except for the fact, of course, that my parents and no one from my childhood or adolescence or even from most of my adult life so far knew what my name was now or where I was living and working or the name of the young woman I lived with and what we did together on those few occasions when we were alone and in bed. And even the young woman herself did not know the truth, and probably never would, for as soon as Zack and I built and successfully set off our bombs, I intended to disappear from her life. I had in fact already cleaned up my room, packed my clothes and books and a few records, and destroyed everything that might connect me to Carol and incriminate her in any way. She had to be able to say, "I didn't know anything about it," and be telling the truth. In thirty seconds, all signs of my ever having lived in that apartment could be erased, and would be.

Otherwise, my life passed for ordinary. If I got caught trying to set off a bomb in the Federal Building in Boston, which was our primary target, or the Shawmut Bank or the eighteenth Precinct Boston Police Station, two of our secondary targets, or if one night, God forbid, down in the basement Zack or I, a little stoned on grass maybe, touched the wrong wires together and blew ourselves and the building to bits—like Diana, Ted, and Terry, when they blew up the townhouse on West Eleventh Street back in '70 —and if as a result of the accident we killed Carol and Bettina and who knows how many others in their sleep, then the neighbors and my co-workers at the hospital and the guys who ran the deli on the corner of Phillips and Bay Streets and the mailman and the guy who read the electric meter and the Greek who collected our rent once a month (in cash, always in cash), they'd all say, *I dunno, she seemed like a nice enough girl, quiet, though, kept pretty much to herself, always paid the rent on time, didn't smile much, didn't socialize with anybody, except her friend, the other girl, the one with the kid. Never came to any of the office parties, didn't hang out in the bars, not even the bar where her friend worked. Really kind of an ordinary girl, I guess. The kind of person you don't actually notice. You could call her a loner. More a loner than a loser. Like whatziname, Lee Harvey Oswald.*

Basically, it was a childish fantasy, wanting to survive your own death so you could overhear the postmortem, read your own obituary, attend your own funeral, and I indulged it often. But at the same time I was aware of something rumbling beneath it, a hidden desire to get caught, to fail in a spectacular, even suicidal way, and it made me very nervous. It was the feeling I sometimes got driving over a high bridge: one quick tug of the steering wheel to the right, and it's over the edge and straight down. I had to force myself consciously to resist that impulse, or else pretend that I wasn't on a bridge—no, I was driving across the Plains, somewhere west of Iowa, nothing but flat, solid, grassy ground beneath me stretching from horizon to horizon.

WHEN HE WASN'T WORKING with me in the basement or driving his cab, Zack had taken to traveling to New York City for days at a time. "I'm making some very cool contact down there with our black comrades-in-arms," he told me. "These brothers, man, they're the forward force of the revolution, the elite corps. A lot of them have been in the joint, some of the brothers are vets back from 'Nam, man. And they're *pissed*. They make Weather look like candy stripers, man."

I asked him if they were Black Panthers, but he said, "No way, these guys are in deep cover, man. And the kind of action they're into is almost beyond politics. These brothers are much heavier than the Panthers." Again, I believed about half of what he told me. But the half I believed lifted my spirits. For years, ever since the Civil Rights movement got taken over by blacks, and the white college kids like me and the white lawyers and clergymen were sent home from the South, leaving us with only the splinters that were left of the antiwar movement—SDS, Weatherman, the Yippies, Diggers, and so on, all of whom were white and middle class—I'd felt somehow cheated out of my true mission, as if in my chosen line of work I'd been deprived of an essential tool, and that tool was black people. Practically from childhood, and especially in high school and college—thanks to my father's old-time New England hierarchy of values, I'm sure, and his heavy emphasis on noblesse oblige—my heroes had been the nineteenth-century white abolitionists, most of whom were educated, upper-class women from New England. Like me. And my father had nothing for those women but unqualified praise and admiration. "Among all our distinguished ancestors, Hannah, those female abolitionists are the ones I hold in highest regard. The others, the men, all they ever did was make money. Until I came along," he'd add, laughing, as if he, a world-famous pediatrician who wrote best-selling books on child care, had somehow managed to avoid making money.

I wanted to know more about these mysterious black proletarian warriors in New York City with whom Zack claimed to have initiated an alliance. But beyond offering hints, winks, and vague allusions to plans for bank robberies and high-jacked armored trucks and heavy weaponry, he wouldn't tell me anything specific or concrete, which disappointed me, and after a while I figured they were largely a blend of rumor and fantasy cooked up by Zack and some of his male friends, the New York–based members of Weather. Radical white-boy wet dreams.

Until the late-winter night that he came banging on our door at two

A.M. When I let him in, he collapsed on the floor in the hallway, bleeding through his jacket, and I knew right away it was from a bullet wound. I'd seen enough of them in the emergency room at Peter Bent Brigham not to confuse a bullet wound with any other kind of injury—it was usually the face of the victim that gave it away, scared, in pain, but mainly surprised. Zack had that look.

I helped him to his feet and led him into the kitchen, where he let go of all restraint and like a child terrified by a nightmare—suddenly awake and safe in his own bed—began to sob. Carol and I carefully removed his torn, blood-soaked jean jacket and shirt, and I saw that the bullet had gone cleanly through his shoulder and seemed to have missed bone and arteries.

"It's not as bad as it looks, but you've lost some blood. You're going to have to get to the hospital," I told him.

"No! I can't! *You* fix it!" he cried, as if I were his mommy.

"Why can't you go to the hospital?" Carol asked him.

"Jesus, *you* tell her," he said to me.

Bettina had come into the kitchen and stood by the door in her pajamas, looking scared and confused. "Carol, take care of Bettina," I said. "I'll take care of him." Carol obeyed and scooted Bettina towards her bedroom. "Zack's okay, honey!" I called to the child. "He just had an accident, that's all!"

I knew enough anatomy and emergency first aid to clean the wound quickly and staunch the bleeding, and when Zack had recovered himself sufficiently to ask for whiskey—a line he probably took from a Western movie—I knew he'd not lost as much blood as I'd feared.

"You going to tell me what happened?" I asked and poured him a teacup of Jim Beam.

Carol had returned to the kitchen, and Zack jerked his head in her direction. "I'll have to tell you later, man."

"Carol, please, we need some privacy," I said.

"This is weird," she said. She walked back into the living room, flipped on the TV, dropped herself onto the sofa, and sulked.

"Oh, man, she drives me crazy sometimes. Now, Jesus, *you*. Fucking public enemy number one."

Carol flipped off the TV, got up, and stuck her head into the kitchen. "I'm goin' to bed, Don. You comin'?"

I was at the sink scrubbing the bloodstains out of Zack's jean jacket and denim shirt, and shot her a dirty look. Then felt sorry for it. All she wanted from me was a little straightforward affection mixed with respect—no reason to treat her like a dumb dog. The bedroom door closed behind her, and Zack was already talking.

He'd blown it, he explained, blown it big time, and we were going to have to leave the apartment, get out of New Bedford, out of the country, probably. We not only, as always, had the FBI sniffing after us, but now we were also being hunted down by these black guerillas from New York City, Zack's very heavy dudes who, he had suddenly discovered, were not Maoist revolutionaries after all, but gangsters, bank robbers, drug dealers. "The real thing, man!"

He'd tried to draw a line, he said, on dealing drugs, specifically heroin, and in Newark, on the way to make a buy, they'd had an argument, a misunderstanding, actually, based not on money, he assured me, but principles. Although they had thought it was about money, which is why the misunderstanding had gotten out of hand, so to speak, and they'd suddenly turned on him. He was lucky to have gotten out of there and back here alive, he said. And now these guys were more dangerous to us than the FBI was, because he knew stuff about them that no one else did, and they knew our names and where we lived, the city of New Bedford, at least, but not the actual street address, he assured me. So we had a little time, maybe a day or two, before they came knocking on the door.

"What the hell do you mean *us* and *we*? What the hell did you tell them about *me*?"

"Nothing, man, just your name in passing, you know, on account of the Weather thing. I mean, you think you're only a peon in the Movement, but you're well known, man, a poster girl. You were sort of like my bona fides, you know what I'm sayin'?"

"Who are these people anyhow? I mean, really? I thought they were SLA or Black Liberation Army. Borderline, but more or less legitimate."

"Well, yeah, I guess at first I did, too. But they sort of work both sides of the street, play one side off against the other. Look, Hannah, I got confused . . ."

"Dawn."

"Yeah, sorry. Dawn. But you know what I mean. Christ, half of Weather and half the Panthers are FBI informers. Half the Klan is on the federal payroll. The Muslims killed Malcolm, and J. Edgar Hoover probably had Martin killed, and who the hell knows who killed Bobby and JFK? Probably LBJ. The point is, there's nobody left who isn't wearing *some* kind of disguise. So who do you trust?"

"You trusted these New York guys, obviously. And I guess they trusted you enough to let you know too much."

"Mistake. Big mistake. On both parts, mine and theirs."

In a strange way, I felt almost relieved that everything seemed to be coming undone, and it was difficult not to show it. "Do they know me as Hannah Musgrave or Dawn Carrington? Or both?"

"Oh, no, just Hannah Musgrave, your poster-girl name," he said, but I knew he was lying.

"What about Carol?"

"She's cool. I never mentioned her. No reason to."

That much I did believe. To Zack, Carol and Bettina were like my houseplants. "Where will you go?"

"Way I figure, it's gotta be back to Ghana, man. Tomorrow. I've got enough bread to get me there, and I know how to get by okay in Accra. It's a very cool city, man, especially for Americans."

"Lucky you. But where am I supposed to go? Tell me that. I've got less than a month's pay in my checking account, and then I'm broke. And I can't just walk out on Carol, not without at least leaving her enough for the goddamn rent. This is fucking ridiculous, Zack!"

"No, no, it's not. You should come with me to Ghana. I feel guilty for this, man. Really. I'll pay your way; it's the least I can do. I'll make a stop at the friendly family trust officer in Boston in the morning, and we can be taking off from Logan on Air Ghana by lunchtime." He said he knew people in Accra who would find me a job. As it happens, people with my skills, hospital skills, Harvard Medical School skills, were highly employable in Ghana.

"It's a chance to start over." He passed his gaze over the apartment. "This, all of it, everything you've got here, this slummy apartment, the little girlfriend, the job at the hospital, even the bomb-making in the basement—it may be your way of stopping the War Machine, it may even be your way of starting the Revolution. But it's bullshit."

"You didn't think so yesterday."

"Yeah, well, yesterday I had more time to play with, time for finding out what's bullshit and what isn't, and yesterday I hadn't been shot yet by a crazed, paranoid black guy who couldn't tell the difference between liberating the people and selling them drugs. I'm outa here in the morning, and with this arm and the painkillers that you're gonna score for me at Peter Bent Brigham, I'll need someone to drive for me. We can commandeer my cab and drop it off at the airport, and twelve hours later we'll be kicking back in Accra."

I stood and walked to the window and looked down at the wet, gray street and the triple-decker houses that lined it on both sides. It was five-thirty in the morning. The sky was pinking in the east, out beyond the bay—in the direction of Africa. *It must be midday in Africa,* I thought. The street below seemed cold and colorless, as if it existed only in grainy black and white, and the radiators hissed and banged as the coal-burning furnace in the basement kicked in, and the darkened hallway smelled of corned beef and cabbage and moldy, wet, threadbare carpeting on the stairs. An empty municipal bus began its roundup of the first-shift mill workers. I could see my car down on the street where I'd parked it, the beat-up old Karmann-Ghia I'd bought in Cleveland. I'll leave the car keys on the kitchen table for Carol, I decided. And a check for what's left in my account.

"Okay, I'll do it. I'll go with you," I said. "Providing we go now, this minute. If I wait around, I'll change my mind."

"Cool. What about Carol and the kid? Doncha wanna wake them up?"

"No. Let's go now. I'm basically all packed anyhow. I've been packed for months. Half expecting this, I guess."

"No shit? Don't you want to say goodbye?"

"I hate goodbyes."

"Man, you are *cold*."

"Who is? Hannah or Dawn? No, you're right," I said and started towards my workroom to get the duffel with my belongings. "I am cold. Both Hannah and Dawn, we're like icebergs."

He smiled. "Yeah, well, you'll see, man. Africa's gonna melt you."

AND SO, LIKE water following gravity, my course and rate of descent more or less determined by the lay of the land and by whomever or whatever happened to lie in my path or by my side, I came to Ghana, a place that on my mental map of Africa was located in the region marked "unexplored." When you let go of your life like that, unexpected turns occur, and before long your life's path has become a snarl of zigs and zags. It's how one comes up with what's called "an interesting life," I guess. And my brief stay in Ghana with Zack was merely that, another zig, another zag—the makings of an interesting life.

It was more complicated than that, of course, but I didn't realize it at the time it was happening. One never does. I was, in a sense, passively following Zack, who knew how to disappear safely and, as it turned out, comfortably in far-off Ghana. But he wasn't leading me, and he certainly wasn't dominating me. He was a facilitator, one of any number of people who could just as easily have played the role as he. Or the role of comrade-in-arms. Or lover. Back then they were all essentially the same to me.

The truth is, I used Zack. Just as I had used Carol. I wasn't as passive as I seemed. Almost without knowing it I'd reached a point, long before I ran out on Carol and fled New Bedford, where I wanted desperately for my old life to be over and a new one to begin. But I had no idea how to go about it—without turning myself in to the FBI. And there was no way I'd do that.

It wasn't the likelihood of spending a year or three or even more behind bars that kept me from turning myself in—I might actually have welcomed jail time, a few years to reflect and pay mild penance; a time to organize my warring memories into a coherent narrative. It would have meant publicly voiding my previous life, however, canceling it out, erasing all its meaning, and I wasn't ready for that. Not yet. My life so far had cost me and everyone who ever loved me and everyone whom I had loved too much, way too much, for me simply to say, "I'm sorry, Daddy, and I'm sorry, Mother. I'm sorry, everybody. I have for more than ten years been making a terrible mistake. And, oh yes, everyone who was led to believe that I was someone other than I am, my apologies to you, too. It was all a dumb mistake, Carol. All of it."

And besides, I had no better alternative life to propose. No meaningful future for me alone or me with anyone else. So it was jail time, and public confession and shame, or get the hell out of Dodge, lady. Disappear. I was like a late-stage drug addict, unable to admit her addiction because of the damage it has done. She goes off the map altogether and no longer associates even with other addicts. I grabbed my duffel bag and my phony passport and followed Zack to Ghana. That way I could keep my mask, and no one could see it for what it was. Except Zack.

WITHIN A WEEK of our arrival in Accra, we had rented from an ex–Peace Corps friend of Zack's a small, two-bedroom, second-storey furnished apartment in a pink stuccoed building downtown, with a balcony overlooking the bustling street below and a view of the vast, open-air Makola market. Another week, and I had a job. Zack seemed to have friends everywhere in this city, at all levels of society—expatriate Englishmen, Ghanaian nationals, African-Americans in search of their roots, American businessmen, and ex–Peace Corps volunteers gone native—and he managed through a pal at the U.S. embassy to get me hired as a medical technician for a New York University blood lab that was using monkeys and bonobos for research on hepatitis.

My job was essentially a clerical one. I worked with the blood, not the monkeys, cataloguing and shipping plasma back to the States. I barely saw our simian donors and never handled them. Two years of Harvard Medical School under the name of Hannah Musgrave and my job, later, in the plasma lab at Peter Bent Brigham as Dawn Carrington had qualified me nicely for a similar, difficult-to-fill position here. In the days before computer checks, nobody checked. You could take off, put on, and mix and match identities like sportswear. You got caught only if you couldn't do what you said you could. Or if someone informed on you.

Once I had my job and living quarters settled, it wasn't long before Zack and I began to fall away from each other. Mostly, it was my doing. Back in the States—starting at Brandeis and finally in New Bedford— I'd been willing to dismiss his egoism and grandiosity as the typically elaborate feathers and coxcomb worn by just about every man I'd ever known in the Movement, without lowering my estimation of his political commitment and integrity. But that wasn't possible here in Ghana. For ten long years, in the vain attempt to create a revolution, I and hundreds of women like me—and, yes, men like Zack—had literally risked our lives and sacrificed our families and friends and given up on the comfortable futures we'd been promised. It was who we were back then and now and who we'd be for the rest of our lives. We believed it. We insisted on it. We needed it. But for Zack, once we'd landed in Accra, all that turned into merely a stage in his life, a phase he claimed to have passed beyond.

I wouldn't have been offended by his having designated those years a phase instead of a life, implying that it had been merely a phase for me, too, and I might even have been grateful for it. It might have provided the start of a way out for me. But in Africa, Zack quickly set himself up as a "businessman" of a particularly embarrassing and loathsome type. At least to me it was, especially then. And that, in turn, flipped him into a defensive posture, which only made things between us worse. For a long time, I said nothing to him about it. But he knew. My presence silhouetted his new life sharply against the brightly lit background of the old, and it made him angry at me, as if I were in charge of lighting.

He'd become a middleman. The bottom-feeder of capitalism. The enemy, as far as I was concerned. The Ghanaian economy had collapsed in the middle 1970s, and the inflation rate of the cedi, the local currency, was doubling by the month against the U.S. dollar. Small farmers and merchants were slipping so deeply into debt it would take generations for them to climb out again. These were Zack's suppliers. He spoke Fanti and a little Twi from his Peace Corps days, and as soon as his shoulder had healed well enough for him to drive, he bought with the dregs of his trust fund a little red Suzuki motorcycle and roared off to back-country cocoa-farming villages and along dusty country lanes from one small market town and city to another and prowled up and down the back streets and alleys of Accra, buying up from desperately frightened debtors their last hedge against financial ruin—ancient Ghanaian artworks and religious artifacts, principally Ashanti gold. He bought the precious objects with American dollars at flea-market prices, then sold them the next day at a colossal markup to the agents and dealers for rich American and European collectors and galleries, who waited for him in the air-conditioned lobby of the Golden Tulip Hotel out by the airport. It was, as he said, "sweet."

He was thriving, and within a month he had bought himself a Mazda van to carry his goods. I remember sitting with him one afternoon at a beach bar called Last Stop that he liked and had made his informal headquarters. It was a Sunday and very hot, and he had talked me into meeting him there "For the breeze," he said, "if nothing else. Who knows, you might actually enjoy yourself for a change and meet somebody you'd like and maybe even fall for." For some reason, Zack was eager to see me involved with a man. "Or a woman," he said. "Doesn't matter to me, so long as you get your own pad if you decide to shack up with him. Or her. Two's company, three's a drag."

We sat out on the terrace and drank the local Gulder beer and watched a gang of small boys and girls chase the surf while their tall, slender mothers stood knee-deep in the water with their skirts pulled up and talked. The breeze off the sea was aromatic and cooling. I kicked off my sandals and showed my face to the sun and admitted to Zack that I was glad I'd come out there.

"Yeah. Too bad there's nobody interesting here today. Probably still too early." He'd completed a successful sale that morning of a half-dozen rare, elaborately carved chieftain's stools to a midtown Manhattan gallery and was more pleased with himself than usual. "Actually, this gig's going so good I'm thinking of setting up a gallery of my own here, with maybe a branch in the States in a year or two. Cut out the middleman, you know?"

"You're the middleman," I said. "Jesus, Zack, do you have any idea how you sound?"

"Look, there's no more trust fund, babe," he said, spreading his empty hands. "Same with you, y'know. No more checks from Mommy and Daddy waiting at the American Express office. This is *Africa*, babe, not Ameri-ka. So lighten up, will you?"

"I never took money from my parents, you know that. And don't call me 'babe.'"

He scowled. "You put me down all the time, but look at *you*, for Christ's sake. Taking U.S. dollars from a university lab that's financed by a U.S. pharmaceutical company that's trying to patent and sell a drug that cures a disease that's been inflicted on the liver of some poor African-American woman who's addicted to another drug that's imported by the CIA from Southeast Asia. Terrific. I suppose that's better than being an upscale African street peddler like me? Because that's all I am, you know. A street peddler. I mean, c'mon, Hannah, which of us is really working for the enemy?"

"Dawn."

"Hannah. We're not underground anymore."

"Dawn Carrington is who I am here. So I'm still underground."

"Yeah. Whatever," he said and flagged the waitress impatiently.

"I used to think I was attracted to dangerous men," I said. "Dangerous to *me*, I mean. And I don't necessarily mean sexually attracted."

"Fuck you. Find yourself a dangerous man then." He waved his hand around the bar like an impresario or a pimp. "A little while and the place'll be full of 'em. The whole fucking city's full of 'em." And it was. In the mid-1970s, Accra, and this bar in particular, along with several others like the Wato and Afrikiko's, were catch basins for First-World drop-ins: anti–Vietnam War draft dodgers, black U.S. military personnel gone AWOL, and ex–Peace Corps volunteers, and probably more than a few of them were CIA agents collecting information on the rest of us and sending it back to Washington. They were Zack's and my tribesmen and -women, although only a few were women. West Africa was peppered with Americans like us in those years.

"You used to think I was dangerous," Zack said. "And now you don't. Is that what you're saying?" He grinned in a manic way, showing me his perfect teeth. With his gingery hair worn in a ponytail he looked more like a Colorado ski bum than a fugitive would-be terrorist. I didn't know what I looked like anymore. Actually, I've never known. I used to tell people that on the FBI wanted poster I looked like a Mexican hooker, but I wasn't really sure and in fact was only asking for an opinion.

"I never thought you were dangerous, Zack."

"Man, you are cold. Just like with Carol, man." He shivered and abruptly stood. "I'm outa here. I'll see you back at the apartment later, maybe," he said and strode off.

I'd hurt his feelings and didn't care, and he knew it. And he was right: from his point of view, Africa hadn't warmed me up. Though we shared the apartment, we kept to our separate bedrooms and were rarely there at the same time anyhow, never ate together, and didn't socialize with the same people. Actually, I socialized with no one, and he hung out with everyone. I liked the city of Accra, though. The huge, bustling city sprawled inland from the sea for miles and was such a glorious and inviting contrast to the gray, old mill towns I'd left behind— those recently abandoned, rust-belt cities like New Bedford and before that Cleveland, which had borne me down almost without my knowing it—that I found Accra irresistible. It was hot, equatorially hot, but thanks to the steady breeze off the Atlantic not uncomfortably humid, and as long as you kept out of the direct sun, it felt ideal—the climate to which human anatomy, after hundreds of thousands of years of evolution, was perfectly adapted. And I liked the Ghanaian people. They were excitable, loud, confident, and in your face, but in an engaging and good-humored way, waving hands, gesticulating, bending, bowing, and spinning as they talked, haggled, hassled, gossiped, and sang. Like the people, the city itself competed tirelessly for your attention and ear with its unbroken din of car horns and buses and trucks without mufflers, radios blasting from windows and open storefronts and hawkers hawking, babies crying, jackhammers pounding. Everywhere you looked Accra worked to catch and hold your eye with bright, busy color—the tie-dyed and beautifully woven wraps on the women and their elaborately coiled, braided, and beaded hairstyles, glossy black, hatlike structures as precarious as wedding cakes; the Chinese bicycles repainted in gaudy colors; the jammed minivans called *tro-tros*, the dazzling heaps of fruits and vegetables in the Makola market; and the barbershop signs with crude, hand-painted portraits of black men wearing spiffy Detroit-style haircuts called "747 Wave" and "Barracuda Zip" and "Concord Up." I liked the street food, especially *keli-weli*—savory little chunks of plantain fried in palm oil and flavored with ginger and hot peppers and served on a banana leaf—and even grew fond of the culinary leftovers from colonial days, a cup of hot Milo in the morning and for lunch at the office a thick sandwich of Laughing Cow cheese and the spongy white bread that Zack, just to get on my nerves, liked to call bimbo bread.

Never much of a cook, evenings I dined alone and mostly in little hole-in-the-wall restaurants in the neighborhood, where I favored the chopped-spinach dish called *kontumbre* and fish and rice *jollof* and the thick, darkly spiced stews. And I liked smoking the very strong Ghanaian marijuana. It was called *bingo* and sometimes *wee*, sold by a dealer named Bush Doctor, who hung out by the pool at the Golden Tulip. Zack bought it by the pound and, whenever he motored off to the backcountry on one of his art-buying jaunts, he carried enough with him to fill a tobacco pouch, leaving the rest carelessly behind at the apartment in a quart jam jar. Those nights when he was away, I'd dip into his jar, roll myself a pencil-size joint with tissue paper stripped off the foil liner of a cigarette pack, get sky high in a single swoop, and sit out on the balcony, hidden in darkness, and watch the thronged street below as if ensconced in a private box at Shakespeare's Globe in seventeenth-century London.

But then a second abyss opened between me and Zack. It was racial, and therefore political, and it surprised me because, until we found ourselves in Africa together, I had believed that Zack and I shared at least the same racial politics. We celebrated the same heroes and models—those white, nineteenth-century radical abolitionists who were devoted to the ideas of absolute racial justice and equality—and loved saying so to each other. We had both committed our lives up to then to extending the blessings and bounty of absolute racial justice and equality to all the dark-skinned peoples of the world. We would smash the Republic, if need be, or die in the effort to liberate our colonized black, brown, red, and yellow brothers and sisters both within and beyond the United States of America. That's how we talked then. Back in New Bedford, night after night, just as we had in college, Zack and I had analyzed the symbiotic relationship between racism and cap-

italism, the evolution from colonialism to imperialism, critiquing ourselves and each other in the attempt to expunge our residual racist atti-
tudes, depriving ourselves of our racial privileges wherever we saw
them lurking, and becoming in the process what we called "white-race
traitors." Together, we ground our racial consciousness to a fine powder.

Our ambition, however, our regularly stated intention, as I was
slowly, reluctantly learning, was little more than a well-intended fantasy. In Africa the racial mythologies we'd grown up with were turned
on their heads. A minority at home was a majority here; the majority
was black, and the minority minuscule in number and white. And like
many of the African-Americans who'd traveled to Africa in search of
their roots, Zack believed that he'd come to a race-blind continent, and
since surely *he* wasn't a colonial, nor, given his radical politics, was he an
imperialist, he could be race blind, too.

It seemed to me, however, that at bottom nothing had changed. Despite the beauty and energy of Accra, when I looked beyond its exoticism
to the day-to-day reality of people's lives, I saw that they were made poor
and weak so that I could be rich and powerful; they watched their ba
bies shrivel in their arms so that my children, should I ever want to bear
them, could be inoculated against the plagues and run in the sun and
someday go to Harvard. I could no more alter my relationship with the
Africans who surrounded me in Ghana than I'd been able in the United
States to alter my relationship with the Americans whose African ancestors had been enslaved and shipped to the New World. In the United
States I'd been stuck with being white; in Africa I was stuck with being
American.

And while this was not a problem for Zack, for me there was no
morally acceptable response to it, other than guilt. Which, to be
honest, was not a problem for me, even though it alienated me even farther from Zack. Over the years, I had learned to live with guilt and had
even come to embrace it, for I was the strictly engineered product of an
old New England puritan line, starting in the seventeenth century and

ending with my parents. With my father in particular, who believed in his bones that one's consciousness of guilt led straight to good works and awareness of God. One's awareness of guilt was a barometer of one's virtue. Absence of that awareness led straight to sinful self-indulgence and damnation. And unlike feelings of mere regret or remorse, which mainly work to separate people from one another, feelings of guilt, thanks to my father's teachings, had always felt warmly humanizing to me. Even when I was a child, it was guilt that had let me join the species. And there in Africa, for the first time in years, those feelings emerged in a pure, de-racialized stream. It was all about class, I decided, not race, and I dove into the stream and swam as if born to it.

I knew I seemed cold to Zack. I couldn't help it. His presence numbed me, as if by anesthesia. Whenever he bragged about how much money he made buying and selling Ghanaian art, I merely sniffed and turned away, and when in response he swarmed all over me with explanations and rationalizations, I could not bother to answer. I was a bitch.

Finally, there came the night that we both had been secretly waiting for. He'd shown up unexpectedly at the apartment where, having thought he was off to buy art, I'd gotten stoned and was sitting out on the balcony, blissfully watching the show below. I had seen him drive up in his van, but felt too heavy and thick bodied to move or put out the joint. He went straight to his bedroom, and changed his shirt for a fresh one. As he started back out he caught a whiff of the sticky sweet smoke from the balcony and followed his nose.

"Where'd you get the wee? Any good?" he asked, laughing and ruffling my hair affectionately. He plucked the joint from my fingers and took a hard hit. "You been copping my shit?"

"Once in a while."

He laughed and handed back the joint. "Just don't leave me an empty jar, that's all. You oughta get outa this pad more. You're gonna dry up and turn into one of those gray, sour-faced old ladies sitting on their verandas. Maybe you oughta get laid, for chrissakes," he said. "C'mon, I'm heading over to Afrikiko's. Let's get juiced, do some dancing, and I'll introduce you to some people."

Afrikiko's was a small, dim bar on Liberation Avenue where American expats sometimes hung out and traded job and housing information and bought and sold drugs, so I knew what kind of people he meant. His friends. Deadbeat dads on the lam, Black Panthers under indictment in the States, dope-smoking white Rastafarians who'd spent too much time in Jamaica. But he was right, I needed to get laid.

The place was crowded with men, most of whom were non-Africans, and a small number of women, most of whom were Africans. We grabbed a table in a corner, and Zack ordered us each a Gulder. When the waitress brought the beers and we'd taken a sip and had visually cruised the bar and hadn't seen anyone Zack recognized or anyone I was in the slightest curious about or eager to meet, I suddenly, without forethought, blurted out, "I'm splitting, Zack."

"We just got here. You are weird."

"No, I mean splitting from Accra. From Ghana."

He studied me for a moment. "Yeah, well, I kind of figured that's what was up. You're ready to cop a plea and go home to Mommy and Daddy. You've had that look for weeks, man. I can read it." He lighted a cigarette, held up his empty Gulder bottle, and waved again for another. "Yeah, no shit. You and Mark Rudd and all the other wunderkinds. You guys bob up at press conferences with famous liberal lawyers at your side after making secret deals with federal prosecutors because you're worried about turning thirty."

"I don't mean that, going aboveground. Besides, I'm already thirty-four. No, Zack, I'm just splitting. Splitting off from you. Going it alone from here on."

"That's not your style. There are followers and there are leaders," he pronounced. "You, you're a follower, believe me. Bernardine, Kathy, Tom, Bill Ayers, even Mark—I mean, they're *leaders*, man. But you, you

are not," he said. "Me neither, if you want to know the truth," he added
and shrugged, as if he didn't much care.

"Maybe I don't have to be a follower *or* a leader. Maybe I can be
something else."

"Yeah? Like what?"

"I don't know. A loner. Myself."

"A loner!" He snickered. "Yourself. Yeah, well, good luck. It's a little late
for that, I think." The waitress finally brought him his Gulder, and he unfolded his long legs and stood as if to say goodbye. He paid her, picked
up his drink, and crossed the room to another table, where a pair of
white kids with matted brown dreadlocks were playing dominoes.
Turning his back to me, he drank and smoked and from his great height
watched them play.

I started to get up from the table, when suddenly Zack turned and
strode over to me, his face red and fisted. "Sit down," he ordered. "I've
got something to tell you."

"Fine."

I sat, and he looked evenly past my mask and into my eyes, as if
about to confess that all these years he'd been in love with me. Or all
these years he'd hated me. Instead, he said, "You're here on false prem-
ises, Hannah, you know that?"

"No shit."

"No, I mean it. I'm gonna tell you something you won't like hearing,
but if you're set on leaving you probably oughta know it."

"So tell."

"You think you had to get out of New Bedford and leave the country, that you had no choice. You think it's because you got caught in a
stupid crossfire between me and some very heavy black dudes, et cetera,
and it was the only way for you to protect Carol and her kid."

"Yes. Something like that."

"Yeah, well, it's not true."

"It's not true? What's not?"

"No. The truth is, I shot myself."

"You what?"

"I shot myself. By accident. Did it with my own fucking gun, too, trying to stash it under the seat of my cab."

I looked away and pretended I hadn't heard him.

"There never was any black dudes or SLA. Or whatever, Black Liberation Army. I mean, there was, there is, but I never knew them, not personally. I only heard about them from some Weather guys in New York."

"Why, Zack? Why'd you blame black men?"

"I don't know. Shit, I guess I thought it would impress you if you believed I was tight with them. I bought the gun in New Hampshire, actually, at one of those roadside guns 'n' ammo shops, and carried it around in the cab in case some jerk tried to rob me. Then I figured I better learn how to use it, so I drove out to some woods on the other side of Plymouth one night to practice with it. I shot off a bunch of bullets, then got worried about the noise and local cops, so I reloaded the damn thing and when I leaned down and tried to shove it back under the seat of my cab, I shot myself. I guess I forgot to put the safety on." He shook his head at the memory. "Pathetic."

"And you're telling me this now? Jesus, why now?"

"I don't know," he said. "In case maybe you want to go home, I guess. You know, to Carol. To the States. And the truth is, the longer you're here, the more guilty I feel about it. So in a way I'm glad you're splitting. I mean, it pisses me off, but it gives me a chance to sort of clear my conscience."

"But why did you come to me? When you shot yourself, I mean. Why didn't you just go to the hospital?"

"I'd bought the gun with a phony ID," he said and smiled wanly. "I was underground, babe. Remember? Like you."

I didn't know what to say to him. I wasn't angry, that's certain. After all, he'd given me exactly what I'd wanted and hadn't dared to ask for. He'd provided me with an excuse to abandon Carol, her child, the New Bedford apartment, my crummy job at Peter Bent Brigham, my sordid and lowly role in the Weather Underground—everything that had become an intolerable burden to me. And along with the excuse, he'd handed me a plane ticket to Africa, a place located as far from my burden as I could have imagined. Here in Africa, I'd enjoyed his protection and advice, and he'd laid his old Africa hand onto my shoulder just heavily enough to make me capable in short order of shrugging it off. And now the dear foolish man was telling me that I was free to abandon him, too. *Go on, babe, split. You want to be a loner now? Go ahead, do it. Do it without guilt, without embarrassment, without regret. You're free, babe, free as a fucking bird.*

I should have said, *Thank you, Zack, a thousand times I thank you.* Instead, I said nothing. I simply got up from the table, turned towards the door, and left my old life and entered a new life, as if walking from one empty room into another.

II

OR ENTERING A DARKENING SKY. And I was following the sun into it, flying like a petrel out along the westering Atlantic coast of Ghana towards Liberia, a tiny country wedged between Côte d'Ivoire and Sierra Leone, a place I knew not at all, where I had not a single friend or acquaintance to turn to, no old Africa hand to aid and abet me in my flight. I had little more than a man's name, Woodrow Sundiata. And all I knew of him was that he was an assistant minister of public health in the government of President William Tolbert and had studied business administration in the U.S. and was said to welcome the arrival in Liberia of English-speaking foreigners with medical training of any sort.

Some weeks earlier, as so often happened, I'd found myself alone one afternoon in the NYU lab office in Accra with no work to do. Bored and restless, I'd opened a file folder marked "Confidential" and had cruised casually through a lengthy correspondence on official stationery between a Mr. Sundiata and my Ghanaian employers, along with copies of letters exchanged between Mr. Sundiata and my employers' American bosses at NYU, including memoranda and cables to and from both employers and bosses concerning the good use to which the directors of the NYU blood plasma lab might put this mid-level West African official who was evidently eager to provide exclusive access to Liberia's large population of chimpanzees, both in the wild and captive, in exchange for American-trained medical personnel and supplies.

> *Such an arrangement could eventually present us with a unique opportunity to obtain at relatively low cost a significant number of animal subjects without violating ITTA regulations and without alerting our competitors to this abundant new source of animal plasma. As we understand the situation in Monrovia, we are to provide Mr. Sundiata's ministry with a few nurses and/or laboratory assistants on renewable six-month contracts, with housing costs and salary to be covered by our New York office, and a single shipment of sterile syringes and miscellaneous antibiotics (quantities yet to be determined). In return, the subject animals are thereafter to be placed effectively under our control. Please explore the matter further at your first opportunity. And confirm the above assumptions re: our anticipated costs . . .*

The night I walked out on Zack at Afrikiko's and abandoned the reality we'd more or less shared since college, I went straight back to the apartment, sat down, and, before I could change my mind, composed a letter to the Liberian assistant minister of public health, asking for a job interview, and the next morning posted it to him. Within a week, I had my answer.

ALL THESE MANY YEARS later, my first meeting with Woodrow still remains vividly clear to me. A ceiling fan turned slowly, stirring the humid air, but not cooling it. My body had been wet with sweat since the moment the plane from Accra landed at Robertsfield Airport. I entered the shabby, disordered office, self-conscious and anxious about my appearance. Compared with the heat and the nearly suffocating humidity here in Monrovia, the weather in Accra had been positively balmy. My hair was frizzled, and my white cotton blouse was wrinkled, and I knew that I had huge, gray sweat circles under my arms. Rivulets trickled between my breasts and down my sides. I felt fat, fleshy.

Seated at his desk, he flattened his hands and splayed his long, slender fingers and slowly, deliberately lifted his face to meet mine. Woodrow Sundiata, Assistant Minister of Public Health of the Republic of Liberia. He was a small, tight-bodied man with a large, nearly bald head, his complexion as dark as a bassoon. He was not a conventionally handsome man, but to me then and there he was sexy. His eyes were light brown, the color of tea with milk. I guessed his age—accurately, it would later turn out—to be forty. He was wearing a pale blue, short-sleeved guayabera shirt, starched and pressed, a heavy gold Rolex on his left wrist, and on his right a bracelet of tiny, white cowrie shells strung on braided leather. No wedding band, I observed.

That first day I saw him as more like an old-time samurai than a modern, post-colonial, West African bureaucrat. It was a first impression that would hold up for several months. There was a visible tension between what I took to be his passionate nature and the means by which he kept it in check—he stood up in a single motion, as if caught by surprise, although Miss Dawn Carrington had been twice announced to him, by phone from his outer office and then by his personal assistant, a young, very tall, very black man named Mr. Satterthwaite, who had showed me in and quickly left us alone.

Woodrow Sundiata stepped back against the latticed window, clasped his hands together high on his chest, and made a little bow. He moved with the confidence of a man used to being in charge of situations and people, I thought, a familiar type to me. He looked directly into my eyes, nowhere else, as if everything he needed to know about me was revealed there. Then, abruptly, he looked away, gestured towards a chair next to his desk, and said, "Please sit down, Miss Musgrave."

Musgrave! I was suddenly dizzy and sat down quickly, more to keep my bearings than to be polite. I stammered, "I'm sorry, but . . . but why . . . why do you say that name?" I was sweating even more heavily than before and had trouble breathing, as much from alarm as the heat and the wet weight of the air, which seemed to have been doubled by his words. *Miss Musgrave!* It had been more than five years since a stranger called me by my father's last name. Even underground no one called me by that name, except for Zack, and then only when trying to antagonize me. Was I no longer underground then? Was my secret out? Just like that?

Relief and fear washed over me in successive waves, each nullifying the other. I felt neither emotion on its own, although I knew as a fact, as data, almost, that I was both immensely relieved and very frightened. No, what I *felt* was simple, mind-numbing shock. Shock at finding myself suddenly no longer underground, for that is what his calling me Miss Musgrave meant. It was now a fact. I said to myself simply, *This is amazing!*

"Yes, well, the American embassy in Monrovia, as you no doubt know, keeps track of American citizens residing in West Africa," he said and slipped me a weary, knowing smile and a conspiratorial sigh. "We help them; they help us. Though we, of course, have somewhat different priorities and concerns than do they." His accent was almost Caribbean, British with a musical, lower-register lilt. "Would you prefer that I call you Miss Carrington then?" he asked.

"No. No, that's fine. I'm a little . . . confused, however. And surprised, I guess. That is, that you . . . that I was allowed to enter the country, I mean."

"I imagine so. But all appearances to the contrary, Miss Carrington, and in spite of our ancient and mostly honorable, historical connections to the United States, we don't work for them. And from the file we received, it didn't seem that your Miss Hannah Musgrave was of any particular danger to the Republic of Liberia," he said. "Are you?"

"Am I what?"

He laughed. He had a pencil-thick gap in the middle of his upper front teeth which was strikingly attractive to me. "Oh, either one. Are you a danger to us? Are you Hannah Musgrave?"

"No," I said. "To the first question. And yes to the second." It was true, I posed no danger to anyone. Not anymore, not after today. Except possibly to myself. And in spite of Dawn Carrington's name in my passport and on my Ghanaian exit visa and my Liberian entry visa, I was indeed Hannah Musgrave. And loved hearing this man say it. My name. And wanted him to say it again. Miss Musgrave. Hannah Musgrave.

We sat opposite each other in silence for a long moment, while I tried letting the name cover my body and my mind. But it wouldn't fit over or around me. It pinched and pulled and seemed too small, as if cut for some other woman's body and mind, a woman who was practically a stranger to me. I was no longer the Hannah Musgrave who'd gone underground in 1970, who'd disappeared from the world of parents, town, college, and university, where she once upon a time had played a central role, or at least a known and recognized role. And I could no more return now to being the old, abandoned Hannah than I could leap forward in time and become the new, nicely recovered Hannah, thank you very much, who tells this story these many years later. I might have been once again dressing myself in Hannah Musgrave's name, but the woman who was born wearing it was gone, apparently forever, as if she were the unexpected victim of a rare, fast-acting, fatal disease. But if I wasn't that woman anymore—and was no longer Dawn Carrington—then who was I? Desperately, that afternoon in Assistant Minister Sundiata's office, I struggled to become the thirty-four-year-old Miss Musgrave freshly arrived in the city of Monrovia from Accra in search of a job, any kind of job, Mr. Sundiata, and housing, any sort of shelter will do, and intelligent company, for I am utterly alone, cut off from all the communities to which I previously belonged. *Oh, and yes, thank you, I would be pleased to have dinner with you this evening, sir.*

"My assistant, Mr. Satterthwaite, will drive you to your quarters, so you can get settled. Perhaps you'd like to take a short nap and freshen up a bit? I'll come 'round at seven o'clock, if that's not too early."

"No, that's fine," I said. "But . . . I'm a little confused. Look, I'm sorry to ask, but I have to. How can I be sure that you're not . . . ?" I paused. "All right, let me say it. How can I know that you won't turn me over to the American embassy?"

He smiled. "To tell you the truth, you can't. But really, Miss Musgrave—may I call you Hannah?"

"Yes! Please do."

"It's a lovely name," he said and flashed his gap-toothed smile. "Yes, Hannah, you wouldn't do us much good wasting away in an American jail, now would you?" He stood and took my hand in his and examined it, and for a second I thought he was going to kiss it. "You're not married, are you." It was more a statement than a question.

"No."

"And you've come here alone. That's quite something. What about your American companion in Accra?" He glanced back at an open file folder on his desk. "Zachary Procter, he calls himself. Not his real name, of course."

"No, it's his real name. He's still in Accra. In fact, I don't think Zack even knows where I am. I don't think he knows I've left Ghana. I . . . I'm quite alone."

"That's good. Good for him, I mean. Because I don't see how we could be as . . . *lenient* with Mr. Procter as we are being with you. But let me assure you, Hannah," he said, and now he did indeed kiss my hand, a gesture that was both comical and elegant, making me smile. "You are no longer alone."

WOODROW'S OFFICE in the Ministry of Health was located off Tubman Boulevard at the southeastern edge of Monrovia in a freshly built, three-storey, cinder-block cube attached to the John F. Kennedy Medical Center. His assistant, Mr. Satterthwaite, drove the ministry Mercedes, a ten-year-old, velvety, dark gray sedan in immaculate condition, and I sat in air-conditioned ease in the back and gazed at the city as we passed through it. Earlier, coming in from Robertsfield Airport some fifty-five kilometers south of the city—packed into an antique Plymouth sedan with six other passengers picked up along the way until I was finally dropped off at the ministry—I had been so distracted by the heat and so anxious and tentative about my reasons for being in this place, this city, this country, this *continent*, that I barely noticed where I was, and if the driver or one of my sweating, placid, half-asleep fellow passengers had told me that I'd been returned to Accra by mistake or had been magically transported to New Bedford, Massachusetts, I might have believed him. That's how disoriented I'd become since leaving Accra. But as I saw clearly now, I certainly was not in New England. And Monrovia was not Accra, and Ghana was not Liberia.

In those days, Monrovia, the capital, was still lovely, if somewhat bizarre looking, at least to my innocent eyes. Innocent, that is, of Liberia's odd history. The principal buildings of government—the copper-domed capitol; the bright, white palace of the president; the supreme court building; the treasury building; and so on; each pointed out with obvious pride by Satterthwaite as we drove into the city from the ministry offices on the outskirts—were miniaturized versions of the same structures in Washington, D.C., as if down-at-the-heels country cousins were putting on big-city airs. Bisecting the center of the city, its spine, was Broad Street, its two lanes divided by a grassy, parklike island and bordered on both sides by towering trees. Here, along the meandering ridge of Cape Mesurado—the rumpled, densely populated, yet still green peninsula where the Mesurado River meets the sea—white wood-frame houses with wide verandahs and floor-to-ceiling shuttered windows sprawled behind neatly hedged and trimmed front yards garnished with meticulously tended flower beds. Scarlet, yellow, and pink bougainvilleas sloshed against porch steps and over walkways, and lawn sprinklers carved glittery pale arcs in the sunlight. The wide main streets and sidewalks were free of trash and cleanly swept, and at nearly every crossing a steepled Protestant church kept the faith. Unpaved side streets and rutted alleys cut downhill from the ridge into brush-filled gullies, where, as we passed, I glimpsed clusters of one-room shanties, small shops, and narrow, single-storey shotgun houses hand built from cast-off lumber and recycled construction materials. The neighborhoods of the poor. But the poor did not look all that poor. As if the men had gone off early to steady jobs someplace else, almost all of the people I saw down there were babies, small children, and women neatly dressed in cotton skirts and blouses and brilliantly colored traditional wraps and headdresses, adults and children alike carrying something—water in plastic tubs, baskets of groceries and garden produce, firewood, bunches of bananas, a chicken.

West of Broad and strung along United Nations Drive towards the cliffs that overlooked the sea were the luxury hotels, the Ambassador and the Mamba Point, half hidden behind high walls and palms. Along Broad and for several blocks off it, public and commercial buildings preened, many of them fronted by tall, neo-classical columns—the Liberian national bank and branches of U.S. and British banks, the municipal police headquarters, the central post office, the Rivoli Cinema, a few small hotels, public utilities, and most imposing of all, the yellow-brick Masonic temple. Oddly, the streets and buildings of Monrovia and the overall ambience of the city, despite its size and sprawl and mix of architectural styles, didn't so much suggest late-twentieth-century West Africa as it did a 1940s sleepy Southern county seat; and the city might have been a set for a sentimental movie about postwar Dixie, *To Kill a Mockingbird* maybe—except that all the actors in the movie, even the extras, were black.

In their dress and demeanor and comportment, and with their slightly diluted coloration, the citizens of Monrovia looked more African-American than African, which in a sense they were, although I knew nothing of that yet. And it was the bourgeois, small-town African-Americans of the 1940s and '50s that they resembled, not of the 1970s, certainly not of today. In Monrovia, even as recently as twenty-five years ago, when the good citizens left their homes, they dressed up. The middle-class men wore seersucker or linen suits and neckties and sported homburgs or Panama hats, and the women wore respectable calf-length, flower-patterned dresses and white gloves, and even carried parasols. Their children walked hand in hand in simple, neatly pressed school uniforms. Occasionally, one saw a batch of Liberian soldiers bully through the traffic in a U.S. troop carrier or jeep, and one remembered the Cold War and Liberia's special allegiance to the U.S. One remembered that the country was our man in Africa, as it were. One saw more heavily armed police officers directing traffic than there were vehicles on the streets; and one noticed cadres of uniformed cops with automatic weapons providing security at the banks and other public and corporate buildings; and one recalled the eagerness with which the three-term president, William Tolbert, and his predecessor, the seven-term president Tubman, both men much admired in Washington, had peddled their beautiful country to foreign investors like entertaining and gracious pimps.

But this was before the bloody coups and the civil war—when the population of the city was still made up almost entirely of civilians. The porticoed homes along the ridge were still owned by the descendants of nineteenth-century African-American settlers, and the people living in the gullies and on the side streets were the descendants of the native Africans the former had displaced, tribal villagers who'd run out of arable land and had come to the big city for work. Down by the harbor nestled the shops and warehouses and homes of the Indian and Middle-Eastern traders and merchants who for decades had been migrating there from Uganda and Rwanda. Everyone seemed to be getting by and getting along. And here and there, striding impatiently through the crowd as if looking for the exit, came the few foreigners, who were white and either in Liberia on business or else attached to one of the embassies—the main one being the American Embassy, pointed out to me by Satterthwaite where UN Drive bent north and east towards the Mesurado River and the bay.

"That the American headquarters," he said, nodding in the direction of a palatial white estate surrounded by high, razor-wired, cinderblock walls. The Stars-and-Stripes drooped from a flagpole, and a spindly forest of antennas and several large satellite dishes scanned the skies from the flat, palisaded roof of the main building. "CIA, FBI, the Marines—all of 'em in there," Satterthwaite said, as if to himself, and chuckled. "Busy, busy, busy."

"Oh," was all I said. And thought: *My country, my enemy.*

I knew almost nothing then of the history of Liberia and its deep and abiding connections to *my country, my enemy.* Piecemeal and from various sources I gradually discovered where I had landed. Liberia is a tiny nation, barely the size of Tennessee and shaped like a thick-bodied lizard, and for generations has given the appearance of being of no newsworthy importance to anyone not actually in residence there. There is fertile land for growing rice and other tropical crops; and rubber, of course, but not much; and beneath the jungle floor a few small caches of diamonds, but hardly enough to sell off or trade away, it was thought. And were it not for the end of the Cold War and, within a year or two, the discovery of a deep and wide vein of diamonds running the length and breadth of the land all the way into Sierra Leone and Guinea, the country might have remained—except to its residents and academic and U.S. State Department specialists—an all-but-forgotten backwater, a misplaced packet of towns and jungle villages and one small city squeezed between its larger, richer, more socially elaborate and cantankerous neighbors on either side, Sierra Leone and Côte d'Ivoire.

To get to the beginning of the modern history of Liberia and to understand its peculiarities, you have to return to the early nineteenth century, when religious, financial, and racial interests in the United States neatly converged over the idea of installing a man in West Africa. In the early 1820s, white Americans, having noticed the presence of a growing number of ex-slaves on the streets of northern cities, began to realize for the first time that they were facing not just a slavery problem, but a *race* problem as well. And while the first problem was political—merely the price a republic had to pay for the economic advantages of owning a self-perpetuating, constitutionally protected slave-labor force of nearly three million people—the second, the "race problem," was moral, emotional, cultural, and, I suppose, sexual. Its dimensions were mythic and deeply threatening to most white Americans' dearly held view of themselves as a morally and racially pure, not to say, superior, people. Besides, the presence of growing numbers of freed black Americans living more or less like white people in cities like Philadelphia and New York was having an unsettling effect on the slave population in the South. Before you knew it, the free blacks would want the vote. Before you knew it, they'd join with the radical abolitionists and in some states would come to outnumber the pro-slavers.

Thoughtful white and some black Americans asked themselves, Why not send the freed slaves back to Africa? Why not create an alliance between northern white Christians and anti-slavery advocates and slaveholders from New York State to Georgia, and give the already free and manumitted blacks some seed money, an ax, and a Bible? And why not raise government and philanthropic funds to purchase the freedom of enslaved blacks—especially the more troublesome ones—give them a one-way ticket to Africa in exchange for their freedom, and let those people go?

Baptist and Methodist missionaries on reconnaissance had already spotted a corner of coastal West Africa overlooked by the British, French, and Portugese slave traders that perfectly suited these purposes. It was a large tract of impenetrable jungle, mangrove swamps, and malaria-infested estuaries, a plot of super-heated, saturated ground that no one else wanted—except, of course, for the fifteen or sixteen tribes of illiterate, black-skinned savages who happened to be living there unencumbered by legal deed or title. The word *Liberia* was not on any map, though surely the native people had a name for the region and for the Mandingo tribal village situated conveniently for coastal trade between the Europeans and the tribes from the hinterlands on a high peninsula at the seaside terminus of a large river. Why not ship forty or fifty thousand mostly literate, nominally Christian black-skinned Americans overseas to Africa, then? Why not send them from the fatherland to the motherland, from the home of their masters to the home of their ancestors, tell them this land is your land, and let them make the place safe for Christianity, civilization, and capitalism?

The place was perfect. The first American settlers—several hundred Christian freedmen and -women and recently manumitted slaves—came ashore in 1825. They named the Mandingo trading village on the peninsula Monrovia, after James Monroe, the fifth American president, who had been an early sponsor of the notion of return. And thus, in short order, was established the first U.S. colony. Soon to be known as the Republic of Liberia, it was organized from the start to operate not as a straightforward colony, but as a covert surrogate, clamped tight to the white-skinned leg of its North American founding fatherland. Consequently, as early as the 1840s, the Americans, unlike their European cousins, had installed in West Africa a home-grown, self-replacing class of overseers—a loyal ruling class made up of tens of thousands of freed and escaped ex-slaves who'd been making Philadelphia, New York, and Boston so scary, and nearly as many manumitted slaves, almost all of them from the South, who'd been offered and had accepted banishment in place of slavery. And for a long time, even to today, the arrangement paid the investors back handsomely.

After the Civil War, of course, it grew increasingly difficult to convince African-Americans to relocate to the soppy, equatorial jungles of West Africa, when they could homestead instead in Kansas or the Oklahoma Territory. Recruitment by the American Colonization Societies, as the founders were called, fell off. In Liberia, however, a diminished ability to recruit new settlers turned out not to be a major handicap. By the 1870s the black American settlers were running things—mainly from the coastal towns of Monrovia and Buchanan—efficiently and ruthlessly enough to generate a wide range of exports at little or no cost to the Stateside importers. Not only was this a feel-good program for white Christians in the United States, but also the resident tribes of savages in the nation were proving to be nearly as economically advantageous as the enslaved African-Americans had been back before the Civil War. The black Americans in Africa had duplicated nicely the old Southern and Caribbean plantation overseer system. It had worked there; it could work in Africa, too. No reason for the whip hand to be white.

By the end of the nineteenth century, just as in parts of the deep South and the Caribbean at the end of the eighteenth, one percent of the population of Liberia for all intents and purposes owned the other ninety-nine percent, and a huge chunk of the profits generated by the back-breaking labor of that ninety-nine percent went straight to the board rooms of America. Where, after the usual executive skim, it got distributed to the white Christian shareholders whose parents and grandparents had put up the original investment. When you pay for the seeds, you get to keep most of the crop. That's why they call it seed money.

Until the turn of the century, the main exports were rice, lumber, spices, bananas, cocoa, and from the hinterlands, ivory. In the twentieth century, with the development of the auto industry, the main crop became rubber. But things change. Not everything, of course; principles of exploitation and use remain the same. Where once there had been enough black-skinned savages and rubber to put treads on every motor vehicle in the West and enough banana trees to put a banana on every plate, by the late 1950s, cheaper, closer-to-home supply sources for both rubber and tropical fruit had been located. The Firestone, B. F. Goodrich, and United Fruit ships turned towards Central and South America and Hawaii, and our man in Africa got left behind.

After that, when it came to Liberia, the Americans seemed interested only in the Cold War. If you happened to be a member of the old boss class—if you were one of those Liberians who, since they couldn't distinguish themselves from the savages by skin color, had turned to calling themselves Americo-Liberians—this wasn't all bad. Having become the true inheritors of the post-bellum mentality of the grandchildren of the old southern slave holders, the Americos were mostly right-wing, conservative Protestants who believed in the moral and cultural superiority of their gene code, which they had inherited from their African-American ancestors. Consequently, to the delight of U.S. politicians and State Department officials, when the Cold War arrived, the Americos turned out to be as anti-Communist as Barry Goldwater, making the Cold War years, for the Americo ruling class, boom years. Foreign aid fluttered down from the skies like manna onto the wide verandahs and lawns along Broad Street from Mamba Point to Tubman Boulevard, missing altogether the rest of the country, where millions of increasingly disgruntled savages lived in near-starvation in mud-hut jungle villages. This, then, in the spring of 1976, was Liberia, the country to which I had fled.

SATTERTHWAITE AND I stepped from the hushed, air-conditioned interior of the Mercedes into dense, wet heat and a cloudburst of cacophonous sound. It came from a distance. It came from a place out of our sight, but loudly surrounding us, as if blasted from speakers hidden in the branches of the cotton tree spreading overhead—an arrhythmic, sustained slamming of thick flesh against steel, crossed by loud, high-pitched, rising screeches. Not human, not animal, something in between; and not in pain or anger, but something of both.

After a moment, the banging and screeches faded to a held silence. Then abruptly they returned, louder than before. Satterthwaite gestured vaguely in the direction of a large, rusting Quonset hut at the rear of the walled-in compound. "Seems like nobody here today, 'cept them chimps," he mumbled.

Close by, facing the red-dirt yard, was a squat, four-square building of unpainted cinder-block that looked like a military interrogation center and that Satterthwaite said housed the administration office and lab. He told me to wait by the car and entered the building, returning at once with a ring of keys, which he handed to me. "S'posed to be some kind of caretaker guarding the place alla time," he said crossly and led me around the main building to a wide, tree-shaded yard behind it, where three small wood-frame cottages with front porches were located side by side. Here the sounds of the chimpanzees were slightly muffled, and for the first time since stepping from the car, I could focus my attention and began to see and hear what was in front of me.

"Them was small-small Firestone houses built for the native foremen. We got 'em moved an' set 'em up special for the Americans who run the blood lab," Satterthwaite explained.

Inside, the units were identical—a single room cleanly swept and minimally furnished with a narrow, stripped bed, a table and two chairs, a kitchen counter with a hot plate, a few plastic buckets, enough dishes and utensils for two people, and a closet-sized bathroom. All three buildings were empty and evidently unclaimed. I chose the cottage farthest from the chimps.

"Can't promise water or 'lectric full time," Satterthwaite said, smiling. "But mostly it comes. I'll check on that caretaker fellow," he added, then dashed back to the air-conditioned comfort of the Mercedes and drove from the compound slowly, almost delicately, as if hoping to be seen by passersby.

I dropped my duffel in a corner. My worldly possessions, entire. Then lay down on the cot, exhausted from travel and the relentless heat and the several shocks of the day, and tried to sleep. But it was impossible. The screeches and banging of metal from the Quonset hut were like an ongoing accident, a slow-motion highway pileup. The racket frightened and confused me. I couldn't stop hearing it, and couldn't get used to it either. I wanted only to replay my meeting with Woodrow Sundiata and savor the details, ruminate on their implications. What was wrong with the chimps? Why were they so agitated? Weren't there people to take care of them, to feed and quiet them down? I'd never seen chimpanzees in the flesh, only on television and in circuses wearing cute costumes—grinning, mischievous little creatures that made us laugh and shake our heads, amazed by their uncanny resemblance to humans and relieved by the difference. But these creatures sounded like huge and powerful beasts. They sounded violent and insane.

I tried covering my head with the thin pillow, but it did no good. Finally, I got up and went into the musty, windowless bathroom, closed the door, and stood in darkness inside the shower stall with the plastic curtain drawn shut on me—and at last could no longer hear them. After a few moments, not so oddly, my thoughts drifted back for the first time in a long time to a rainy night in 1967, standing in line for a movie in Durham, North Carolina, at a small art-house theater. The theater was located across the street from the county jail, a high, dark-brick building with bars in the third-storey windows facing the street and the line of moviegoers below. I'd been sent to North Carolina to help organize SDS chapters at Duke and Chapel Hill, and I remembered the movie—it was *Easy Rider*, of all things—because it was the only movie I saw that entire fall and I came away loathing it. While I waited in line for the theater to open, a few of the prisoners, men barely visible to the moviegoers on the sidewalk below, started shouting down at us, perhaps at first as a joke or to harass us, hollering obscenities and curses. *Hey, you assholes! Motherfuckers! Hey, you cocksuckers, suck on this!* And so on. Then other prisoners joined in. I imagined that all of them were black, although surely some were not. In seconds there were dozens of them calling down to us, and their hollers had turned into wild, uncontrolled, enraged screams, and they were banging metal objects against the bars, their tin cups, I supposed, or maybe just their fists—a clamorous, outpouring of anger that so shocked and frightened me that I wanted to break out of line and flee down the rain-soaked street and into the night.

When at last the door to the theater opened and we were able to get inside, the sudden silence of the lobby was even more terrible than the noise outside. It was as if we had become prisoners ourselves. We looked around the lobby at the posters, inhaled the familiar, friendly smell of fresh popcorn and candy, caught one another's scared gazes, recognized them as our own, and quickly looked elsewhere.

Lost in the memory of that night, I slowly sank to the cool, dry floor of the shower stall—when suddenly something with claws darted across my ankle and calf. I half leapt, half fell from the stall onto the bathroom floor, pushed open the door to the outer room to let in light, and looked carefully back. A brown rat the size of a man's shoe stared at me from a dark corner of the shower stall. I reached around for something to club it with, something to protect myself from it. Nothing. The bathroom was bare—just a toilet without a seat, an empty plastic pail for a sink. And then I saw the cockroaches. I hadn't noticed them earlier, though surely they'd been there all along, watching me. Despite the sweltering heat, my body went cold, as shiny, dark-brown packs of brooch-sized cockroaches moved in undulating waves across the walls and over the crackled, lime-green linoleum floor. Scrambling to my feet, I heard again the undiminished screams of the chimps and the clang and bang of large, hard bodies being hurled relentlessly over and over against the steel bars of cages. It was the noise of bedlam, the cries from a madhouse or a torture chamber.

I ran from the bathroom, slammed the door shut behind me, and leaned against it, breathing hard. Though the room in the fading, evening light was half in darkness, I could now see cockroaches there, too—whole legions of them marching across the cot and pillow where minutes earlier I had lain my head. Why hadn't I seen them before? Had I been that disoriented, that distracted by fatigue and the noise of the chimpanzees? The insects swarmed over my duffel, scattered from clusters on the kitchen counter, and regrouped on the hot plate. They raced across the dusty surface of the small dresser in the corner. They were everywhere, spreading over the formica-topped table as if spilled from a pail and shuddering over the floor and across the threadbare braided rug—hundreds of cockroaches, thousands, fleeing from my sight into pockets of darkness between walls, behind and beneath furniture, plates, and utensils, as if I had unexpectedly caught them doing a forbidden thing, a black mass or an obscene sexual act.

I held my breath and didn't move. The cockroaches seemed to do the same, as if watching, waiting for me to attack them or run. I began to tremble, from my hands up my arms to my body and onto my face. I felt my lips purse involuntarily, and my right cheek started to twitch, as if with neuralgia. *What is* wrong *with me?* I wondered. Even though alone,

I felt embarrassed. *But this is the way things* are *in Africa,* I reminded myself. *It's the tropics, for heaven's sake!* What did I expect in a house that's been empty for weeks or months? I'd had to displace cockroaches and rats before, in my apartment in Accra and before that in dozens of rented rooms and filthy apartments and so-called safe houses in the States, and had disinfected my living quarters, set traps, put out poisons, washed floors with lye and scrubbed counters down with ammonia water. And though the chimps were louder and more raucous than I might have expected, I'd heard laboratory animals before—monkeys and bonobos yelling to be fed at this time of day—and had not been frightened by them, only worried that someone might not be there to feed them on time and clean their cages and change their water.

Slowly, carefully, as if walking on loose sheets of paper, I crossed the room and stepped onto the small open porch. *The dirt yard needs sweeping,* I noticed. *I'll buy some candles and mosquito coils at the little corner shop we passed coming in, and tonight when I sleep I'll burn them near the bed.* With relief, I saw a bundle of mosquito netting tied to a ceiling hook above the bed. *Tomorrow I'll scrub down the cottage and put out traps and poison. Tomorrow I'll dispossess these tenants and take over the place, make it my own. I'll meet the people who are supposed to care for the chimps, and I'll learn their schedules and tasks, so that I can fill in for them when they're late or for some reason can't come in to work. And, in fact, right now I'll see if I can figure out how to calm the chimps myself somehow. Perhaps all they need is fresh water, and maybe what and how to feed them will be obvious to me. As soon as I can, possibly this very evening, I'll present myself to the woman who Mr. Sundiata said runs the lab and the man who feeds the chimps and cleans their cages, and they'll tell me what sort of work I am to do here. I'll work hard, very hard, and they will quickly find me irreplaceable. I'll find good friends here, men and women. Liberians speak English, after all, and they're said to like and admire Americans. It will be easy and enjoyable. I may call myself Dawn Carrington, or I may say I am Hannah Musgrave, and I'll make a useful, satisfying, aboveground life for myself here in Liberia. And someday I'll return to the United States, and at last I'll see my mother and father again.*

These were my thoughts as I crossed the compound and approached the door of the Quonset hut. I neared the windowless building, and the screams of the chimpanzees rose in volume and intensity, as if the animals could somehow see and hear me coming. The door was padlocked, like the doors to the cottages. I took from my skirt pocket the ring of keys that Satterthwaite had given me and tried the keys at random until one of them snapped the lock open. Removing it, I swung back the heavy door and faced a black wall of impenetrable darkness.

A vegetative stench gushed from the interior and washed over me. It was oily, hot, and dense, like composted fruit mixed with fresh barnyard manure, but cut with an ingredient that I had never smelled before, something acidic and glandular and starkly repellent, like the brain chemicals of a psychopath. The howls and screeches of the chimpanzees and their compulsive, arrhythmic banging against their cages had merged and become a congealed and hardened quantity of sound, as if it were an object, a quarried thing, a room-size block of stone. My eyes grew slightly used to the darkness, enough to make out a light switch on the wall just inside the door. I reached in and flipped it, and the building filled with cold fluorescent light. Then I stepped across the iron threshold and entered.

The barred cages, racked in two layers from the front of the Quonset hut to the rear, were actually not as small as I'd pictured, not as small as the cages they'd used in the lab in Accra. These were the size and dimensions of a large kitchen appliance, a stove or dishwasher. At first I couldn't see the creatures inside the cages, and for a second I wondered if the cages were empty and all the noise were just a tape-recording being played at high volume, some kind of special effect, as if a bizarre fraud were being carried off here. I looked around the large chamber, half expecting to see a wizard of Oz playing a diabolical noisemaker in the corner. Then I saw the chimpanzees—saw their wild eyes and pink lips and flared, flat nostrils, their almost human faces, their thickly knuckled hands wrapped around the bars, their hunched bodies—and I thought, *Oh, my God, they're much too large for their cages, they're huge, much bigger than I'd ever imagined. They're the size of human beings!*

There were some who were children, looking stunned and almost comatose, lying in the corners of their cages. Others, with barely enough room to pace a few short, angry steps, back and forth, back and forth, were evidently adolescents. A half-dozen more, full-grown adults—females, I could tell from their huge genitalia—were forced to stand bent over, nearly filling the cages with their bulk. Farther down, I saw four or five even larger adults shaking the bars with terrible force—clearly males, with surprisingly small penises, although I didn't know why I was surprised and was embarrassed for having noticed at all. The big males spat at me and threw garbage and chunks of their feces in my direction, glowered, and showed me their cavernous, wide-open, nearly toothless mouths. I couldn't understand. Why were they toothless? Their teeth, their powerful canine teeth, must have been removed, yanked out with pliers. The chimpanzees' shoulders and chests were scabbed, and they had pulled out patches of hair all over, the young as well as the old. And, good Lord, what a stench of brutality filled that place! The animals were in more physical and emotional pain than I was capable of imagining. *Why is this happening? Who has done this?*

I could not absorb what I was seeing. It had no meaning. The scene bewildered me, as if it had been contrived by a species other than human, a species as clever as ours, as organized and rational, but demonic. I stood a few feet inside the doorway and stared at the dark faces of the chimpanzees, and I couldn't stop myself, I suddenly began to weep. I cried for them, certainly, their pain and suffering, and then I wept for the humans who had imprisoned them. And then I felt my stomach knot and unknot, and in confusion I cried for myself. When, suddenly, I felt a touch on my shoulder. The dead weight of a hand. I glanced at my shoulder and saw a black hand with long, slender fingers lying there, and I leapt away from it.

"Ah, forgive me, Hannah. I didn't mean to startle you."

It was Woodrow—Mr. Sundiata to me then—facing me with a

benign smile. It was the dark-brown face of the man whom in a few short months I would marry, the man whose three sons, in less than two years, I would bear. The husband whom I would deceive and abandon and to whom I would later return. The man who would betray and forsake me and who would later beg for my forgiveness and receive it. The man who would be chopped down and killed before my eyes. You may not believe me, but in those few brief seconds I saw what was coming. It was as if in the darkened room of my future an overhead light had been switched on and immediately, as soon as the room was illuminated, turned off again, dropping the room back into pitch darkness, and though I would remember what I had seen, the way one remembers a week-old dream, I would not glimpse it again until after it was long past and gone.

"I'm a bit early, I know," Woodrow said, still smiling. "My apologies, dear Hannah. But I wanted to show you a little of our fair city before darkness descends."

I fell into his arms, weeping freshly, out of control, ashamed of myself and feeling foolish, a silly, weak-kneed American girl falling into the arms of a big, strong African man. But I couldn't explain, I couldn't tell him what it was that had made me weep and practically ask him to hold me. I didn't know if it was the sight of the mutilated, imprisoned chimpanzees that had made me weep or this awful, roach-ridden, rat-infested place. Or the fear of Africa, of being so alone this far from anything or anyone familiar to me. Zack, who had made Africa seem almost friendly and as already known to me as it was to him, was no longer there. I'd come so far away that everyone I had ever known was gone from my life now. Then I thought that perhaps it was the shock and relief from having suddenly found myself no longer living underground. Yes, that's why I'm weeping, I decided. Replacing my false identity and the fears and comforts that accompanied it with my ill-fitting old identity and its fears and comforts had to be a sharp blow to the psyche. It had happened so suddenly and unexpectedly that I was reacting to it only now.

Or was it the quickly fading vision of my future?

Or all of these at once?

Woodrow eased me from the building to the yard outside, where it felt comparatively cool. For the first time since entering the building I inhaled deeply. Woodrow drew the heavy door shut behind us, clicked the lock onto the hasp, and walked me slowly towards the waiting car, all the while murmuring into my ear that I was surely exhausted, that I needn't worry about the chimps. He had roused their attendant, Haddad, from a nap, and the man was on his way over now to feed and water the poor beasts. And a nice air-conditioned ride about the city would revive me, and then, over a leisurely dinner on the terrace of the Mamba Point Hotel overlooking the sea, we would get to know one another better and more personally.

"Hannah, I want you to know that I have decided to take an interest in your situation," he said. "Does that please you?"

I didn't answer him. But the truth is it did please me. It pleased me immensely.

FOR THE FIRST few months of our courtship, as in the old days with Zack, I felt that one of us, Woodrow or I, was wearing a mask. But I had no way of knowing which. With Zack, it had been as if both of us peered through eyeholes, so no problem: Zack and I were each two people, and knew it.

Maybe it was this *courting* business. Over the years I had been involved with many men—not many, actually, even though it's the sixties and early seventies we're talking about here, and my twenties. *Numerous*, let's say. And I had believed at least twice that I was in love, once for as long as six months, both times wrongly and inconsequentially. They were crushes, infatuations, fixations, maybe, and there's no point in my going into detail here. The truth is, I had never really been in love. And, perhaps more important, I had never been courted before. This was new and strange and exciting, and although the process confused me, I plunged ahead anyhow.

I wondered if this was how it had been for my mother and father. "When your father and I were courting . . ." my mother's illustrations from her youth frequently began, but when it came to matters of the hearts and minds and men and women and the language used to portray them, I was a pure product of my generation and thus hadn't a clue as to what she was talking about.

Two or three times I'd stopped my mother's story and asked directly, "What do you mean, 'courting'?"

"You know, dear, when Daddy and I were first together. When he was in med school and I was still at Smith . . ."

"What do you mean, 'together'?"

"Well, *dating*, I guess. And all that. Getting to know one another. The way one does," she said, her voice rising. "Before one marries, I mean." Her eyes darted nervously away from my gaze, as if I'd accused her of having done something disgraceful. "Why are you asking this, Hannah? I was only telling a little story."

Why, indeed? I knew what my mother meant. I knew my mommy's language, her silences and euphemisms, her code words and coy abbreviations, knew them better than I knew the language of my friends. My mother was right to feel defensive and angry. I was attacking her. But for what? For her timidity concerning the subject of sex, I suppose. For her placid reliance on words like *courting* and *dating*, as if they meant the same to every woman of every age and thus could be used politely under any and all circumstances to conceal as much as they revealed.

I wanted to say, Do you mean when you and Daddy were first *fucking*, Mother? Is that what you're remembering at the start of your twenty-times-told tale of the day that he took you to meet his parents for the first time? And while you all sat in the parlor—it was a *parlor*, not a living room, right?— waiting for the maid to call you to lunch, the three of them, Daddy and Grandfather and Grandmother Musgrave, silently read, Grandmother from her Bible, Grandfather from the *Wall Street Journal*, and Daddy from a medical textbook; and you, Mother, sat alone on the wide, hard sofa with your legs crossed primly at the ankles and stared at your lap, silenced by the silence of the others, as if the three of them were not reading but were lost in private prayer.

Courting. And now here I was myself dealing with a man in the same way, meeting him for lunch and dinner three and four times a week, talking on the telephone almost daily, giving and receiving little gifts, meeting his friends, and soon, soon, he promised, his family, but plenty of time yet for that. I was dealing with Woodrow Sundiata in a way that I knew could only be called courting.

And we weren't fucking. We were barely kissing. We held hands when walking along the moonlit beach, but rarely in public, and were held in each other's arms when dancing at the Mamba Point Hotel or at the several government and Masonic balls that Woodrow invited me to. Mostly, though, we talked, talked to one another, talked in the way that is specific to courtship, speaking at first, as all lovers do, through a mask to a mask—long hours of talk that over time, weeks, months, slowly, atom by atom, transformed the mask of the other into an actual face and made one's own mask as invisible to the wearer as to the viewer. It was how one lost track of the masks and how one came to know oneself anew. I thought: So this is what it's like, being in love! I get it. You become a new person! A person unknown.

I told him the story of my life, most of it, a version of it, and he told me his, and in the telling both storytellers came to believe that their stories were true. *I'm the person I'm describing*, I thought, *I really am!* I knew that I was editing the story as I told it, but not to hide anything or to protect myself—I believed that I wanted Woodrow to know everything about me, no lies and no secrets that mattered. But I was telling my story to a man, not another woman, and therefore edited it accordingly. And I was revealing what I knew of myself to a black African, not a white American, to a Christian, not an atheist, to a conservative government official, a member of the True Whig party, and

not to a neo-Marxist fugitive under indictment by her own government for acts of civil disobedience and suspicion of terrorism. I had no
choice but to alter, delete, revise, and invent whole chapters of my story.
Just as, for the same reasons, I am doing here, telling it to you.

And Woodrow was doing it, too, I was sure. He was the person he
was describing—at least I believed he was, even though he, too, must
have been editing his story in hundreds of large and small ways to protect me from my abysmal ignorance of lives like his and to assuage my
fears of the vast differences between us. He was doing for me what I
was doing for him and now for you. As my mother and father had
surely done for each other long ago during those months when they
were courting, before they were married, so that when finally they did
agree to marry and started fucking, each knew whom she or he was
fucking and was confident that the other person did too.

Which is almost how it happened for me and Woodrow. I remember a night in May: Woodrow and I were returning from a policeman's
ball at the huge, yellow-brick Masonic temple at the center of the city.
There had been a considerable amount of drinking and hearty male
laughter at our table, which was not the head table, of course, where
President Tolbert and his half-dozen closest ministers and their large,
tulip-shaped wives had sat, but close enough to it for me to gain a considerable amount of favorable attention from the important men. That
night, Woodrow proposed marriage to me.

Not exactly proposed marriage, but I knew it's what he meant, and I
didn't exactly accept, but he knew what I meant, too. We were in the
back seat of the Mercedes, with Satterthwaite driving, as usual, watching us in the rear-view mirror, as always. Woodrow was uncharacteristically voluble. He was happy and a little drunk. All evening long, from
the tone and tune of the greetings he'd exchanged with the big men—
from President Tolbert himself to the American ambassador to the chief
of police—and from the way the big men had so politely flirted with me,
it was becoming clear that Woodrow was about to enter the next inner
circle of power, where at the center the president stood alone. And far

from hindering his progress towards that center, the young, white American woman—whose past was known among the Americo-Liberian community to have been "adventurous" and possibly even a little politically dangerous, especially for a woman, the woman named Hannah Musgrave, whose passport still had her name as Dawn Carrington—that woman was in fact an obvious help to him. In that circle I glamorized the otherwise dull and officious little assistant minister of public health, for I knew that's how they viewed him, as one of the cadre of boring, competent, American-educated bureaucrats whom the president used to keep the government running and the Americans happy. Woodrow was one of a contingent of Liberians whose business would have been business had they been of Lebanese or Indian descent or Mandingo, but because they were black Africans of at least partial African-American descent, their business was government.

Satterthwaite pulled the car over at the gate to my compound and shut off the headlights, but kept the motor running. He stepped from the car and walked slowly around to my door, as he always did when Woodow returned me to my residence, and waited for his boss to say his goodnights, spread my shawl gently over my shoulders, and reach across me and open the door.

Woodrow, however, placed his left hand onto my knee. "Hannah," he said in a descending voice, as if about to deliver unexceptional bad news. "It's time that I introduced you to my mother and father and my grandmothers. My people." He cleared his throat and continued. "We have reached a very important point in our relationship, you and I."

"Oh!" I exclaimed. "Good! I'm eager to meet them." And I was. It had been nearly four months by then that we had been courting, and from the beginning Woodrow had spoken of his family members with a respect that bordered on awe, as if they, too, like the president and his cronies, made up an inner circle of power and prestige that he very much wished to enter.

"Also my father's other wives," he said. "And his brothers and sisters and their wives and husbands, and my brothers and sisters, too, and their wives and husbands and children."

I laughed abruptly, involuntarily, but he went on as if he hadn't noticed. "It's the time that we go to visit my people," he said, placing heavy emphasis on *people*. I knew that his father was a farmer, an elder in the Kpelle tribe, and that the household was located in a tribal village in Bong County, about seventy miles inland from Monrovia. The family was Christian, Woodrow had told me in a reassuring way, although like most Liberians, especially country people, they practiced what he called "the old religion" as well.

I viewed myself as a firm atheist, so didn't mind that at all. I reasoned that, since one superstition was pretty much like another, two or more practiced together were weaker than one alone. I was more threatened by a Baptist who believed only in the resurrection of Christ than I was by a Baptist who believed in both the resurrection of Christ and astrology. Thus I was more concerned about Woodrow's own strict Christianity than about his Christian family's reliance on "the old religion." After joining the government, he himself had become a deacon in the United Methodist Church in Monrovia. He attended services every Sunday, and on several occasions had invited me to join him, until finally I was honest with him. "I'd feel like a hypocrite," I said.

Woodrow seemed pleased. "Spoken, Hannah darling, like a true Christian."

"What on earth do you mean?"

"Well, you view hypocrisy as a sin, a thing to be avoided at all costs."

"Nearly all costs."

"Yes, yes, nearly. Quite right. Don't worry, my dear, the Lord has His ways and plenty of time. But never mind," he said and smiled benevolently down upon me, as if having uttered a silent prayer for my conversion.

"I'm not worried," I said. But I was. *Look at me*, I thought. *I'm in love with a Christian, a black African man who believes more in the god of my par-*

ents than in the gods of his. How had this happened? I was in the midst of its happening, but still I had to ask. I was intelligent enough and sufficiently self-aware, even back then, to have tried viewing it as merely a reaction to my isolation and loneliness. During those first months in Liberia, I was utterly alone at the so-called plasma lab, except for the chimps and their caretaker, a man who fed them twice a day and who once a week made a half-hearted attempt to clean their cages, and the woman who took the blood samples from them. Everyone else I knew in this country, even the Americans posted at the embassy, I knew only through Woodrow. These people, all the foreigners, in fact, I deliberately avoided anyhow, regardless of Woodrow's assurances that I was safe in Liberia under his protection, and that I *never*, he emphasized, would be extradited to the United States.

And you can be sure that I'd questioned the racial aspect of my love for Woodrow. I had dealt with that in the Movement long ago, after I'd gone through a rather lengthy period, eighteen months or so, of wanting to sleep only with black men. And did, with way too many of them, until finally, one night in Cleveland after a long, grueling, self-critical session with my Weather cohort, I saw myself as a racist commodifier of sex, acting out the age-old exploitation of the colonized by the colonizer. At least that's what I confessed to. It wasn't long afterwards that I began my first love affair with a woman, a white social worker named June.

But all that had faded, blown away like wisps of clouds after a storm. Now I can't even remember June's last name. Irish, I recall that much. June was Irish and had gone to Antioch. Of the too many black men I slept with, with the exception of the two or three I'd worked with in the Movement, I remember not even their first names. Calvin? Daryl? Walker? Why even call up the names of those poor men? It was long ago. And wrong.

So what was it about Woodrow Sundiata that brought me to believe that I had fallen in love with him and that made me, after a few short months, decide to marry him? My initial attraction had been mostly sexual, and within weeks, once I got used to his rigid, nearly ex-pressionless face and constricted manners, had weakened somewhat. I no longer saw him as an African samurai. What, exactly, then, did I see in him, other than a benefactor and protector? If it wasn't the color of his skin, perhaps it was the fact that he was African. That he was point-edly not American. In those years, I was bone weary of my war against everything American. The war against American racism, the war against the Vietnam War, the war against the System—all of it. It felt like I'd been at war my entire life, even as a child and adolescent waging the war against my parents. I hadn't realized it until after I'd left Ghana and Zack, my last links to the Movement, but by the time I arrived in Monrovia, I was in a sense shell shocked.

Here in Liberia with Woodrow, it was peacetime for Hannah, almost as if all those old wars had been won, instead of lost or merely abandoned. Never in my life had I felt as free of anger as I felt then. That old, constant, edgy watchfulness, an irritated grasping after right-eousness that I could never really trust anyhow—I felt none of it there. This was *Africa*, and the people who surrounded me and the man who was courting me were *Africans*. American racism, the Vietnam War, even the Cold War and the System that fed off it, and my parents—they mean nothing to the Africans, I thought then. And, presumably, could mean nothing to me, too.

Later, of course, I would think differently, but for the time being, floating between two identities, the one called Dawn Carrington, and the other Hannah Musgrave, I was at peace. A woman with two names I was nameless, with so many pasts I had no past. Leaving Ghana and Zack behind, I'd come to Liberia and had stumbled into bliss. It was in a state of surprised blissfulness, then, that I had met Woodrow Sundi-ata, and now I was about to meet his people and, if they approved, to marry him. Which, I knew, would take me even farther away from my wars, my parents, my pasts, than I had managed so far.

"When shall I meet them?"

"Saturday. I've sent word ahead, so they can prepare for your visit.

This will be a significant day for them. In my family I am the only one who has not yet married. You've not yet been to the back country, have you?"

"No, I guess not. How ... what shall I wear?" I felt foolish asking, but I knew that in an important sense this was a ceremonial occasion. I kept thinking of my mother's first meeting with her future in-laws, the anxious silence in the parlor as the people who would become my father and grandparents read their respective Bibles, and the girl from Smith College sat alone on the sofa and looked from one Musgrave to the other, wondering who these people were, that such weird behavior could seem natural. And when they had finally been called to the dining room by the maid in her starched black uniform with the white collar and everyone was seated, Mother Musgrave said to her son, "Bernard, will you say grace?"

The college girl watched the others, and when they lowered their heads and closed their eyes, she did the same and for the first time heard her fiancé pray aloud to God and His resurrected Son. When he had finished, *In Jesus' name, amen,* she opened her eyes and saw the cold, clotted vichyssoise suppurating in the dish before her. Oh, dear, she must have thought. What have I gotten myself into?

No one spoke. Silver clanked. The father slurped. The maid arrived with bread and soundlessly paddled back across the thick carpet to the kitchen. Finally, the son, the Yale medical student, cleared his throat, placed his soup spoon carefully down, and said, "Mother? Father? I have an announcement to make."

The others looked up and placed their soup spoons as carefully down as he. The college girl did as they and put her hands in her lap. The mother dabbed at the corners of her thin, lipless mouth with her napkin. The girl did the same. The father turned in his chair to face his son, as if interviewing him for a position at the bank.

"Announce away!" Father Musgrave ordered.

The son, a tall, too-thin boy of twenty-four with permanently tousled brown hair and a large Adam's apple, cleared his throat again and said, "Well, I've asked a girl to become my wife." He looked across the table at the girl who would become my mother and smiled nervously, and the girl smiled back in a way that she hoped was reassuring and proud. "And I'm happy to say that she's accepted!" he declared and laughed awkwardly. "How about that?"

There was a brief silence. His father turned back to his soup, as if deciding not to hire the boy after all.

His mother said, "That's nice, dear," followed by a long pause. "Who's the girl?"

The story always ends there, its point, as far as my mother was concerned, made. She was the only one who told it, and she never told it with my father present and of course never in front of my grandparents. She believed that it was about her, after all, not them. But I had always wondered, what happened then? Did the girl get up from the table and run out? Did the boy try to smooth over the sudden rumples in the occasion by quickly excusing himself from the table and following his fiancée to the foyer? She already had her coat on and buttoned, tears of shame and humiliation in her eyes, and he held her by the shoulders and explained that she mustn't take it personally, his parents were cold only because they were frightened.

"That's what powerful people do when they're frightened, darling, they go cold on you." I can hear him now, his voice seductively calm, so reasonable sounding—a kindly, wise man, even back then, when he was little more than a college boy. "They have only me, you know. And they're afraid of losing me to you."

They touched hands lightly, and the girl took off her coat, wiped her tears away, and the two returned to the table as if nothing untoward had happened.

But I know it didn't go like that.

The girl who would become my mother didn't leave the table. She wouldn't dare. She sat there instead with a sickly smile pasted onto her face and wondered, as she would for the rest of her years, if she had been insulted, which was why she told the story repeatedly. And the boy who became my father, his voice raised a register, as if driven by excitement rather than fear, said, "The girl I've chosen to marry is right here with us today! It's Iris!"

My grandparents turned their hard gazes on my mother, and both of them nearly smiled, as if suppressing frowns. My grandmother said to my mother, "Well, then, welcome to the family, Iris."

"Yes," my grandfather said. "Welcome."

And my mother said, "Thank you. Thank you both."

She herself had no family to which she could welcome them and thus, struggling to find something appropriate to say, could only say thank you, over and over, and in time came to believe that her gratitude was genuine.

Except for an aunt in Windsor, Ontario, my mother was alone in the world. Her parents had been killed in the crash of a small private plane piloted by her father, my other grandfather. He had been a speculator in Canadian farmland, very successful. He and his wife were returning to Windsor from a combined western holiday and the auction of a cattle ranch in Alberta, when, somewhere over Lake Superior, with my grandfather at the controls, the plane entered a suddenly rising zone of thunderstorms and didn't come out the other side. Their bodies were never recovered, and my mother's aunt, her sole surviving relative, delayed telling my mother for nearly a month, waiting for the girl to finish her exams at Smith. It was my mother's freshman year, the first time the girl had been away from home, so no need to make things worse than they were, losing both parents like that, by obliging her to postpone or cancel her end-of-semester exams. There was no funeral to come home to, anyhow, and my mother's aunt, who had been managing her now-deceased brother's office for years, while he flew about the continent buying and selling tracts of land, could easily take care of any legal and financial matters that came up. She had power of attorney, and the girl was a minor.

My mother seemed to have spent her entire life in a state of low-grade mourning, which was why she never wanted more than one child. She still loved her own prematurely lost childhood too much, or so I believed then, to give it up and try becoming an adult.

With my father, it was different. But only in degree, not kind. In fear of his parents' disapproval of any family structure unlike theirs—a mother, a father, and a single, obedient, overachieving child—he had cut his life to fit their template. He became a pediatrician, eventually, and through his child-rearing books, a world-famous pediatrician, not out of a love of children, but as a secret rebuttal to his parents' unwillingness to love their single, obedient, overachieving child. And because all the world's children were his, none was. Except me, of course. I was his child. But much of the time when growing up, I felt less his child than his test case, the proof in his pudding, exhibit A-to-Z put forward to an adoring public as evidence of the wisdom and practicality of Dr. Musgrave's theories on progressive and humane child-raising in America at mid-twentieth century.

But all that was before 1968, before the Chicago Democratic Convention and 1969 and the Days of Rage and my arrest, indictment, and flight, and before the years in the Weather Underground, the bombings, the robberies, the terrorist campaign against the war, against colonialism and U.S. imperialism—all that was before Africa.

WOODROW WASN'T EXACTLY sure, but he thought that altogether he had forty-two brothers and sisters. Maybe more.

My mouth dropped. Woodrow smiled. An old joke. But that was counting all his father's children by his four wives, he said, still smiling. From his father's first wife, he farther explained, there were only five children, of which he, Woodrow, was the youngest, which is why he had been allowed to attend missionary school and from there enroll in a preparatory school here in town, in Monrovia, and then, on a church-sponsored scholarship, travel to the United States, where he had studied business at Gordon College, a Baptist school in Beverly, Massachusetts, only a few miles from Emerson, the town where I had grown up. Woodrow's older brother, Jonathan, and his three sisters had stayed in the village, because of their responsibilities to the family. Woodrow had met his responsibilities to the family by finding jobs for about twenty of his half-siblings and cousins so far, in the government of President William Tolbert and in the True Whig party, of which he was a national officer, as were all cabinet ministers and sub-ministers. He was able to do this, he said proudly, because his mother and grand-mother were Americos, descended directly from the African-American founders of the Republic of Liberia, and not full-blooded Kpelle like his father and grandfather, who were headmen descended from headmen.

Woodrow's family pride was much greater than mine. It colored his every reference to them, and I envied him that pride. I admired it. I wanted it for myself. "Woodrow," I said, as he reached across me to open the car door, "would you like to stay with me tonight?"

I had startled him. He blinked, frozen in mid-reach. I'd startled myself as well. Where had *that* come from? I hadn't once, all evening long, thought of sleeping with him. I'd enjoyed attracting him and was aware that the attention I'd received from the big men at the head table had aroused Woodrow, but making love with him? Now? It had not crossed my mind. This was not usually the case—for no other reason than because he was an African, I actually thought Woodrow sexually unusual, let's say, and wondered almost constantly what he would be like in bed. Tender or rough? Gentle and generous, or harshly demand-ing? Knowledgeable of a woman's body or, like almost every man I had slept with so far, woefully ignorant of it?

He was a small man, small hands and feet, small ears. I liked small men.

"Well, yes, of course," he said. "Of course. Yes, I would like to stay with you tonight. But, no. No." Then, regaining his balance, "It's not the right time, Hannah darling. Not yet. I don't mean to seem a prude, you un-derstand. Or to suggest that you're not desirable to me. Quite the op-posite. No, it's just—"

"I am really embarrassed," I said, interrupting. "I guess . . . well, I thought that was what was on your mind."

He laughed, affecting the big African man's deep, dark laugh. "Always! Always! But first things first. As you Americans say. Hannah, I want you to meet my people. Then . . . then we will be free to follow our desires." He chuckled the Englishman's chuckle.

"Is that customary?" I asked him. "Do you usually have your family meet a woman before you sleep with her? Am I being too frank, Woodrow?"

"No, not at all, not at all. Not too frank at all. It's only the American way of speaking, isn't it? I like the American way of speaking, even in a woman. But in answer to your question, you are the first woman I have invited to meet my people. Remember, I'm inviting you to meet them, not inviting them to meet you. I'm my own man, Hannah, not theirs. This meeting is for you. For you and for me. Not them."

He pressed the door handle, and Satterthwaite opened it wide for me to exit. Woodrow kissed my hand, as had become his custom by then, and smiled sweetly, and I stepped from the car. "When you have met my people, then we can sit down and decide what we will do next. Together. Goodnight, Hannah," he said.

"Goodnight," I said. "I'm sorry, Woodrow, if I misunderstood." I felt almost bawdy, what my mother used to call "cheap." I turned away before he could respond, and made for my cabin. The car pulled out onto the road. Halfway across the compound I stopped and watched its taillights fade and disappear and then stood for a long, lingering moment in thick darkness, letting a flurry of images of slow, comforting sex with Woodrow and marriage to him and bearing his children and settling into a permanent life in Africa flutter randomly down, obliterating neat, orderly thoughts of tomorrow and the next day and the next, the mundane details of my daily routine. I was bored by the thoughts of tomorrow and my ongoing days, one by one by one—but, oh, the images of a permanent life in Africa, though they frightened me, they were exciting and made my skin prickle. They signified a future! I hadn't had a vision of an actual, believable future in a long time, not for years.

A wedge of shadow darted past my ear. A bat. In the distance a dog barked once and went silent, as if kicked. There was a rustling noise coming from the Quonset hut at the rear of the compound, and I started quickly for my cabin. Before I reached the porch steps, a single chimp had begun to pant and hoot, and in seconds another had joined in, then more, and by the time I opened the door of the cabin, the chimps, all of them, were howling and banging against the bars of their cages.

WOODROW ARRIVED AT the compound early the following Saturday, chauffeured in the ministry car by the faithful and ever watchful Satterthwaite. He hadn't answered my question the night before about what to wear, and I was shy about asking him again, but figured I'd better dress like a proper white lady—a pale yellow cotton sundress, a floppy, broad-brimmed hat, and sensible, low-heeled shoes, purchased in town the day before. Which turned out to be correct. My usual daytime uniform of jeans, tee shirt, and sneakers would not have cut it. It troubled me slightly that, bit by bit, week by week, my African wardrobe was coming to resemble my mother's collection of resort wear.

Woodrow's outfit that day resembled nothing from my father's closet, however. He wore a starched, white guayabera shirt, pale blue Bermuda shorts, brown British shoes and knee socks, and a new pair of round tortoiseshell eyeglasses. Beside him on the seat an old-fashioned pith helmet lay at the ready. Evidently, when a government sub-minister goes to his village, he does not want to be mistaken for a villager.

I got in back and kissed him on the cheek. "You look like a missionary, Woodrow," I said and smiled: *Just teasing, honey.* He frowned. I kissed him again.

"You don't approve?" he said. His frown became a scowl.

"No, I like the look. Especially the eyeglasses. I mean, you seem very . . . official. For a family visit, that is."

"Yes, well, in a sense I suppose this visit is somewhat official."

The car sped along the road, splashing through steaming puddles of water. It had rained earlier, and sunlight flashed like strobes off the overhanging, bright green foliage and fronds. We were headed north from the compound, which was located east of the harbor on the inland edge of Monrovia. I hadn't been out this way before. My travels in Liberia so far had been strictly limited to the immediate neighborhood of the plasma lab and to the commercial area downtown and west of the city out to the beaches and hotels beyond, where I'd gone solely in Woodrow's company. Due to the attention I attracted, especially from other white people, and my residual underground paranoia— which I clung to in spite of Woodrow's assurance that there was no possibility of my being arrested by the Americans or anyone else—I was still wary of traveling about the country on my own.

Pavement turned to gravel, and the brightly painted, air-conditioned homes of the affluent Monrovians, with their close-cropped lawns and iron-spike fences and the occasional security guard on patrol, gave way to one-room roadside shops and small, rectangular, daub-and-wattle cabins, many with zinc or thatched roofs. Manicured lawns and flower gardens were replaced by vegetable patches and burned-over fields ready for planting and long stretches of dense brush, then solid, continuous jungle. Soon the road was red dirt, and there were fewer and fewer vehicles: Chinese bicycles wobbling under two and three riders, handcarts pushed by shirtless boys, and now and then a crowded rattle-trap of a van or mud-spattered pickup headed for the city.

A crippled yellow dog—Satterthwaite refused to slow for it or adjust speed or direction an iota—heroically dragged its hindquarters across the road just in time to avoid being hit. People walked alongside the road, mostly women and girls with babies strapped on their backs and heavy loads of garden crops balanced on their heads. They watched us blow past and, expressionless, as if the Mercedes were weather, turned away from the wake of dusty wind that followed and resumed trudging towards Monrovia and the weekend market there.

"My father's name is Duma," Woodrow said. "Duma Sundiata. He's the headman of his quarter in the village. Not head of the village its own-self, which has a chief, a paramount chief, above the headmen. So some people like to say my father Duma a small-small man." His voice had dropped a register, and he had slipped into rapid-fire Liberian English, usually with me a sign of easy intimacy. But today he sounded anxious. "But he's *abi-namu*," he said. "That means he's a direct descendant of the Kpelle ancestors, and he has many farms and many children, so even the paramount chief of the village thinks very well of him and invites him to the most important palavers."

"Palavers?"

"For settling disputes and such amongst the peoples. The village name is Fuama. Fuama is very small, very isolated. Small-small. Only a village. Fuama is about fifty miles from here, three and a half, maybe four hours."

I couldn't tell if he was worried more about the impression I would make on his people or the impression his people would make on me, so I said nothing. Reassuring Woodrow was not my strong suit then. He was still too much a mystery to me.

"My father, Duma, he comin' to receive us," he continued. "But him want to present us to the chief and to the other headmen, prob'ly. Same for my mother, Adina, and the other headmen wives. Alla them know why we comin' out," he added.

"Oh. They do? Why exactly *are* we coming, Woodrow?"

He turned to me, eyebrows raised above his glasses, surprised by my question. "Well, it's to tell them of our plans, Hannah darling," he said, his low-voiced Liberian-English turning subtly British again, almost a patrician drawl.

"Plans?"

"Our plans to marry. So they won't be surprised and have hurt feelings when they find out about it later. Since we won't be able to do it in Fuama, and certainly not in the traditional way," he said.

"I don't know why not. I can handle that. I might even prefer a traditional wedding," I said. "But, look, Woodrow, you haven't actually proposed marriage to me. Not formally, I mean." I tacked on a small laugh. *Keep it light.*

"Ah!" he said, as if suddenly remembering. He smiled gently, but his nose and forehead and upper lip were shiny with sweat, as if the conversation were becoming a wee bit uncomfortable. "Yes, well. Yes, I assumed, after our talk the other night—"

"No, no, that's okay, I assumed it, too," I said, interrupting. "I didn't expect you to get down on one knee and ask for my hand, and you can't very well go to my father and ask his permission. No, it's okay. I knew what you were saying. And I agree. I mean, I accept your proposal. Consider it accepted." I didn't want to make him say what he seemed reluctant or maybe unable to say, but at the same time I wondered what else had I missed all these weeks we'd been together? What other exchanges had I agreed to, other offers accepted?

"Tell me what you mean," I said. "That we won't be able to do it in Fuama in the traditional way."

"Well, you . . . you're a foreigner. And there are certain important conditions that a Kpelle girl, that any native girl, has to meet."

"Conditions?"

"A certain type of education and experience. And it's . . . it's rather too late for you. It would be too late even if you weren't a foreigner, because a woman learns it as a child, as a young girl. She learns it from her family and her people. She learns it from the older women, and in a special way that's not known to men. We males, we learn other things." He was silent for a moment, and his face was shut, as if he were trying to remember the words of an old song. "We . . . the people, they have societies for this," he said with slight embarrassment. The societies for the girls and women were called *Sande*, he explained, and *Poro* for the men, secret, highly ritualistic associations, a bit like American college sororities and fraternities, I gathered, except that the Sande and the Poro were ancient and engaged the entire community in their rites and governance. They had strict rules and harsh punishments for violators of the rules; they had officers and emblems of office, secret signs and words, and elaborate regalia and ceremonies that the ancestors had established long before the Europeans arrived. Sande and Poro connected the living to the dead, the physical world to the spiritual world, girls to women and boys to men and men and women to each other, and through rite, secret knowledge, and shared belief they organized and facilitated a person's transition from one state of being to another.

"But that's not a problem," Woodrow assured me. "Your being a foreigner and all. Not for me, certainly, because, as you know, I'm a modern man. One of the *twi*, as the people call us. No, no, we'll get married in town, in Monrovia, in a proper church way," he declared. "We'll have a Christian marriage. It will be fine and good, you'll see. The president may even come and celebrate with us. He sometimes does that, President Tolbert."

"Yes," I said. "That would be nice."

THE ROAD, up to now a shaded tunnel through the crowding green jungle, had opened on both sides to the geometrically laid out orchards of a rubber plantation—row after row of tall, high-branched rubber trees protected against wandering cattle and human beings by barbed-wire fencing. At each tree a man in tattered shirt and loose pants stood tapping latex into a white plastic tub, as if collecting his winnings from a casino slot machine.

"Firestone," Woodrow said. He sucked his lips for a moment and stared out the window. "Everybody from here and people from far away works for them now. Good money, best they can get." He paused and examined his carefully manicured fingernails. "But the people, they got to *buy* food now, instead of growing it. Even rice. A big problem," he said, his brow furrowed with worry. "Big-big problem."

Woodrow's politics, like those of most educated Liberians, were conflicted. He was all in favor of President Tolbert's so-called Open Door
policy of making it cheap and easy for foreign, especially U.S., companies to acquire monopolistic, long-term leases to vast tracts of land and
ownership of everything on and under it, avoiding taxes and tariffs,
unions, and regulations on wages and working conditions. But he was
aware of the price being paid by the natives.

"It's the fastest way to civilize the tribal people," he went on, switching back to town talk. "And this country is mostly tribal people, you
know. The foreign companies build schools for the children of the
workers and make bush hospitals and company stores for them, so the
workers will leave their villages and live close to the plantation." He
paused. "And they help our balance of payments. Something the Peace
Corps does not do," he said, smiling. "And it brings hard currency into
the economy."

Right, mainly in the form of bribes, I thought, but did not say—
payoffs and misdirected foreign-aid funds siphoned into the pockets
and secret bank accounts of President Tolbert and his inner circle of
ministers and bureaucrats. Nothing trickling down to Woodrow Sundiata, however, whose Ministry of Public Health had little to offer the
representatives of foreign corporations and governments and no power
to restrict their field operations. Once the necessary under-the-counter
payments were distributed in Monrovia, the companies were free to
loot whatever they wanted from the land—rubber, citrus, rice, cocoa,
and in recent years a small but growing quantity of diamonds. With
Liberian government collusion and assistance, they rounded up and, on
contract, hired tribal people and made them into indentured workers,
paying them a dollar a day to help extract the raw materials, and then
processed what they'd taken and sold it abroad at a colossal profit.
Sometimes they shipped and sold it right next door—rice to Guinea,
flour to Sierra Leone, powdered milk to Côte d'Ivoire. They even peddled Liberia-grown crops back to the Liberians themselves, dumping
foodstuffs at inflated prices for credit or cash on the Lebanese and

Indian traders in Monrovia, who in turn marked up and distributed the goods to every small shop and market in the land.

This troubled Woodrow and depressed him. He explained that his father, Duma, who owned many farms, on instructions from the village headman had leased the land under his control to a Norwegian company that insisted he plant nothing but rice on it. In the evenings, Duma's four wives cooked rice that had been grown and harvested on Duma's land, carried in bulk by truck to Monrovia, shipped to Nigeria for bagging, and sent straight back to Monrovia, where it was purchased for cash at the village shop in Fuama by Duma's wives at a triply inflated price.

"The people eat poorly now, much worse than in the past. It's a bad system," he pronounced. "But we got nothing else available. Except communism, socialism, whatever you want to call it. And we're not stupid, we see what happens when you try that. We see what happens to African countries when they get big socialistic ideas. The devil you know is better than the devil you don't know. And America we know. England and so on, them we know, too. China and Russia, them we *don't* know. So we live with the system we've got. Besides, communism, socialism, no matter how I might like some of their ideas, in the end they're no good for anybody. At least capitalism is good for some of us. Right?"

"Right," I said, and nothing more.

WE RUMBLED ALONG the rutted dirt road through scattered crossroads towns and small villages and after a while wound slowly up to a more populous highland district. Now I saw large numbers of ordinary Liberians everywhere—the tribal people, poor people, men, women, and children bent over hand-tilled rows in their small burned-over fields. Also great numbers of people who seemed to have no work—knots of idle boys and men sitting in the shade of a tree as if waiting for a boss in a truck who would never come and crowds streaming alongside the road aimlessly, it seemed, as if having just departed from a sporting event.

We passed an old man and woman holding hands, both blind, tapping their way with sticks, abruptly stopped in their path by a sleeping black pig. They stood and poked at the pig with their sticks, trying to determine what was blocking them. A plaintive-faced boy, machete in hand, watched over a row of fresh coconuts for sale on the ground. Leaning against the front of a bamboo roadhouse—above the open door, a scrawled tin sign, Champion Sam's—a pair of teenaged girls in unbuttoned jean jackets, miniskirts, and plastic spike-heeled shoes flashed us with their long black legs and tobacco-colored cleavage. In the middle of a field adjacent to the roadhouse, a tall, thin, shirtless man stood, wiped his brow with the back of his hand, lay his hoe on his bony shoulder, and watched his toddler sons, little more than babies, lug a burlap sack of seed across the field towards him.

I gazed on the Liberians as we drove swiftly past them, poor people eking out their day-to-day livings and enduring terrible hardships and humiliation in the process, and all of a sudden, with no warning or buildup, I felt a powerful urge to ask Satterthwaite to stop the car. Let me out of this air-conditioned chariot, let me be one of *them*, not one of *you!* Let me walk unnoticed with them along this dusty road to the market and not ride smoothly over it. Let me mingle out there with the men, women, and children whose backbreaking labor and suffering are used to pay for this German car and its driver, to pay for the power and privilege of the man beside me, my future husband, also to pay entirely for me, for my safe, secure, undeserved life!

My eyes filled, and I was breathing hard. And even though it caught me by surprise, it was an old impulse, one all too sadly familiar to me, this desire to separate myself in the dance of life from the people who had brought me and become one instead with the people excluded from the dance, the people who set up the chairs, served the food and drinks, provided the entertainment, and cleaned up afterwards. I knew the desire was illicit. It wasn't rooted in compassion or altruism; it wasn't even political.

In a voice louder and bolder than I intended, I called to Satterthwaite, "Stop the car! Please!"

"What's the matter?" Woodrow asked. "Are you ill?"

Satterthwaite brought the car to a halt in the middle of the road. In the tangled brush next to the car, a goat looked at me through the window glass. It was an ordinary red-haired goat with large, fly-clustered yellow eyes, a scrawny female with a swollen udder and a thin piece of rope trailing from her neck into the dense, thorny bushes behind it.

"No! I just . . . I need to get out of the car," I said and opened the door and stepped outside, face to face with the goat. A bulky wave of cooked air broke over me, nearly knocking me down. I shut the door and took several unsteady steps away from the car and toward the goat, which seemed suddenly afraid, backing away, wide eyed.

A gang of naked and half-naked children appeared out of nowhere, round-bellied babies and boys and girls, some on the edge of adolescence, the girls with rosebud breasts, the boys with man-sized hands and narrow shoulders and spindly arms, all of them barefoot, their legs covered with road dust, sores, old scars, their noses and eyes running. They extended the pale palms of their hands to me and murmured, "Gimme dash, miss, gimme dash, miss, gimme dash." I heard Woodrow behind me shout at them through the open window of the car in a language I didn't understand, Kpelle, I supposed, and the children backed off a ways and gazed at me in silence.

Except for the buzzing of the flies, all the noise of the world seemed to have been banished, and after a few seconds even the flies went silent. There was only the heat, the impossible heat. And the face of the goat staring wide eyed through the heat at me as if I had no other wish than to kill it and had all the power to do so. And me staring back. Somehow that broken-down, used-up animal's pathetically scared gaze had turned for one brief moment into the central reality of my world, erasing everything that surrounded it, shutting out everything that had preceded it, memories even, blotting out Woodrow's presence and Satterthwaite's, and erasing my reasons for being there today. It wasn't a symbol of the world that surrounded me; it was the world itself, as if I'd suddenly been made incapable of perceiving anything else.

I'm describing this moment from memory, obviously, many years afterwards, but while inside that moment I had no memories to associate with it and thus had no correct understanding of it and no context for it. I'm not sure I understand today what happened alongside the road to Fuama that day, except that afterwards I was a subtly changed person, and Africa no longer frightened me.

I approached the goat, put my arms around her neck, and drew her to me and held her tightly against my breast. Strangely, the animal didn't resist or pull away; she gave herself over to my embrace.

Sounds began to penetrate the silence, first the buzzing of the flies, then the children, murmuring again, "Gimme dash, gimme dash," and Woodrow saying, "Come now, Hannah, come back inside the car." I felt his hands on my shoulders. Slowly, I let go of the goat and stood away from her and allowed Woodrow to help me back into the car.

Before he joined me there, Woodrow tossed a handful of coins into the air in the direction of the children, sending them scrambling after the money. The goat had disappeared, swallowed by the bush. People, most of them adults standing on both sides of the road, watched us impassively, as if we had merely slowed in our passage through their village but had not stopped.

"All right, Satterthwaite, drive on now," Woodrow said and closed the window on the universe. "We have a long ways to go yet." Without turning, he said to me, "From now on, my dear, when dealing with the tribal people, you'll have to stay close to me and follow my example and my instructions. Understood?"

"Yes, I understand. I'll do that," I said. "It's a promise."

*   *   *

BEFORE LONG, we passed beyond the villages and small farms into a region that was even less populated. Here the isolated roadside settlements, small clusters of daub-and-wattle huts with thatched roofs, looking more like family encampments than communities, were separated from one another by dark green jungle too thick with trees, vines, head-high ferns, and flowering bushes for any earthbound animal to penetrate. Snakes, lizards, and insects might make their way unimpeded along the ground, but otherwise it was strictly parrots and arboreal animals like monkeys and tree sloths that ruled. When suddenly a human being appeared—a man with a machete or a woman and her baby—it was as if he or she were emerging from a wall of green water, stepping gracefully from the jungle onto the road ahead, usually carrying a large bundle of cut sticks or a gunny sack stuffed with groundnuts.

The sky, floating overhead, was a creamy ribbon. Here below, the road was its shadow, growing rougher as it narrowed, with deep pits, potholes, and corrugated ruts carved in the red dirt by the morning and evening daily downpours—not by motor vehicles, surely, for there were no tire tracks anymore, save ours. To avoid the holes and ruts, Satterthwaite drove more slowly and elaborately now, cutting from one side of the road to the other as if on an obstacle course. Every few hundred yards we passed people walking towards us and away, always walking, never just standing, never idly waiting, men, women, and children and sometimes elderly people, all of them walking with bundles on their heads and in their arms—sugarcane stalks, firewood, baskets and swollen burlap bags and large and small babies strapped to their mothers' backs or clinging to their hips—everyone, regardless of the burden, moving along with a lovely, easeful, straight-backed carriage. They wore loose clothing, brightly colored, traditional, topless and over-the-shoulder wraps on the women, the men usually shirtless in baggy shorts or trousers, battered straw hats or sometimes baseball caps on their heads, most of them barefoot or in broken-backed sneakers worn as slippers.

We slowly drew abreast of them and passed by. The people turned and looked at us. A Mercedes sedan carrying a white woman accompanied by two black Africans in Western city clothes way out here in the bush had to be an unusual sight, extraterrestrial, almost; yet the expressions on the native people's faces remained unchanged, placid and incurious—as impenetrable as the jungle itself. At least to me they were. I could not know how, or even *if*, Woodrow and Satterthwaite read them.

By this time, after nearly six months in Africa, I had learned the names of some of the trees and flowers, although it was difficult way out here to separate and identify individuals from the tangled, green throng. As we passed strangler figs and huge cotton trees with gray, winglike extensions at the ground, I named them to myself. For miles we drove alongside a closed palisade of thick bamboo, then a grove of ferns high as a house, and everywhere liana vines, blooming epiphytes, wild coffee plants, aloes. Swatches of frangipani and oleander blossoms tumbled to the roadside. Among the fan-shaped traveler's-trees and papaws and in thickets of the malagueta pepper plants that so excited the early English traders that for a century they called this place the Pepper Coast, I saw black hornbills pecking for seeds with their ax-like beaks, and dusky plovers and parrots. And wherever there was standing water, usually a pool covered with water lilies or a shining green swamp, I saw kingfishers in flocks, egrets, and herons.

This inland territory, the bush, was ancient. Primeval. From before the Fall, it seemed. Here the needs of nature and humanity were collaborative and far more peacefully meshed than back along the coastal region, where Monrovia, the capital, and the other, smaller cities of Liberia—with their modern industrial spoilage and smoke-spewing cars and diesel trucks and buses—waged warfare against the jungle that surrounded them. Down there, from the border with Côte d'Ivoire in the east to the border with Sierra Leone in the west, human beings and their machines were chewing their way inland, greedily devouring the land and everything on it.

It was like that all over equatorial Africa then, especially on the coast, and is even worse now; but in the mid-1970s, when this journey took place, the upland region of Liberia still remained essentially untouched by industry and technology, by modernity; and as we moved farther and farther away from the coast and the plantations on the lower plateau, I felt myself steadily slipping backwards in time. The twentieth century disappeared behind us, then the nineteenth was gone, the eighteenth, and the seventeenth. Lost to my mind were the crowded, rapidly swelling coastal cities, the rubber plantations, the railroad lines, even the roads that had spread inland from the seaside trading stations built first by Europeans and then Americans. The iron mines hadn't yet been established, the gigantic mahogany and cotton trees still loomed overhead, blocking out the sun, and diamonds hadn't been uncovered and sold for guns. Chimpanzees hadn't been captured, caged, and bred for the development of multibillion-dollar drugs. They and all the other now-decimated species were still out there in the jungle, abundant, invisible, silent, watching us pass. This, I thought, is as close as I will ever get to West Africa as it was when the first Europeans arrived.

THE ROAD, barely a grassy trail now and no wider than the car, led to the edge of a slow-moving, brown river. A large raft made of cut poles lashed together with vines was waiting at the bank and the half-dozen men beside it, barefoot and wearing loose shorts, watched us approach as if expecting our arrival. The river was not wide—a boy could toss a ball to a boy on the other side—and a thick vine tied to a tree on both banks crossed the river just above the sluggish surface of the water.

"Beyond this river is my village," Woodrow said. "Fuama."

These were the first words he had spoken to me since I'd stepped from the car nearly two hours earlier and had been overcome by . . . what? A vision? A seizure. If I don't know what to call it now, I certainly didn't at the time. It had been a sudden, thoroughgoing confusion of needs and desires, I knew that much, even when it was happening, and little else. But looking back these many years later, I see it more clearly now, and if it was a vision, then it must have been the felt aftereffect of a collision between two conflicted desires that had been germinating in my subconscious for months. One desire had been generated by the woman named Hannah Musgrave, who wanted to become wholly herself again, free to go back to her parents and homeland; the other by the woman named Dawn Carrington, who also wanted to become wholly herself, but hoped in the process to disappear from her pursuers safely into Africa. My decision to marry Woodrow was turning both women—the lost but still loving daughter and the fugitive revolutionary—into a bourgeois African man's loving American wife. It had set Hannah's and Dawn's opposing desires on a collision course. If I married Woodrow, Hannah would never go home again, and Dawn would not disappear into Africa. It would be as if neither woman had ever existed, as if both had been from the beginning nothing more than fictions. In deciding to marry Woodrow, I was deciding to abandon my dream of assuming the identity I had been given in childhood and youth, as well as the identity I had replaced it with.

I glimpsed that fact that day, and it terrified me, and when I fled from the safety and comfort of the ministry car and embraced that poor, pathetic, female goat, it was not to comfort her, but somehow to induce her to comfort me. To help me believe that what I saw coming towards me would not arrive.

THE CAR COASTED from the road onto the raft and stopped. To the man in charge Satterthwaite spoke a few words in the man's language and dropped a coin into his hand. Satterthwaite closed the window and let the motor and air-conditioner continue to purr, as the crew of muscular men, like a team in a tug-of-war, somberly, rhythmically pulled on the thick vine and drew us slowly across the river, where I saw gathered on the farther bank a large, rapidly growing crowd of naked and near-naked men, women, and children. They were a somber group, like a photo from an old *National Geographic*, the women with large, pendulous breasts, the men with tightly muscled arms and chests, the children with round bellies and protruding navels—a passive, yet withheld and slightly suspicious-looking crowd, as if waiting for us to make our intentions clear, not exactly welcoming, and not in the slightest ceremonial. I suppose I expected feathers and masks and drums, elaborate headdresses, leopard-skin capes, and woven breastplates, not, as they seemed, a loose collection of poverty-stricken hunters-gatherers. Woodrow's people. His family. Soon to be mine.

Satterthwaite drove the Mercedes slowly from the raft and onto the mudded clearing, parting the crowd, and shut off the motor.

"End of the road," Woodrow said and chuckled. He put his pith helmet on and, checking himself in the rear-view mirror, squared it.

"End of the road," Satterthwaite repeated, and he, too, chuckled. He stepped from the car and opened my door for me to exit, then jumped to Woodrow's door.

Immediately, as soon as we were out of the car, the people surrounded us, all of them talking at once in loud voices pitched at the same high, flattened tone, their rapid-fire cries, calls, and speeches directed entirely at Woodrow, who shook hands with the men like a visiting plenipotentiary, smiled and nodded politely to the women and children, but said nothing in response to anyone and did nothing to present or even to acknowledge me. Satterthwaite, leaning against the hood, arms folded across his chest, waited by the car and with a sly smile on his face watched Woodrow and me in our city shoes and clothes make our awkward way up the slippery embankment.

Woodrow reached the top of the bank before the rest of us and without a pause plunged into the forest there. The crowd, focused entirely on Woodrow—their village champion returned from a far country in triumph—followed him, and I followed them, more or less ignored, except for the smallest children, the babies, who stared at me with wonderment and a shadow of worry on their brown faces, until their mothers caught them looking and turned them around, shifting them to where they couldn't see me anymore or else covered their faces with a flattened hand or a large leaf torn from a nearby tree.

It was very hot, and the ground was wet and muddy, and the path was narrow and half-covered with wet, overhanging ferns and bushes. I had difficulty keeping pace with the others and at one point, hurrying to catch up, slipped and fell, smearing my dress, hands, and lower legs with red mud. I blurted, "Shit!" but no one looked back. No one paid me the slightest attention. To everyone, it seemed, except for the babies, who'd been all but blindfolded by their mothers, I was practically invisible. Which, before I arrived there, may well have been what I wanted. I wanted to see them but didn't want them to see me. It was not, however, what I'd expected. And now that it was happening, it made no sense to me. *Some welcoming party*, I thought.

Soon the others had gotten so far ahead that I couldn't see them anymore, and then I couldn't hear their chatter and ululating calls to one another. I was alone and damned near lost in the middle of the jungle, and I was growing angry. Furious.

I felt like Katharine Hepburn in *The African Queen* and almost laughed out loud at the thought. *Woodrow in his pith helmet and eyeglasses as Bogie?* But I slipped and skidded and stumbled on, and after a while, a half-hour or so, the path brought me face to face with a palisade nearly eight feet high, made of thick poles roughly cut and peeled and lashed together with vines. The path split right and left alongside the wall, with no indication of which way led to the entrance to the village. I could see on the farther side of the wall thatched roofs like conical hats and the green leafy tops of fruit trees and caught the aroma of wood smoke and roasting meat.

I chose to go left and, like a princess locked out of her castle, made my way along the wall, looking for the drawbridge or gate, a doorway, a hole in the wall, a tunnel—any way in. I heard drumming, high, thin, rapid-fire patters at first, then a heavy bass drum joined in, and the click of sticks on a log, and singing—those high-pitched female ululations orchestrated cleanly into a chorus now. The sun shone aslant in the sky, behind the trees, but it was still very hot and humid, and I was sweating and muddy. The mud had a cold, metallic stink to it. I took off my shoes, and carrying them like pathetic gifts, one in each hand, walked along the path barefoot, whimpering with frustration and anger and confusion. Where was the damned gate? Where had everyone gone? What was going *on* in there? Why hadn't Woodrow or someone, *anyone*, stayed back to lead me into the village? It was turning into one of those awful dreams of rejection and repressed rage that you think will never end. When, after walking for what seemed like hours but could not have been more than twenty minutes, I realized that I had actually walked full circle around the village without having come to a door or a gate and had arrived back where I had started, and I was suddenly afraid.

There must have been something important said or done back at the car that I utterly missed, I thought. I'd been distracted, confused, when we came to the river, not paying attention. Back there, when we crossed the river, a gesture, some sort of instruction or lead, must have been given to me by Woodrow or Satterthwaite or by one of the people who greeted us, something that would have told me what to say and do when we arrived and thus, as a result of my not having said or done it, would explain what was happening to me now. I must have unintentionally insulted Woodrow or his people. Perhaps I offended one of their ancestors or broke one of their taboos. Good Lord, I thought, this is Alice's Wonderland—the rules are different here, and I haven't a clue as to what they are, and everything I do is wrong!

Barefoot and muddy, sweating and scared, my shoes in my hands, my hair damp and in stringy tangles, I grimaced and began half to laugh over my plight and half to cry. I felt like a traveler from another planet whose compatriots had left for home too soon. A shadow crossed mine, and when I turned there was a slender boy of fourteen or fifteen standing beside me. He was silent and motionless, as if he'd been transported there by magic. Shirtless and barefoot, wearing little more than a loincloth, he was a pretty, almost girlish-looking boy who smiled slightly and gestured for me to follow him. Turning, he walked gracefully downhill a short ways, looked back once to be sure that I was coming along behind, then stepped into the bushes and disappeared into the bright greenery, and when I arrived at the place where he'd become invisible, I saw a narrow footpath and took it.

In seconds, the path had joined a wider path, a trail, actually, that soon broadened and swept beneath a head-high, earthen trestle overgrown with ferns and tall grasses. As I passed beneath the bridgelike structure, I glanced up and saw the high palisade above it and realized that in my search for an entrance to the village I had simply walked across the top of it and had missed the gate entirely. I followed my lissome guide under the bridge and entered the village of Fuama.

It was a large, circular compound of ten or twelve daub-and-wattle, whitewashed, windowless huts, each with a single, low doorway facing a packed dirt yard the size of a basketball court. A crowd of people, which I recognized as the same crowd that had greeted us when we first stepped from the car, was loosely gathered around a fire pit. Two large, skinned, piglike carcasses, headless and without hoofs, were slung across the red coals alongside a fifty-gallon drum whose steaming contents I could not see but assumed was a soup or stew, made no doubt from the heads, hoofs, and innards of the beasts roasting on the fire. While the children mostly held hands and watched in silence from the edge of the crowd, men and women of all ages drank from gourds and soda pop bottles, laughing and talking excitedly with one another and every few seconds breaking into scraps of song. It was a party, a drunken celebration. Off to one side were the drummers—four sweating, muscular, young men—eyes closed, heads thrown back, as if each were chained to a private, throbbing world of sound. And there, behind the drummers, rising above the crowd on a dais at the entrance to a hut significantly larger than the others, stood a very tall, elderly man in a white, short-sleeved shirt and trousers, four older women in colorful wraps, and Woodrow.

Standing next to Woodrow and slightly behind him, yet making herself visible to the crowd, was a young woman with a thick, pouty upper lip. A naked baby was perched on her wide, outslung hip. The woman was very dark, almost plum colored, with glistening hair that was braided and coiled like a nest of black snakes and wore a bright yellow-and-white sash across her bare breasts. She stared at me un-blinking. Everyone else seemed not even to notice my presence. Woodrow, too, ignored me. Or perhaps he just hasn't noticed my ar-rival yet, I thought. Or maybe he didn't notice my absence in the first place.

I flipped a small, discreet wave in his direction. *Over here, Woodrow!* He saw me. I know he saw the tall white woman standing at the edge of the crowd. How could he have missed me, for heaven's sake? But he seemed to look right through my body, as if it were transparent, a pane of glass between him and his people.

I didn't know what to do. I turned to my guide, the boy who had brought me here, and said, "What should I do?"

He smiled sweetly and shrugged.

"Do you speak English?"

He nodded yes and said, as if reciting from a textbook, "I learn it at missionary school. I go to missionary school."

"Like Woodrow. Mr. Sundiata."

"Yes."

"What's your name?"

"Albert," he said. "I am Sundiata, too. Same like Woodrow. My father and Woodrow's brother the same-same."

"Should I go over there?" I asked. When I pointed towards Woodrow and the others on the dais, they were stepping down from the low plat-form and entering the hut, one by one.

Albert shrugged again. Smoke from the fire bit at my eyes, and my nostrils filled with the smell of roasting meat. The women in the crowd had resumed their high-pitched singing, and the drumming rose in volume with them. A wizened, toothless old man shoved a gourd in front of my face, and the vinegary smell of palm wine momentarily dis-placed the smoke and the aroma of the meat. I grabbed the gourd and took a sip from it and shivered from the sudden effect, felt my heart race, and found the courage to make my way quickly through the lively crowd towards the hut.

I passed through the low doorway and stood inside. It was dark, and I thought I was alone in the room. Tricked. A prisoner. The hut was stifling hot, the air heavy with the sour smell of human sweat. I stepped away from the entrance, let in a band of sunlight, and saw Woodrow seated on a low stool against the far wall. On either side of him, also on low stools, sat the tall, elderly man and the eldest of the four women. The others, including the young woman with the baby, lay on mats on the floor nearby, watching me.

"Woodrow, I hope—"

"Please sit down," he said, cutting me off. "Welcome."

I looked around in the dimly lit space and followed the example of the other women and lay my long body down on a mat by the door.

There was silence for a moment, an embarrassing, almost threatening silence, until finally Woodrow said, "This is my father, and this is my mother. They don't speak English, Hannah," he added.

The old man and woman seemed to be examining me, but they said nothing, and their somber, inward expressions did not change. It was as if I were being tested, as if everyone knew what was expected of me and were merely waiting to see if I could figure it out on my own. If my ignorance or lack of imagination forced them to tell or show me what was expected, I'd have failed the test. They were an imposing, almost imperious group, but at the same time they were utterly ordinary-looking people. Commoners. Working people. It was the context, the social situation, not their appearance, that gave them their power over me.

Woodrow's father's skin was charcoal gray, his face crackled and broken horizontally and vertically with deep lines and crevices. His neck and arms had the diminished look of a man who'd once been unusually muscular and in old age had seen everything inside his skin, even the bones, shrink. His hair was speckled with gray and, except for a few thin tufts on his cheeks and chin, he was beardless. The old woman, Woodrow's mother, was very dark, like Woodrow, and small and round faced, with a receding chin, also like Woodrow. I could see him in her clearly. In twenty years, the son would look exactly like the mother.

I hadn't noticed, but Albert, my guide, had followed me inside the hut and was now squatting by the door. Woodrow rattled several quick sentences at him, and the boy leapt to his feet and went back outside, as if dismissed. We continued to sit in silence. I dared not break it. What would I say? Whatever words came from me, I was sure they and my voice would sound like my mother's—that insecure, coy, jaunty banter she always fell back on when addressing black or working-class people, as exotic to her as the people of Fuama were to me. I waited for one of the Africans to speak, any of them, in any language, it didn't matter. I longed for the sound of human speech, regardless of whether I could understand it, as long as it wasn't me doing the talking.

Then suddenly Albert was back, lugging a basket filled with steaming chunks of what looked like roast pork and a handful of palm leaves, which he distributed to everyone, starting with Woodrow and his father. He placed the basket on the ground before Woodrow and disappeared again, returning at once with a large open gourd filled with a thick, gray stew. Woodrow gave him another order, and the boy left again, this time returning carrying a batch of pale Coke bottles filled with what I assumed was palm wine.

At the sight of the food and drink, Woodrow's father's expression had changed from unreadable impassivity to obvious delight, and he reached across Woodrow and with one hand grabbed a Coke bottle and with the other picked up his leaf and snatched a piece of the meat from the basket. He took a mouthful of the wine, mumbled what I took to be a quick prayer, and spat a bit of it onto the ground before him, then swallowed, smacking his lips with pleasure. He tore off a large piece of the meat with his teeth and, almost without chewing, swallowed it—his eyes closed in bliss—and then a second large mouthful, and a third, by which time the others had joined him, and the hut filled with the sounds of chewing, slurping, swallowing.

The young woman on the mat opposite me lay back and ate in a leisurely, luxurious way, as if at a Roman banquet, nursing her baby at the same time. She glanced over at me, smiled to herself through half-closed eyes, casually passed a Coke bottle to me, then returned to eating. Woodrow's sister? His father's youngest wife? Or Woodrow's village wife and baby? I didn't know how to ask and was afraid of the answer. Flies buzzed in the darkness, cutting against the thick, muffled noise of the drums and singing outside. I took a small sip of the wine and as the others had done spat half into the dirt before swallowing. With leaf in hand I plucked a small piece of the pork from the basket.

I glanced around and realized that everyone had ceased chewing and was watching me with friendly but inexplicable eagerness. And then, of course, it came to me. This was bush meat. The skinned beasts roasting on the fire were adult chimpanzees, their heads and hands and feet removed and boiled with their innards for stew, their cooked haunches, shoulders, ribs, and thickly muscled upper arms and legs cut into steaks and chops. It was bush meat —a profoundly satisfying, probably intoxicating, delicacy to be savored in celebration of the return of Fuama's favorite son and the foreign woman who had agreed to become his wife.

I slowly returned the chunk of meat to the basket, wiped my hand on my dress, and stood up. "Woodrow, I . . . I'm sorry," I said. "But I can't." His face froze. The others simply stared at me, uncomprehending, confused, as if they and not I had made the terrible mistake. I knew that it was an insult to them, an unforgivable breach of decorum, and Woodrow was being humiliated before his people. But I could no more eat the flesh of that animal than if it had been human flesh. I'm not in the slightest fastidious about what I eat, and have devoured the bodies of animals all my life without a tinge of guilt or revulsion. I've eaten snakes and insects, badgers, woodchucks, bison, and ostrich. I could have eaten dog or cat or rat, even, if that were traditional and were expected of me as a way of honoring the hospitality of family and tribe. But not chimpanzee. Not an animal so close to human as to

expect from it mother-love and grief, pride and shame, fear of abandonment and betrayal, even speech and song.

I turned and left the hut and made my way back through the crowd
to the gate, where I retraced the path back to the palisade, where Albert
had first found me. No one tried to stop me from leaving the village,
and no one followed me. I was alone again, and familiar to myself again.
My thoughts were mine again—safe, known, fixed.

From the palisade I slowly, carefully, walked back along the path
through the jungle to the riverbank, where down by the river Satterthwaite leaned against the hood of the Mercedes, smoking a cigarette
and chatting with a teenaged boy, one of the crew that had pulled the
car across on the raft. The raft, I saw, was halfway across the river,
empty, on its way back or over, I couldn't tell. Satterthwaite looked up
and smiled pleasantly, as if he'd known I'd arrive like this, a woman
alone and angry and frightened and glad to be back at the car, and he
knew exactly how to make me feel better.

"You finish, Miz Hannah?" he said.

"Give me a hand," I said and started down the steep embankment
towards him. He came forward and, just as I was about to slip and fall,
grabbed my arm, righting and easing me to level ground, reeling me in
like a kite. "Thanks."

"No trouble," he said and flipped his cigarette into the brown river
water and swung open the rear door of the car. As I passed him, he
placed one hand over his crotch, looked down at it, then at me. I stopped,
halfway into the car, halfway out, and returned his look. He said,
"Anyt'ing I can do to make you a little more comf'table? Gonna take a
while before Mr. Sundiata turn up. Be dark soon, y' know." His smooth,
dry, hairless face was close to mine, and his breath smelled strongly of
palm wine. I'd never been this close to him before and saw for the first
time that he was a very young man, much younger than I'd thought,
probably not yet twenty, and reckless and naive and dangerously curious.
Dangerous to me, possibly, but definitely dangerous to himself.

I slipped past him and sat down in the welcoming shade of the leather-upholstered interior. I reached out and touched his wrist with my fingertips and said, "Can you find me something to drink? Beer would be nice. Or some of that palm wine you've been drinking. And some fruit to eat?"

He smiled broadly—beautiful teeth, I noticed, also for the first time. "Not a problem," he said and went to the boy, spoke quietly to him, and handed him some coins. The boy ran along a riverside path I'd not known was there, in seconds disappearing from sight and taking the path with him. Satterthwaite strolled back to the car and said, "Want the air-conditioner? Can turn it on if you like. We got plenty of gasoline still."

"Yes, that would be nice," I said and closed the car door. He slid into the front, turned on the engine and the air-conditioner, then slung his arm over the seat back and looked at me with—oh my, yes—a handsome, elegantly formed, young man's look of lust. The dark, leathery interior of the car smelled like ripe peaches. I leaned back in the seat and let the cooled air flow over me. It pleased the skin of my face and neck, my bare arms, a breath from the arctic blowing across my legs, and I drew my mud-spattered dress up a few inches to my knees and closed my eyes.

"When the boy come back wit' the wine and fruits, I can make him go 'way." He spoke in a voice that was barely more than a whisper, as if reluctant to wake me from my reverie.

"Fine," I said. And after a few seconds, "When do you think Mr. Sundiata will come back?"

"Oh . . . not till long time. If him not come before dark, then not till mornin'."

We both spoke very slowly, as if under water. "He won't come looking for me?"

"Naw. He gots him a heap of fam'ly bus'ness to settle first."

"All right, then. I can wait."

"Me, too. Us two can wait together." He extended his pack of cigarettes, I took one, and he lighted it with a flip of his heavy, chromium Zippo.

I cleansed my mouth with smoke, and thought, *So this is how it's going to be, married to Woodrow.*

A SHARP WHISTLE woke me. I pried open my eyes and peered from the car. It was blue outside, dawn's first light. A pale exhalation of thin mist floated above the river. Hands on hips, feet apart, Woodrow, in his explorer's outfit, stood at the water's edge, peeing into the river. *Doctor Sundiata, I presume.* He zipped up, whistled a second time, and waved impatiently at the figures of the three men and a boy sprawled sleeping on the raft drawn up on the opposite bank. They sat slowly, stood, stretched, and made ready to bring the raft over.

Satterthwaite's first name was Richard—I'd learned it during the night. He lay snoring like a gigantic rag doll flung across the front seat of the Mercedes. I was in back, alone now, and a good thing, too. I felt poisoned—the raw palm wine we'd drunk, which had tasted so fine going down, was hammering nails into my brain, and my mouth, which last night had been so warm and wet and open, felt sewn shut and dry as parchment. The car was rank with stale cigarette smoke and vine-gary fermentation—or else it would have stunk of sex. A pair of empty, cork-stoppered Coke bottles lay scattered over the floor in back. I shoved them into a far corner of the seat, then quickly buttoned and straightened my clothing, finger-combed my hair, and licked my finger-tips and wet my eyelids.

Woodrow pulled open the door beside Richard and shook him awake. "Hey-hey, Satterthwaite! C'mon, wake up, boy! Time t' leave," he said in a rough voice. "You better not been runnin' that air-conditioner all night long, usin' up all the gasoline."

"Naw, Boss, don' worry none 'bout dat," Richard said and started the engine. "We got plenty-plenty still!" he declared, a little too loudly. He seemed suddenly foolish, a boy in fact.

Then Woodrow was beside me in the dank interior of the car. He removed his ridiculous hat and placed it carefully on the floor, leaned his head back on the seat, and took off his eyeglasses. He closed his eyes and yawned. And said not a word.

Nor did I. Until nearly an hour had passed, and we were coming down onto the plateau, passing into the region of rubber plantations and small farm villages. As we approached one of the larger roadside settlements, Woodrow instructed Richard to pull over and find us some breakfast. Richard parked the car beside a tiny, windowless, mud-walled shop, and got out. When he disappeared inside, I turned to face Woodrow for the first time since our departure from Fuama.

"I'm sorry about yesterday," I said to him. "I really am. But I didn't know what to do. Why did you ignore me for so long? And then, when I needed your help, you wouldn't help me. You and the others. Your people."

"I might ask you the same question."

"What do you mean? What did I do wrong? I know I refused their . . . hospitality, I guess. But bush meat! Really, Woodrow! I just wasn't ready—"

He interrupted with a long-suffering sigh. "Hannah, there's too much to explain. Too much . . . difference."

"Between you and me? No, I don't believe that, Woodrow."

"Not between you and me. Not that." He paused and rubbed his jiggling knees. His face was clenched like a fist. "Too much difference . . . between me in the city, the person you know already . . . and the me back there," he said and pointed behind us, towards his home. His origins. His ancestors. "I made a mistake, Hannah. I shouldn't have taken you to Fuama with me, I should have come alone this time. You weren't ready. I wasn't ready," he quickly added. He shook his head from side to side, sad and puzzled, and studied his hands as if seeking a solution there. "Maybe later it will be all right, but not now. I don't know how to explain certain things. It's very difficult to . . . what can I call it? It's hard to *integrate* things. To mix the worlds together. I have Monrovia, the city world, and my position in the government. I have my education and my travels and all the different kinds of people I know and do business with. All that. And I have the world of Fuama, too. Both worlds are very strong inside me, Hannah. But you know nothing of Fuama, and I know everything. It's not like that with your people. I know much of them. Remember, I have lived in your country and gone to a college there with American boys and girls. White people. No," he said, "you did nothing wrong, Hannah darling. I did. Even before we got to Fuama, back on the road, I saw that it wouldn't work, and I became angry with myself. But you," he said, "no, you did precisely the *right* thing."

"I did?"

"Yes. You went back to the car and patiently waited for me to return. And when I returned, you didn't press me to explain. Until now, when we're nearly back in our world and can speak in private again. We're back in the world we share. I thank you for that," he said and reached across and took me in his arms and self-consciously kissed me, as if he thought we were being photographed.

Over his shoulder I saw Richard approach from the shop, carrying meat patties and what looked like bottles of Fanta. I pulled away and said, "Come, Woodrow, let's have something to eat. I'm starved." I opened the car door and stepped into the blinding bright sunshine, then leaned back in and said to him, "It's all right. And thank you for explaining. We don't have to go back there, Woodrow. Not until after we're married. And not even then, if that's what you want."

He followed me into the sunshine, a broad smile of gratitude spreading across his face. It said, *Married! We're going to be married!*

WE FOUND STOOLS beneath a cotton tree and settled there to eat and drink, the three of us. I noticed a group of idle villagers a short distance away who were watching us and said to Woodrow, "Back in Fuama, when the people first met us at the river, all the mothers tried to keep their babies from looking at me. They kept covering the little ones' eyes. Except for that young woman in the hut, the one with the baby. Did you notice that, Woodrow?"

He shook his head no and went on eating.

"Who was she, Woodrow?"

"Who?"

"The woman in the hut."

"Just a woman from the family," he said. "Her name is Marleena."

"Who is the father of her baby?"

He didn't look up from his food. "She didn't say. The father is probably away from the village. Must be working in the mines or some place like that. The young men from Fuama, they stay at the mines and come back only once in a while."

"Why didn't she cover her baby's eyes, like the other mothers did?"

"I don't know!" he said. "Why you asking so many questions anyhow! Eat your food. You said you were hungry, didn't you?"

I gave up and did as instructed. But it didn't matter; I knew the answers to my questions.

For a while we three ate in silence, and then Richard spoke. "You know 'bout Mammi Watta, Miz Hannah?" he asked.

"Who?"

"Mammi Watta. She the spirit of the river an' all that."

Woodrow said, "It's nothing. A story. A bush people pickney story is all."

"The peoples use it to scare the picknies when they bad and for makin' them do good," Richard said.

"Has it got something to do with me?" I asked him.

"No. Nothing at all," Woodrow said.

"Excep' Mammi Watta a white woman an' come from the river," Richard said and gave a goofy little laugh.

"It's just that you're probably the first white woman those little picknies have ever seen, that's all," Woodrow continued. "And the mammis all know it's impolite to stare at people, 'specially grownups."

"Tell me the story," I said.

"It changes all the time," Woodrow said. "And there's different ways of telling it in different villages. I mostly forget it anyhow." He stood up and brushed the crumbs from his shirt, finished off his warm Fanta, and said, "All right, we better get moving. I got work to do. And so do you, Satterthwaite." He looked pointedly at Richard, who quickly got up and headed for the car.

As we neared the car, Woodrow leaned down and in a low voice said, "That boy's getting to be one uppity nigger. He's my cousin's son, but I frankly don't know if I'll keep him."

"Oh, do!" I said. "He's good at what he does. He's just a little foolish sometimes, that's all."

"I suppose you're right," he said. He put his arm around me as we walked. "Thank you, my darling," he said, "for being so understanding."

"Oh, think nothing of it, Woodrow. We all have our little secrets. Especially women and men."

"Yes!" he said. "Especially women and men!"

IT WAS PERHAPS a little odd and certainly not characteristic of me, but after returning from Fuama, as soon as I was alone, the first thing I wanted to do was write to my parents. Hundreds of times over the years, I'd wished that I could simply sit down and write them a letter, even a short note—any form of written communication would do, my voice on the page to their ears, calling their fading voices back to me. But I couldn't. Mostly because it was too dangerous, but also because, as the silence between us stretched into months and then years, it grew nearly impossible for me to imagine what I would write to them. If I ever got the chance to communicate with my parents directly and freely again, where would I begin? Where would I end?

Dear Mother and Daddy,

This letter comes to you from very far away, as you can see from the postmark and return address. All the way from Monrovia, in the African nation of Liberia! How I got here is a long, complicated story, and I hope someday I can tell it to you. But for now, just know that my being here is

*what lets me contact you directly for the first time in years. Even though
it's still possible that you'll never receive this letter or if you do that it'll
arrive already opened and read and copied by the FBI. But you don't
have to worry about that (I think) as I'm more or less safe here in
Liberia, and nothing I write to you will be in the slightest incriminating
of you, or of me, for that matter. Although I do wish I had a good
American lawyer, Kunstler or Ramsey Clark or one of your guys, Daddy,
available here to check it out first. Anyhow the point is that for the first
time in almost seven years, since my indictment in Chicago, actually, I'm
not taking a risk or putting you at risk by writing to you.*

When I was underground, a telephone call had been out of the
question—too dangerous, unless it were prearranged and placed pay
phone to pay phone. In those days, everyone I knew more than casually
simply assumed that the FBI was tapping his or her phone. What
could my parents and I have said to one another, anyhow, what intimacy could we have shared, knowing that it was being heard and tape-
recorded by a pair of government agents eating jelly doughnuts and
drinking coffee in a van outside the house? It wouldn't have been my
voice to my parents' ears or theirs to mine—we'd be too circumspect,
too self-conscious and coded. We were nearly that as it was, under the
best of circumstances. Besides, in those years our need to communicate
with one another directly never seemed quite desperate enough for us
to be willing to go all clandestine, as if we were mobsters or Soviet
spies. As a result, from the beginning until the end of my underground
years, we resisted going through the elaborate dance of setting up calls
between pay phones outside a convenience store, one for my parents in
Emerson, Massachusetts, the other for me down the block from a safe
house in Cleveland or New York or New Bedford. Daddy wasn't the type
to endure that. If it weren't in response to a verifiable, life-threatening
medical emergency, he would have regarded any such arrangement
with contempt and as beneath his dignity, even if it meant depriving
himself of his daughter's voice. And Mother certainly wasn't the type. If

she'd been told by me or Daddy that every time she left the house she was followed by an FBI agent, she'd probably have had an old-fashioned nervous breakdown, a paranoiac seizure that would have paralyzed her and sent her to her bed for weeks. I exaggerate, I know, but not by much.

I've been out of the States for a while now and therefore haven't heard anything about Daddy in the news, which in recent years is the main way I kept track of you two, you know, and as a result I'm left hoping but not knowing for sure that you're both okay, in good health, etc. So I hope you'll answer this letter with news of home and family. Maybe you should run it by your lawyer first, though, just in case I'm being legally reckless. If you wish, feel free to show it to Mitchell Stephens or Ron Briggs or whoever represents you nowadays, Daddy. I've been assured by a friend here—he's sort of my boss, actually, a man positioned fairly high up in the government—that the Liberians won't extradite me. I'm working for a blood plasma lab doing research on hepatitis with chimps. Not really doing the research, just supplying and shipping chimp blood to the U.S. It's sort of a NYU, U.S.A., and Liberia jointly funded operation, and it is interesting work but has gotten stressful for me because of the chimps and what we have to do to them, so I'm not sure how much longer I can work at the lab. I have no intentions of leaving Liberia in the foreseeable future, however, and even if I wanted to, where could I go? Anywhere else and I'd risk being arrested and would have to go underground, which, believe me, I never want to do again as long as I live.

For years, Mother and Daddy and I relied on go-betweens, people in the Movement or Weatherman who, to the best of our knowledge, were not being followed or tracked by the FBI. From Mother's point of view, no news from me was not necessarily bad news. It left her free to fantasize that, in spite of appearances, everything was actually hunky-dory, as if I were living on a hippie commune somewhere in Oregon and "going through a stage." I never sent messages to the house or Daddy's office at the clinic. From time to time, maybe once every three or four months, I did leave word with one or another of Daddy's lawyers or his literary agent in New York, messages that I hoped would provide some small comfort to my parents without at the same time putting them or me at risk. I'd say to a receptionist or an answering machine, "Please tell Doctor and Mrs. Musgrave that their daughter is safe and in good health," and then hang up.

> *Mother and Daddy, a lot has changed in me since I left the U.S. Not my underlying political beliefs, Daddy, I'm sorry to say, although you'll be happy to know that I have pretty much separated myself from Weatherman and have no contacts with them anymore. That's a whole other story, which I hope to be able to tell you someday in person. But something that's possibly even deeper in me than politics has been changed. My mentality? My underlying temperament? I don't know. But for the first time in my adult life I'm not part of a movement, I'm not a member of a group or organization dedicated to political and social change. I'm alone. Wholly alone. And it's a little bit weird for me. A lot weird, actually, and I can see that it's changing me in unpredictable ways. Who knows, Mother, I may turn up one of these days with a husband and a baby asking to swap recipes and gardening tips. No, not likely just teasing. Actually, there is a man here with whom I've become seriously involved, but there's nothing about the relationship that I need to burden you with, not just yet anyhow, if ever. Trust that he's a good man, however, very kind and helpful to me.*

In the months since I'd arrived in Africa, the literal physical distance between me and my parents had grown so great that for the first time in years I found myself unable to imagine their daily lives, and I think that's what made me suddenly want so badly to communicate with them. Somehow, even though back in the States we'd been unable to speak or safely write to one another, as long as we were located close enough to get to one another in a matter of hours if need be, I'd been able to imagine Daddy and Mother going through their usual day-to-day activities and not feel especially worried about them. Once in a while I'd catch an item about Daddy in the news—his arrest at an antiwar protest with a dozen other distinguished citizens, people like William Sloan Coffin and Arthur Miller and the Berrigan brothers, an interview or essay under his byline in *The Nation* or *The New Republic*, his appearance on TV as a Mc-Govern delegate at the '72 Democratic Convention, and so on. Sometimes an item showed up on the book pages or in the culture section of the *New York Times*, usually having more to do with his liberal politics and exemplary personal life than his best-selling books. I could tell that, through it all, Mother was still playing her lifelong role as the loyal, selfless Wife of the Great Man. She was occasionally photographed at his side, although during those post–Civil Rights years when he was seen arm in arm with like-minded, earnest white men of a certain age and position, if a woman other than my mother was present, she was usually a famous folk singer.

Now, however, with no access here in Africa to those reassuring, though distant, glimpses of my parents, I had begun to worry about them. I fretted mainly about their health. They were in their sixties, and back then, in my mid-thirties, that seemed elderly to me. With no clear prohibitions against my contacting them by mail, I had on several occasions sat down to write them a letter. But I didn't know who they were anymore; nor was I sure of who I was. So what on earth could I say to them?

> *What else can I tell you that won't take pages and pages? It feels so strange writing to you like this. I wish I could tell you about the country and the people, about my life here and about how I came to be here in the first place, but I'm not sure how to say it yet. Just know that I love and miss you both very much, that I'm all right and in good health, mentally as well as physically, and that I feel safe here.*

Better to say nothing, I decided, and again and again tore up the letter and put away my pen. Until that evening when I returned from my first visit to Fuama. I sat down at the table in my cottage, and by the light of a kerosene lamp—the electric power was off, and Woodrow

still hadn't been able to locate a working generator for the compound—
began finally to write my letter.

> *Write me back, if this letter reaches you. If yours reach me I'll let you*
> *know by return mail, and then we'll once again be in touch, after so long,*
> *too long, all these months and years. I hope you know how grateful I am*
> *for the way you both have stood by me throughout those years, even*
> *though out of necessity we've had to remain at such a distance. I'm sure*
> *it's been difficult for you, especially since our political beliefs, though they*
> *overlapped, never quite matched. But despite everything, they are not lost*
> *years. I know that my actions and their consequences have been hard on*
> *you, painful and frightening, and I often wish that it could have been*
> *different. I love you both and always have, and I think of you all the time,*
> *even way out here in deepest Africa.*
>
>   *Love,*
>   *Hannah*

The impulse to write my parents satisfied, I mailed the letter and
quickly forgot about it. Then, two weeks later, I was leafing through the
day's mail, the usual packet of lab reports from the NYU administrators of the project, who still seemed to think of me as their field agent,
someone who could make sense of the charts, graphs, and statistics
they'd derived from the blood samples I'd shipped them months earlier
and who was therefore eager to read them, along with the odd jumble of
official Liberian government pamphlets and studies financed by the UN
and USAID and distributed to every agency in the Liberian government, regardless of its area of expertise and responsibility or lack thereof.
From the day of my arrival at the lab, I had not read more than the
opening paragraph of any of these reports and had simply dumped
them unopened into the trash for burning later. But this time a stiff,
white, business-size envelope fell out of a report on the practicalities of
developing a fish-farming industry on the St. John River. It dropped
into my hand as if seeking it out.

My dear Hannah,

How thrilling and, after so long, what a relief to receive news of you and to receive it from you directly! Your mother and I literally wept with joy when your letter arrived. I cannot begin to express the pleasure it gave us (and you may be pleased as well as surprised to know that it arrived unopened, with no evidence of its having been tampered with). I hasten, therefore, to answer it. I will be discreet and discursive, as you were, so as not to compromise your situation in any way.

I'd known at once what it was—I'd seen that envelope a thousand times before, since childhood. It bore the return address of Daddy's clinic, his familiar letterhead, and I recognized in my name and address the typeface of his equally familiar IBM Selectric, probably typed by Ingrid, Daddy's doe-eyed Danish assistant, and I thought, Damn him, he can't even write my name and address by himself and in his own handwriting, he has to dictate the letter on his little tape recorder, probably on a plane to Houston or someplace, and on his return have that poor, lovelorn sad-sack, Ingrid Andersen, type it out and leave it on his desk for his signature. She'll even fold and seal the letter and lick the stamps for him. Suddenly I was sorry that I had written my letter and wanted to toss his into the trash. It was stupid of me to have contacted Daddy and Mother, stupid and self-indulgent and sentimental, and now I'd pay the price, and the price was having to open and read my father's answer.

We were delighted to know that you are safe and in good health, although astonished to hear from you at such a vast distance. I looked up your country in the atlas and encyclopedia (I confess, I barely knew of its existence) and am learning quickly as much as I can about its rather intriguing history and culture and its perverse connection to the roots of our homegrown racial conflict. I feel almost as if you have joined the Peace Corps and have been stationed out there for two years, and I do wish it were so, for, sadly, I fear that your stay may run a bit longer, no? I

do believe, however, that someday there will be a general amnesty declared
for all of you who put yourselves on the line against the war and the men
who ran, and continue to run, this country as if it were their own private
fiefdom. I won't go into specifics here (as I'm not confident, all
indications to the contrary, that our letters are not being copied by the
FBI for J. Edgar Hoover to peruse at his leisure), but there are signs,
thanks to Jimmy Carter, that clemency is in the air, and not just for
Agnew and Nixon this time. It may take several or perhaps five or more
years for it to happen, unless, of course, someone like the idiot actor who's
currently cast as governor of California becomes president after Carter,
which seems extremely unlikely to me, after what this country has been
through. But who knows? I've guessed badly on presidential elections
before. Remember Nixon vs. Humphrey?

By the time I entered the sixth grade I'd passed to the left of my
father. It was either that or go to his right. His liberalism, cleansed of
anger and tainted by melancholy, ill suited my temperament, and temperament always trumps ideology. He was like Adlai Stevenson. He
even looked like Stevenson, a tall, angular version with the same high
forehead, the same sad eyes and too-pretty mouth. He believed in non-
violence because he himself was incapable of committing a violent act
and, to work his will on others, frequently resorted, therefore, to manipulation. He was charming, articulate, witty, and of course intelligent
and reasonable, and if you valued those qualities—and who among us
did not?—then you bent your will to his. Which was all he wanted, the
mere concession that he was right and that you, as a result, were wrong,
implying, if you persisted in your belief and acted accordingly, that you
were unintelligent, unreasonable, witless, inarticulate, and boorish.
And who among us valued *those* qualities? He was a hard man for a wife
and a female child, an only child, to resist.

Well, I did not mean to get into politics. I'm sure that's not what you
want to hear from me. Despite everything, your mother and I are fine,

one might even say happy, except of course for the continued absence of
our beloved daughter from our daily lives. Even at our advanced age—
not so old, really, still hale and hearty at 68 and 66—we're as engaged
and busy as ever, me with the clinic here in Emerson and over at the
hospital, although I've cut back some on the latter, and with my books and
a certain amount of political activism, and your mother with the house and
her gardens and bonsai collections and with helping me. She continues to
be, as always, my irreplaceable amanuensis. I've had to travel a great deal
in the last year or so, more than I like, mostly lecturing in the U.S. and
Western Europe, where they find my ideas on child-rearing a little more
challenging than useful, perhaps, but worth listening to nonetheless.

After my father died, I hoped that I'd find among his papers the
first letters I wrote to him and Mother, their only child's letters home
from Saranac Lake Work and Arts Camp, a funky, pseudo-socialist,
overpriced retreat for privileged kids from the suburbs. The camp was
located in the Adirondacks, not many miles from my farm here in
Keene Valley, as it happens. For five summers, my liberal parents
shipped me off to the wilderness to be with other rich white kids with
liberal parents, until I began to see through the hypocrisy and cynicism of the camp directors and was finally old enough to insist on
staying home in Emerson doing volunteer work at the hospital.
Saranac Lake Work and Arts Camp is defunct now—not enough affluent parents in the 1980s and '90s, the Reagan, Bush, and Clinton
years, wanted their kids to experience the rigors of manual labor,
which happened to save the camp considerably on staff, food, and
maintenance costs, or learn the words to folk songs that helped us love
and admire the oppressed, exploited workers of the world and ignore
our own mild version of it. But I was innocent of all that then, at least
at first, and for eight weeks every summer was free of my mother's
hovering, fearful shadow and my father's constant, watchful evaluation
of my behavior and development—I was always his Exhibit A, don't
forget, the visible proof of the wisdom of his theories on child-rearing.

And every week for five summers, from that happy, unguarded center of consciousness, I wrote a letter home. After he died, I wanted to hold those letters in my hands and read them, to reconnect my adult self, inasmuch as I had a self, to the girl I was then. During those eight weeks at Saranac every summer, I was truly happy and as near to being my natural self as I have ever been, before or since. I never questioned then the simple fact of my own essential reality. It's why, so many years later, when I went looking for a farm to buy, I came up here to the Adirondack Mountains and bought Shadowbrook Farm and why I have settled permanently here, hoping to find again that lost self, and finding it, cling to it. My father, as you might have guessed, did not save those long-ago letters from Saranac. Nor did my mother. Among his papers were the letters written to him over the years by the readers of his books, his colleagues, ex-students, ex-patients, state governors, cabinet officers, and presidents, and even the letters written to him by my mother from Smith when he was at Yale Medical School. But nothing from little me. I had even less hope of finding anything from me among my mother's papers. Daddy, who'd always intended to write his memoirs, saved everything he might someday want to refer to; but there was nothing in Mother's life, other than her relationship to Daddy, that she deemed sufficiently memorable to preserve for posterity. Predictably, when it came time for me to sift through her papers, I found every love letter and note, every Christmas and birthday card, that Daddy had written to her over the years, starting with his formal invitation to a mixer in New Haven in 1939 and ending, forty-five years later, with his final instructions to her on the dispersal of his personal library and manuscripts. But not a shred from their daughter. Before Mother died, I asked her why she and Daddy hadn't saved my early letters from camp or any of the hundreds of letters I'd written from boarding school and college and later from the South during my Civil Rights stints and when I was organizing mothers on welfare in Cleveland, before going underground. "Well, after you were indicted and didn't show up for the trial and disappeared," she said, "Daddy thought it would be wise if we destroyed them. I think he showed them to Ron Briggs, his lawyer, and he advised it. To keep them from being used against you by the government or the press or whomever else might want to hurt or expose you. So we burned them. Besides, you know how protective he was of his private life. Don't forget, Daddy was famous practically from before you were born."

> We miss you, my darling, and pray for your continued safety and well-being. Speaking of prayer, Bill Coffin was here this past weekend, and we took the liberty of sharing with him the good news of your letter (the fact of it, not the letter itself, of course). He sends his love and prayers. We continue to be as circumspect as possible in all matters regarding you. Many, many people ask after you, of course, both your friends and ours and also numerous longtime supporters from the Movement, who come by from time to time or who call and/or write me at the clinic. In any event, inasmuch as it's somewhat unclear to us how careful you want us to be regarding your current whereabouts and circumstances, we remain utterly discreet concerning both and shall continue to do so. There will come a day, I know, in the not-too-distant future, when we shall all be together again. In the meantime, please remember that we love you.

Fame is like a drug, and when one person in a family is famous, it affects everyone else in the family, shaping and deforming it in many of the same ways an alcoholic or drug addict does. You can't ignore fame—it colors everything—but you're not allowed to acknowledge it openly, either. It's why you prefer to associate with other people who are famous or who have someone famous in their family. They understand. You can trust them the way an addict trusts his fellow addicts and enjoy their company the way an alcoholic enjoys the company of drunks. They make you feel normal.

> And now that we are at least in touch by mail, if there is any way we can be of help to you, anything we can send to you, medical supplies,

clothing, books, or money, whatever, just tell me and I'll have it sent at once. Do you, by the way, have access to a telephone? You could call us collect anytime, you know. Of course, that may still be a little too much exposure. In which case, your mother and I will happily rely on your letters.

With love,

Dad

BM/ia

Another two weeks went by, and then came my mother's letter, handwritten on her embossed, peach-colored, personalized stationery. Still, such a lady. I hadn't answered Daddy's letter and didn't for many months, and when I did, kept it short and impersonal, for reasons suggested, I assume, by his letter to me and for reasons I'll likely explain later. Mother's, however, I answered at once. Hers to me first. Then mine to her.

Dear Hannah,

I was so happy and relieved to hear from you again and to know that you're safe and sound, even if you are in far-off darkest Africa. I can well imagine you out there, believe it or not, as it somehow seems almost like an extension of your unselfish and adventurous nature. I am sure that your generosity of spirit and lifelong compassion for the poor are contributing mightily to the welfare of the people there. In fact, I wonder if it's possible that your social commitment can be put to even better use among the Africans than it could here at home, where there is little but opposition to change.

Mother always viewed my political commitment the same as she viewed her own, as noblesse oblige, as a modest way of acknowledging that one had only by accident acquired social and financial privilege. It wasn't that the poor and downtrodden were exploited; they were merely less fortunate. In that way, one avoided contending with any self-incriminating guilt and felt free not to surrender one's privilege.

I've been remembering so much lately, ever since your letter arrived, remembering you as a child, my blond, blue-eyed baby girl with the heart of gold who used to bring home all the lost and abandoned animals in the neighborhood, and even some that hadn't been lost or abandoned and had to be returned to their owners, and a few years later bringing home all those bedraggled, sad-faced children, your schoolmates from Huntington Chase, "the losers," as you once explained to me when I asked who were these children, and when you went off to Rosemary Hall how every Thanksgiving, Christmas, and Easter break you would come home with the students who for whatever reason couldn't be with their families for the holidays. Do you remember the girl named Anna from Jordan, or was it Turkey? I remember sitting up late one Christmas Eve with her, decorating the tree and telling her the story of each of the tree ornaments, how they were passed down from your father's family and how every Christmas we added three new ornaments to the collection, one for each of us. I told Anna how every ornament had a special emblematic meaning in our family. You were out on a date, as I recall, and your father couldn't get home until halfway through Christmas dinner the next day, but your friend Anna loved the stories, all those Musgrave associations going back to the early 1800's, when the tree ornament collection first began, and she and I were able to get very close that night. And of course I've been remembering your college years, when political activism became so central to your life, the summers in the South working with SCLC registering black voters, when we were so worried about you that your father went South, too, and joined the marches himself, although of course he was there mainly because of his own passionate commitment to civil rights. That was the period when your principles and character had begun to change and shape ours, which leads me to say what I wanted to say at the start of this letter: that your principles and character have probably had a greater impact on my life, and I dare say on your father's, too, than ours have had on yours. And I want you to know, Hannah, that despite the difficulties and anxieties we've experienced as parents in the last twelve or fifteen years, we are grateful to you for that. Many is the time when late at night, taking the measure of our lives (as we long-married couples sometimes do, my dear), your father and I have said to each other, "If it weren't for Hannah, we'd have probably ended up a couple of country-club Republican fuddy-duddies." That possibly sounds funny coming from me, but it's true, and I want you to know it. We are thankful to you, Hannah, and thankful for you.

My mother's letter, more than my father's, brought with it a flood of memories. As she had intended, no doubt. They were not, however, the memories she had hoped to evoke. Within the structure of our family, we each from the beginning performed different, supportive functions, and our memories of the early years more clearly reflected those differences than the overall structure of the family itself. Over the years, on my farm here in Keene Valley, I've seen that a river or a stream running through a valley or plain or tumbling over rocks across and down the side of a mountain, like an artery or vein, brings that otherwise immobilized land to *life* and implies the existence, embedded like a heart, of a separate source of life. Without the Ausable River running through it, my farm would be inert, stilled, and were it not for the wind in the trees—a noise from the sky, not the earth—the land would be utterly silent. It may seem arrogant, but in my youth I sometimes felt that I was the river running through the lifeless, soundless landscape of my dry little family. Yes, I abandoned them and ran off to sea, as it were, and disappeared there for years. But I never forgot the pleasure and meaning that I took from my perceived role in the family as life-giver, as the creator of movement and change. It gave me a sense of power that I got from no other source. My mother's letter brought all that back to me. Living up to that role had seemed my life's destiny. An only child, I had, practically from birth, felt best defined in terms of my relation to my parents. Our family was a trihedron, a closed, three-sided, geometric form. In deserting my mother and father, running off as I did to change the world by any means necessary, I broke the thing apart, depriving all three of us of an essential aspect of our shared and individual identities. I knew at the time what my desertion would do to them, but I didn't care then. I knew that, without my ongoing, supportive presence as one side of our three-sided family, they would break off into a pair of monads, and each of them would end up with a solitary life for which neither had the slightest preparation. Or else they would pretend that I had not left at all, that the river still ran through their pastoral valley, somewhat dwindled, perhaps, reduced to a trickle, but still there, still flowing, greening their grasses and causing their flowers to bloom and the leaves on their trees to bud and open in the sun.

> Well, I almost started to cry, writing that. I may have to re-write this letter entirely if I can't stop being so maudlin. I do want to assure you that both your father and I continue to enjoy good health—although I had my gall bladder removed last summer, which was no big deal, really, and actually helped me shed a few excess pounds, thanks to the two-month-long nonfat diet that preceded the surgery. We're as physically active as ever, especially your father, who has taken up bicycling lately with the same discipline and energy that he devotes to everything in his life. I'm content with tennis (mostly doubles nowadays) and golf in the summer months and swimming at the club pool in the winter. We've kept up with most of our old friends, all of whom constantly ask after you, of course, and we even took a white-water rafting trip down the Grand Canyon this spring with Bibby and Marsh Mansfield and John Kerry and his lovely wife (he's a young Kennedy-type liberal Democrat running for Congress in the 5th district, a man who many of us think has presidential potential, certainly more than Teddy, but don't get me started there). We don't travel quite as much as we used to, although your father still does a fair amount of lecturing and book promotion for his publishers around the country and abroad. The Carter administration has asked him to join several federal commissions on health and childcare and so on, but he has

steadfastly refused. He does serve on a number of corporate boards now, however, which take up a lot of the time that he once devoted to political activism. But with the war in Vietnam over and the struggle for civil rights behind us, he is much less active in politics, as am I, of course. Mostly, we're engaged now by local and environmental issues, where we inevitably end up siding with the young idealists against the greedy capitalists. So, not too much has changed, I guess!

When I was a little girl, from as early as I can remember, we had a dog who loved me the same way I loved her, a white female Samoyed named Maya. Her name suggested Daddy's taste, surely, not Mother's, but I didn't think of it that way then: Maya's name came with her, and she embodied it, just as I did mine. I had no invisible friend to keep me company, and never wished for a brother or sister. I had Maya. Before all others, I loved Maya, and knew her, and she loved and knew me. We were authentically whole *individuals* to each other, unique and irreplaceable. Not that I thought she was human or that I was a dog— our species difference mattered less than if we'd had different genders We played and studied together, slept together, even talked to one another in a language that only we two understood. But Maya grew old faster than I did, and when I was eleven and she was eleven, she developed arthritis and took to snoozing in the shade under Daddy's car. Her habit was to lie under the rear bumper after she'd gone outside in the morning and had finished her business, as if the effort of peeing in the side yard necessitated a short period of private rest and reflection afterwards. This was before I went away to Rosemary Hall, and every morning, when he was not traveling, Daddy drove me to school at Huntington Chase. *His* habit was to start the car and run the engine for a minute before backing it out of the driveway, to give Maya time to crawl from beneath the car. But then, inevitably, there came the day, a blustery, unseasonably warm, spring-like February morning, when Daddy turned on the ignition, waited the usual ninety seconds before putting the car into reverse, and as soon as the car began to move, we heard and felt a bump underneath, and he and I knew instantly that he had run over Maya and killed her. I had just begun to insist on being called Scout then, and Scout didn't cry when her dog was killed by her father. Without looking up from the open schoolbook in her lap, Scout said simply, "You ran over Maya." I remember Daddy practically leaping from the car and lifting Maya in his arms. He held her as if she were a full-length fur coat and stood by the open car door, looking back at me with a strangely puzzled expression on his face, as if he couldn't quite believe what he had done. "I'm so sorry, dear," he said. I didn't respond. In my rapidly hardening heart I knew that he'd grown weary of her inconvenience and the demands that her old age put on us and for an instant had willfully blocked out the fact of her existence. I had no word for it yet, but I believed in the unconscious and knew that it was very powerful, especially when it came to adult behavior. He said, "I think she was already dead, though. She was very old. Old and weak. I think she must have died before we came out. Or she'd have moved from under the car the way she always does. We'll bury her in the backyard, okay? We'll stay home this morning, you from school and me from the office, and we'll bury her by the pear tree. How does that sound, Hannah?" "Scout," I said and went back to my book. "Scout," he repeated, his voice dropping to a whisper. Mother suddenly appeared at the door behind him. "What happened to Maya?" she asked. Daddy turned and showed her, and she said, "Oh, my! Are you all right, Hannah dear?" "Scout," I corrected. "I'm fine," I said and looked up at her. "It's Maya who's dead." "Yes, of course. Yes. Poor Maya," she said. I turned back to my book and pretended to read, while my parents stood there by the car, my father with the dog in his arms, my mother wringing her hands uselessly, the two of them staring in hurt confusion at their cold child. Without looking at them, I said, "It's not like Maya's a person, you know. A human being. And we don't have to bury her by the pear tree. We can take her to the vet's, and they can do whatever people do with dogs that die of old age." And then I told my father to hurry up and drive me to school or I'd be late.

> *Dear Hannah, how I would love to be able to hug you and sit face to face with you and talk the night through. I wonder if it's possible for us to visit you there. I understand, of course, that you can't visit us here, but maybe we could fly over to Africa and be with you for a few days. It would mean so much to us if we could all be together again, however briefly. I would love to see where you work, meet your friends (especially this mysterious new man-friend you mentioned), and travel about the countryside some and "see the sights." Neither your father nor I have been to Africa before, you know, although your father keeps saying he wants to go to South Africa and support the anti-apartheid movement in some fashion that's appropriate to his profession and his public standing here in the U.S., probably by forming an international organization of physicians opposed to apartheid. It's possible that we could come first to Liberia for a few days or a week and then fly on to South Africa. What would you think of that? Naturally, we wouldn't want to inconvenience you in any way and would stay in a nearby hotel, rent a car, and so on, and would amuse ourselves quite capably while you were at work. We could hire a local guide and go sightseeing, then meet up with you afterwards. The very idea of it is exciting to me, and when I suggested it to your father, he was thrilled.*

It amazed and disappointed me to see the ease with which my parents, simply by presenting themselves to me, could turn me into that cold child again. I read their letters and was transformed into Scout. Here I was, a woman in her middle-thirties who had accumulated a lifetime's experiences that her parents would never even know about, let alone experience for themselves; yet, in their presence, even in as disembodied a form as an exchange of letters, my world shrank to the size and shape of theirs, as if I'd never left it.

I've gone on and on, especially for a letter that I'm not one hundred percent sure will even get to you, and so I really should close now. I love you, darling, and miss you terribly. Please write back soon.

All my love,

Mother

I didn't take the time to refold her letter and put it back into the envelope, before I was writing my answer. My hand trembled as the words scrawled across the page, and when I had finished, I did not bother to reread what I had written. I immediately sealed it, slapped on an airmail stamp—one of those famous Liberian chimpanzee stamps printed in small editions for foreign collectors—and headed straight for the little neighborhood post office, where, after a ten-minute wait for the postmistress to return from lunch, I handed it to her.

Dear Mother,

The last thing I need is for you and Daddy to show up at my door! How can you even think of doing such a thing! I'm not a post-deb taking her Grand Tour in Africa and I'm not in the Peace Corps, thank you very much, Daddy. Please understand that my situation vis-à-vis the government of Liberia and the U.S. State Department is extremely delicate, and I'm more or less free to stay here solely by their leave. And I mean that, more or less free. And by their leave. The American authorities pretty much run the show in Liberia and they know who I am. I'm no longer underground, but as you surely must remember, Mother, there is still a federal warrant for my arrest that could be acted on any time they wish, for any reason they wish. Relations between the two countries are conducted not as between equals but rather on the basis of what's in the best interests of the U.S. At the moment, because of an acute shortage here of medically trained personnel, it's in the interests of the U.S. State Department and probably a few congressmen from New York and New Jersey to allow me, even with my low-level skills, to be employed basically as a lab assistant for an academic front financed by some huge, politically connected pharmaceutical company. The university is doing research that requires blood from chimpanzees, an animal that happens to be abundant in this region, research that, if successful, will some day produce the patent for an anti-hepatitis drug that will generate enormous profits for the pharmaceutical company sponsoring the research and in the end will make the shareholders of the company obscenely rich. Thus the complicity of the U.S. government and thus their interest in having me employed here. (I can't believe I have to explain this to you!)

Mother viewed people as either lucky or unlucky, Daddy saw them as overprivileged and underprivileged. He failed to note, however, that the underprivileged among us could not be eliminated without first doing away with the overprivileged. Nonetheless, in my parents' dreamy, meandering, hand-holding march towards universal justice—where the downtrodden would be uplifted and the sick and the starving healed and fed—Daddy was a step ahead of Mother. He was a logical man, a decent and kind man, but a liberal. He believed that no one's property need be confiscated and redistributed on the long march towards universal justice and that none of the overprivileged would have to be lined up against a wall and shot and none of the underprivileged would have to be deliberately sacrificed along the way. Thus he saw no reason why, for the duration of the Revolution and for as long as desired thereafter by him and his descendants, his own pocket could not stay filled.

Besides, I know that the American embassy has someone watching me just to be sure that I'm not engaged in any anti-American political activity. The Liberians probably watch me, too. In spite of Liberia's willingness to do the U.S.'s bidding in Africa by turning itself into a CIA listening post and its one airport into a B-52 base, this is not an especially stable country. There are many groups and individuals who would love to see the present pro-American government overthrown and replaced by one allied with the Soviet Union or China or God forbid with the non-aligned nations of the Third World. As a result people like me (who are not tourists or Peace Corps volunteers) are viewed with suspicion by all sides. It's as if I'm under house arrest, Mother, and if you and Daddy or anyone else from my past suddenly shows up here calling attention to yourselves by hiring guides and poking around the country "sightseeing" (and you know what Daddy's like when he travels), I'll very likely be extradited to the U.S. and sent to prison for a long, long time.

I'm no longer the same person I was when this exchange between me and my parents took place. But I can see how, just in telling you about the exchange, I revert, not quite to my childhood state of mind, but to adolescence, or even to pre-adolescence. Both my parents are long dead now. In the intervening years I've been married, widowed, and borne three children; I've perpetrated a hundred large and small betrayals and abandonments; perfect lovers have been replaced by other perfect lovers, men have replaced women and boys have replaced men, and Africans have replaced Americans, who have been replaced by Americans again; chimpanzees in cages have replaced a childhood pet, and Border collies, free-roaming farm dogs, have replaced the chimpanzees; and I've gone on alone, untouched, undeterred, unbetrothed, a woman whose essence is a white shadow, a spirit of the river, one of those mammi wattas. Yet despite all that, today, in telling of a brief correspondence back in 1977 between me and my parents, and in the process bringing my father and mother wholly back to my mind, the person I was so long ago returns to me, invades and inhabits me.

In writing to you and Daddy I took a small chance that I'd be compromising my position here slightly. All I wanted was an intimate exchange of family and personal news so that we might not feel so estranged from one another. But after reading Daddy's letter and now yours, believe me I feel more estranged than ever. I know you mean well, and no doubt Daddy does, too, but please, please, please, try to respect the difficulty of my position here and my feeble attempt in spite of it to reach out to you. In very different ways the two of you seem unable to know me as a person. Daddy's still addressing me as if I were one of his young, awestruck interns, and you act like I'm a troubled teenager emerging from her rebellious years. I think it would be better—since we now know that all three of us are still alive and well—if we didn't try to communicate any farther, at least for the time being. I'm sorry to have to write that to you, but I see no useful or safe alternative.

Love,

Hannah

But there came a time several months later, after my marriage to Woodrow, when I first learned that I was pregnant, and I felt a powerful need to break my silence once again. I wanted my father to know, of course. Not of the marriage, necessarily—though I had no reason to keep it a secret. I wanted him to know of my pregnancy. I wanted both my parents to know that they were going to be grandparents. I was also motivated by a desire to shock my father, perhaps to frighten and hurt him. That was Scout operating.

Daddy,

I'm writing to tell you that I am married and ten weeks pregnant with my husband's child. You may inscribe in the big old Musgrave family Bible that my husband's name is Woodrow Sundiata. He is 43 years old and is the Deputy Minister of Public Health for the Republic of Liberia. We were married in Monrovia by a Methodist minister on September 12th 1977. Witnesses were Hon. William Tolbert, the President of Liberia, and my husband's close friend and colleague, Hon. Charles Taylor, who is the Minister of Public Services. Rest assured that I'm healthy and receiving the best possible medical care here. I will let you know when there is anything more to tell you about my ongoing life. Mother keeps me well informed as to your ongoing life, so you need not answer this.

Love,

Hannah

My father did not write back. Nor did my mother.

*   *   *

YOU THINK IT'S never going to end. First the fucking. Then the pregnancy. The delivery. The infancy. And then it actually ends.

It's not that any one of them goes on forever—some, like the fucking and the actual birthing part, last only minutes or hours. But all of them, while they last, seem without beginning or end, and whatever stage of the two-year-long process you're enduring, from fucking to the end of infancy, it seems to be all there is. And I went through it twice, overlapping—first with Dillon; then, just as I finished nursing him, with the twins, Paul and William.

First you think, *This is what my life is now. This is who I am.* My life is this endless grinding and thumping, being ground and thumped. Then you think, no, my life now will be spent floundering clumsily inside and around the thick waters of my own strangely misshapen body. No, it's shitting red-hot coals to give birth. Turning myself into an inverted volcano. Then you think, no, I'm the leaking person who gives her sore breasts over to another creature's sucking mouth, and when the baby is filled, cleans up its vomit, piss, and shit.

Over and over, the same cycle, month after month. *This is what my life is now,* you think. *This is who I am.* And everyone, especially if she's a woman, assures you that you will love all the stages of this life, that each stage will make you feel for the first time increasingly like a fully realized woman, an expanded and deepened version of your old self.

THIS IS THE END *of my history,* I thought. *My life has become a series of endless moments. There's no more story to it.* I got pregnant right away, probably the first time Woodrow and I fucked. Sorry about the language, but I can't call it "made love." I don't think Woodrow and I ever actually *made love,* although, Lord knows, we fucked constantly, at least in the early years we did. At his urging always, never mine. From the very beginning, Woodrow's way of making love to me, and consequently my way of making love to him, was chilled, methodical, obligatory, and, even when slow and drawn out, brutal. It was the same for years as it was on our "honeymoon" at the posh beach house south, along the coast, loaned to Woodrow by Liberia's friendly World Bank representative.

That first night, still half-drunk from the reception champagne—ten iced cases of Dom Perignon delivered to the reception by the president himself—and exhausted and confused by the crowd of people I barely knew, and weirdly, unexpectedly desolated by loneliness, I went straight to the bedroom that looked out on the moonlit beach and crashing surf beyond, doused the lights, undressed, and literally tossed myself onto the enormous, king-size bed and stared up at the slow-moving, overhead fan, and said to myself, *Thank God that's over!*

And then thought, *But, Lord, Lord, what have I done?*

I could hear Woodrow where I had just left him, prowling proudly through the house, patting the leather-upholstered furniture imported from Miami and checking out the brand-new, stainless-steel kitchen appliances from Sweden, opening liquor cabinets and linen closets with undisguised glee and rising dreams of gluttony. He was delirious with happiness. And because I knew the reason he was happy, I hated him. And because I was the reason, the agent for his happiness, I hated myself, too. He had a Christian wife at last, and better yet, a white Christian wife, and better still, a white Christian American wife!

His marriage ceremony, to be sure, had been a little unusual— his bride had invited to the wedding no family members or friends of her own to raise toasts and share in the hosting or to present her, and had offered him no dowry, not even a single cow or a meager plot of arable land; she had brought him and his family nothing. I had arrived like a captured bride, booty. Nonetheless, an ordained Christian minister had presided over the nuptials, and at the reception in the grand ballroom of the Mesurado Point Hotel, where the air conditioning and sound system broke down fifteen minutes into the party, Woodrow Sundiata had been visibly honored by all the elite members of government in attendance and by the chief representatives of business, foreign and domestic. Woodrow's people had come in from Fuama village,

nearly thirty of them in elaborately feathered and wooden tribal costumes, carried to Monrovia in the back of a flatbed truck, and had
danced, drummed, and sung for him and his bride and their guests all
the hot afternoon long, and his father and mother had declared publi-
cally (although they'd had to do it in their native language rather than
in English, and no one seemed to hear them) their pleasure and pride
in this marriage, or so I was told by Woodrow, and there had been
many florid toasts and speeches from members of the government. Not
from the president himself, of course, but several of the more lugubri-
ous ministers spoke. And despite my shortcomings, because of *what* I
was rather than who I was, there was now a certain glamor to Woodrow and an almost enviable modernity. Suddenly Woodrow Sundiata
possessed visible evidence that he was a city man, a worthy member of
the Liberian elite, clearly a man fit for the president's inner circle. If he
had married a Liberian woman instead, even a descendant of the old
African-American ruling class, he would have remained the same little,
slightly boring, American-educated bureaucrat, the clever, but not too
clever, missionary-boy from the bush. (By now I saw how he looked to
others and was beginning to look to me, as well.) With me as his wife,
however, Woodrow was exotic, a little sexy, and possibly dangerous, as
if his newly consecrated American connection gave him access to
power and information that were unavailable to other Liberians, even
among the elite. Women flirted with Woodrow now, showed him their
bare brown shoulders, large bosoms and butts, their big, bright teeth.
Men sidled up to him and spoke confidentially to him of deals and possibilities and newly conceived alliances, then reported back to their
brethren: *Hey, my brother, you see? Even the Belgian representative of the
World Bank has given the man the use of his private, very lovely, very expensive
beach house for a honeymoon cottage. He's now a man to keep track of.
Woodrow Sundiata sleeps on fine Belgian cotton sheets tonight. The sub-minister
sleeps with a white American woman tonight and every night. And she will connect him to the big American and European world out there beyond Liberia*

where, mysteriously, people get quickly rich and end up with power over other people's lives and livelihoods. Woodrow Sundiata, my brothers, has become a man to deal with.

He strolled into the darkened bedroom, where I lay splayed on the bed in my underwear, lost in morbid thoughts of having somehow lost my history, of being trapped inside an endless moment. I couldn't explain it to myself. I wondered if, when my politics disappeared, my only hope for an autobiographical narrative had disappeared, too. It had happened piecemeal, in small erasures, going back to New Bedford and barely noticed at the time, and now I seemed to be living outside of time, without cause or consequence.

Woodrow's sudden presence in the bedroom hadn't interrupted my thoughts. I was barely conscious of my brand-new husband's silent body, even though I could smell him—alcohol, cigarettes, sweat—and in the half-light could see him. As if I were alone, I rolled off the bed, undid my bra and took off my panties, and slid under the covers.

"Ah, I see that you're ready for me," Woodrow said. He had already shed his jacket, shirt, and shoes and now slowly unbuckled his belt and dropped his trousers and shorts, stepping from them with knees high as if from a tub. He was erect and surprisingly large sized. This was the first time I had seen him naked. He still wore his socks and garters, like a man in an old-fashioned pornographic film.

I remember asking him if he had a condom.

"A *condom?* You're not serious," he said and gave one of his British chuckles, a low, belching sound that came from his chest. He spotted a candle on the dresser and matches and sashayed over and lit it. The long shadows of the blades of the overhead fan passed slowly across his dark brown chest and shoulders. "Ah, that's better!" he pronounced. In the flickering candlelight his erection gave me a good-natured, straight-armed salute.

"Of course I'm serious," I said to him. "I don't want to get pregnant. Not yet, anyhow. Not this week, or even this year, maybe. Woodrow,

I'm still absorbing the idea of being *married*, for God's sake." I pulled the cool outer sheet to my neck and tried to make a winsome smile. "One thing at a time, Woodrow. Okay?"

He laughed. "Hannah darling, this is a matter in which you must do as I say." His erection, I noticed, was starting to droop, as if fatigued.

"Oh, come on. Now *you're* not serious."

"Decidedly so," he said. His face darkened. He reached forward and with one hand grabbed my wrist and with the other whipped the covers away, and, lo, his erection had returned and was again at full salute.

Oh, dear, oh, dear, I thought in my mother's voice, and said in mine, "Wait, Woodrow, please! You don't have a condom. You didn't bring any condoms? Let me at least . . ." I began, with no idea how the sentence should end, thinking that maybe there was something I could do to myself that would protect me from being made pregnant. Why hadn't I anticipated this, bought a box of condoms myself in Monrovia? Surely they sold them at the Mesurado Point for the American and European men who were afraid of disease as much as I was afraid at this moment of becoming pregnant. I had thought of it, actually, many times, in sober anticipation of this very night, my wedding night, when for the first time Woodrow and I would make love, but each time had realized that in Liberia the women who bought condoms were likely to be prostitutes, so had put the idea out of my mind, until now, when it was too late. Too late. Too late, as Woodrow forced my legs apart with one knee between them and, scowling, spit on his hand and glistened up his cock, and then, too late, he was on me and in me.

I remember the fact of it, but not much more, because after that first time it was always the same with Woodrow, who never seemed to lose his erection and rarely came. He merely grew weary or sleepy or bored or had to leave for an appointment elsewhere, and that's what finally, after long hours of it, stopped him. He could not follow a natural arc of rising passion—the drive toward orgasm, and the post-climactic, floating lassitude afterwards. No beginning, middle, or end for him, and consequently, none for me, either. Not once in all those years. I don't think he knew that such an arc was possible or even desirable. He thought this was good sex, good for him, good for me, and was proud of his ability to keep us grinding away for hours like a pair of millstones groaning on wobbly axes, the thump of the bedstead bumping against the wall like a drum beaten by a dumb, arrhythmic drummer, on and on, making me first sore and then numb, until before long I was outside my body, floating somewhere overhead, thinking penny thoughts and making lists and averting my gaze from the two of us humping below like a pair of mechanical dolls that never finished what they'd begun but only ran slowly down until they finally stopped, batteries drained, and were still and silent.

And so ended one endless moment, the fucking, and another took its place. In a matter of weeks, Woodrow had come back at least once, and I was definitely pregnant, and in June of 1978 I bore Woodrow his first son, whom he named Dillon, after his mother's father, to affirm the lad's Americo heritage, and Tambu, after his father's father, to maintain his lineage connection to the Kpelle, and Sundiata, to declare to all the world his own proud paternity.

Dillon Tambu Sundiata. Later the boy-soldier known as Worse-than-Death.

A beautiful baby. Everyone said so. Even I could see it, although I couldn't at the same time keep from seeing my baby as an alien, a member of a different, non-human species. Not *sub*-human, but *different* and possibly superior.

The truth is, I wasn't as bad a mother as I probably sound now, looking back all these years later and judging my past self from this distance. I'm less confused and turbulent now than I was then. But with regard to myself, less forgiving. When my sons were babies and little boys, certainly when they were newborn infants, I was diligent and careful and nurturing in all the ways of a good mother. No one faulted me then and no one can now, not even I. But nonetheless I was detached from my babies, detached in an unusual way, and I know this, and knew it at the time, too, because, with regard to my chimps, I was not detached and could tell the difference. I could look into the round, brown eyes of the chimps, even the eyes of the large and often fierce adult males, and could see all the way to their souls, it seemed, deep into the mystery of their essential being. But never, not once, could I see that deeply into the blue eyes of my sons.

I tried. I would wake in the middle of the night ashamed and in distress and would slip from bed and make my way to the crib and gently wake and lift Dillon in my arms. Sitting by the window, while the moonlight washed over my baby's face, I gazed unblinking into his eyes and tried to see him, truly see *him*, for what and who he was, a person separate from me and yet a part of me, seen, known, honored, and protected; and every time, my gaze came bouncing back, as if reflected off a hard, shiny, opaque surface. I was like Narcissus staring into the pool.

It wasn't his physical appearance that made Dillon seem alien to me—he was perfectly formed, straight boned and firmly muscled, even as an infant, and his skin was reddish, almost copper colored, and burnished, and his tiny face glowed in sunlight and shone in moonlight. His eyes were dark blue, almost black, though they later turned bright blue, like my father's sapphire eyes. His head was large and round, like Woodrow's, and symmetrical as a piece of fruit. His thin hair, the color of fresh-brewed coffee, was like a lace cap, and his tiny ears were perfect whorls, natural wonders, as if carved out of soft stone by trickling water, and I loved to touch them. He was a beautiful baby. I thrilled to his pomegranate smell and used to nuzzle him with my nose. And the quality of his attention—from the moment I first took him from the hospital nurse's arms into mine and lifted his face to my breast and he began to suck—was refined and as selective and focused as a camera's on the world that surrounded him: first the nipple of my breast, then my face, my eyes and mouth, and behind me Woodrow's proudly smiling face, eyes, and mouth, the room, the light streaming through the open window, the noise of children playing outside, cars, buses, and trucks passing on the street.

But he didn't seem to belong to the same species as we did,

Woodrow and I. *How could this infant, this* stranger *have emerged from my body?* I kept wondering. The nine months of pregnancy had seemed like nine years to me, interminable, and though for the better part of it I had felt him moving inside me, shifting positions down there in the watery darkness, despite that long familiarity with him, when he was finally born he seemed to have arrived from another planet. His physical appearance kept surprising me, as if some other woman had borne him. Because he was male, I suppose, and had a penis attached to his body, and because his skin color and the texture of his hair were so unlike mine. *He must be another mother's child,* I kept thinking.

You were the cutest little pink thing when you were a baby, with silky straight blond hair that I couldn't bear to have cut until you were nearly six and your father insisted on it, and then I cried and cried, although for some reason you seemed extremely pleased to have it cut short. When my boys were infants, my mother's voice in my ears plagued me. It was as if she were always standing just behind me, watching and commenting constantly while I washed, fed, and clothed my babies, brought them into the living room to show the guests, took them out in the carriage, held them up for the praise of strangers and friends alike, for Liberians love to make a fuss over newborns, and their attentions made me feel less like an alien myself.

It was only when Dillon was a few months old, and I could place him in the daily and nightly care of Jeannine, Woodrow's eighteen-year-old niece who had come in from Fuama to keep house for us during my pregnancy and got promoted to governess, that my mother's voice began to fade and eventually go silent. I no longer saw myself through her eyes and instead began once again to see myself through my father's, which, while not ideal psychologically or otherwise, was preferable. It was, at least, familiar.

Then in short order I was pregnant again, another nine endless months of it. Pregnant with twins this time—although I didn't know that I was carrying two babies until they had already arrived on the planet—and, as there were two of them, a matched, identical pair, they turned out to be even more alien to me than Dillon had been. And here came my mother's voice again: *Twins! They're so adorable, like peas in a pod. I always wanted twins, you know. Especially when you were a baby. You were so cute and loveable that I wanted two of you. But you have to be careful and not name them similarly, calling them Florence and Francis, for example, or Ronald and Donald; and don't dress them alike, or else they'll have trouble separating from each other when they get older. Your father, you know, wrote about that in his second book, which, by the way, you have never read, have you? I don't know why, Hannah, you refuse to read your father's books, especially now that you have children of your own . . .*

We named them William and Paul—William after Woodrow's elder brother; Paul after Woodrow's uncle, his father's elder brother—and gave them both the same middle name, Musgrave, to indicate their mother's lineage, with the last name Sundiata, to claim their father's. It was William Musgrave Sundiata and Paul Musgrave Sundiata who became, years later, the boy-soldiers known as Fly and Demonology.

BUT I WASN'T going to get into that. Not now, anyhow. Not until I can first bring you to a sympathetic understanding of my sons and what happened to them and can keep you from being frightened of them. Just as there are certain things about me that I won't reveal to you until your understanding of what happened to me early on and later is such that you won't be afraid of me, either, and won't judge me as you would a stranger. Like my sons, I, too, was once upon a time an infant, a child, and adolescent, all in a particular time and place with most particular parents; and like Fly, Demonology, and Worse-than-Death, I, too, was shaped, formed, and deformed by time, place, and parents—although, in the case of my sons, time and place were more influential in the creation of their fates than were parents. For me, probably, it was the opposite.

Even so, my hope and my intention is that you know us and not be afraid of us.

*   *   *

GIVING BIRTH, like being pregnant, like fucking, did remake me, just as everyone who had been through it themselves said it would. But it didn't make me *more of a woman*, as promised. It made me more of a stranger to myself. I went from being a whale with a porpoise in her gut to an emptied snakeskin, a wrapper. Until slowly, with the baby and one year later the twins finally out of me, I filled again, swollen now with blood and milk that spilled, dripped, trickled, and sometimes squirted from my body, and I realized that I had become a leaking food source, a supply ship. Depersonalized. Objectified. My body a vessel no longer connected to my past self.

I was not a natural mother. Was not born programmed like most women with a mother's instincts and abilities. Had to be taught nearly everything by Jeannine, sweet-natured Jeannine with the round, brown face and puffy cheeks, whose kindness and endless patience in those first years of my marriage astonished me. It's almost as if I was, and still am, missing the gene. There are things that I am naturally good at, skills that seem to have been part of my DNA—math, mechanics, linear thinking, classification, etc.—right-brain stuff that we usually associate with males and that early on got me my father's favor, my teachers' and later my professors' wary admiration and, from boyfriends who needed help with their calculus homework and tuning their cars, mistrust and envy. Women, including my mother, and other girls worried about me or merely felt superior. But thanks to my father's constant delight and his proud endorsement of these tendencies and skills, I never minded my mother's worry or my girlfriends' superior airs or the wariness of the males. I courted it.

As a girl I was a full-blown tomboy. Wouldn't wear a bathing suit top to cover my flat chest until I was almost thirteen and no longer flat. Took Scout for my nickname when I was ten, and from fourth grade until eighth insisted on being called by it and would not answer to Hannah, except when it was used in anger by my mother or father. Otherwise, it was, "Hannah? Who's Hannah? I'm Scout." Entered science fairs in grade school, always the only girl to win a prize. A fact that in the 1950s was worth an article in the *Boston Globe*, which Daddy clipped, framed, and hung in his office like one of his degrees. Built a tree house in our backyard with leftover scrap lumber the summer Mother had her garden house put up. Won a Westinghouse scholarship to study engineering at Brandeis (another article in the *Globe*), then switched to pre-med in order to impress a biology professor I'd developed a sophomore crush on. In the Movement ran and kept patched together with tape, spit, and baling wire the old Multilith presses we used then, when everyone else, especially the men, were or pretended to be hopelessly inept, and later in Weather was one of the half-dozen members nationwide who could be trusted not to blow themselves up while making bombs from dynamite and blasting caps stolen from construction sites. Though was never trusted to place and set the bomb itself, a job reserved for only the more charismatic comrades, so had to read about it in the papers afterwards if it went off successfully. And still had the gene-firing proteins in Africa whenever I needed them—building cages for the chimps, devising and installing a cistern for the house, replacing the busted radiator on the Mercedes with a radiator from a wrecked jeep when Satterthwaite couldn't find anyone in Monrovia clever enough to do it. And years later still had it, the right brain clicking away, when I took over the farm here in Keene Valley, impressing Anthea and the girls and the local men with my ability to tune and maintain the vehicles, build stockades and fences, fix the furnace, and build a windmill from scratch. Talked trucks, tractors, guns, and plumbing with the guys down at the Ausable Inn, packing back brewskies with the boys while a football game raged from the TV at the end of the bar. And whenever one of them, drunk and reckless, put the moves on me in the parking lot, I'd punch him lightly on the shoulder and say, "Frank, for Christ's sake, keep your hands in your pockets. Don't you know I'm one of the guys?" And Frank or Pat or Chuck would laugh and shuffle his feet on the packed snow and say, "Sorry, Hannah, guess I forgot, heh-heh-heh," and hoped like hell it

never gets out that he got so drunk one night down at the Ausable Inn
that he tried to fuck Hannah Musgrave, who is white haired and must
be sixty and is probably a lesbian anyhow. But it does me no harm to
have them think that I'm different from other women, that I'm not like
their wives and daughters, that I'm Scout, a tomboy grown old. Safe.

IN AFRICA, especially early on, when the boys were babies and for
many years afterwards, I had no such ruse to protect me. Especially
around home, where my natural abilities were inappropriate or at best
useless—except, perhaps, to the chimps, although even there
Woodrow wanted me to delegate the physical work, give it to the native
men and women who worked at the lab. My proper job, other than to
function as Woodrow's consort, was to supervise the household staff
and to mother and raise his sons as little Americo-Liberian gentlemen.
Consort and chief of staff were mindless tasks that I could handle in
my sleep, practically. Turning myself into mommy was something else,
however.

It was, as I said, Jeannine who taught me what I needed to know to
get by. She showed me how to fake it as a mother, and when I couldn't
fake it, substituted for me altogether. She was little more than a child
herself, barely eighteen years old and freshly arrived from the village of
Fuama, not quite literate and, under her uncle the deputy minister's tute-
lage and protection, eager to become a Christian. She had been part of
the family dance troupe that performed at our wedding, and afterwards,
at Woodrow's request, although he didn't tell me at the time, had remained in town and moved into his house, now my house, to cook and
clean for us.

The house itself, up to now strictly a bachelor's quarters, was owned
by the government, one of a dozen or so that had originally been private
residences built or bought by foreigners who'd afterwards moved up the
housing scale or gotten themselves assigned to some other African capital. The houses had been acquired over the years by the government to

dispense as favors or small rewards to ministers and VIPs and came with a staff, a car, and a driver, all paid for out of the national treasury. The residence assigned to Woodrow was a sprawling, white, single-story structure with a wide front porch and floor-to-ceiling windows, high ceilings, and large airy rooms—an American-style residence probably built in the 1940s, the sort of house a small-town southern lawyer would have built for himself. Except, that is, for the eight-foot-high, cinder-block wall that surrounded it and the heavy iron gate and Woodrow's pair of huge, black, drooling Rottweilers roaming the grounds.

There was a small patio at the side of the house, where we often ate dinner, and a master bedroom fit for a Jamaican plantation owner, with a four-poster bed and private bath and French doors that opened onto a flower garden and a second patio, where Woodrow and I sometimes took our breakfast. There was a small bedroom that would soon become the nursery, a bathroom, and two additional bedrooms, and behind the house a servants' quarters and a laundry and utility room. There was even a gardener's shack for Kuyo, the part-time yardman—another of Woodrow's close relations come in from the country for the support and protection of his cousin, uncle, nephew, or half-brother—the deputy minister. I was discovering the age-old Liberian system of exchange between the powerful and the powerless, a form of indentured servitude that more closely resembled slavery than nepotism.

The house had been outfitted with modern plumbing back when the city water system still worked, but the municipal pumping station and delivery pipes and valves had long since fallen into disrepair. Consequently, faucets ran only in a trickle and for a few hours a day, while outside on the street water poured from broken mains day and night. We had electricity and all the usual appliances, a TV, too, but even in those days, when the country was still relatively stable, we rarely had power for longer than three or fours hours a day, usually in the mornings, and relied on kerosene lamps and candles at night, and more often than not we were obliged to cook with charcoal on a backyard tin stove.

To me, it was a luxurious setting, however, almost embarrassingly so, compared with how most Liberians lived. A comparison, incidentally, that I rarely had the opportunity to make—because of Woodrow's insistence that I account for every minute of my day when he wasn't in attendance and his use of Satterthwaite as a keeper and spy as much as a driver and bodyguard and his refusal to allow me to go anywhere in the city alone. "You must not forget who you are," he insisted. "Please, Hannah darling. The wife of a high government official must not be confused with a Peace Corps volunteer."

The truth is, I *had* forgotten who I was. That's what marriage and motherhood had given me: the upshot of the fucking, the pregnancy, the birthing of my sons and their infancy was that I wasn't more of a woman or less; I was a different woman. You probably think of me as strong and independent, and I believe that I am—now. I was strong and independent when I was young, too, back before I came to Africa. But in the years between? No. Emphatically no. I was different then.

My weakness and dependence on Woodrow and other men—and in time I'll tell you about them, too—caused terrible pain and harm to many people. To my sons, especially. Who was that terrible woman, and how do I deal with her now? And the chimpanzees, my dreamers—I need to know who betrayed and abandoned them, too. Was it Hannah darling? Was it Dawn Carrington? Was it Scout? Whom must I hate? And what will be the sentence for her sins and crimes?

IT WAS JEANNINE who taught me how to buy groceries at the Saturday market at Congo Square, and how to cook Liberian style with palm oil, peanut, or groundnut oil, with coconut milk and plenty of hot peppers. There wasn't much meat available that wasn't tinned—plenty of fresh fish, however, and chicken, and occasionally pork and goat and stringy chunks of beef. I knew all too well, of course, the local habit of eating chimps and monkeys, bush meat—an atavistic throwback to cannibalism, as far as I was concerned. But it wasn't merely the country people in the distant villages who relished it and offered it up as a special tribute to distinguished guests. The townspeople loved bush meat, too, and considered roasted ape a luxury item, a delicacy. By then Woodrow had come to accept my abhorrence of bush meat—crediting it to my affection for the chimps at the lab and later the sanctuary and perhaps a white American fastidiousness—and ate it himself only when he dined out without me. "It's actually very sweet," he said. "Cooked correctly, it's better than any pork, and no kind of mutton compares. In fact, in Sierra Leone that's what they call it, 'spring mutton.'"

No, at home we ate *jollof* rice, rice *fufu*, coconut rice, rice and beans, curried rice, check rice with greens, rice balls. With Jeannine at my elbow, I learned to cook them all. We ate plantains, breadfruit, yams, gari, or cassava mixed with fish or chicken, one-dish meals mostly. Desserts were fruit salads, banana fritters, tapioca pudding, and shredded coconut balls. The gorgeously colored vegetables and plump fruits were always fresh, firm, a pleasure to cut, chop, mix, fry, roast, steam, and chill.

This was a whole new enterprise for me, who'd never paid much attention to cooking or even to shopping for food. Food had always been fuel, already there on the table before me, or if not, then prepared as quickly and easily as possible, and eaten the same way. Nourishment, that's all. Now, however, it had become an intricately linked sequence of deeply satisfying, sensual, spiritual, and social rituals. In the past, I'd never really cooked, not even when keeping house back in Cleveland, where the preparation and consumption of food and cleanup afterwards were rigorously communal, or in New Bedford with Carol and Bettina—Carol had done all the cooking, actually. I did the cleanup, like a good husband. In the months when I was living alone at the lab compound I'd depended on expensive, Western-style groceries and imported canned goods purchased at what passed for a supermarket, Dot-Dot's, on Ashmun Street. But after Woodrow and I were married, the marketing became a Wednesday- and Saturday-morning ritual for me and Jeannine that continued for years, long after I was capable of handling it alone. It was one of the few occasions when Jeannine and I stood on more or less equal footing, when I was less than the mistress of the house and she more than my servant. For a long time I didn't know how much more, and back then, especially when we shopped for food, I thought we were friends.

I remember walking with her to the square, enjoying the beauty of the crowd, the thronged streets, and then, looking for a particular herb or spice, taking side trips down the alleys and side streets to the shops of the poor. I remember putting my face and hands forward in gestures learned from watching Jeannine haggle and gossip with the shopkeepers in the market, who were all women, many of them from outlying villages, at first feeling foolish for it, awkward, inauthentic, somehow condescending, until it became natural and almost intimate.

But how I wished I were invisible. My white skin was a noise, loud and self-proclaiming. It declared my caste and status for all to hear. And I was both hated and envied for it. For a long while, whenever we went to market, hard looks and cold shoulders greeted me. Then, when it became known among the higglers and shopkeepers that I was Deputy Minister Sundiata's wife, visibly pregnant by the minister, and was in Liberia to stay, coldness alternated with servile deference, as the shopkeepers bypassed the locals in line to serve me ahead of the others. One or the other, hatred or envy, rejection or servility, would have been endurable, on some occasions maybe even desirable, but coming together as they did, they were like a sty in the eye—a cause of pain, but one's only means of seeing the world.

And it stayed painful, even after I had become a fixture in town, no longer exotic with my brown babies in tow or pushing a carriage. As soon as he could walk, Dillon went ahead hand in hand with Jeannine, while the twins, magical beings to Liberians, lay tucked into the carriage that I insisted on pushing, after the usual argument with Satterthwaite, who was still under strict orders to drive us in the car and wait while we did the shopping. I carried the money, and though Jeannine translated for me—for I understood almost no Liberian English then and even after years of hearing it daily got lost whenever native speakers wanted me lost—and did most of the actual bargaining, I did all the numbers, until Dillon decided he wanted to do the calculations himself. And I let him, a proud mamma, for it was his special gift. Early on, it had become obvious that Dillon was precocious with numbers. Good at math, as they say. Though not yet two and still clinging to Jeannine's hip, he would call out numbers for no apparent reason, "Seventeen! Twelve! Twenty-nine!" And because neither Jeannine nor I could determine the source or meaning of his numbers, we assumed they were random bits, numbers overheard from Woodrow talking on the telephone to someone in the ministry, just meaningless sound scraps that he was repeating for the simple pleasure of it. Until one day I happened to notice that, just before calling out a new number, he would stare intently at the number plate of a nearby parked car, and it dawned on me that he was calling out the sum of the numbers on the plate. He shouted, "Seventeen!" and I looked where he had been looking and added the numbers, five plus seven plus two plus three—*seventeen*.

It was the first recognizable sign of his precocity, of his love of numbers and preternatural skill at using them, and it was how he quickly became his father's favorite. "The boy is a genius at math," Woodrow proudly declared to anyone who asked after his sons. "Like me." The twins, however, Woodrow regarded with a strangely anxious wariness, as if the two boys knew things that mere mortals didn't and perhaps shouldn't know. Which in a sense was true, because each twin knew another person better and deeper than any of us ever could. It's dangerous, that much knowledge. They understood each other's breathing and cries in the night and were able quickly, silently, to comfort each other and developed their own language long before expressing any willingness to use ours. It separated them from the rest of us, and it bound them together. The twins were like the chimps. Dillon, too—inasmuch as he had an ability that we did not, an ability that might be dangerous.

At first, my daily routine was surprisingly liberating to me. Then oppressive. Never before had I been so free, yet never so confined and controlled by others. Controlled by Woodrow, of course, and to some small degree by Satterthwaite, whose responsibility was to be on call for any driving I might require. At Woodrow's direction, Satterthwaite was to leave the office whenever I wanted or needed to go out, whether to the doctor, the market, or to the stores downtown, where there was very little on the shelves that I wanted or needed anyhow. As for our past indiscretion, Satterthwaite's cynicism matched mine. An exciting risk, that's all it had been. The same for him as for me. We'd chanced it, and we'd gotten away with it, and that moment, that exact degree of risk, would never appear again. The danger would always be greater and therefore not worth it, or less, and therefore not exciting enough. He remained a boy who was employed by my husband, and I was his boss's wife and practically middle aged. Without once having to say it, we both knew the same thing.

I was controlled, too, by the people who worked for Woodrow at home—the yardman, Kuyo, until he left that job to work full time at the sanctuary; the many village girls and boys who came and went, working for a season or two and sometimes longer as housekeepers, laundresses, cooks, and drivers; and Jeannine, who was at first by herself the cook and maid and then became the nanny all of whom actually answered to Woodrow, not to me, and knew their jobs better than I anyhow and didn't need any supervision. So I made lists, menus, schedules; tried, ineptly, to help with the flower gardens; and shopped; and arranged entertainments—dinners, teas, lunches—for Woodrow's colleagues and friends among the Americo-Liberian elite. I'd ended up with my mother's life.

In those first years in Liberia, it was of course mostly my own doing, falling into my mother's life. It was a thing difficult to avoid. As soon as we were married, Woodrow had insisted that I quit my job at the lab. Not "seemly" for the wife of a minister of government, he pronounced. And I complied. For a long while I had been eager to quit the lab anyhow and hadn't already done it only because until now in the entire country of Liberia there was nothing else available to me, nothing for which I was not over- or underqualified. And, of course, there was the matter of the chimps, my dreamers.

Until I married and moved into Woodrow's house, I had nowhere else to live than in my cabin at the lab. Before long, however, the job had changed for me, and to my surprise I had actually become attached to it. Attached to the chimps. In the beginning, the work had been suffused with tedium. Every day it was the same—a simple, mind-numbing set of tasks associated with recording and tracking plasma samples taken from the chimps and shipping the samples back to the U.S. for testing. The chimps had been deliberately infected, and the progress of the disease had to be recorded month by month, until the subject, the infected chimp, died, date and cause of death carefully recorded. They'd been infected at different ages, depending on when they'd been brought to the lab, and I noted that; and gender, duly noted; and background (subject's general health before infection; conditions of birth, i.e., born and raised in the wild or captivity; birth order, if known; location of early habitat; place and means of capture . . .)—all duly noted.

At the same time, my days were edged with the slow approach of despair, despair that later became intolerable, because of the condition and fate of the chimps. Those same tedious details, the data, however impersonal and repetitive, gradually provided the individual chimps with individual biographies and identities. They were nameless and were differentiated one from the other by a file number, each file containing the chimp's entire life history. Number 241: male, age approx. 14 years; captured in Maryland County, mother killed by poachers; purchased at market in Gbong by Swedish businessman, seized from him by customs officials at point of departure from Liberia; age at capture, approx. 6 months; age when turned over to U.S. lab in Monrovia, approx. 2 years; infected with hepatitis C at age approx. 4 years; total time in confinement 12 years, 3 months, 4 days at time of most recent extraction of plasma sample. . . .

Gradually, over time, each number came to contain within it a single chimp's story. But it was a kind of obituary written in advance, for once a chimp was placed inside one of our cages, its life was effectively over. I worked in the office, a cinder-block bunker that hummed with the sound of the air-conditioner, but still it couldn't blot out the noise of the chimps when they were hungry or angry or frightened. It was always one of those three—hunger, anger, and fear—and the chimps reacted to them like people who were mad, with wild screams, shouts, calls, and cries beyond weeping. It was like working in an insane asylum. Sometimes silence fell, and, as in an asylum, that was bad, for it usually meant that the patients were hurting themselves.

I did not handle the chimps myself and in the early days rarely saw them. I was the clerk of the works, as I called myself, the only one trusted with the numbers. The woman and man who actually took care of the chimps and drew the blood plasma from them and infected them with the diseases shipped in dry ice from the U.S. were local Liberians who had been recruited and trained by American physicians long before I arrived on the scene. Elizabeth Kolbert, a practical nurse, was in her late forties, a large, slovenly woman, very black, with six or seven kids—it was never clear exactly how many. Sometimes she said six, sometimes seven, sometimes simply "many." Underpaid, with no husband to help provide for the kids, she got by as well as possible, but always came late to work and left early and sometimes didn't show at all.

The other employee at the lab was Benji Haddad, also in his late forties, a light-skinned con man with a nasal voice, a toothpick in his mouth, and pomaded hair shaped like a helmet. He worked nights dealing blackjack at the hotel casino and part time at the lab, drifting into the compound around noon for a few hours to feed the chimps and clean up their cages, and because he hated doing these tasks, for they were beneath his dignity and understanding of his own status in town, he made things as difficult and uncomfortable for the chimps as possible, banging the bars with his shovel, spraying them with the hose as if in fun. It was he who knocked the chimps out with darts so Elizabeth could extract the blood samples and inject the viruses. Knockdowns, they were called. It was he who extracted their large incisors. And both Benji and Elizabeth talked about the knockdowns, extractions, and biopsies as if they were car mechanics discussing oil changes and tune-ups.

As clerk of the works, I was also the paymaster, which went a long way towards shaping my relationship with Elizabeth and Benji. They desperately needed their regular paychecks, a rare and luxurious thing in this country. Their monthly pay, drawn on the lab account at the Chase Bank in Monrovia, exceeded the average annual income for most Liberians and let Elizabeth and Benji and their families live modestly. It let them send their kids to school, rent a little house close to town, and even provided Benji with a car, a beat, old hand-me-down Ford.

Because of the way he treated the chimps, I was not fond of Benji, and he knew it. I could not keep a disapproving scowl off my face when in his presence. He was not especially fond of me, either, and we were barely civil to each other, except on payday, when I was officious and he as smooth as wet glass. But I liked Elizabeth. She was jolly, and although she viewed the chimps the way most people regard house cats or squirrels or caged birds—as if the creatures were without feelings, memories, or emotions and with no needs other than physical—she seemed to find them amusing and interesting. And she seemed to like me and enjoyed hanging out at the office telling stories about her kids and neighbors and now and then local politics.

It was Elizabeth who told me of the atrocities, told me in a way that let me for the first time believe the stories and rumors that I'd heard earlier, stories of how the soldiers, especially the president's personal security force, took drugs and roamed the city at night looking for women and girls to rape; how they wantonly butchered people from the tribes not currently in favor, that is, killed people who were not members of the president's own tribe, the Americo-Liberians, or the most populous and best educated of the native people, the Kpelle, though they had no qualms about torturing and killing Americos and Kpelles if it was on the president's orders. Elizabeth told me also of rumors of cannibalism, of rituals among the stoned soldiers that consisted of disemboweling people and eating raw their hearts and livers and drinking their blood. These rumors I discounted, however. *African urban legends*, I thought. Stories told to scare the white lady. These guys might be murderers and thugs and rapists, and maybe they relish eating chimpanzee flesh, but they're not cannibals. Not in this day and age.

THE DREAMER THAT my records called Number 34, when finally I was able to put a face on the number, was the first one I named. After a few months at the lab I had taken to visiting the chimp house when no one was around, mid-afternoon, when the chimps, having been recently fed by Benji, were usually relatively quiet and settled. I went there for company, strangely enough. My days were lonely, and somehow visiting the chimp house after the humans had left it diluted my loneliness. The animals were kept one to a cage, the babies housed by themselves in smaller, half-size cages. The cages were padlocked, constructed of thick steel bars that might have come from a maximum-security prison, and stacked on metal racks. For ease of cleaning, the floor of each cage was grated to allow feces and urine and uneaten food to fall through, the way chickens are kept in poultry farms. I'd gotten used to the rotting, vegetal smell of the place, the claustrophobic heat, and the sorrow that the creatures exuded with every breath. But something about that sorrow drew me forward and out of my habitual, brittle self-absorption. Paradoxically and without a scrap of shame, I felt comforted by their sorrow, soothed and reassured by it. Theirs was a reality greater than mine.

I walked alongside the cages and peered in, and the chimps came cautiously forward, and for a second, with knuckled hands grasping the inch-thick bars, their round, puckered faces peered back at me. Some of them rolled up their lips and bared their huge mouths to warn me off; others, lips pursed, on the edge of speech, it seemed, ready to exchange a small word or two, saw me approach and shyly withdrew and became sullen or sour faced; and there were a few who were clearly psychotic, screaming, wild eyed, terrorized.

Number 34 was a large adult male, and I kept coming back to his cage and lingering in front of it, perhaps because after my first few visits, he, more than the rest, was able to return my gaze with the same mixture and degree of apparent curiosity and fear that I was feeling towards him, and he seemed neither enraged by my presence nor intimidated by it. The others, when I looked directly at them, if they came towards me at all, if they did not cower in the corner of their cages or, like autistic children, bang their heads against the bars, leapt at me or bared their teeth in rage or spat. They tried to throw things at me, uneaten food, feces, water bowls, and sent me on my way, frightened and disturbed and embarrassed.

This was before I learned how to approach the chimps—eyes lowered, teeth covered, face slightly canted, as if in deference. It was Number 34 who taught me. From the first, he'd been neither angered by my presence before his cage nor frightened of it. With him, I had a chance to experiment, mimicking his approach to me and afterwards applying it to the others, who gradually began to accept my approach, then, over time, seemed to welcome it. *Hello, brother ape. Greetings, sister ape. How are you today? What are your thoughts, brother ape? Is everyone in the chimp house okay? No one sick? No one injured?*

I looked steadily at Number 34, and he looked steadily back. He was the boss, I decided, the chief. That's why he's given me the time of day and hasn't been frightened or angered by my dumb lack of ceremony. He's seen that I'm just an ignorant human, and because I'm not Benji or Elizabeth and haven't been involved in the capture and transport and imprisonment of him or any of the others, I'm relatively harmless. He was long faced, with a grizzled muzzle and a huge paunch and a habit of pouting with his lips as if about to whistle. His facial expression reminded me somehow of a surgeon, scalpel poised, ready to cut—thoughtful, concentrated, deliberate. I named him Doc.

I suspected that Elizabeth and even Benji had favorites among the chimps and might even have given some of them names. But I told no one about Doc, and gradually over the following weeks I named them all, one by one, even the babies. There was Ginko, a scrawny adolescent male who had a pale, greenish cast to his skin; and Mano, a stubby, tough-looking male whose full name I realized later must be Mano-a-Mano; and Wassail, round bellied and freckled and reminding me of Christmas somehow, one of Santa's elves; and Edna, a slope-shouldered female with dark, stringy hair who made me remember for the first time in years a crafts counselor I'd had at Camp Saranac the summer I was nine, a kindly woman mocked by all her charges, including me, for her slow speech and low, mannish voice. Their names bubbled into my head as if sent by thought-transference from the chimps themselves, and it was only later that I'd realize I was naming them after people whom the chimps reminded me of, people I'd long forgotten. The names were sounds that for mysterious reasons I liked saying to myself, sounds that were keys capable of unlocking blocked memories, lost sensations, ignored associations.

Words replaced the old file numbers, absorbing the data that made up each chimp's biography, and just as with a family member or a close friend, the name became the same as the bearer. I knew that I was making a mistake and soon would no longer be able to see the chimps as numbers, as data, and that in time I would want to free them from their cages. But I couldn't help myself. For my job had lost its tedium, and the edge of despair had begun slowly turning into a cause. An old pattern. It's how since childhood I have made my daily life worth living, by turning tedium and despair into a cause.

In any case, by the time Woodrow and I were married, I had come to love my job.

"BUT WHO'S GOING to replace me?" I asked him. It was the very first morning after we'd returned from our two-day honeymoon. We were finishing breakfast on the terrace adjacent to our bedroom, and

Woodrow had informed me that I might prefer to stay home today, since I no longer had to work. I would not have to give notice that I was quitting; he'd already done that for me. Jeannine refilled my coffee cup and padded barefoot back through our bedroom to the kitchen.

"Not your problem who'll replace you, Hannah. The woman, Elizabeth, she can fill in for you until the Americans send someone over. They know about the need, I've already informed them that you will have to be replaced. They tell me they have some big, rich foundation ready to expand funding for the position, so they can afford to send an American graduate student over soon, which is nice and what they prefer anyhow. One of their own. The new person should be along shortly. A matter of weeks. Maybe days. So you needn't concern yourself. Nothing will be lost in your absence, my dear."

"Terrific. Great. Elizabeth is barely literate," I said. "She'll screw everything up. Do you have any idea how long it took me to get those records straight and reliable when I first took over, after she'd been 'filling in' for the previous clerk of the works? It took months!"

"Hannah darling, they're *chimpanzees*. Animals. Animals and numbers, that's all. Anyhow, what does it matter?" He touched the corners of his mouth with his napkin and stood up to leave. "It's just a way to keep money flowing from one hand to the other."

"No, it's science! Medical science."

Woodrow looked down at me as if I were a child, and laughed, genuinely amused. "I'll see you this evening, my dear little bride," he said, and strolled to his waiting car.

Woodrow was right—the lab was a shabby, inept operation, and it was ridiculous to call it a "lab" and think of the work done there as science, much less medical science. It was the broken-down tail end of an elaborate scam, a way for a pharmaceutical company to gather data that would back up its claims for a product; a way for a university to get funding for professors' and graduate students' salaries and brand-new lab equipment, possibly a whole new university department; a way for Woodrow's underfunded ministry to get a few American health workers and some decent medical equipment into Liberia and paid for by someone else. And it had been a way for me to finance my stay in Africa, avoiding arrest in the U.S., and most important, a way for me to come up from underground.

Everything in Liberia worked like this. No one in the country gave a damn if a system or an organization didn't work; no one cared if roads financed by U.S. aid weren't built or buildings never finished or machinery, trucks, buses, and cars never repaired—as long as the money to build, finish, and repair kept moving from one hand to the other. The country was a money-changing station. Corruption at the top trickled all the way down to the bottom.

AND SO BEGAN the period when my life made no sense to me. I stayed home and shopped and cooked with Jeannine and supervised her care of my sons, the care of my house, even the care of my husband, and did little else, and acted as though it were normal, even desirable, to live this way. Time passed quickly, as it does when you don't question the role you're playing, when you're barely even aware of it as a role. Everything and everyone else fits—the script is written, all the other actors know their cues and lines and where to stand, and the play continues without intermission or interruption day in and out, twenty-four hours a day, season after season, year after year, until you don't even know you're in a play.

All the while, however, the larger world of Liberia was following a different script. I was little aware of it—oh, I listened to the news, the gossip and rumors, Woodrow's nightly reports, heated discussions among our friends. But because I was not a Liberian myself, I listened as if they were talking about events in a distant land. Instead, I let myself be caught up in the solidly quotidian details of the daily life of a genteel Americo wife and mother—living like my mother in the fifties and sixties, who, until her daughter managed to get herself onto the FBI's Most Wanted list, went sweetly and quietly and cooperatively about her proper business—clipping flowers for the table; making lists and menus for the cook, guest lists for parties, travel arrangements for her husband; shopping for curtains, clothing for her children; making doctors' and dentists' appointments for her children; enrolling them in uplifting and socially advancing classes.

But there was so much else that I could and should have been doing with my life then that it embarrasses and hurts me to be telling it now. For this I *do* feel guilt, and not mere embarrassment. What *was* I thinking? A woman in her mid-thirties, out from under the shadow of her parents at last, no longer underground or on the run, I was free to float, moved only by the current of my real character. And my character had led me into this quiet eddy of nearly stilled, slowly circling water. I'd washed up in a small, backward, provincial country in Africa, where I was a privileged member of the elite, not merely an expatriate or a foreign national employed by her government or by some huge American or European corporation, like all the other white people here. Distinct from the other whites in spite of my skin color, I was rather grandly financed by a man who held a high government position. I had three small children to keep me distracted and more or less busy, a handful of practically indentured servants to leave me time for naps and leisurely walks in my garden, a ready-made social circle of men like my husband and women whose roles matched mine, except for the fact that they were all native Liberians and preferred to keep relations with me, the unavoidable outsider, superficial and strictly social. I was neither one thing nor the other, neither expat nor Liberian national, and thus had no responsibilities to anyone but myself, my children, and my husband, who essentially made no more strenuous demands on me than a small den of Cub Scouts might make on their den mother.

And everyone wanted me to stay exactly where I was. *You're beautiful, Hannah darling, don't ever change. Stay in your box.* Woodrow liked boxes. He liked keeping his colleagues, his friends, his sons, me, and his people all in separate compartments, one stacked upon the other, like the cages that held the chimps. His life at home, his work at the ministry, and his political and associated social lives were one stack of boxes, which he kept in the city. A second stack he stashed in the bush, in Fuama, where, for all I knew, he had a second or even a third wife in a box and had other children, though he certainly never mentioned that possibility, and I did not ask. Nor was I at all clear as to where the box with me inside was positioned, other than in the city stack. Somewhere near the middle, probably, once we were married. That box, unbeknownst to me, was slipping gradually towards the bottom.

The Liberians we saw socially in Monrovia preferred to position me at the polite edge of their circle, men and women alike, which was understandable, given my ignorance of their deeper ways and experiences and our vast differences of background, and which was how I preferred it myself. It made it easier for me to keep track of who I really was, to keep my several not-quite-serial identities from overlapping or becoming confused with one another—Hannah Musgrave, Dawn Carrington, Hannah Darling, Mammi, Miz Sundiata, each with her own past, present, and, presumably, future. Since childhood, compartmentalizing had been one of my strengths, after all. That and numbers. Like Woodrow, perhaps. Not boxes inside of boxes, or in a vertical stack like his, but rather side by side, boxes next to boxes, a row of them stretching from one horizon of my awareness to the other. And I could slip unseen from one to the next, as if each had a secret doorway connected to the box beside it.

When I look back now, so many years later, an old lady sitting on her porch here in Keene Valley or sipping her beer at the Ausable Inn or out on the lawn in the shade of a maple tree, telling my story to a friend and remembering the world I lived in then, I know what I could and should have been doing with my time and riches and my abundant privileges. I was surrounded daily, after all, by abject poverty so pervasive and deeply embedded that, though I could never have alleviated it in the slightest, I could have altered significantly the lives of at least a few individuals, people to whom I was related by marriage, for instance, and people who worked for us, and even neighbors, for, although we lived in one of the poshest neighborhoods of Monrovia, there were huts and tiny, sweltering, tin-roofed cabins tucked into the warren of back alleys nearby that housed whole families just barely scraping by and always on the verge of starvation. But even within that small circle of desperately needy family members, friends, and neighbors, I provided no meaningful, lasting help. Whether the poverty inside that circle was truly unalterable, like that of the rest of the country, I couldn't say even today, but it seemed to me then a fixed and hopelessly unfixable condition, as permanent and unalterable as a gene code.

Beyond that small circle, of course, poverty was indeed fixed. If I bothered to walk ten blocks beyond our Duport Road enclave, I'd find myself in the middle of a workers' quarter jammed with mostly illiterate young men from the country, tens of thousands of them with only a farm boy's skills who had drifted into the city to find work, and finding none, had stayed to see their lives die on the vine, unplucked. They became thieves, pickpockets, extortionists, and beggars. They became drunks and drug addicts. Or they joined the army solely for the shelter and clothing it promised, and because they almost never got paid, they continued to steal, extort, and beg, only now with a gun in their hands. Joining them, plying their trade on these narrow streets at night, were loosely organized troops of prostitutes, most of them girls from the country following the boys, or girls kicked out of their villages by their husbands for having gotten pregnant in adultery or by their parents for having gotten pregnant out of wedlock. There were the so-called rope hotels, muddy, room-size squares of ground surrounded by a head-high cinder-block wall with a thatched roof on poles. Inside the walls, at the height of an adult's armpit, ropes were strung like clothesline across the enclosed space. For a dime, a homeless man or woman could drape his or her weight over the rope like a blanket and sleep all night, dry and more or less safe from the dangerous streets and alleys. Babies, naked and crusted with fly-spotted sores played listlessly in puddles of sewage. Vast midden heaps at the edge of the city were ringed by settlements of huts made from refrigerator cartons, the rusted carcasses of wrecked cars, cast-off doors and broken crates—whole villages of human scavengers sifting the towering, constantly expanding piles for scraps of cloth or paper that could be used or sold, kids and old women fighting with the rats and packs of wild dogs for bits of tossed-out food. It all seemed so hopeless to me that I averted my gaze. I did not want to see what I could not begin to change.

Yet at any time, once my babies were born, I could have put my shoulder to the wheel of one or several of the dozens of volunteer and nongovernmental charitable organizations that were stuck to their hubs in the mud of Liberian corruption, cynicism, and sloth. I could have distributed condoms, medical supplies, food, clean water, information. It was eight years between my marriage to Woodrow and my first return to America (an event I'll tell you about very soon), and in those years I could have taught a hundred adults to read. I could have bribed a hundred parents to keep their daughters from working in the fields or on the streets and paid for the girls' secondary-school education. I could have been a one-woman Peace Corps with no nationalist agenda, a one-woman charity with no religious program, a one-woman relief agency with no bureaucracy or salaried administrators to answer to. It wouldn't have changed the world or human nature, and probably wouldn't have altered a single sentence in the history of Liberia. But it would have changed me. And, a different person, I might have avoided some of the harm I inflicted later both on myself and others.

Instead, I gave out tips and Christmas bonuses and little presents on Boxing Day, a holiday that Liberians, not letting a good thing pass unappropriated, had borrowed from Sierra Leone. I dropped dimes and quarters into the cups of crippled and deformed, leprous, and amputated beggars on the streets of Monrovia, gave pennies to children who clustered around me whenever I stepped from the Mercedes, and although I myself did not attend services (a girl has to have some principles, I suppose), I supported Woodrow's church by sending our children to its Sunday school with dollar bills for the collection plate tucked into pledge envelopes.

It was as if the people who lived there and the events that took place in those tumultuous years were deadly viruses, and I lived behind glass, a bubble-girl protected against infection from the outside world. Meanwhile, beyond my bubble the president and his cohort, which, despite my husband's best efforts and advantageous marriage, still did not include him, grew fatter and richer and ever more flagrantly corrupt. They skimmed the cream off American foreign aid, blatantly stole from any and all non-governmental and UN public service allocations, took their cut from World Bank and IMF grants to the financial sector, and pimped the country's natural resources, selling off at special, one-day-only rates Liberia's rubber, sugar, rice, diamonds, iron, and water, peddling vast stands of mahogany and timber to companies owned and run by Swedes, Americans, Brits, Germans, and, increasingly, Israelis. Foreign distributors of beer, gasoline, motor vehicles, cigarettes, salt, electricity, and telephone service haggled over lunch for bargain-priced monopolies; by sundown they had the president's fee safely deposited in his Swiss bank account and, after the celebratory banquet, partied the night away at the Executive Mansion with Russian hookers, smoking Syrian hashish, snorting lines of Afghan cocaine, and guzzling cases of Courvoisier.

The few Liberian journalists and politicians who dared to criticize the president and his cronies simply disappeared. As if sent on permanent assignment to Nigeria or Côte d'Ivoire, they were not mentioned again in public or private. Newspapers were locked down by judicial fiat, and radio stations were silenced, until the only news, little more than recycled releases from the president's press office, was no news at all. Meanwhile, the president's personal security force grew larger in number and actual physical size—big, scowling, swaggering men in sunglasses looking more and more like an army of private body guards than an elite corps of enlisted men—while the men in the regular army seemed to diminish in number and size, their uniforms tattered, torn, and dirty, their boots replaced by broken-backed sneakers and plastic sandals. Compared with the glistening black AK-47s carried by the president's men, their rifles, obsolete U.S. Army leftovers from the Korean War, looked almost antique and were without ammunition. More like dangerous toys than deadly weapons, they were used mainly as clubs.

I knew all this as it happened, saw it with my own eyes, and learned the details and background and the names and motives of the people involved from Woodrow, from the few of his colleagues in government who, like Charles Taylor, trusted him, and from our social acquaintances—and, of course, I learned of it from Jeannine, who loved showing me that she knew more about the world of Liberian big men and their affairs than I did, and from Elizabeth, who had taken over my old job at the lab and whom I visited daily to be with the chimps. For, when it came down to it, the chimps had become my closest friends in Liberia, my only confidants, the only creatures to whom I entrusted my secrets, and whose secrets I kept and carried.

EARLY IN 1979—I think it was April, because the rains were about to begin—President Tolbert tacked a ten-cent-per-pound sales tax onto the already inflated retail price of rice. That winter's measly crop had been worse than usual, and supplies of rice had diminished to a dangerous level. Rice was the country's staple food. Without it, the people, especially the poor, faced starvation, and the nation faced famine. Stores and shops had emptied out, and black marketeers selling rice from Guinea and Côte d'Ivoire were getting rich at prices only the rich could afford.

"Why on earth do you need so much for a little one-pound bag of rice, Jeannine?"

"On account of it so dear now. Them don't got no more at Dot-Dot, an' none at Congo Square, neither. Peoples only can buy rice these days from the Arab, y' know, an' he sellin' it very high priced."

A Costa Rican freighter loaded with sacks of rice grown in Louisiana, meant originally for Haiti, and stamped USAID NOT FOR RESALE, lay at anchor in the harbor, waiting to be off-loaded. So far, on the president's orders, the off-loading permit had been refused by customs, and the captain and crew hadn't bothered to come ashore. For days, stevedores, dockworkers, retailers, and crowds of hopeful higglers with their gunny sacks, and women and girls from the countryside with empty pails and plastic buckets had gathered at the docks, waiting for the ship to tie up and the sacks of rice to be carried off and distributed among them.

While the people waited hopefully in the rain day after day and night after night for their rice to come in, it was a continuous, twenty-four-hour party, an informal, spontaneous carnival, with people dancing and singing in little groups on the docks, drinking raw palm wine, roasting scavenged groundnuts on charcoal fires, all good-naturedly, optimistically marking time. Each morning, as I passed in the Mercedes on my way to the lab, I saw that the crowd had grown larger. They seemed to be saying to themselves, *We are hungry now, but we won't be hungry long.* Everyone believed it.

Then one morning the voice of President Tolbert himself came over the radio, and he announced the new tax on rice, a "people's contribution" it was called, a way for Liberia to free itself from foreign debt, he said. Since rice was the main food for all Liberians, every single man, woman, and child would now be able to contribute to the nation's independence. The legislature would pass the decree today, and then the ship currently waiting in the harbor of Monrovia would be off-loaded, and the rice distributed. And there were more ships coming, he promised. Ships from Nigeria, Brazil, and America were on the western horizon. Soon everyone would have plenty of rice—jollof rice, rice fufu, coconut rice, rice and beans, curried rice, check rice with greens, rice balls. . . .

The ten-cent tax per pound effectively doubled the street price at that time. No one, rich or poor, held any illusions as to where the money would end up. Having extracted as much as they could from foreign governments and corporations and sold off for a pittance nearly all the nation's natural resources, the president and his colleagues, resorting to autocannibalism, had turned to devouring their own and had begun the meal with the most numerous and defenseless of their own, the poor. There was no meat on those bones, however. The poor had nothing left to give to the wealthy, not even ten cents per pound of rice. Having nothing more to lose, as soon as the president went off the air and no longer seemed to be watching them, they rioted.

It began shortly before I passed by the harbor in the car one morning on the way to the lab, which was located on the south side of the city near the JFK Hospital. As we approached the harbor front, we saw black clouds of smoke pouring into the gray sky. There were tires burning in the lot beside the dockside warehouse, and large crowds knotted around the fires, people shouting at one another, as if angry at themselves, rather than the president. They shook their fists, men and women alike, their faces dark with anger.

"What's wrong with them?" I asked Satterthwaite, more curious than frightened.

Satterthwaite half-turned in front and said, "It on account of the tax."

"What tax?" I asked.

"Ten cents a pound for rice. President Tolbert say it this mornin' on the radio."

A battered pickup truck with a half-dozen men in the back waving machetes crossed suddenly in front of the Mercedes. Satterthwaite hit the brakes and swerved away, bumping over the curb onto the harbor-front parking lot. Another vehicle, a small red taxi, pulled in behind us, and the pickup truck followed us over the curb onto the lot, swerved, and stopped in front, effectively blocking the Mercedes. The driver and another man jumped down from the pickup to the pavement and walked towards us.

"Don't get out, don't open the window, don't say nothin'," Satterthwaite said. I heard the door locks automatically clunk into place.

A gang of men appeared out of nowhere and surrounded the car. They began to rock it from side to side and bang on the trunk and hood with their fists like hammers. Most of them were shirtless, unshaven, their hair in long, springy coils. They waved their machetes and stared wild eyed into the back of the car, trying to see through the tinted glass—though I could see plainly enough their detonating faces, huge and black and wet with rain.

Two of the men thumped purposefully on Satterthwaite's window, the leaders, evidently, ordinary workingmen in tee shirts and loose trousers. They had the faces of men who wished to negotiate. Satterthwaite lowered his window a few inches and spoke rapidly to them in pidgin.

In response, the men were shouting at Satterthwaite, as angry as the others now, apparently confused or not believing him, but he kept talking rapidly in a calm, low voice, until finally they grew quiet and listened and then at last instructed the others to back off. Satterthwaite turned and explained, "Them think we come from the president to tell the ship to give the rice to the government. Them think we the tax collectors, but now they see who we are, Miz Sundiata and her driver, so them say it all right for us to go."

"Thank you," I said.

It went suddenly quiet inside the car again, and the pickup pulled away from the Mercedes, freeing us to leave. Satterthwaite put the car in gear and inched forward and gave a gentle, grateful wave to the men, who politely, almost apologetically waved back.

At that moment, as if they'd been watching and waiting for us to leave the scene, a pair of army trucks filled with helmeted soldiers appeared, engines grinding, and blocked the departure of all three vehicles, the pickup, the red taxi, and the Mercedes. Two jeeps braked to a quick stop beside our car, and dozens of soldiers jumped from the trucks and jeeps and dragged the drivers from the pickup and the taxi, beating the heads and faces of the men with rifle butts, sending their now pathetic-looking machetes clattering to the pavement, kicking the men, rolling their bodies away from the Mercedes like logs. Blood sprayed from noses, ears, broken mouths, and from inside the car I heard muffled howls cut by the sound of human bones being cracked and splintered. The wild men with machetes who moments ago had terrified me were transformed with terrible efficiency into sacks and tossed into the rear of the trucks.

I yelled at Satterthwaite, "For God's sake, get us out of here!"

A soldier waved us on. Satterthwaite hit the accelerator, and in seconds we were back on Gamba Boulevard, headed south and out of the city. I gazed out the windows through the steady rain at the nearly empty streets and alleys. Abruptly, halfway to the lab, I told Satterthwaite to turn around and drive me home. "Take the back way, stay out of town," I said.

And so it was back to the bubble, then. When we pulled into the yard, Woodrow was standing at the door, arms folded across his chest, waiting. The dogs posed alertly beside him like sentries. He'd returned home from the ministry as soon as he learned from the radio what had happened down at the docks and was now spreading to all parts of the city.

We watched and listened to the Rice Riot, as it came to be called, from behind the high, gated wall that surrounded our home on Duport Road. The riot sprawled uphill from the waterfront, as the crowd of ordinary folks broke away from the soldiers sent to subdue them quickly became a mob led and egged on by gangs of boys and young men drunk on palm wine and high on marijuana and Lord knows what else. They stormed up the long ridge into the center of town, smashing windows and burning trash, then looting stores, dressing in looted clothing and lugging TVs, radios, tape decks, electric fans, and blenders like trophies. They overturned cars, massed in the squares and at crossroads, swelling in size and noise as they went, beating on stolen pails and cook pans, blowing whistles, chanting, dancing. It was a headless beast, thrashing in pain and confusion.

Woodrow and I and the boys, Satterthwaite, Jeannine and Kuyo, we all peered from behind the barred windows of the house and watched the smoke rise in smudged clouds, billowing skyward through the rain, first from one district, then from another, more distant district, and felt relieved that the rioters seemed to be moving south and west, away from our neighborhood and in the direction of the Liberian government buildings and the foreign embassies, towards the dead end of palm-lined Gamba Boulevard, where the bright white Executive Mansion ruled, as if the beast were moving blindly, instinctively, towards the source of its pain.

It was unclear, however, what the mob expected to do once it reached the palace. Stand outside in the thousands and raise their fists in anger and frustration? Try to tell of their sorrow and pain and hunger, their fear of having to watch their children die? Tell the foreigners of their plight, yes, tell the world, if possible, but especially tell the president, the hulking, glowering man in the blue, pinstriped Savile Row suit and exquisite Italian necktie, who looked down from his office window, gazed across the mint-green lawns and gardens to the ten-foot-high wall of wrought-iron spikes protecting the palace grounds from the street, where his people cried out and clung to the iron bars and banged against them with sticks, machetes, and fists. Tell the president, who, after a few moments of contemplating the crowd, its growing size, its fury and suicidal desperation—suicidal because they had come to the Executive Mansion, the most protected building in the country, where they had effectively trapped themselves in a cul-de-sac against an iron wall—walked calmly from the window to his desk, picked up the telephone, and called his minister of security.

Shortly after that, clanking and snorting like mechanical bulls, the tanks appeared, three of them, grinding along the boulevard towards the huge crowd, slowly passing the European and Israeli and American embassies, whose gates were locked shut from inside, the bridges over the moats raised, and behind the tanks marched a battalion of soldiers from the president's security force. These grim men were not regular army enlistees. They came helmeted, wearing full battle gear, carrying M-16s and AK-47s. These men were not riot police, like the men we battled in Chicago in '68 and '69. They weren't National Guardsmen, ill-trained reservists given unfamiliar weapons and called unexpectedly to duty, like the frightened boys who'd shot students at Kent State. No, these were men who were trained and armed and brought out of their barracks today for one purpose only, to shoot down as many people as their officers ordered, even if they had to run down and fire point-blank at members of their own tribe, killing their friends and neighbors, possibly even family members, men, women, and children, all of them unarmed, helpless against the tanks and guns.

BBC radio parroted the official Liberian News Agency's report that seven civilians had been killed and three soldiers, and that the soldiers had fired only in self-defense. But we learned afterwards—not from any newspaper or radio broadcast, but from hushed conversations with friends and servants—that hundreds, as many as six hundred, some said, of poor and hungry, utterly defenseless Liberians were shot dead that day. Jeannine said the hospitals were filled to overflowing with injured people and had begun to turn away anyone who could not walk in and, after receiving emergency repairs, walk out. Hundreds of people had been shot point-blank, others had been crushed beneath the tanks: children in their mothers' arms; the mothers themselves; teenaged boys and girls caught up in the riot merely because they happened to be on the streets that day, choosing a wild, out-of-control block party over a day in the classroom; men and women who may well have hoped for a coup to grow out of the riot but were not themselves guilty of plotting one, merely of hoping for one; and opportunistic, drunken thieves and looters living out a materialist fantasy. It was said that dozens of young men had been carried off in trucks and coldly executed, their dismembered bodies destroyed in vats of hydrochloric acid or secretly burned and buried in the bush. It was said that a U.S. destroyer had anchored offshore, and another, filled with U.S. Marines, was steaming over from Freetown to join it. We were told that American helicopters had been on their way from Robertsfield Airport to remove all embassy personnel, if necessary, and carry out any U.S. citizens who considered him- or herself in danger.

Which did not include me, of course. As long as President Tolbert, my husband's boss, remained in charge of the situation, my children and I were in no danger. And Tolbert remained in charge. By evening, a nervous, fearful calm had descended over the city, over the entire country, in fact, and the following morning the loud, hearty voice of the president boomed from the radio, telling us that thanks to the courage and discipline of the Liberian armed forces, a coup had been averted, the back of the rebellion had been broken, and a communist-inspired revolution had been thwarted. Once again the Republic of Liberia had been preserved by the brave, freedom-loving men and women of Liberia who had remained loyal to the president's True Whig party. And to reward the people for their faithfulness to him and his party, the cruel tax on rice, which had been imposed by the Congress while secretly under the influence of certain devious and disloyal elements in the opposition, had been rescinded by presidential order. Three cheers for the True Whig party.

"Hip, hip, hooray!" the president sang. *He's drunk*, I thought.

Woodrow said, "Well, I guess that settles things. We can't allow ourselves to be ruled by mobs."

I agreed. The good wife. Satterthwaite sagely nodded. *Yas, Boss.* And Jeannine hurried out to buy rice.

THE TRUE WHIG PARTY had run Liberia almost from its nineteenth-century inception, back when the country, supposedly no longer the African stepchild of America, was first declared a republic. No one we knew was opposed to the president or belonged to any party other than his. In spite of my husband's backroom role in these events—for he was, after all, a member of the president's administration—and in spite of the fact that my three sons were, like their father, citizens of the Republic of Liberia, my personal connections to the events remained tangential. I was like an asteroid passing through the farthest orbits of the Liberian planetary system, crossing on a long elliptical path determined eons ago in a different solar system. My and my family's orbits had a barely measurable effect on one another. I still believed that as long as my children, my husband, and I were physically safe and reasonably comfortable, the country and I were nearly irrelevant to each other.

Then one rainy November night in 1979, seven months after the Rice Riot, I remember waking very late to the sound of deliberately lowered male voices, Woodrow's and that of another man, coming from the living room. Their rumblings, anxious and urgent, rose slowly and then quickly fell, as if they'd remembered freshly that they didn't want to be overheard. I slipped from bed and in the dark made my way down the hall towards the living room, and just as I reached the entryway, saw the silhouette of a large, broad-shouldered man leaving by the front door. It clicked shut, and Woodrow sat down at his desk, sighed audibly, and lighted a cigarette.

"Was that Charles?"

Without looking at me, he said, "No." Then, after a pause, "Yes, actually. He sent you his love, but had to rush off."

"Why was Charles here this late? Is something wrong?"

"No. Business."

"Really? Business? It's almost three, Woodrow."

"Business."

"Oh."

He sighed a second time, giving up for the moment—too much effort to lie. "Yes. Dangerous business, actually. Charles has gone and formed a political party. To oppose the president." He paused again. "Seems like a terrible idea. Especially now, so soon after the riots."

"You told him that."

"I told him that. Yes." He explained that Charles had tried to convince Woodrow to join this new party, to be called the People's Progressive Party, and help him organize a referendum to cut short the two years remaining on Tolbert's eight-year term. If the referendum passed, a new election would be held in the fall. And Charles was thinking of putting himself forward for president. "He wants me to declare against the True Whig candidate and run for the Senate from Gibo, where Fuama is located. My home district."

"This is a ridiculous idea, right? To cut yourself off from the president and the party? To oppose him?"

"Oh, definitely! Definitely ridiculous. Hopeless. But Charles is an ambitious man. And a rather reckless one."

"And you're not?"

"Ambitious, yes. But not reckless."

We both remained silent for a long moment. He poured a drink from the open bottle at his desk and drank it down. Then looked up at me, half surprised to see me still standing there at the door in my nightgown. "Go to bed, Hannah darling," he said.

"Are you safe, Woodrow?"

"Yes, yes, of course. I turned him down flat. Go to bed."

"But does this put you against Charles now?"

"No. Not really. He may not see it that way now, but he will."

"What about him? Is Charles safe?"

"He'll be fine, as long as his referendum never gets held. And it won't. There's no way the president will permit it. And with no referendum, there'll be no early election. Good night, my dear. I still have work to do," he said, and turned back to the papers strewn across his desk. His jaw clenched and unclenched, like a nervous fist. "Hannah, please," he said without looking up. "Go to bed."

He's frightened to death, I thought. *He's pretending to work so as to avoid visions of his own imprisonment and execution. And ours.* I suddenly realized that it was a thing he had been doing for many months now. Possibly years. He knew that his life, and therefore ours, mine and my sons', were precariously held. *How stupid I've been!* I thought. Too self-absorbed, too obsessed with my own memories, dreams, and reflections to see the danger that surrounded us. And for the first time, I, too, was frightened.

*   *   *

YET IN SPITE of my fear, or perhaps because of it, I kept inside my bubble and stayed deliberately detached, rigorously uninvolved, all the way through a series of cascading events, one falling hard upon the next, that threatened to crack the bubble open like an egg. These were events that no one, least of all I, could have anticipated. Charles Taylor did indeed form his People's Progressive Party and called for a nation-wide referendum to void the remaining two years of the president's term. A week later, the Senate of Liberia unanimously passed an act specifically banning the party, and Charles, to avoid arrest and probable execution, fled the country. He was said to be the house-arrested guest of Libya's President Ghaddafi, who refused to extradite him back to Liberia. It was a small favor, easily given, one that might someday elicit ample repayment—either from Tolbert, for having kept Charles under lock and key, or, if Tolbert fell, from Charles, for having refused to extradite him.

Back in Monrovia, everyone suspected that Tolbert had lost the support of the Americans. It was thought that the Americans had begun to mistrust the president's engorged ego and greed and his increasing recklessness and were about to abandon their man in Africa, cutting him loose both of their restraints and of their protection. If you want a big dog, the Americans believed, you have to give him a long leash. But not too long. For a decade, William Tolbert, the president of Liberia, had been one of the Americans' big dogs. Maybe now they were switching the leash to Charles Taylor. Maybe Charles would return in triumph from Libya and become the next president of Liberia.

It was a not-uncommon syndrome in Africa in those years, in which a puppet president gradually became a self-deluded despot who no longer remembered who was really in charge of his country. After years of feeding and lavishly housing the leader and his cronies, the citizens finally grow hungry and angry enough to riot in the streets. The leader calls out the army and brutally shuts down any and all opposition. Soon, however, the army, unpaid for months, becomes demoralized, and the officer corps gives evidence of increasing unreliability—a reluctance to follow orders passed down from the commander-in-chief, loud demands for back pay or, with national cash reserves having long since dried up and no cash money available, demands for increased emoluments and political payoffs and perks—until finally, with the leader no longer able to buy their loyalty, the officers come together and plot the leader's overthrow and replace him with one of their own.

Around four o'clock of the afternoon of the coup, Woodrow telephoned and said he had to stay late at the ministry and might have to remain there overnight. "There's a bit of a crisis over here," he said with typical understatement. "And by the way, you'd better keep off the streets until tomorrow at least. There've been reports of a few rows between the army and the police out there. Nothing serious, you understand, but I'll send Satterthwaite over, if you like," he added.

"We weren't going anywhere, anyhow. No need to send Satterthwaite. He'll just want to hang around and read his comic books," I said blandly, Satterthwaite having become my least favorite member of the household. The truth is, though Jeannine and I had grown somewhat more cautious in our movements through the city since the Rice Riot a year earlier, by the same token, because the anger of the rioters had not been directed against our home, we felt oddly, perhaps unrealistically, protected by our high wall and locked gate, our brave dogs, and our status.

"Stay as late as you like. We'll be fine," I said, not in the least curious as to the nature of the crisis at the ministry. About once a month, due to a "bit of a crisis" or an unexpected cabinet meeting or the sudden need to entertain a visiting foreign dignitary or corporate chieftain, Woodrow did not come home until dawn or midday the next day, arriving rumpled, exhausted, smelling of whiskey, cigar smoke, and cheap perfume. I never asked him where he'd been. I could guess easily enough, of course, but had no desire to confront him. By then I had come to welcome his shabbily contrived absences. I saw them as earning moral capital for me; moral debt for himself. We were drifting steadily apart, each of us in a different way, I thought, preparing for the inevitable split.

The night of the coup, however, Woodrow surprised me and did not stay out till dawn or beyond. Instead he arrived home around one a.m. Jeannine and I rushed from our bedrooms to the living room to see who or what had caused the dogs to bark. I flipped on the light, and there he was, standing by the door like a burglar caught in the act.

"You're home early," I said.

"Yes." Then, speaking slowly, almost with a drawl, he said, "I'm lucky to be home at all, if you want to know the truth. Have you been listening to the radio?"

"No. I was at the lab till supper, and Jeannine was with the boys all afternoon outside. Why? Did we miss something?"

"You missed something, yes." Quickly, he told us what had happened that afternoon and evening and gave us an indication of what would likely happen tomorrow. A dozen enlisted men led by an illiterate master sergeant named Samuel Doe had pushed their way into the Executive Mansion, and facing barely token opposition from the president's personal security force, had captured Tolbert and placed him under arrest. Their boldness and the suddenness of the attack had bought them sufficient time and unpredictability to let them capture and imprison in a single afternoon all of the president's ministers, including, of course, Woodrow, along with the Chief Justice of the Supreme Court, and the few generals still loyal to William Tolbert. The soldiers simply walked into the offices, homes, and restaurants where the officials happened to be working or dining and took them at gunpoint to the damp, windowless cells at Barclay Barracks. By midnight, Sergeant Doe and his men had released several of the lesser ministers, again including Woodrow, and the generals, in exchange for their pledge of support for the coup. They announced over the radio that they had overthrown William Tolbert's corrupt and barbarous regime. Sergeant Doe stammered and stumbled his way through the announcement, as if making it up as he went along. Then he and his men eviscerated the president with their bayonets and tossed him and his guts from the window of his office to the lawn below.

"These boys mean business. They're going to clean house," Woodrow said, and poured himself three fingers of whiskey and drank it off.

"What are you going to do? What are the Americans doing?" I asked.

"The usual. They're evacuating most of their embassy staff and any U.S. nationals who want to leave. The cultural attaché over there, Sam Clement, called to check on you and the boys, actually. Kind of surprised me. I guess they still regard you as a U.S. citizen over there. Anyhow, I told him we'll be all right," he said.

"Are you sure?"

"These new boys, they know they're going to need a few people like me just to keep things running. They're enlisted men is all, soldiers, sergeants and corporals, mostly illiterate Krahn country boys, and they're already scared of what they've done. They even want Charles Taylor to come home and help them run the country," he said, and abruptly gave a pleased cackle. "Ha! I may come out of this with a promotion!"

Jeannine in her nightgown and cotton robe, castoffs I'd given her, stood listening at the door, half hidden in the darkness of the hallway. "You wan' some supper, Mistah Sundiata?" she asked. She rubbed her eyes like a child wakened unexpectedly from sleep.

"No, no, I'm fine! You two go on to bed. I've got to check through my files. There are some things I'd just as soon keep out of the hands of anyone who might come looking," he said, and poured himself another drink. "Can't be too careful at a time like this." His face was covered with a film of sweat, whether with excitement or fear I couldn't tell. Possibly, in this climate, it was the whiskey: Scotch is a northern-latitude drink. Woodrow's consumption of alcohol had gradually increased over the last year or so, and I'd begun to suspect that he was becoming an alcoholic. I'd never lived with an alcoholic before and wasn't sure what to expect or how to measure the disease's stealthy approach.

"I'll fix you some chicken," Jeannine said and headed for the kitchen.

"Fine, fine, fine. I'll eat it in here!" he hollered.

"Good night, Woodrow," I said, and turned and walked slowly down the hallway to my bed. I wondered if the symptoms of alcoholism were different for Africans than for Americans, for blacks than for whites. A drunk is a drunk, I decided, regardless of his race or culture.

A while later, from the bedroom, I smelled paper burning. The living room fireplace was mostly for decorative purposes and had a lousy draft, but was cheering on a rain-chilled evening. Woodrow was cleaning out his files, erasing paper trails that might link him to the doomed and despised president and his inner circle, a circle that Woodrow had for so long tried to join but that, despite his best efforts at flattery, servility, and faithfulness, had rebuffed him. No wonder he seemed almost pleased by the coup. No wonder he'd cackled with delight at the prospect of his good friend Charles Taylor's triumphant return.

Sometime later, I was wakened by a woman's light laugh. Jeannine's? Then silence. I could still smell the smoke of burnt paper, but it was old, cold smoke now. It was nearly dawn, birds were making their first chirps, and Woodrow still hadn't come in to bed. Then I heard that all-too-familiar thumping, the sound of my headboard being bumped against the wall by Woodrow's tireless thrusting—only this time, for the first time, it wasn't my bed, our bed, and the wall wasn't the one behind my pillow. I knew at once that Woodrow was with Jeannine, and the bed was hers, the wall the one behind her head in the small room beyond the boys' bedroom. I lay there curled on my side like a question mark, listening, unable to shut out the sound of my husband fucking his niece, my sons' nanny, my friend, perhaps the only human friend I had in those days. And did I want to do the normal thing— leap from my bed, run down the hall, fling open the door to Jeannine's room, and shriek bloody murder at the treacherous bitch and bastard adulterer of a husband? Did I want to expose and humiliate them both? Would my relationship with the two of them be forever changed?

No. None of it. It was as if they had been doing this for years, since the first week of our marriage, and I had come to accept it as normal and even necessary. Simply, it was how we lived now, Woodrow and the boys and I. And, of course, it was payback for my little tryst with Satterthwaite. We were all adulterers. I knew that, restless, agitated, still exhilarated by having come so close to death and escaped, Woodrow had walked into Jeannine's room and slid into her bed, spread her legs, and begun to fuck her. He was exercising his prerogative as head of the household, and she had merely accepted his heavy, sweating presence atop her as natural and inevitable. I grabbed Woodrow's pillow and covered my ears with it, muffling the sound of his betrayal and Jeannine's easy compliance.

A moment of relative silence, the only sound my own throbbing pulse, and then the thumping of Jeannine's bed against the wall gradually began to filter through the pillow, and I could hear them again. I took the pillow away and lay on my back listening, as on and on it went, like the steadily pounding piston of an engine, while the ground doves outside my window began to gurgle and pepperbirds began to sing, a rooster crowed, a car drove slowly past the house, and someone in the house next door, in the kitchen just beyond the terrace outside our bedroom, turned on the radio. A man was speaking from the radio, his voice a weird blend of authority and confusion—Samuel Doe, the new head of state for the Republic of Liberia. He was announcing the execution of the president and the arrest of fifteen traitors and giving the time and place of their upcoming public execution.

Later that day, in a now-infamous episode, Sergeant Doe and his men hauled thirteen of the ministers, the Supreme Court justice, and the major general who had run the president's security apparatus down to the beach a mile south of the city, where, before a huge, cheering crowd, they erected fifteen telephone poles in the sand, stripped their victims, most of them fat, old men, to their underwear, tied them to the poles, and shot them literally to pieces. The executioners were drunk, and consequently had to fire hundreds of rounds into the bodies to be sure that the old men were dead. Many in the crowd snapped photos and videotaped the event, and all day long, with loudspeakers mounted on truck beds blaring juju and reggae, the people sang and danced in drunken celebration, while buzzards circled overhead and small yellow dogs worked their way closer and closer to the fly-blown carcasses tied to the poles—meat rotting in the sun.

THOUGH WORSE WAS to come, 1983, my eighth year in Liberia, was a hard one for me. But who knew what was coming? Certainly I didn't. I was forty now and honestly believed that the truly difficult part of my life was behind me. Oh, sure, I knew I'd have to face individual crises in the future—who doesn't? My three sons, as they grew into adolescence and beyond, were bound to create episodes of fear and trembling; my marriage to Woodrow someday soon would have to withstand the blows of middle-age, mine as much as his, and the eventual departure of the boys from home, and the culmination, disappointing, of Woodrow's career, for I knew by then, even though he'd been made minister, a full member of the cabinet, that he was never going to get inside the inner circle of power that was now centered on Samuel Doe. I was already hearing anxious grumbles from Woodrow about my own career—although I still hesitated to call it that, my work with the chimps, my dreamers.

But I pictured these coming events and crises as separate beads on a string, individually not too heavy to bear, collectively merely the defining weight of a life, my life, anyone's. In the last year, however, I'd begun to believe that all my future dark days, like those of most people I knew, even here in Liberia, would be matched about evenly by future days of brightness. Darkness would be canceled by light, neutralized, evened off, so that when I grew old and died, I'd come out at zero. In the game of life, all I expected, all I hoped for, was to come out even, a zero-sum game.

These aren't low expectations for a life, exactly. They aren't high, either. But for me, as I entered my forty-first year, my expectations and hopes had at last met one another and were a solid fit, a balanced scale, yin and yang, hand in glove. No more dreams of revolution, no more millenarian expectations, no more longing for utopia. I called my newly achieved state of mind *realism* and almost never used words like *bourgeois* anymore. I was standing on solid ground now. Terra firma. Yes, indeed—realism. My mother and father were still afloat in clouds of unknowing, maybe, but I had finally created for myself a life that neither imitated theirs nor stood in simple reaction to it. After all these years, I could say to myself that I had freed myself from my parents. It may have taken rather too long, but I'd done it.

I'd even begun talking with Woodrow about returning to the States with the boys to visit my parents. Their American grandparents. Could he arrange it with the American embassy, possibly through the cultural officer? Whatzisname, Sam Clement? Or could he speak informally to the U.S. ambassador himself about issuing a passport for Dawn Sundiata, née Carrington, with the boys traveling on Woodrow's Liberian VIP passport, so there'd be no nasty surprises when we arrived in the States?

"It can be arranged, of course," Woodrow said. "Bit of a turnaround, though, wouldn't you say?"

We were at dinner at home, eating on the patio, the five of us, a peaceful moonlit evening at the end of the rainy season. For the first time in months, I could hear the dry clatter of the palms in the warm breeze. "Don't jump the gun," I said to him and poured myself a third glass of wine. The boys had left the table and were being bathed now by Jeannine. "I'm only giving the idea some idle consideration," I explained. "I've been thinking about them a lot lately, maybe because hitting forty makes me realize how old they are. I've started to worry about their health, actually. And I'm feeling more guilt with each passing year, Woodrow. Guilt for the distance between us. And there's the boys to think of. Really. I don't want the boys to grow up without knowing anything more about my parents than they would if I were an orphan."

"Ah, well, that's true for me, too, you know." Woodrow lighted a Dunhill cigarette, pushed back his chair, and crossed his legs. He watched me carefully, as if he thought something new and puzzling might be happening here.

"The boys know *your* parents. It's mine I'm talking about."

"I mean that I myself sometimes think of you as an orphan. But you're not, are you?"

Most of what Woodrow knew of my past he'd learned years ago, when I first came over from Ghana, from a small sheaf of information gleaned from that file folder slipped to him by the same American cultural attaché, Sam Clement. I didn't know what was in that file and wasn't sure I wanted to know, so hadn't asked. It wasn't until nearly a year after we were married that Woodrow had actually showed me the folder, and he did it for his reasons, not mine.

He brought it from his office one afternoon and carried it out to the lab compound, where I was sitting at my desk logging genealogical data on the baby chimps. He dropped the folder on top of my logbook, and I opened and read through it quickly and in silence, while he sat on the corner of my cluttered desk and waited. An oscillating fan on the desk hummed and drifted back and forth, riffling the papers in the folder. It wasn't much, barely two single-spaced, typed pages and fuzzy copies of the photos used for the FBI's Most Wanted list in 1970, after the Greenwich Village townhouse bombing that sent me and the entire Weather cohort permanently underground.

I sighed heavily at the sight of my old face. It brought me reluctantly to grieve all over again for someone I'd loved and whose death I thought I'd gotten over, not the three friends who'd been killed in the explosion—I never really knew them more than slightly from the various national SDS conventions—but the late, unlamented Hannah Musgrave. Here it all was again: the names and dates, the tired facts of my biography up to then, the description of my few skills and talents. It was the CV of a small-time, would-be domestic terrorist. Sad. Pathetic.

"Why are you showing this to me now? You had it when I got here, when I first came over from Accra, didn't you?"

"You're my wife now. If I'm ever asked, I should know what's true and what's a lie. In case I have to defend you. I've seen files like this before, you know; the president has a cabinet stuffed with files just like this, and they're mostly lies, lies and false confessions. But bits and pieces are true."

"Yes," I said. "But everything's pretty much true, what's in there."

"Pretty much?"

"Except . . . well, except that I never knew what was happening anywhere other than where I myself happened to be, and I wasn't responsible for anything that I didn't do personally. Which wasn't much, believe me. We weren't that stupid or naive. We were in these small cells, what we called *foco* groups, and mine was in New Bedford, Massachusetts. So when that townhouse blew up and killed those three people, I was as shocked as everyone else. I hadn't heard from any of those people in years, didn't even know if they were still part of Weather or not. Same with the Pentagon bombing and most of the others. The New York police stations. All of them, actually. That was the idea, to keep the cells separate. Only the three or four people at the top—the Weather Bureau, we called them—knew what all the cells were *supposed* to be doing, and they knew only in a general way. We were instructed to invent and implement our own individual attacks on the government cell by cell. Some of the cells were really creative and bold. But others, like mine, were incompetent and timid and more or less driven by fantasy. You have to understand, Woodrow, most of us were like actors in a play that on a barely conscious level was mainly about disappearing. About breaking with your past. You know?"

"Your past. I don't understand."

"Well, that was *me*, husband. I was mainly trying to break from my past. Of course, what I *thought* I was doing . . ."

"What was wrong with your past?" Woodrow interrupted. "I mean, that you wanted to break from it?"

He was never going to get it. No matter what I said or how far back in my life I went with him, my pain and sorrow and my anger and shame were too weirdly American for Woodrow to grasp what had transformed me from a college coed worried about keeping her real name on the dean's list to a hard-as-nails terrorist on the run under a false name. Or what had transformed the terrorist into the two-named wife—three names, actually—of the Liberian minister of public health, the mother of his sons. How could he be expected to get those changes when I barely understood them myself? If I told him everything that had been left out of that thin folder, if I made the story of my life *real* to him, like I'm trying to do for you, he'd be afraid, rightly, that I could be transformed yet again into something equally strange. Or even changed back into what I had been before. The coed. The political activist. The fantasist. The maker of bombs.

I wasn't going to put that fear onto him, I decided, not after all he'd done for me so far and showed every sign of continuing to do. Despite all, Woodrow was a good and generous man, there was no denying it, and I loved those qualities in him and benefited from them and fully expected to benefit from them for the rest of my life. I was not altogether sure, even early in our marriage, that I loved *him*, however. The essential Woodrow. Whoever, whatever, that was.

I understood, perhaps better than he, that I could no more make sense of his past than he could mine. We were a husband and wife who could not imagine the texture and content of each other's consciousness as they had existed prior to the day we first met. Woodrow, too, had been transformed many times. A boy from a West African village had turned into an American college student, a black-skinned foreigner with an exotic accent, a young man who, in time, had become a Liberian cabinet minister married to a white American woman. If I knew his story, the whole of it, I, too, might be frightened by the possibility of still farther transformations to come. What if he became again the boy from a West African village? He seemed on the verge of it whenever we visited Fuama. What if he still secretly was that boy, now become a man, with a second and third wife and still maintained sexual control over his female cousins and nieces? Not just Jeannine. Or became again the black African college boy imitating the white American college boys, drinking too much, playing with drugs, screwing the coeds whether they liked it or not? I'd known some African students like that at Brandeis, although most of them had been enrolled elsewhere, the technical and business schools in Cambridge and Boston proper, out looking for hot, guilt-ridden, liberal white girls turned on by negritude but scared of American blacks.

Consequently, neither I nor Woodrow had sought to learn the other's story. The rough outline, a few typed pages in a file folder, was enough. No details necessary. No late-night connubial reminiscing for Mr. and Mrs. Sundiata. No lengthy descriptions of anyone other than the husband and wife sitting across from each other at the table right this moment, the man and the woman lingering over the last of the evening's wine, with the dinner dishes and serving bowls cluttering the space between them, palm trees flipping their fronds in the breezy dark, tree frogs advertising their wares, the giggles and splashes of the boys in their bath, and Jeannine's low, monitoring scold as she hurries them to dry and into their American pajamas, Bugs Bunny, Daffy Duck, and Pluto.

WHEN IS IT TIME to flee your country? "When they shoot your dogs," is what people say. There was no warning—there seldom is—not even the sound of a car or truck pulling up at the high, chain-locked gate. The dogs barked once, more in surprise than fear or anger, a yelp of astonishment, then a rapid set of gunshots, six or seven, and the two Rottweilers were dead. Andy and Beemus—Woodrow's pride, his beautiful black thugs imported from Zimbabwe, goofy, meat-eating playmates for his children and fierce protectors of his household—lay in the driveway between the rear of the Mercedes and the iron gate, large mounds of bleeding black dirt, as four helmeted soldiers carrying automatic rifles opened the gate as if they had the key—wait, they did have the key: in the dark we saw that one of the soldiers . . . no, it was a civilian with them, a man wearing a navy-blue suit and tie, looking as if he'd just come from a board meeting, a man whom both Woodrow and I recognized at once, in spite of the soft gloom that surrounded him, when he looked across the yard at us and dropped the key in a showy way into the breast pocket of his suit jacket, at which point Woodrow and I heard a truck rumble to a stop on the street beyond the gate and wall, and a second later the yard was filled with soldiers.

As many as twenty, I would later recall, but to do so I had to concentrate on where in the driveway and yard, patio and house the soldiers had positioned themselves, which was difficult for me afterwards, because mainly I remembered first the dogs' being shot dead in a single burst of gunfire, Woodrow leaping from his chair and knocking the wine bottle onto the tile floor, where it smashed into tiny green slivers, and my realization that the boys were barefoot.

"Stay inside!" I shouted to them. "Don't come out here!" I wasn't as frightened yet of the stone-faced young soldiers as of the broken glass that could cut my babies' tender, pink-bottomed feet. "Don't come out here till I sweep!" I yelled, when Woodrow and I were suddenly surrounded by these men, Samuel Doe's own personal security force. I noticed that much, but since they were with, possibly led by, our friend and Woodrow's colleague, Charles Taylor, then the soldiers had no imaginable reason to be here.

I remember feeling oddly distant from them and unafraid, in spite of what I knew about these men, their cold-blooded brutality and sadism, their fearful capacity for murder, rape, torture, and worse. The stories I'd heard—rumors is all they were—of drug-fueled ritual dismemberments, amputations, cannibalism, were of a savagery beyond anything I'd ever read or heard of before and still I had not yet decided whether to believe them. One *couldn't* believe those stories; human beings just don't act that way. Anyhow, this wasn't happening to me. It was as if I were watching a movie, an amateur movie staged as some sort of training exercise made for new recruits from the countryside. This is how you bring in an important man for questioning by the leader. You kill his dogs first.

Then with a key obtained earlier from the man's caretaker—who may well be his nephew or brother-in-law, but not to worry, the man will know the consequences if he refuses to turn over the key—you simply open the gate and quickly seal off all means of escape from the compound. You place the important man and his white American wife under guard with four of your men, the same four who shot the dogs and were the first to enter the compound, while the others round up the three terrified little boys in their pajamas, their useless, hysterical nanny, the sleeping maid—the children and the servants to be kept under guard in a room of the house well out of sight of the mother and the father, preferably a room without windows, the utility room at the back. All this is to take place in thirty to forty-five seconds, during which time you slap handcuffs on the important man. Treat him roughly, as if he were a goat going to slaughter. And keep between him and his wife. Push her against the outer wall of the house. Don't look at her eyes, her strange, pale blue eyes. Everyone, even including the civilian in charge of the operation, Charles Taylor, who will be known personally to the woman and the important man, will speak only in Liberian, so she won't understand what is happening or else she's likely to interfere and complicate matters. Her husband, the important man, will understand all too well.

I remember that their eyes locked, Woodrow's and Charles's, and I realized that one of the two had betrayed the other, or perhaps not yet; but both knew that, if it hadn't happened yet, the betrayal was coming. It was a strange, fierce exchange of gazes between the two men, the minister and the man who had been sent to fetch him by the leader, that illiterate ex-sergeant, Samuel Doe, the master of the coup that had executed the previous president and his cabinet three years earlier. I knew him; we all did. Liberia is a small country, and we all knew what kind of man he was. His paranoia and secrecy and penchant for torture had kept the country loyal out of fear of him, starting with his ministers and judges in particular, but the small men in government as well, all the way down to the non-commissioned officers in his personal security force, the enlisted soldiers in the army, customs officers, cops in the street, the private guards at the banks, even the caretakers and watchmen. The leader's cruelty and greed and his limitless lust for power in his petty kingdom had corrupted his subjects from top to bottom, including the two men facing each other here on the patio, my husband and his friend, two minor ministers in the cabinet, one evidently sent to arrest the other by the leader himself, who, in his enormous, white, limestone house on Mamba Point was at that moment probably swilling fifty-year-old Napoleon brandy and crowing with delight, because, as I soon learned, he was convinced that the two of them, Charles Taylor, the Gio, and Woodrow Sundiata, the Kpelle, both of them clever village boys, American-educated college boys, had been stealing from the president's personal cache of millions of dollars originally sent to Liberia as American foreign aid. The leader knew this was true. The Americans had shown him the proof. The leader was a shrewd judge of character and circumstance and no doubt believed that Sundiata was the weaker of the two ministers, weak because he was married and had children, and therefore would betray his friend Taylor very quickly, very easily, probably by midnight, especially if Taylor were the one sent to arrest him. And then the leader would have both thieves in his grasp, instead of only one, as would have been the case if he'd chosen to arrest Taylor first. That man, Taylor, was too angry and too strong inside to confess or incriminate anyone else. Taylor would have let the leader's men torture him to death—not to protect Woodrow, whom he felt superior to, like all the Gio, but to infuriate the leader, whom he loathed and whose power and wealth he coveted.

Charles and Woodrow spoke in Liberian pidgin, and I could barely understand them. Even so, right away it was clear that something much more complicated and dangerous than a mistaken or false arrest was taking place, for Woodrow seemed to understand very well why the Minister of Public Services, his good friend and longtime colleague, had invaded his house, shot his dogs, terrorized his family, and clapped him in irons. And Charles—I knew him well enough now to call him Charles, I'd danced with him and shared fond reminiscences with him of Massachusetts, where he'd attended Bentley College—seemed disgusted with himself, as if he'd fallen for an old trick, as if he knew that somehow Woodrow was not the prisoner here, he was. Woodrow spoke too quickly for me to translate, but I knew that he was making a plea. Yet he was not exactly pleading. He was asking Charles to be sensible.

Charles told him to shut his fucking mouth. I understood that. Then in English, Charles said to me, "It's all right, he'll probably be home by morning. But you stay here, stay with your children and your people. Don't let anyone leave the house until Woodrow returns. You understand me, woman?"

I nodded, and Charles walked quickly away, followed by Woodrow and the four soldiers who held their guns on him as if they expected him to make a run for it. Then all the soldiers left, but one, who took up a position at the gate. When the truck was gone and Charles's black ministry car had rolled into the darkness behind it, the lone soldier strolled into the house and returned with a bottle of Woodrow's whiskey. He lighted a cigarette from a fresh pack of Woodrow's Dunhills, squatted down by the gate, and took a long pull from the bottle. The soldier saw me watching him from the patio and extended the bottle, offering me a drink. I shook my head no, no, no, and hurried inside to my children.

It all happened so fast that it hadn't fully registered with me, until, halfway across the living room, my legs suddenly turned to water. The room spun, and I tipped and nearly fell to my knees. I reached out to break my fall with one hand on the cold tile floor, when from the tiny, dark laundry room at the rear of the house, Jeannine, trembling, gray faced, her eyes darting around the room, led the boys out.

They saw me and let go of Jeannine's hands and tumbled towards me like baby birds falling from a nest. I caught them in my arms and pulled them close and stroked their heads, the four of us on the cold floor, tossed together in a tangled heap the same way we sometimes played mamma lion and her cubs in the cave, except this time, for the first time, the boys were terrified and crying, all three of them, and I was struggling not to cry myself, saying in a low, crooning voice, as if all four of us and also Jeannine had been wakened by the same nightmare, "They're gone now, the soldiers have gone away, they're gone and won't be back, my darlings."

The twins were quickly comforted and settled themselves peacefully against me, the nightmare over, but Dillon pulled away and, looking over my shoulder and around the room, said, "What about Papa? Where's Papa?"

"He'll be fine, Dillon. Don't worry about Papa."

"Why did the soldiers take him away?"

"He'll be back soon. The leader wanted to speak with him, that's all. Your papa is such an important man that the leader wanted to see him and couldn't wait for tomorrow, that's all, so he sent some of his own special soldiers to fetch him."

Dillon looked at me with his steady, skeptical gaze. He knew I was lying, but accepted it, so as not to further frighten his younger brothers. I knew that, had we been alone, though barely seven years old, Dillon would have pushed me for the truth, or else a more complex and believable lie. That was his way. And possibly mine. Children are usually more concerned with justice than truth. And a strong lie sometimes gives as much strength to the one being lied to as to the liar.

The twins merely wanted comfort, not the truth. That was their way. Jeannine, too, wanted comfort, and accepted my reassurances with evident relief, clasping her hands together as if in prayer, although she surely knew that Woodrow, her uncle, her employer, her sometime lover, the man whose power had brought her out of the tribal village into this magically softened life in the city, the person on whom she depended utterly for safety, physical comfort, nourishment, even health, was in danger of losing all his power, possibly his life, and that therefore she, too, was in grave danger.

I disentangled myself from the boys and stood and helped them to their feet, tugged and straightened their pajamas, and kissed them each and in as normal a voice as I could manage told them to hurry along to bed now, it's very late. "When they're in bed, Jeannine," I told her, "there's broken glass on the patio."

"Yes, m'am," she said, and drew the boys to her and led them down the hall towards their bedroom. Then I remembered the dogs. Good Lord, the poor dogs! I walked to the door and looked out at their black bodies between the car and the gate, where the soldier squatted and drank Woodrow's whiskey and smoked his Dunhills. If I left the house, I'd have to negotiate the space with him somehow. As long as I stayed inside, he'd stay outside. Better to send Jeannine for Kuyo tonight and ask him to come over to the compound right away and remove the bodies of the dogs and hose the blood away before the boys got up in the morning and, when they asked where are the dogs, Mammi? I'd have to lie again and say that Mr. Doe had admired them and wanted them to guard the presidential palace, and Papa had decided that it would be a nice thing to give the dogs to him. Wasn't that nice of Papa?

All at once I seemed to be living a wholly different life from the one I'd been living barely an hour ago, with different rules, different intentions, and utterly different strategies for survival. I flopped down on the sofa, exhausted. What should I do? What *could* I do? I glanced at the telephone squatting on the table beside me and instantly decided to call Charles Taylor. It wasn't exactly the next logical step, but I had no idea what was. Maybe Charles would say something that indirectly indicated where I should turn next; or maybe he would even tell me outright what I should do to save my husband. He surely was still Woodrow's friend. My friend, too. Whatever he was doing tonight, it was against his will. He was acting on the leader's orders, that's all.

A quick search of Woodrow's rolltop desk in the cubicle off the living room, and I had Charles's home number. After a dozen rings, a woman picked up.

"Mist' Taylor, him na home," the woman whined, as if wakened from a deep sleep. One of Charles's harem girls, I supposed.

"Fine, fine," I said. "Ask him to call Mrs. Sundiata as soon as he returns. No matter how late," I added, although I knew at once Charles would likely not get the message and, even if he did, would not call, not yet. I shouldn't have called him. A mysterious and scary business was unfolding, and Charles was no mere messenger boy for the leader. There was more to come, surely. He owed me nothing anyhow. He was possibly in danger himself, and my call might have made things worse for him. At that time, I rather liked Charles Taylor. Of all Woodrow's friends and colleagues, he was the most worldly and congenial, and in his relations with me he was downright charming. A ladies' man, I'd decided, even before I learned of his harem, a claque of teenage girls and very young women, most of them from the backcountry, beautiful, interchangeable parts in Charles's domestic life and rarely appearing with him outside his compound and never at a government function. I'd seen them mainly at his home, when visiting with Woodrow for drinks and dinner. They were gorgeously plumed birds kept in cages, nameless, for Charles never bothered to introduce them to me. One doesn't introduce one's servants to one's dinner guests. Actually, they were more like groupies than servants. Charles had a rock star's charisma and presence and generated a sexual force field that made him glow and allowed him to treat those who warmed themselves at his fire with benign neglect.

I'm not sure how benign it really was, though. Each time Woodrow and I visited Charles's compound out on Caret Street, the girls I'd seen there previously had been replaced by new, younger girls, and I wondered what happened to the caged birds they'd replaced. Set free, flown back to the country? Not likely. More likely they'd become prostitutes, and were possibly now among those who entertained Woodrow and Charles and their friends and colleagues on those increasingly frequent nights when Woodrow didn't come home from the ministry until dawn. I knew, of course, what went on. A wife always knows, and besides, this was Liberia, not Westchester County. After a while, when new birds appeared and boredom with the old ones set in, Charles probably just recycled the girls by passing them down the chain of command—first to the Assistant Minister of General Services, then to the Administrative

Officer for the Ministry of General Services, on to the Director of the
Office of Temporary Employment of General Services, all the way to the
lowest clerk in the ministry, who could not afford to house or feed anyone but himself and family, and so the girl would turn to the soldiers or
hit the streets, which amounted to the same thing.

All night long, I waited to hear from my husband—a phone call or,
more likely, as I persisted in thinking, his actual return, angry and humiliated by his treatment at the hands of the leader and his one-time
friend, Charles Taylor. You may prefer not to know this about me, but
secretly, deep in the dark chambers of my many-chambered heart,
Woodrow's arrest pleased me. It wasn't very wifely of me, I know, and it
certainly was not in my best interests or my sons', for we were as dependent on Woodrow as his niece Jeannine was. The entire household,
even the chimps, were dependent on the man. He had insisted on it. It
was, especially for Woodrow, the only way to live together, it was the
African way, and all of us, Jeannine and Kuyo and I, had happily complied.

I sat there on the couch and considered my situation and how helpless I had suddenly become. I remembered my vows as a teenage girl and
later as a grown woman never, never to become dependent on a man's
fate. I'd seen early on how it had paralyzed my mother, and from that
vantage point, still a girl's, I had looked ahead at what the world would
offer me when I became a woman, and had pledged that I would take it
only on my own terms. I would gladly accept from a man responsibility,
commitment, recompense, and reward, but only if they were reciprocal
and I were free to walk away from the man when and if he broke the
contract or became a danger to me. The years in the Movement from
college on had only reinforced this pledge, educating me as to its inex-
tricable link to my personal freedom. I fought with my male classmates
at Brandeis, who called me a bitch, a dyke, a cock-teasing, ball-busting
feminist; and I argued with and sternly critiqued my male comrades in
SDS and Weather, the boys who called themselves men and the women
girls and said they really appreciated my contribution to the discussion,

*but let's go back to my room and fuck and then you can make breakfast for me in
the morning.* Later, underground, I demanded of my cellmates total up-
front clarity and agreement on splitting equally all financial, household,
and childcare responsibilities and labor, even when the child was not
mine and neither of the parents my lover.

Lord, all those vows, all those promises and contracts—broken,
abandoned, nearly forgotten! Throughout the night, I lay in bed waiting for Woodrow's return, for, all evidence to the contrary, I still believed that this was, at worst, another of the leader's ways of
intimidating and keeping loyal one of the most loyal members of his
government. The other members of his government, more dangerous
than Woodrow, had long since been disposed of. It was a move typical
of Samuel Doe. He was famous for it. Arrest the man for a night, and
send his best friend and fellow minister to do the job. It'll keep the both
of them in line.

While I waited, tossing restlessly beneath the gauzy mosquito netting, I let myself play out little scenarios, dimly lit fantasies that up to
now I'd kept pretty much hidden from myself, like a secret stash of
pornography tucked in the dark back corner of a closet. I saw myself
settled in a small house, like the old Firestone cottage I'd lived in when
I first arrived in Liberia, only with an extra bedroom for the boys to
share, and located a few miles inland from Monrovia. The four of us
would take care of the chimps, my dreamers. That's all, a simple life. I'd
school the boys at home, and I'd read to them at night, and they'd play
with the children of the village, while I socialized with the other mothers, went to market with them, and cooked native food the native way
on my own. A very simple life. Just me and the boys and the dreamers
and the villagers and the jungle.

And when I grew tired of that fantasy, or it grew too complicated
and was no longer sustainable, I envisioned a life here in town, a con-
tinuation of my present life, except that now Woodrow was no longer a
part of my life, and I was free to be the white American woman with
three brown sons living in the big white house on Duport Road with

the view of the bay, the woman who ran the sanctuary for the chimpanzees, the woman with the mysterious past who could never return to her native land, who was occasionally seen at one of the better restaurants in town on the arm of an official from one of the European embassies, was sometimes mentioned in the society column of the *Post* as one of the guests at an embassy party. Or even, why not, seen dancing at a Masonic ball with Minister Charles Taylor. Which would indeed complicate things, no?

Fantasies of escape really are like pornography. They have to remain simple and untainted by reality, or they cause anxiety. I imagined myself and my sons, all three wearing small backpacks, Americans in Africa, as they board a plane at Robertsfield, leaving Liberia. Then here we are departing from the plane after it has landed at Logan Airport, in Boston. My mother and father, unchanged after all these years, greet us at the gate. Embraces and tears of joy and mutual forgiveness all around. No one else is there, except for other arriving passengers and the people waiting to greet them. No reporters covering the return of a one-time fugitive on the FBI's Most Wanted list, the last of the Weather Underground come in from the cold. No U.S. Marshals or FBI agents to arrest me. No customs officer asking to see our passports and confiscating mine.

It would be simple, oh so simple, if Woodrow stayed arrested—stopped, frozen in time at this moment, and not jailed or tortured or beaten or killed, not shot dead by one of those iron-headed men with the AK-47s, big, cold-eyed men from the country. I didn't want *that*. As I lay there in my bed and dawn light slid through the shuttered windows, as pepperbirds started their pre-morning ruckus, my tumbling fantasies gradually slowed and then, top-heavy with growing complexity, ceased to move. They buckled under the weight of reality and collapsed. Leaving me to contemplate the undeniable fact. My husband had been arrested by the most powerful man in the country, a man who, with impunity and without reason, was more than capable of killing him. And where would that leave me, me and my children?

*   *   *

BY DAWN THE SOLDIER guarding us had disappeared from the yard. And Jeannine and Kuyo, I discovered, had fled during the night—not until after Kuyo had removed the bodies of the dogs, I noticed, and Jeannine had swept up the broken glass. They'd gone back to Fuama, where, by noon, news of the arrest of Woodrow Sundiata, the village's one big man in Monrovia, would have sent every member of Woodrow's immediate family into hiding, where they'd stay for as long as it appeared that Woodrow was an enemy of the leader, even if it meant hiding in the bush for years or until the leader was overthrown and replaced.

I didn't care, I was glad they were gone from the compound. Their presence, no matter how useful their service, oppressed me. Their role in my life, even after all these years, had never clarified itself. They weren't servants or employees, nor were they family members, the kind you can count on in a crisis to provide aid and comfort. I didn't know what they were, or who. They weren't even hangers-on, the sort of people you can shoo away when they've become a burden or a bore.

So they were gone, and the house, for the first time since I moved into it, was empty. Fine, then; that settled it. I made a plan. It was more a piece of theater than a plan, however. In my life here, I had been acting in a play not of my making for so long that it was all I had. A role. *As soon as I have fed the boys their breakfast, I'll dress them the way Woodrow likes to see them, in blazers and ties, like little brown gentlemen enrolling at Choate, and I'll dress myself accordingly in my long, white, chiffon dress and carry the silly, saffron-colored parasol and wear a soft, wide-brimmed hat against the sun, and with my sons in tow I'll march into the leader's office like a latter-day Scarlett O'Hara and demand the immediate release of my husband. After that, I'll make up another little piece of theater and play it out. And then another, and if necessary, another.*

When I had the boys fed and properly dressed, tasks I normally left to Jeannine, but not today, maybe not ever again, I telephoned Woodrow's office. To my relief, Satterthwaite—Richard, as I now freely called him—answered. He'd already heard that his boss had been taken in the night by the leader's security force. Richard was scared, I could tell by his shaky voice, usually so suavely controlled. He was sure that he was about to be arrested, too.

I told him not to be ridiculous, Woodrow would be released quickly, it was all a mistake and would be settled in a few hours. He partially believed me. I was the boss's wife, after all. In reality, all I cared was that he make it possible for me and the boys to be driven to the leader's door in a ministry car chauffeured by the minister's personal assistant. It was in the script.

"The best thing you can do now," I said to Richard, "if you want to keep your job in the ministry, is help me get Woodrow home quickly and safely. Which you can do by driving me and the boys directly to the presidential palace, as if no one has done anything wrong. Because no one has. Have they, Richard?"

"No. No one. Not Mister Sundiata, for sure," he said.

"And certainly not *you*, Richard. The car is still here at the house, the soldiers left it. So come over here right away."

THE BOYS AND I stepped one by one from the tinted interior of the Mercedes onto the white-gravel walkway to the ignominiously named White House, a faux plantation house with tall white columns and verandas, office and residential wings right and left, and tall windows and porticos—like a set for an antebellum movie, *Mandingo* maybe, or *Roots*.

"Wait for us here, Richard," I said. "We shan't be long." I snapped open my parasol, lined the boys up behind me like ducklings, and marched up the wide steps to the guard box at the top, where I waved off the guard with a regal flip of my free hand, as if he had come forward to escort me in rather than to stop me, and kept moving. It was never done, but I was a woman, a white American woman, with her children, and so it was permitted. I and my three somber-faced boys, who must have been as much in awe at that moment of my queenly entitlement as of the colossal scale and splendor of the building that we seemed to have taken possession of, swept on unimpeded, all the way up the wide, curving, carpeted stairs to the second floor, through the outer office and past the startled secretaries to the antechamber of the office of the leader himself, where finally we were stopped, not by a member of the staff, but by a white man emerging from the inner sanctum just as I and my ducklings arrived at the wide, polished mahogany door.

It was Clement, Sam Clement, the fellow from the American embassy—in his early forties back then, fair haired and southern, a Princetonian with a tennis-court tan and the beginnings of a bourbon paunch, and wearing, just as you'd expect of our man in Africa, a rumpled, straw-colored, linen suit. I'd caught him by surprise, and he took a backwards step, recognizing me, and delivered his sweet, sad smile, a Virginia Tidewater all-purpose smile passed down in the family, father to son for generations.

"Why, hel-lo, *Dawn!*" he said, putting lead-footed emphasis on the name, as if to remind me that he still remembered my real name and, while I might fool the natives, I was no mystery to him. "Missus Sundiata," he added.

I gave him a curt nod and pushed past and through the doorway. "I'm here to see the leader," I announced and entered the large, bright, sunlit room. I brought the boys to my side now, clustering them around me, and heard the door snap shut behind us as if with smug satisfaction, and faced the leader, who stood behind his desk, a small, tight smile on his lips. *He grows larger every time I see him,* I said to myself. Taller, wider, thicker, like a hippopotamus.

"Miz Sundiata," he pronounced, as if announcing my arrival at a formal ball, then chuckled. *He may be illiterate, an ignorant pig of a man, but he knows how to play the chieftain,* I thought. He clasped his hands below his chin and looked us over like a judge about to issue his verdict. He wore a double-breasted, dark gray suit, bright white shirt and paisley tie, with a floppy silk handkerchief dangling from his breast pocket. "Wife of the esteemed Minister Woodrow Sundiata. And his sons, too, I see," he added and smiled down at them.

I knew I had only a little time before he grew impatient with the occasion and had me removed. "President Doe, what are the conditions of my husband's release?"

His eyebrows rose into his forehead, then lowered, and his round face darkened from brown to nearly black. I half-expected smoke to blow from his nostrils and ears, his eyes to glow red as coals, and I drew my children closer to me. "You in naw place fe' makin' demands, Missy!" he told me, lapsing into pidgin, speaking rapidly, almost losing me. Because I knew the subject and could read his emotions from his face, I was able to follow him adequately and look for openings. He told me that my husband was a traitor and a thief. A bad man, top to bottom. Not fit to be the father of these beautiful boys or the husband of a nice lady like me.

"Me curse de name of de man!" the leader of Liberia declared, and he spat on the vast Oriental carpet.

My sons grabbed the folds of my dress and moved tightly against me. They knew now that I had lied to them last night. Papa was not the friend of the leader after all. I'd probably lied about the dogs, too. And much else. I calmly stroked their heads and waited for the exhibition, for I knew that's what it was, to run its course. The man ranted, he roared, he glowered and lowered his voice to a weird whisper, then roared again. This was his theater, his play, too, and he loved it.

I began to catch the gist of his complaint. Over one million dollars had been secretly extracted—"Em-*bezzled!*" he kept repeating, as if he'd just learned the word. The money had been taken from funds allocated to the General Services Agency by the State Department of the United States of America. It was money that had been embezzled, therefore, from the generous citizens of the United States. And did I know who was in charge of the Liberian General Services Agency? Did I? Of course

I knew! Charles Taylor, my husband's closest friend and ally, was in charge of the General Services Agency! Over one million dollars, one-point-four million U.S. dollars, to be exact, were missing from the books, gone, fled the country, probably in Switzerland in a secret bank account in the name of Charles Taylor and Woodrow Sundiata, waiting to be wired back to each of their separate accounts here in Monrovia as soon as they thought no one was looking for it anymore!

"But dat naw goin' t' happen," he solemnly declared. "It naw goin' fe' take place," he said, and then suddenly returned to speaking English and was calm again, as if the two languages determined his emotions rather than served them. "You want your husband freed, Missus Sundiata?" he asked.

"I do. Of course."

"No problem." He strode to his wide, mahogany desk, an ornate Victorian box, its top entirely free of paper, with a box of Cuban cigars, a chrome martini shaker, and a red telephone on it. He picked up the receiver and without dialing said just two words, "Release Sundiata." And hung up. "See? No problem," he beamed.

"Then why . . . why did you arrest him?"

"To flush out the bad man, Charles Taylor. His co-conspirator." He kissed the word.

"And . . . ?"

"Your husband a good boy. Too bad me didn' think t' grab him sooner, though, because ol' Charles Taylor, him gone out of the country now. Skee-da-delled. Wal, not quite. He be halfway 'cross the ocean now. But when him land in New York City," the president said, smiling broadly at the thought, "there be a big surprise waitin' for him."

"Aha!" I said. "That's why Mister Clement was here." I pictured Sam Clement calling his superiors in Washington, ordering the arrest and detention of a Liberian national arriving from Monrovia this afternoon at JFK. I said, "You are a sly fox, Mister President. And my husband? What about him?"

"Nuttin'. He give me what me want. Now me give him what him want."

"Which is . . . ?"

He herded me and my sons towards the door. "You ask him yourself, missus, when he come home today. G'wan home now, or him be there before you. G'wan home," he said. "An' pack your suitcase," he added and closed the door solidly behind me.

WOODROW AND I were alone for the first time all afternoon and evening. Finally. He stood in his shirt and loosened necktie and white undershorts and socks, carefully placing his suit jacket and slacks on hangers and into the closet, a tumbler of scotch and ice on the dresser next to him. I sat on the bed, brushing out my hair, and watched him slowly, delicately, almost lovingly, remove and hang his clothes—a man of bottomless vanity. He'd been holding court with relieved friends and neighbors in the living room for hours and was a little drunk. The boys were asleep in bed, Jeannine and Kuyo were back, and except for the dogs, everything seemed to have returned to normal. Throughout the day, since his release, friends and relatives had been dropping by, as if on a casual, neighborly visit, to verify the truth of what they had heard, that Woodrow Sundiata had been arrested by the leader, held for a night, and released unharmed, a sequence almost unheard of in Liberia in those years. Even more unusual, he had kept his old position as minister. The leader was telling people he'd made a mistake. Woodrow was a good boy; Charles Taylor was the bad man, and him the Americans had arrested in New York, caught fleeing the country. Unfortunately, millions of dollars were still missing from the General Services fund, and only Charles Taylor knew where the money was hidden.

That was not true, of course, and no one believed it. Samuel Doe owned Woodrow now, just as he owned the one-point-four million U.S. dollars that, according to Woodrow, Charles Taylor had siphoned off the General Services fund, transferred to the Barclay's Bank on Grand Turk in the Turks and Caicos Islands, then carried back in cash in a ministry briefcase when returning to Monrovia from a Caribbean holiday with one of his lady friends. He'd stashed the cash in a safe-deposit box controlled by Woodrow and Charles at the Barclay's in Monrovia. Now, thanks to Woodrow, President Doe had the cash in *his* safe deposit box, and Charles Taylor would soon disappear into an American prison. My husband, I knew, would henceforth be like one of the president's pet bonobo apes, only a little bit free, with a short chain clamped to his thin ankle. I could not believe his stupidity.

"So, you did steal the money. You and Charles."

"No, no, not at all. Charles did that. Charles was the culprit," Woodrow said and gently bit his lower lip, as if his mind were elsewhere. He picked up his glass and took a sip of his drink. "I was merely looking into the General Services budget for a little help from the American aid for my own programs. Help I need and deserve, but that the Americans never see fit to provide. They prefer roads to medicines, you know."

"Yes, Woodrow, I know." I didn't believe him. I studied his hairless legs and wondered anew why they were so scrawny, almost as if he'd had a terrible, wasting disease as a child that he refused to tell me about. And he'd grown thick and soft around the middle in the last few years, making his legs seem even skinnier than they were. I was sure that he and Charles had schemed together to steal as much as they could for as long as they could—it was part of a Liberian government minister's job description, practically. And I knew that, once arrested, Woodrow had betrayed Charles, who had skee-da-delled. Then Woodrow had purchased his own release by turning over the stolen U.S. funds, now safely in cash currency and part of Samuel Doe's burgeoning secret treasury, his French Riviera retirement fund. I figured that the leader's original plan, to have Charles and Woodrow betray each other, hadn't quite worked. Charles must not have implicated Woodrow, or they'd both be either dead or lying battered and broken in some hut in the bush. Charles, uncharacteristically for a Liberian, had refused to play by the rules of the game. But it had all turned out fine for the leader, since he'd ended up with the money in one pocket and the health minister in the other and Charles, the bad one, the hard one, the dangerous one, tucked away in an American jail many thousands of miles from Liberia. Better than killing them.

"You turned over the money to Samuel Doe, then?"

"No, not exactly. I merely knew where it was located."

"Oh."

"You're angry with me?"

"Oh, no, of course not!" I snapped. "You realize, of course, what you've risked? And how it might have affected me and the boys? And still may? What were you thinking?"

"Please. This whole mess has been Charles Taylor's doing, not mine," he said.

"Well, yes, you're free, and Charles's not, and you still have your job. So I guess that proves it," I said, suddenly feeling a little bit sorry for him. Also, I was exhausted and wanted to sleep, not argue. Then, when I turned my face up to his, I saw that he was terrified. He took a hard swallow from his drink and closed his eyes tightly, then opened them wide, as if hoping the world had changed. I remember thinking, *He won't live out the year*.

He did, of course, manage to live out that year and the following seven, too, and he lived them rather well, both with and without me at his side. But at that moment, to me he was a dead man, and I had already begun preparing my grief, for I knew that it would require a certain amount of conscious, willful preparation. I did not love him anymore, if I ever had, and I would not miss him. But I didn't want him to suffer, and I still needed him. Needed him for my sons and, to a lesser degree, for myself.

"There is, however, one condition that the president has set for my freedom," Woodrow said in a low voice. He kept his gaze averted from me and unbuttoned his shirt very slowly, as if wanting it to last a long time. "If you can call it that, freedom."

"Oh?"

"Yes. In exchange for the information he wanted, I asked the leader for safe passage out of the country for you and the boys."

"Out of the country? *Why?*"

"To get you out of danger. But he said—"

"What danger are *we* in?" I demanded, very loudly, cutting him off.

He inhaled deeply and, inflated with slight disgust, looked down at me, as if he thought me a fool. "Because, Hannah, this country is no longer as safe as it once was for the wife of Woodrow Sundiata. And since I myself cannot leave without permission from the leader . . ."

"There's a condition for your so-called freedom?"

"Yes. There is."

"And . . . ?"

"You."

"*Me?* I'm the condition?"

"In a sense, yes. He wants you out of the country."

"My God," I laughed. "Why?"

Exasperated, Woodrow sighed, as if thinking that I just didn't *get* it. Women, American women especially, do not understand how the real world works. "Hannah darling, Samuel Doe probably believes that your presence here makes it more difficult for him to control me than if you were not here. If you were a Liberian woman, instead of . . ."

"It's not a problem if I'm just another village girl, right?"

"Well, yes, quite right. You're a complication, let us say. He's a little bit afraid of you. Of you and who you know and who knows you." Again he loudly sighed, a man who dreaded what was coming next.

"And the boys? What about them?"

"I'm sorry. They can't go with you."

"I *must* go, but my sons *can't* go? That's it? What the hell are you talking about? Who says this?"

"He says it. Doe. The president."

"*Why?*" I screamed at him, and it felt very good. I almost never shout, and I never scream.

"Because the boys' presence will help him control me."

"Whereas my presence will have the opposite effect."

"Exactly."

"Woodrow, please! This is *insane!* Besides, where does Samuel Doe think I can go on my own? If I go back to the States, I'll be arrested as soon as I get off the plane, just like Charles. And he can't expect me to leave my children behind!"

"No, it's not insane. It's coldly sane, very calculated, very shrewd. President Doe knows exactly what he's doing. And you won't be arrested when you get to the States. That won't happen. The Americans have agreed that you are not Hannah Musgrave. You are who your passport says you are, my dear. You are Dawn Carrington."

"Sam Clement's part of this, then. And my sons? What will happen to them without me?"

"They're my sons, too. And they'll be fine with me and Jeannine and my people. Until I can arrange to send them to you, which really shouldn't be all that long a wait. I can't speak of it yet, but Samuel Doe is not president for life, you know. This is just something that we're going to have to do, regardless of what we might prefer to do. Things will change."

"How long . . . before things change?"

"I don't know. Not long. A year. Two, maybe more. Although I hope not."

It seemed unreal, unfair, and altogether unexpected. I certainly hadn't desired it, but once put in front of me like this—once it was clear to me that I would have to abandon my husband and children and return alone to the United States, once I saw that I would be alone, safe from prosecution—I realized, gradually at first and then in a rush, that it was exactly what I had wanted all along.

I was being severed from my African husband and torn from my African sons. I was being released from my obligation to care for the chimps. And I had no choice! It was all being forced upon me by my husband's stupidity and weakness and by the Liberian leader's greed and paranoiac need to maintain control over his subjects, and by the American government's desire to use the Republic of Liberia as a chip in a game with stakes too high to bother chasing down a middle-aged, one-time member of the Weather Underground traveling on a phony passport.

I'm not making excuses, I'm just trying to tell you the truth as I understand it now, not as I understood it then. At the time, I didn't realize that I was once again seizing an opportunity to abandon one life for another. I thought I loved Africa, my new and, compared with my homeland, relatively innocent country. And although I knew that I was not in love with my husband, I thought that I was loyal to him. And my sons—I did love them, but I was not a woman for whom motherhood was a fulfilling, natural role. I'm still not. It's always been an act. It was only with the chimps that I felt like a natural mother, but I did not love them individually and for themselves, the way I did my sons. I was only leaving my sons temporarily, I told myself. I may have been acting there, too, but I was playing before an empty house. In all my relations with both my sons and the chimps there was a disjunct, a powerful, buried conflict that made it possible for me to abandon both with such remarkable and awful ease that today, when I look back on it, I'm ashamed. I would try to make amends later and promised myself that I would return to all of them, to Africa, to my husband, my sons, and my chimps, and would never leave them again.

Finally, he was undressed. Standing naked before me, he finished his drink, then lit the mosquito coil, snapped off the light, and slipped into bed. When I followed and was lying on my back beneath the top sheet, he flopped an arm across my belly and pressed his face against my breasts, his signal that he wanted sex.

"No, Woodrow. Not tonight," I said as gently as I could manage.

"Really?" he said, mildly surprised and disbelieving.

"Really."

"As you wish, then." He was silent for a moment. "It may be your last chance for a long, long time, you know."

"Oh, Lord, Woodrow," I said, turning to him, and smiled into the darkness at the gods of sex who knew everything I knew and more. I felt Woodrow stiffen against my thigh and took him into my arms.

* * *

I WOKE JUST before dawn with a boulder of rage lodged in the middle of my chest and a desire to break someone's skull with it. But I didn't know whose head to aim it at. Woodrow lay snoring beside me, a secondary target. I shoved his bare shoulder. He blinked slowly several times and yawned like a house cat, all teeth and tongue.

"I'm going to wake the boys and tell them," I said. "I thought you'd want to know."

"Tell them? Now?" He licked and smacked his lips. "We'll tell them together. It's better that way."

"No. I'd rather do it alone." I pushed the pale shroud of mosquito netting aside and left the bed and in the cool half-darkness began to dress.

"What will you say to them?" he called.

"Oh, you needn't worry, Woodrow. I won't tell them the truth. I'll lie. I'll protect you. I'll even protect the president."

"How? What will you say to them? They're too young to understand."

"Yes. Well, so am I," I said. "I don't know, I'll make it up, for Christ's sake."

"Please, Hannah, don't swear. Is there coffee? I don't smell it."

"It's too early. No one else is up. Not even Jeannine," I said, and swept from the room, righteous and wrathful. It was an act, however, sweeping from the room. The boulder of rage still weighed me down. I may talk to my husband with rare animation and force, I may look swift to him, perhaps even graceful; but I felt inside as if I were pushing the words and my body through pudding.

I strode past Jeannine's cubicle and with customary but useless irritation noted that the door was shut ("What if they woke in the night and needed you, Jeannine? What if they needed you to kill a snake?") and entered the boys' room. The curtains were drawn, but even in the dark I knew where everything was located and strode through the small, cluttered room as if the lights were on. Their three small cots were positioned side by side along the far wall, as in a barracks. Wheeled toys, trucks and tractors and excavators, lay scattered about the room. Stacks of picture-books, balls and bats, and Dillon's plastic guns were everywhere, and crayon drawings like primitive graffiti, a map of the world, and photos of African animals cut from old copies of *National Geographic* were taped to the walls. In corners and atop the dressers lay piles of clothes, sneakers, and costumes and dishes and plastic cups from bedtime snacks. It was the overstocked bedroom of pampered and privileged little boys from anywhere in the Western world. I could make out only outlines in the shadowed room, but all their stuff, here in the heart of equatorial Africa, suddenly looked weirdly out of place to me, as if it belonged instead in a suburb of Boston. I was already starting to disappear from my sons' real, everyday life, as if going underground again.

From a block away came the first call of a backyard rooster. Doves gulped and gurgled on the dew-wet grass just outside the window, and palm fronds nicked one another in the soft, offshore breeze. Up close, I saw that Dillon was awake. He stared at me through the gauzy netting, expressionless, as if he'd been anticipating my arrival and I'd arrived late. The twins in their cots lay sleeping in identical parallel positions, facing the wall away from me and from the world at large.

I drew back the netting and sat down on the edge of Dillon's narrow bed. "You're awake early," I said and stroked his cool, bare arm. He said nothing and continued gazing at the spot by the door that I had filled seconds ago, as if an afterimage lingered there—my fading white shadow. Without getting up, I reached with both hands to the twins' cots, brushed the netting away, and gently held each boy's ankle, waking the two as if waking one. They turned, rubbed their eyes, sat up in tandem, and smiled.

Paul and William, though not delicate or fragile, were small for their age, almost preternaturally quiet, and except with one another, kept their own council. From infancy the twins had remained a mystery to me, unlike Dillon, who seemed more and more to resemble the child I had been. Paul dominated his brother William, as one twin always will, but gently, politely, and neither was shy or insecure. Paired, the two more than made up for their lack of size and loquacity and made a fiercely combative team, especially when threatened by their older brother. He, on the other hand, was tall for his age, rangy and prematurely muscled. Dillon was a natural athlete and was already, at seven, the size of a boy of ten. Woodrow had recently enrolled him in twice-a-week tennis lessons and had begun asking me about colleges in the United States where a boy could learn to play "top-level tennis."

Princeton, I'd guessed. Probably Stanford. But how on earth would I know? I demanded. Wasn't he being a little premature? The boy was barely seven, for heaven's sake. Which Woodrow had laughed off, noting that his parents and mine had set us upon *our* paths as early as five or six, had they not? And unless we wanted our sons simply to follow in their father's footsteps, we would have to show them right from the beginning a different and better way of life. We did not want our sons to follow the same path as their father, did we? Not that there was anything wrong with that path, of course. Woodrow simply felt that his sons should rise above their father—above their mother as well, I assumed—to the same degree as he had risen above his.

Maybe Woodrow's dream of his handsome brown sons playing tennis at Princeton was no less realistic than any other. They had advantages he'd barely dreamed of, after all. They were the sons of an educated, high-up city man. They were half American, their mother from a "good" American family. They were half white. Sometimes, when sitting up late and in his cups, he would declare, "My sons will be very big men in the big world! Captains of industry, Hannah! Head of the United Nations! Presidents! *Big men!*"

It was more a promise than a prediction, as if it were up to him. I wondered what broken-promised path we were setting his sons on now. *His* sons? *My* sons. It was a faint and overgrown path, winding both into the jungle and out of it, and we had no map to give them, no way to guess where it led. I was about to abandon my boys, to leave them in the care of this weak Christian man, their poor father, confused and self-divided, who had recently become a barely tolerated enemy of the state, and his extended family, hopelessly impoverished, powerless people whose language and culture were to me so far beyond exotic as to be practically meaningless and unintelligible. What clearing in the jungle would these people find for my little boys? And what guiding role in their future lives would I play now? I had only Woodrow's vague assurance that soon I would be able to rejoin them, either here or in the United States. But how soon? It all depended on the life expectancy, political or otherwise, of Samuel Doe, the unpredictable and treacherous president of the Republic of Liberia—an eventuality that neither I nor Woodrow could effect in the slightest.

I had never left my sons for longer than a single day and was as new at this as they. I told myself that I had no choice in the matter, none, and quickly hardened wholly into stone. To my freshly wakened, still sleepy little boys, I said, "I'm going to have to go away for a time and leave you with Papa and Jeannine."

Dillon turned to the window, as if seeking a way out of the moment without having to push past me. The twins opened their eyes wide and made little Os with their mouths and at once turned for an explanation, not to me, but to each other. None of the three could look at me. I said that the president wanted me to go back to the United States for a visit, but he couldn't let them or Papa go with me just yet—Papa because his work for the government was too important, and them because they were Papa's sons and, like him, were Liberians. I knew it made no sense to them, but couldn't think of an adequate lie. *Because* the truth made no sense, I wanted them to hear it, as if by punishing them with nonsense I were somehow punishing their father. "It's not my fault," I said. "I would like to stay here, or else take you with me. But the president won't let me. The president is a very strange man," I told them. "He thinks if I'm not here with you and Papa, he'll be able to keep Papa working for him and not helping the people who are against him. That's silly, of course, but it's what he believes, and he's the president. And he thinks if you go to America with me, then Papa will want to go, too."

With his back to me, Dillon asked "Will you come back someday?"

"Someday? Of course! And it won't be someday. It'll be soon, as soon as possible."

"Okay, then. Go ahead," he said. He slipped out of his bed and in tee shirt and shorts, barefoot, headed for the door, and was gone. The twins watched him leave and began to get out of their beds to follow.

I said, "What about you two? Is it all right with you, that I have to go away for a while?"

They stopped by the door and turned back and smiled sweetly, both of them, as if they'd already discussed the subject and had reached an easy agreement. Paul said, "Yes, Mammi. It's all right. You can go." Both twins waved goodbye to me, and ran to catch up to their brother.

When you part with someone you love, there's usually an aura of grief attached. But saying goodbye has never been difficult for me. I do it quickly and with little felt emotion, until afterwards, when I'm by myself and it's done and it's too late for any feelings that might slow or clog my departure. I sat at the foot of my eldest son's rumpled, empty bed alongside the two empty beds of his brothers and saw that for the first time in nearly eight years I was alone again. And for the first time since the day I went underground, I felt strong and free.

The room slowly filled with hazy gray morning light, gradually bringing into sharp focus the clutter of the boys' toys and clothing, all the defining props and evidence of their ongoing existence. Though I had been the one to clip and tape the pictures, maps, and drawings to the walls, the boys had chosen them. And though I had purchased most of their possessions, it was with money given me by their father. To my eyes, there was nothing of mine in that room, no evidence that I existed.

MY LEAVE-TAKING from Liberia in 1983 went nearly as unremarked as my arrival had back in 1975. I packed my old duffel and said my goodbyes quickly and easily, as if flying to Freetown or Dakar for a holiday weekend with friends. The boys, naturally, were afraid they were being abandoned by their mother, but they could not admit it, even to one another.

The night before I left, Sam Clement dropped by the house on his way home from the embassy, to wish me bon voyage, he said, and to reassure me that he'd keep an eye on my boys, including Woodrow (wink wink), until I got back, when in fact he was merely making sure that I knew that my departure from the country was under the protection and in the interests of official U.S. policy towards Liberia and the administration of President Doe.

Later, the president himself telephoned to say that he hoped I had a "superb" holiday in America and used the word *superb*, his new word of the week, I guessed, twice more, in reference to my sons and to characterize my company, which he said would be very much missed during the upcoming national holiday. As an expression of his personal affection for me, he was providing Woodrow with a bit of a cash bonus to help pay my travel expenses and would send it to me via Woodrow's trusty assistant, Satterthwaite.

Woodrow, who left early for the ministry the next morning and did not see me off later, was clearly relieved to have me gone from his household—it was saving his life, after all—but had to say that he would miss me terribly. Then Satterthwaite arrived with the car around three that afternoon and handed me the packet given to him at the office by Woodrow. It contained my one-way ticket to JFK and an envelope with fifty crisp, one-hundred-dollar bills inside. Satterthwaite looked at the ground and said to me, "I hope you come back soon-soon, Miz Sundiata," but I knew he was thinking, *Damn good t'ing dis bitch finally outa here, 'cause someday her gonna get mad at de ol' man an' tell 'im what we done once way back den an' mek de ol' man fire me or wuss.*

Jeannine stood woefully at the front gate as Satterthwaite drove me from the yard, tears running down her round, brown face, her fingers crossed in a behind-the-back hex designed to keep me from ever coming back, making the house hers, my children hers, my husband and his wealth and power hers.

No one else took account of my departure from Liberia that day. It happened so quickly, of course, that there was little occasion for a farewell party or visits with the half-dozen or so people in Monrovia whom I counted as friends. And they weren't really friends, anyhow— merely acquaintances, the wives of Woodrow's colleagues and business associates. Elizabeth and Benji, who had been running the lab on their own for the last seven years, were not my friends, though I knew them well and had seen them nearly every day on my visits with my dreamers. The university had not bothered to replace me after I left my post as clerk of the works and had withdrawn all but minimal support for the project, providing only enough funding to keep the chimps caged and alive. This was before AIDS research had gotten under way in earnest, when a new reason would arise to infect the animals with disease and monitor their reactions. If they'd been allowed to do it, the university officials would have had the animals put down, cheaper than releasing them to the wild and easier on the animals, most of whom had been traumatized by capture and confinement and had gone through a simian version of the Stockholm syndrome and had so thoroughly substituted their captors' desires for their own that they were incapable of living naturally in the wild.

Early the morning of the day I left Monrovia, even before packing my bag, I went out to the lab, ostensibly to say goodbye to Elizabeth and Benji, but actually it was for a final visit with the chimps, for, without my ongoing vigilance, I did not think they would live long under their keepers' care. The machinery that paid Elizabeth and Benji their monthly salaries was permanently in place, it seemed, and did not depend on there being any chimpanzees in those cages. Corruption thrives on process, not product, so it didn't matter to them or anyone else if the chimps starved or sickened and died, if the cages one by one were emptied out, because Elizabeth and Benji would still be paid by the American university for maintaining its research facility and animal subjects in Liberia, and the university would still be paid by the multinational pharmaceutical company based in New Jersey, and the pharmaceutical company, through tax write-offs and federal grants, would still be paid by the American citizenry. Though I had come dangerously close to loving the product, the dreamers caged in a Quonset hut out at the edge of the city, I was merely a witness to the process, helpless to change it at any level.

I rode out on my bicycle, as had long been my habit, and as usual no one was at the lab. Elizabeth's and Benji's routines had long since been reduced to showing up twice a day for only as long as it took to feed the chimps and hose down the floor of the Quonset hut and conduct whatever little side business the two ran out of the all-but-defunct lab. They had sold off piecemeal most of the office furniture and the household goods and furnishings from the three cottages—after taking as much of it as they wanted for their own use—and were renting out the cottages on an hourly basis, I suspected, for I had on several occasions seen strangers, men with women, arriving and leaving at odd and unlikely hours. I never entered the cottages to see for myself who was living or working there—prostitutes, I assumed—and never confronted or quizzed Elizabeth or Benji about the use they were making of the compound.

They could strip it bare, for all I cared, or trash it or turn a profit from it any way they wanted. I had no loyalty to the university that financed the project and did not believe in the purposes for which the facility had been established in the first place. To me, it was a prison whose inmates had been deranged first by the circumstances of their capture and then by their lifelong confinement, inmates rendered incapable of functioning outside their cells, kept there now solely for their own safety. I made sure that they were properly fed and watered twice a day—either by Elizabeth and Benji or, if they didn't show up, by me—and that their cages were washed down, and when on occasion one of the chimps injured itself or fell ill, I nursed it back to health, and, as happened several times over the years, if one of them died from an undiagnosed illness or simply from sadness, I buried the poor creature out behind the Quonset hut and erected a wooden marker with the dreamer's name painted on it, *Hooter* and *Livingston* and *Marcie*. And grieved.

The dreamers had come to trust me, to welcome my twice-daily arrival with a joyful chorus of pant-hoots and hand-claps. We communed together, usually for an hour, sometimes more, in the mornings after my sons had been washed and fed at home and dressed for the day and placed in Jeannine's care, and again in the late afternoon, when it had begun to cool and I did not mind riding my bike out to the compound and back, a thirty-minute ride each way that took me to the edge of the city and the beginning of the jungle. My time with the dreamers was the most peaceful, restorative two hours of the day for me, and I had quickly become dependent on the visits for what little peace of mind I had then. Without it, I feared I would come undone, for, despite the leisurely pace and apparent stability of my daily life as wife and mother, that life felt fragile, as if it were someone else's and at any moment I would be exposed as a fraud, a counterfeit wife and mother, not at all who I seemed or claimed to be. And not anyone whom I knew, either. It was only when alone with the dreamers that I knew myself.

In those years, there were, as there is now, a large number of baby chimps being bought and sold illegally on the streets of Monrovia and in the marketplaces all over West Africa and many more babies being captured and smuggled out to labs in Europe and North America. I knew about this terrible trade, knew that to capture a single baby in the wild it was first necessary to shoot its mother and as many as three or four of the other adults who always tried to protect the baby from the human beings. Over the years, whenever I came upon one of the little wide-eyed, terrified creatures locked in a tiny cage or at the end of a chain in the market or alleyway, I purchased it myself, and after nursing it back to health, for the babies I bought were almost always malnourished and swarming with parasites, carried it out to the compound, where, with a terrible sadness, I imprisoned it with the others.

A baby chimp cannot survive alone in the forest, and I had no way of returning it to its lost and probably scattered and decimated family. The best I could do for it was provide a less cruel form of imprisonment and deprivation than the one that would lead inevitably to an early death. Baby chimps are like young humans, playful and clever and eager to please, and they respond to kindness with delight and gratitude. But after a few years they become troublesome, hormone-fueled adolescents and then adults, very powerful, willful, and highly intelligent creatures for whom the human order of things is perceived as a challenge, a regime to be overthrown. An adult male chimpanzee can weigh as much as an adult male human and is five times as strong and capable of extreme violence against objects and other animals, including human animals and its fellow chimps. When a pet baby or even a laboratory chimp becomes an adult, unless it is caged, it is almost always executed, killed simply for being itself.

In purchasing the babies I came across in the marketplace and locking them into a prison, I was saving their lives. But for what? Every time I walked along the rows of cages and pushed melons, bananas, cucumbers, and armloads of greens through the bars or passed the food directly into the hand reaching through the bars towards me, every time I returned the direct, deep-water gaze of the dreamers in my charge, and every time we spoke together, they in their language, and I in mine, I asked myself, why can't I set them free? Lord knows, I wanted to do it, and hundreds of times I imagined doing it, simply unlocking the cages and taking them by the hand—for all of them now let me hold hands with them, and we even groomed one another—I would lead them under cover of darkness to the edge of the forest and there let go of their hands and turn and walk alone back into the city.

But it was too late for that. They were like ruined children, incapable of surviving on their own. Humans and chimpanzees have to be taught by their kith and kin how to be a human or a chimpanzee, how to find proper food and shelter, how to relate to others of its species in ways that are mutually useful and satisfying, how to reproduce, how to care for the young and the old and the infirm—or else we perish as a species. Every chimp in my care had been captured as a baby and had been confined for its entire life so far, and did not know, therefore, how to be itself. And I had made myself the warden of their prison, and by default had become their caretaker and had made them dependent on me for their food and shelter and protection from the humans who would as soon neglect them and let them starve and die in their own filth as sell the babies for pets and kill the adults and sell their bodies for meat, their hands and heads for souvenirs. And now I was about to abandon them.

They greeted me that morning with their usual clamor and applause and loud declarations of hunger and thirst, which I quickly satisfied. Neither Elizabeth nor Benji had shown up yet and possibly wouldn't arrive till evening, if at all, but I had arranged with Woodrow to have our yardman, Kuyo, who had developed an affection for the chimps, replace me as caretaker. Woodrow promised me that he would see to this, but I carried his promise to Kuyo myself, to impress upon him the seriousness of the job. Starting this very evening, I told him, his job as yardman would include purchasing the chimps' food in the marketplace once a week and feeding them and washing down the floor of the Quonset hut twice daily. Woodrow's office paid for the food from the general fund supplied by the grant from NYU, the same fund that paid Elizabeth's and Benji's salaries every month. Kuyo said he'd like that. "The monkeys-dem, we come to be friends now for a long-long time." I felt, therefore, replaceable in the lives of my dreamers. But were they replaceable in mine? I wasn't sure. Everyone else in my life, even my children, saw me as replaceable. Somehow I felt that in my sons' eyes, just as in Woodrow's, I had become extraneous to their lives, merely a witness, a sympathetic bystander. To Jeannine I was a pretender to the throne. To everyone in Liberia who knew me I was Woodrow Sundiata's white American wife. I was a woman whose absence would barely be noticed.

Except by the dreamers. When I was no longer there mornings and afternoons with armloads of food and plenty of fresh water and kindly murmurings and filial touches on the hand and arm, they would know I had left them. And they would miss my pale shadow on the far side of the bars greeting their dark shadows, my blue eyes peering into their brown eyes and seeing there some essential part of myself, some irreducible aspect of my being, which in turn gave them back the same reflected version of themselves, revealing to me and to them the face of our ancient, common ancestral mother, caught and given shape here and now in her descendants' mirrored gaze. The dreamers and I took each other out of the specificity of personal time and physiognomy. When in their presence I was in sacred time and space, and they were, too. I was convinced of it.

I know how this probably sounds to you, but I don't care. Any more than a born-again Christian cares what she sounds like when she tells an atheist of her personal relationship with an itinerant Jewish preacher who was crucified in Jerusalem two thousand years ago. There are parallels between my meetings with the chimpanzees and the Christian's encounter with Christ. When I first saw the dreamers, like a Christian touched by her savior, I wept uncontrollably. Later, through the daily rituals associated with caring for them, like any steadfast acolyte, I gradually got myself close enough to see them for what they truly were, a gate that led me straight to that ancestral mother. The spirit of the river, the one they call Mammi Watta.

I tell you this even though I know you might think it little more than spiritual bilge, a weird form of New-Age hogwash, because I've come to trust your kind patience and open-mindedness. I'm not a conventionally religious woman. I'm not religious at all. But until the dreamers entered my life, I was locked into a material world whose only exit lay in an imagined future, a utopian fantasy. Until I met the dreamers, I was stuck with a mere *ideology* of exit.

Slowly I walked from cage to cage, as if passing along the stations of the cross, with my head slightly bowed, my teeth carefully covered, hands loose at my sides, and the dreamers quieted one by one and silently watched me, babies and adults alike. I said to them in a low murmur, *I'm leaving you today and do not know when I will return. And I pray that this is a riskier, more worrisome thing for me than it will be for you. And I pray that in my absence neither of us will fall back to being what we were before. That we not become imprisoned isolates. That we not become monads.*

That we not become as we were, motherless brothers and sisters unable to recognize one another as kin. I passed along the cages, and when I returned to my starting point, repeated my slow walk and said the prayer again, and did it a third time, making of it a ritual act. And then I bowed my head and backed slowly out of the building into the glare of sunlight and closed and locked the heavy door behind me.

III

THE SIGHT OF SO MANY white people rushing to get through passport control and customs at JFK nearly sent me running back to the plane. I had not seen a majority of white people gathered together in one place in nearly ten years. There were some blacks in the crowd, of course, men wearing safari jackets, guayabera shirts, or dashikis, women in long, colorful wraps—my fellow travelers from Africa. Another cluster of weary, well-dressed families whose very foreignness made them look comfortably familiar to me had come off a flight from Delhi. Most of the white people, me included, wore jeans and sneakers and tee shirts, summer travel apparel for European tourists in the States and Americans returning from abroad. Many of them, as did I, wore small, papoose-sized backpacks. They were my people, members of my tribe.

But the whites didn't look quite human to me. Their faces were all the shades of an English rose garden, from chalk to lemon yellow to pink to scarlet, and their noses and ears were too large for their heads, their hair was lank and hung slackly down and, where it wasn't held in place by a cap or hat, seemed about to slip off their skulls and fall to the floor. They looked dangerous, so self-assured and knowing, so intent and entitled, as they rushed to stand in neat rows and handed their passports to the uniformed officers waiting in booths like bored ticket takers at an amusement park.

When my turn came, before presenting my passport, I opened and glanced into it, half expecting to see there a photograph of a black woman—someone who did not resemble these white people—and surprised myself with the face of a woman named Dawn Carrington, who did indeed resemble the white people. The officer, a gaunt man in his forties with strands of thinning black hair combed sideways over the top, took the passport and examined the photograph carefully and matched it with my face. He breathed through his mouth as if suffering from a cold. He flipped the blank pages, then paused over the page that had been stamped years earlier, first in Accra and when I came over to Liberia. He cleared a clot of phlegm from his throat and said, "You've been away for quite some time."

"Yes. I was married there," I said. "To an African."

"And your husband? Is your husband traveling with you, Mrs . . . ?" he looked again at my photo. "Carrington."

"No."

"I see." He hovered over the information for a second, then pursed his lips as if about to whistle. "So you reside in Liberia, then?"

"Yes. I have . . . I have children born there."

"I see. How many?"

"Three. Three sons."

"I see." Another long pause. He gazed over the heads of the swelling crowd and into the distance. "How long will you be away from your husband and children, then?"

"I'm not sure. Not long. I'm here to visit my parents," I quickly added, surprised to hear it said like that, so frankly and easily. Surprised to find myself telling him the truth.

"I see." He handed the passport back and stared at me for a second, as if he knew me from a distant past, and I returned his stare, as if he did not. He twitched his narrow, red nose, wrapped it in a hanky and blew. "Well, welcome home, Missus Carrington," he said and blew again.

*   *   *

BY THE TIME I got out of the terminal, it was mid-morning, and the air was already hot and humid and gritty with soot—New York City in late July. I rode into Manhattan in a taxi driven by a very large, middle-aged black man whose shaved head glistened with sweat, and I started to feel safe again: I'd made it through passport control and customs and had gotten away from the white people. From the name posted on the divider, Claude Dorsinville, I guessed that the cab driver was Haitian. Yes, he said, from Port-au-Prince, but he had lived in Brooklyn for fifteen years. His children were Americans. I asked him if he wanted to return to Haiti someday. "Yes, yes!" he said. "But not till America go down there an' bomb the hell out of my country and get rid of the Duvaliers. Just like they did in Grenada," he added.

A half-hour later, when I walked into the cavernous space of the main concourse at Penn Station, I looked around and found myself surrounded once more by white Americans—prosperous, well-fed, loud, and purposeful men, women, and children, with only a sprinkling here and there of black people. Suddenly, I was sure I was being followed. I glanced behind me and scrutinized the faces of the commuting businessmen and -women, the Eastern seaboard travelers, the college students, even the children standing in line with me for tickets. *Who among you knows who I really am and is waiting for me to give myself up? Who among you will reveal me to the others?* An ageless woman wrapped in a tattered tan overcoat and wearing gloves and a knit cap scuffled unnecessarily close and seemed to study my face for a second too long. Was she a panhandler? Why didn't she ask me for money? I tried to appear distracted by deep thoughts. Just another traveler, an ordinary citizen heading wearily home. I tried to look like what I was—an American, upper-middle-class, white lady in her natural habitat. But it was as if I were back traveling underground, incognito and in danger of being suddenly recognized and denounced by a stranger, exposed, my artful disguise ripped away, the bomb hidden in my duffel carefully removed and defused, my backpack emptied and false IDs laid out on a steel table in an interrogation room, while I am forced to look down at them and answer the question *Which of these women is you?*

On the train, I managed to find a seat alone at the rear of the last car, where I could watch the other passengers without being easily watched back. By New Haven, I had calmed sufficiently to realize that maybe I wasn't so much paranoid as merely exhausted, jet-lagged, and hungry. Cautiously I made my way forward to the café car, bought a plastic-wrapped tuna sandwich and a cup of coffee, returned with them to my seat, and later slept and did not wake until the train pulled into Boston's South Station. End of the line.

Whenever I'd been asked, whether by the officer at JFK or at home by Woodrow or the boys or by Sam Clement or anyone else, whom in America I planned to visit, I had said the obvious and expected thing: *Why, I'm going to visit my parents, my mother and father, in Emerson, Massachusetts.* In a vague and general way, though it was the truth, it was not so much a travel plan as merely a way of postponing the choice of a destination. Until the moment that I actually arrived in Boston and walked out of South Station into the rusty, fading, early-evening light and crossed to the line of taxis waiting at the curb and realized that, once in the cab, I would have to tell the driver to take me to a house in the suburbs, 24 Maple Street in Emerson, *Don't worry, I know the way and will give you directions,* until that moment, I had not been committed to a specific travel plan. I'd had no itinerary.

There were alternatives, of course. Thanks to the generosity, if you want to call it that, of Samuel Doe, I had enough cash in my backpack to go anywhere in America. Although I hadn't communicated with them in years, I knew that without too much trouble I could make quick contact with old friends and associates from the Movement, people who would welcome me back into the fold from the cold, who would let me sleep on a couch or cot until I found a place of my own, who would provide me with a new name, social security number, and driver's license, and would pass me from safe house to safe house, from friend to acquaintance to complete stranger, until I ended up separated from myself by seven or eight degrees, living in some small town in eastern Oregon, working as a school nurse and sharing a double-wide trailer with a divorced lineman who thought I was who I said I was.

It was 1983, the war against the war was long over, Ronald Reagan was president, and young Americans were more interested in getting rich by the time they turned thirty than in refusing to trust anyone who'd already turned it. It was, in a sense, the perfect time for me to have returned, the perfect time to show my back to all that I had thought and believed and dreamed and done and failed to do, and start over. I could become a so-cial worker in Albany, a caterer in East Lansing, Michigan, an ambulance driver in St. Louis. Or I could go back to New Bedford, where Carol was probably still living with her daughter, Bettina, and waiting tables at the same seafood restaurant, maybe still renting the same third-floor walkup apartment, and if in the meantime she hadn't hooked up with one of those wiry, ponytailed men with tattoos crawling over their chests and arms whom she seemed irresistibly drawn to, she would let me have my old room back. Or I could simply strike out on my own, wade into America's vastness and anonymity, bobbing up someplace I'd never been before, with a new life story already forming, one bit of false information sticking to another, like the beginnings of a coral reef that someday will seem to have been there all along, as substantial and self-evidently true as the continent itself.

That's the real American Dream, don't you think? That you can start over, shape-change, disappear and later reappear as someone else. That you can survive the deliberate murder of your personal past and even attend your own funeral, if you want, and watch the mourners from the shade of a grove of trees a short way off, be the stranger at the edge of the crowd, her presence barely noticed or remarked upon. *I don't know who she is, a friend of someone in the family, I guess.* And when everybody has finally left the cemetery, and you're alone there, you come forward and pluck a flower from one of the baskets left at the graveside, put it in your hair, if you want and, like a happy ghost, walk off with the secret knowledge that down in the darkness under the dirt the coffin is empty, there's only sawdust inside it or rocks or a dummy stuffed with straw.

I pushed my duffel ahead of me into the back seat of a taxi and got in. The driver, a flat-faced Boston Irishman wearing a Red Sox cap, half turned to me. "Hiya, how ya doin'?" he said. "Where ya wanna go?"

BY THE TIME the cab stopped in front of number 24 on gracefully curved, tree-lined Maple Street, it was almost dark. Lawn sprinklers carved silver arcs above the mint-green lawns. Wide, sloping paved driveways led to two- and three-car garages, breezeways, and screened side porches. The thick-leaved trees along the street were maples, of course, forty and fifty years old. The neighborhood was long established, a planned community from the early 1920s of large, neocolonial homes planted on nineteenth-century farmland and lately painted in neocolonial colors with names like baguette, flannel, and persimmon, with coiffed hedges and manicured yards the size of boarding-school playing fields. They were comfortable, oversize houses that had been designed to shelter well-educated, calm, orderly families with inherited money for up to three generations before being sold off to strangers with new money. My parents' house—a three-bedroom Cape Cod with dormers and an attached el for my father's study and home office—was slightly more modest than the others. They'd paid cash for it with a gift provided by Daddy's father shortly after I was born, only a few years into their marriage and Daddy's medical career. Except for dorm rooms at Rosemary Hall and Brandeis, until I was in my midtwenties, it was the only home I had known.

I walked up the driveway, crossed to the breezeway at the side of the house, and approached the kitchen door. In all those years away, nothing had changed—the smell of moist, freshly cut grass; the cluttered breezeway and the wooden glider; Daddy's rusting, rarely used grill; Mother's meticulous flower gardens in back; the tool shed by the crabapple tree. And balanced in the crotch of the old oak in the farthest corner of the yard, my tree house, a lean-to tacked to a small platform, a nestlike, secret sanctuary and watchtower that in summer became nearly invisible in the leaves of the oak tree.

I was trapped in a time warp. On the other side of the window, my mother sits at the kitchen table with a Manhattan in front of her and waits for Daddy to come home late again and gets a two-cocktail jump on him. The table has been set, and their supper stays warm in the oven, and she's probably thinking about tomorrow's schedule, making mental lists of things to do and menus and guest lists, which she'll write out later before bed, after she's checked with Daddy to be sure she's included everyone he wants and has not listed anyone he'd prefer not to see, to be sure she's remembered to unwrap the punch bowl and glasses and hasn't forgotten to ask the housekeeper to work late and help serve the canapés and hors d'oeuvres and clean up afterwards.

I stood by the door watching my mother as if she weren't real, as if studying a tableau vivant, amazed by how lifelike it was, when suddenly she moved her hand and raised her glass to her lips, and I jumped, startled by her movement. She turned towards the door, and saw me. She wrinkled her brow as if puzzled and then squinted like a bird watcher trying to remember the correct name of an unfamiliar type of sparrow. For a long moment, we stared at each other through the glass, mother and long-lost daughter. Or was it daughter and long-lost mother? She had grown old. Her crepey throat and arms belonged to an elderly woman, and her back was rounded, and her hair, still carefully cut and set in the shape of a tulip, had gone white and was a fluffed, thinned outline of what it once had been. She wore a pale blue short-sleeve blouse and loose madras skirt and L. L. Bean docksiders, the off-duty summer uniform of an elderly Yankee matriarch.

I opened the door and entered, shucked my backpack, and set my duffel down. Mother half rose from her chair, then sat slackly back. Her mouth opened in astonishment. There was a film of fear over her face, as if she expected her feelings, in a cruel and unexpected way, to be suddenly hurt. This was the sort of moment that Mother tried at all costs to avoid. She only had old roles for it, half-forgotten lines from other, slightly different scenes, gestures and words that may or may not come off as appropriate. In a loud, flattened voice, she said, "Why, it's Hannah! What a wonderful surprise!"

I moved close to her and put my arms around her bony shoulders and kissed her dry, crinkled cheek. Her body smelled the same, lavender and rye, but it was a shrunken, fragile version of the body I so clearly remembered. She made a dry, chugging sound and began to cry. She grabbed my wrists and drew back from me. "It's really you, Hannah! It's really *you!*"

"It's really me."

"Can you stay for dinner?" she asked, grabbing a line at random from some other surprise visit. "If I'd known you were coming, I'd have prepared some—"

"I can stay," I said, cutting her off. "I can stay for as long as you like. And I'm sorry I didn't warn you. But I didn't know until the last minute that I'd be able to get here. I didn't want you and Daddy to make plans for me and then not be able to come."

"No, no, that's fine, Eleanor made up a beef stroganoff this afternoon before she went home, and there's plenty for both of us. We'll have a nice bottle of wine and celebrate. I think there's a tart, an apricot tart that I bought yesterday at this excellent little bakery that a lovely young couple just opened in town—"

"Mother," I said, cutting her off again, more for my sake than hers. "It's fine. Anything is fine. I didn't come home to eat. I came home to see you and Daddy. To be with you and Daddy."

"Of course, dear. I'm sorry. It's just that . . . I'm so excited to see you, and so *surprised!* Will you be able to spend the night? There's plenty of room, naturally. Your old bedroom . . . it's right where it always was, a little bit redecorated, of course, more in the order of a guest room now, as the old guest room is where Eleanor sleeps when she stays over, which she does from time to time. You remember Eleanor, don't you? Oh, no, I don't think you ever met Eleanor. She came to work for us after you went to Cleveland, I think, but you've heard us speak of her, she's lovely and has been such a help to me . . ."

"Mother, I'll stay the night. I may stay many nights. Where's Daddy?"

Her reading glasses hung from her neck by a thin silver chain. She lifted them and carefully placed them before her eyes, as if I'd asked her to read her answer from a manual. "Sit down, Hannah. Yes, Daddy's not . . . well. He's not here," she declared. "Would you like a drink?" she asked brightly.

"Jesus Christ, Mother, no! I mean, yes. Why not? What do you mean, 'not well'? And 'not here,' for Christ's sake."

"Please, Hannah, you don't need to swear. I'll tell you everything. Just let me . . . let me gather my wits. This is *such* a surprise. What would you like to drink?"

"Anything. Gin, I guess."

"Ice? With vermouth?" She got up and went to the liquor cabinet next to the refrigerator and started rummaging among the bottles.

"Anything, Mother. Anything. Tell me about Daddy. If you don't mind."

"No, of course not. I'm sorry. It's just   the surprise and all, I didn't expect . . ." she trailed off, fussing with my drink. I sat down at the table and said nothing and waited. She set the glass before me. "No vermouth? I can make it a martini. Your father loved his dry martinis."

"No, this is fine, thanks. Tell me about Daddy, Mother."

"I didn't know if I should write you, it's been so long since we'd heard from you, and I wasn't sure where to write. And I didn't want to upset you unnecessarily, especially with you being as I supposed way out there in Africa and unable to do anything for him anyhow . . ."

"For God's sake, Mother, get to it!"

Her lower lip quivered. She was about to cry. "I don't . . . I'm sorry, it's just, it's just that it's hard to know how to talk to you, Hannah. You're so . . . I didn't expect . . ." and she started to weep. My cue to embrace and comfort her. To feel guilty and apologetic for demanding simple, unadorned information. To be punished for trying to evade her manipulation of my emotions. In a way all too familiar to me, with her tears Mother was making herself—and not Daddy and my desire to know what had happened to him—the subject.

And, naturally, I responded with no response. Just as I did all those years ago, starting when I was a child and discovered that the only response useful to me was no response—it kept my emotions intact and still my own, and it punished her back, punished her for her self-absorption, her relentless shifting of the subject, no matter how dramatic, poignant, or dire, to herself.

My mother was a closed circuit. All her poles and the pronouns that represented them were reversed. Of strangers, she would say, "She hasn't met me yet." Of people who passed for dear friends, she would say, "I'm her dearest friend." It wasn't a psychological disorder; it was a metaphysical disfigurement. It was beyond her control, and I should have been kinder towards her. But at that moment in the kitchen I couldn't give her what she wanted—an embrace, an apology, an expression of concern for her, not for Daddy, and surely not for me. And even though I *was* concerned for her, I chose not to respond to her weeping. I ignored it, as if she were merely pausing to organize her thoughts. Which in a sense she was, if tactics unconsciously deployed can be viewed as thoughts.

"I'm terribly sorry, dear." She sniffled and took a bracing swallow from her drink. "It's been a . . . a very difficult time for me. I've been so alone," she said and began to weep again, caught herself and bravely plowed ahead. "Three weeks ago, Hannah, your father suffered a massive stroke. A cerebral hemorrhage."

No response. I said nothing. And consequently almost felt nothing.

"I was here in the kitchen, preparing dinner. I'd let Eleanor go home early that day, it was Friday, Fourth of July weekend, and Daddy was in his study, and I heard a loud noise. A thump. It was like the sound of a dictionary being accidentally dropped," she said, an image she had no doubt memorized, rehearsed, and taken on the road, where it must have played well. "I called to him, 'What was that, dear?' I called again, 'What was that, dear?' But the study door was closed, as usual when he doesn't wish to be disturbed, so I assumed he hadn't heard me and it was nothing serious and I went back to cooking. I was making my famous porcini risotto, and for another thirty minutes that took all my attention. Because of the stirring and the slow addition of the chicken stock, you know. That and the salad and setting the table. I even went outside and cut some flowers for the table, and I never knew a thing was wrong, until dinner was ready to be served, and I went to the study door and knocked and called to him. 'Dinner is served, Bernard!' No answer." She took another sip from her drink, which would soon need replenishing. I remembered how she loved to finish her Manhattans like an adorable child by sucking the cherry from her fingertips with a pouty flourish, and wondered if she'd wait until she finished her story, the story of how she experienced her husband's stroke.

"I called a second time," she went on. "Still no answer. So I opened the door. I had an awful feeling that something was wrong, a foreboding, almost, and then I saw him. He was lying on the floor beside his desk, and I realized that what I'd thought was the dictionary falling had actually been *him*! *Daddy!* And I felt awful for it, for having all that time been fussing about in the kitchen and dining room, while he was lying on the floor only a few feet away and needing me but unable to call out for me."

Now she began to cry in earnest, for it was the climax of her story, and from here on she'd have trouble keeping it from being Daddy's. Grudgingly, I said that she couldn't possibly have known what had happened to him or done anything other than what she did, and nudged her forward.

He was unconscious, she said, and at first she thought it was a heart attack and regretted that she'd never learned CPR. Not knowing what else to do, she called 911 and waited there beside him, with his head in her lap, for the ambulance to arrive. "It was the worst fifteen minutes in my life, waiting for that ambulance," she said. "Do you want another?" she asked.

"I'm fine," I said. "Tell me the rest. I assume they did an MRI and CAT scan. And operated on him at once."

"Oh, yes, of course," she said brightly and brushed those old tears away. She smiled into her now-empty glass, plucked the cherry from it, and popped it into her mouth, sucked for a second, chewed, and swallowed. "Ralph Plummer, he operated that very night. Immediately. At Mass General. Ralph's the best in the business. I stayed with Daddy all night, of course, except when he was those seven hours in surgery, and I've been right there by his bed most of every day since. He's still at Mass General. In the intensive care unit. We're trying now to decide where he should go next, Ralph and I and Freddie Rexroth, along with several of Daddy's old friends and medical colleagues."

She continued her story, but I barely listened now. Between the instant that the artery in Daddy's head burst and when he arrived at the hospital for diagnosis and treatment, more than an hour must have passed. I had enough medical experience and training to know what happened. While his skull was filling with blood, his brain was being compressed inside the skull case, cutting off the circulation of blood and oxygen to other parts of his brain, until the cells began to die and neurons started blinking out, darkness sweeping across his mind like a power failure spreading across a city grid, one neighborhood after another plunged into the gloom of permanent night. The prescribed treatment—a hole drilled in the skull, surgery to alleviate the pressure and tie off the burst vessel and siphon off the clotted blood—would have caused more damage to his brain than the hemorrhage. Tissue would have been inadvertently, unavoidably, removed. My father's brain was no longer my father's brain. And his body was no longer his body. If three weeks after surgery he was still in the ICU at Mass General and hadn't been moved to a rehab facility, then there would be no recovery, no return. He was alive, thanks to modern medical technology and the surgical skills of Dr. Ralph Plummer, "the best in the business," but he no longer had a life. Unless, of course, Mother was exaggerating.

I realized that she had asked me a question and was waiting for an answer. "What?"

"I said, 'Why did you stop writing to us?' I'm sorry to bring it up, but we worried so. And wondered. We wondered about your life, Hannah. Especially after you wrote us that you had married a man out there, a Libyan."

"Liberian."

"Yes. Liberian. Why did you stop answering my letters?"

"What letters? I wrote you about Woodrow and said that I was pregnant, remember? After that I never heard from either of you. I know, I know, my tone was probably a little harsh, that's the way I was in those days. But still—"

"That's not *true*, Hannah. For a long time, both your father and I wrote you. We did. And then he stopped. Because of his wounded pride. But I kept on for a long time, Hannah. Then I just sent cards, Christmas cards and birthday cards. Finally, I gave up, too." She looked at her hands in puzzlement, as if trying to recognize whose they were. Then she looked at mine. "I see you're wearing a wedding ring," she said, almost wistfully.

"Yes. All those letters and cards, were they addressed to Hannah Musgrave, Mother?"

"Of course."

"Well, I'm not Hannah Musgrave. Haven't been for years."

"You're *not*?" Genuine astonishment. "Who are you, then?" Genuine curiosity.

"Good question." I got up and walked around the kitchen and poked into the cabinets, the refrigerator, even the freezer. Everything was the same and in the same place as when I last looked, fifteen years ago—the china, the glassware and silver, cutlery, pots and pans, the canned goods and packaged food. In fifteen years, nothing in this room had changed. I leaned against the counter, arms folded, and said, "I'm Missus

Woodrow Sundiata. First name, Hannah. Mother of three sons, Dillon, William, and Paul. Or maybe over here I'm Dawn Carrington. That's what my passport says, anyhow. A fugitive. Still underground."

"Three sons! Oh, my! I'm a *grandmother!*"

"Yes, you are. Congratulations. But your letters and cards—if they were addressed to Hannah Musgrave and were mailed after I got married to Woodrow—disappeared, no doubt, into the famously inept Liberian postal system."

"That explains it, then," she said brightly. "Your father, you know, made some inquiries a few years ago. He met someone in the foreign service, an American who was stationed out there; he met him in Washington once at some official State Department dinner and asked after you. Discreetly, of course."

"Of course. What'd he learn?"

"Nothing. The man said he'd check when he returned to Liberia, which he did, and he wrote back to Daddy that there wasn't any record of an American woman named Hannah Musgrave residing in Liberia. So we assumed that you'd left the country. We thought you might even be in the United States. Underground. Like before. And that we'd hear from you eventually. Like before. But, Hannah," she said, smiling, her eyes suddenly glistening with apparent joy, "I'm a *grandmother!* How wonderful. Tell me about my grandsons. I'll warm up Eleanor's stroganoff for us," she said, and went to the refrigerator, flipping the oven on as she passed the stove. "Tell me *everything!* Oh, if only Daddy could hear this. You'll see him tomorrow, dear," she said in a comforting tone, switching emotional levels too rapidly for me to keep up.

I tried, however, and soon found myself switching topics with the same reckless abandon. I described Dillon first, his temperament and good looks, and then told her a little about our house on Duport Road, mentioning in passing that in 1976 I'd traveled from the States first to Ghana and then to Liberia on a phony passport, which I'd used when leaving Liberia and returning now to the States as well, and explained briefly and in a vague way why I'd been obliged to leave without my sons or husband, which utterly confused her. So I returned to my sons themselves, telling her about the twins, and then a little about the country itself and Woodrow's family in Fuama, whom she thought "charming" and "interesting."

She asked me if I had pictures of Woodrow and the boys.

"No. I mean, not with me."

"You *don't?* Why on earth not, Hannah?"

I had to think for a minute. "I stopped carrying pictures of family years ago, Mother. When I was underground."

"Oh," she said. "Yes, when you were underground. Are you still underground, then?"

"In a sense, yes."

"Oh."

I told her about my work at the lab and how it had ended and then later had evolved into caretaking the chimps, which she also found "charming" and "interesting," causing me to switch back to the subject of Woodrow and his precarious position with the government of Samuel Doe, without telling her what I knew about Samuel Doe, whom she knew as the more or less democratically elected, anti-communist leader of an African nation, someone much favored by the Reagan administration.

"I read everything I can about Liberia," she said. "The *New York Times*, of course, and just recently a novel by Graham Greene that was pretty depressing, to tell the truth, but it gave me the flavor of the place—"

"*The Heart of the Matter?*"

"Yes, I think that was it."

"That's Sierra Leone, Mother. And a long time ago."

"Oh."

I asked her to tell me more about Daddy, his condition, the effects of the stroke and surgery. But it was almost as if she didn't know the answers. She was as evasive and vague about his condition as I had been about Samuel Doe. She kept saying, "You'll see tomorrow. I'll arrange to have his doctors speak with you. He's pretty incapacitated, dear, so prepare yourself. I always try to be cheerful and optimistic when I'm with him. But it's difficult. And sometimes when I leave his room I just break down in tears. Shall I open a bottle of wine? It is a special occasion, after all. How about a special red?"

"Fine," I said. "Whatever. Will he be able to recognize me?"

"Oh, my goodness," she said and set napkins, plates, and silver on the table. "Of *course*, he will."

THE NEXT MORNING, Mother and I drove into Boston, and before seeing Daddy, we met first with the surgeon, Dr. Plummer. I had insisted on it. I was still hoping that Mother had exaggerated the seriousness of Daddy's condition. The surgeon strolled into the waiting room where we sat on overstuffed, turquoise easy chairs and stood over us, poking through a folder that I assumed was Daddy's file. He was a Top Gun type, a forty-year-old athlete with a military buzz cut, titanium eyes, and a mouthful of very white teeth. He wore pressed chinos and a tight-fitting, navy blue polo shirt, all muscle and sinew and as clean as an action figure.

"Looks like an intracerebral hemorrhage," he said, shuffling through the papers as if reading them for the first time. "Big bleed. Caused probably by high blood pressure. That and blood vessels weakened by old age. The scans indicated the stroke was catastrophic."

"Catastrophic," I said.

"Yes." He checked his watch.

"That means he'll die from it?"

"No, it doesn't," Mother interrupted.

"Yeah, usually it does. With someone your father's age, death usually occurs within a few hours of the event. Or at the most a few days."

"And when it doesn't?" I asked.

"Not my area," he said.

"Will he get better? Will his condition improve?"

He glanced through the sheaf of papers. "Hard to say. Age's against him. Guess he's otherwise in good shape. Heart, lungs, et cetera. Once he's in rehab, they'll make an evaluation."

"How long might my father have to remain in intensive care?"

"Not my area," he said again. "Speak to the attending physician on that." He checked the file again. "Doctor Rexroth."

"Freddie. Freddie Rexroth," Mother said. "A dear."

"Surgery went okay, though. A case like this, we don't like to opt for surgery. The age thing. A batch of tissue, brain tissue, always gets scraped off, no matter how good you are. And I'm good. Some guys want to try a spinal tap first. But with a lumbar puncture you can get cerebral herniation. Brain tissue, because of the pressure inside the skull, gets sucked through the transtentorial notch into the cerebellum and the stem. Bad news. So we opted to cut," he said, closing the file with relish, as if the memory of the cutting had unexpectedly pleased him. "Anything else?" he asked, and smiled.

"No," I said.

MOTHER ENTERED Daddy's room ahead of me. "Good morning!" she chirped. "I've brought someone to see you, Bernard. And you'll never guess who it is." She waved me onto center stage. "Ta-*da!*"

I came slowly forward and stood at the foot of his bed. His head was wrapped in a gauze turban. Wires monitored his heartbeat and blood pressure, and plastic tubes snaked in and out of his nostrils, mouth, and the veins of both wrists, pumping oxygen, nourishment, and medications into his body and removing spittle and phlegm and urine. My father's heart, liver, and kidneys were strong. He had taken good care of his body and had exercised it regularly, drank moderately, never smoked. But he'd been attached to this elaborate apparatus for twenty days, and he probably looked the same today as he had when they first wheeled him in from the operating room. He'd look the same in twenty weeks. Twenty months. Twenty years. His body was outliving him.

"Stand over here, dear," Mother said, sotto voce. "On his right side. It's his left that's paralyzed, and they think his vision on that side is still impaired, too. Poor thing."

I obeyed and passed behind her. There were bars along the sides of his bed to keep him from tumbling out, but with all the tubes, cords, and wires, I couldn't imagine him moving. His head was propped by a pillow, and he wore a white hospital gown. A tuft of gray chest hair fluttered above the collar of his gown. I avoided looking directly at his face, as if I knew I'd learn there a thing I did not want to know. The skin of his forearms and hands was like yellowed parchment. His fingernails were clean and professionally manicured.

Finally, I dared to look at his face. And it was like seeing my father in his coffin, as if Mother and I were attending the funeral of Dr. Bernard Musgrave, my dead father, her late husband, who lay there with his eyes closed imitating sleep. The color of his face was a little too bright against the white background, and his chin and cheeks had been freshly shaved by a stranger, a patch of three-day grizzle missed here, another there. The hair keeps on growing after the rest of the body has died, doesn't it? Like the fingernails and toenails. My father's internal organs might still function, thanks to the machines attached to them, but it was the same sort of meaningless continuity as the ongoing growth of his beard and fingernails.

"Look who I've brought!" Mother exclaimed. "*Look*, Bernard!"

His eyes flashed open, then closed. "Let him be, Mother," I said, turning to her, catching the anger on her face, shocked by it, but then, just as quickly, not shocked.

"No, see, he's awake," she said.

I turned back, and he was staring straight up, as if at the ceiling. "Hello, Daddy," I whispered. "It's me, Hannah."

"You'll have to speak up. He isn't wearing his hearing aid."

"Hearing aid? Daddy has a hearing aid?"

"He's had it for years, Hannah. But they won't let him use it here.

Because of the battery or something, with all the electronics," she said and tossed a disdainful wave at the bank of blinking monitors.

I reached down and touched his dry cheek. He watched my hand descend, but didn't move his head. He still hadn't looked at me. I was afraid to raise my voice, afraid it would crack, and I'd cry. I didn't want to cry. I wanted to be tough, clear headed, rational. I knew what I was supposed to *feel*; I needed to know what to *think*. I couldn't count on Mother for guidance; she had neither feelings, with the probable exception of anger, nor thoughts, except for a set of self-revising strategies for attention.

"Bernard!" she said in a loud voice. "Look who I brought to see you! It's *Hannah*, Bernard!" Then, in a stage whisper, "It's the medication. He's very heavily sedated, you know."

I positioned myself directly over him, cutting off his view of the ceiling, and saw my face reflected in the pupils of his eyes. For a long moment, we stared at each other like that, unblinking, dry eyed, as if staring into the distance through fog. But we were only inches away from what we were trying to see in each other's eyes, the thing that had always been there, from my infancy on. I can remember it from almost that far back, when he would look down at me in my crib, and we would fix our gazes on one another's eyes. I saw him, and at the same time in the same way, he saw me, and in that instant he and I became real to one another and to ourselves. By that means we both came into existence. My father had given life to me, whether by accident or intention, it didn't matter; and I had given it back to him, an exchange begun probably at my birth.

It was an exchange from which Mother had been excluded. Not because Daddy or I wished it, but because we both knew that she was incapable of truly seeing anyone, even herself. All my life, whenever I tried to see into my mother's eyes, I saw two tiny, mirrored disks that bounced my gaze back at me. I never shared with Mother the eye contact that secures for you the knowledge that you are as real as the world itself, as certain of your own existence, regardless of its meaninglessness and contingency, as you are of the world's. The opacity of my mother's gaze deprived me of that certitude and security and made me resemble her from time to time in ways that would later shame me. And by now you know some of those ways. How I saw, or more precisely, how I did *not* see, my sons, for instance. Or my husband. It wasn't as though I could have seen them, if only I'd tried. Like my mother, I was incapable of seeing them. It was beyond my capacity. Woodrow was always *my black African husband, Woodrow*. He was never simply Woodrow. And my sons were *my black African husband's three sons*. *The eldest* and *the twins*. They were never Dillon, William, and Paul. It's why I was able to leave them with such ease and so little regret. Simply, they weren't as real to me as I was to myself. They weren't even as real to me as my dreamers. Not until later, much later. And by then it was too late.

And now my father was no longer real to me, except in memory. A dry, white crust of spittle was stuck to a corner of his mouth. I wet my fingertips and washed it off. His face was the one I'd known all my life, but it wasn't my father's face anymore; it belonged to one of my ancestors, a pale, lipless Puritan with a beaked nose and cold blue eyes. It was more a mask than a face. A death mask. I made one last attempt to see if the person peering through the eye holes was still alive, and I said, "Daddy, are you in there?"

"Speak loudly," Mother said. "He can't hear you. The hearing aid."

I turned and said, "Mother, just shut the fuck up."

She looked scared, as if I'd struck her, and pasted a thin smile onto her lips and, with thumb and forefinger, mimed locking her mouth with a key and throwing the key away. The sickly smile and her rage-filled eyes made her look like a happy executioner. *Is this my mother? Is this who she really is?*

"Leave us alone for a few minutes, okay? Why don't you see if Doctor Rexroth is in the building. We should speak with him later."

She nodded, turned, and left the room, closing the door softly behind her.

I leaned down and reconnected my gaze to my father's, as if resum-

ing a deeply familiar ceremony that had been briefly disrupted by an er-
ratic member of the congregation, someone with a coughing fit who
had politely removed herself from the hall. I kissed his forehead, and
his eyes slowly closed. "Hello, Daddy," I said. *You're not going to recover
from this, Daddy. You're not coming back to us. It took too long for Mother to get
help, too long to get you onto the operating table, too long for me to come home.
And now it's too late for me to be of any use to you. Too late for me to thank you
for loving me. You loved me almost in spite of yourself. But it was enough to
make me capable of being thankful, at least, no matter how late it's come. I am
who I am at bottom and who I am not because of who you and Mother were and
were not. It's because of who you were, Daddy, that I'm able to be someone at all.
If I hadn't had you, if all I'd had was Mother, I would be her. I'd be no one. An
absence. You saved me from that, Daddy. You—*

"My name." He said the words in a small, child-like voice.

"What, Daddy?"

His eyes were wide open, staring into mine. "My name."

"Your name is Bernard. Bernard Musgrave. Doctor Bernard Musgrave."

"My name." It was a statement almost, not a question, with equal
stress on both words.

"Want me to say *my* name? Is that what you want, Daddy?"

"My name," he said. "My name. My name."

"My name is Hannah. Hannah Musgrave, Daddy."

"My name."

"*Your* name, then. It's Bernard—"

"My name." He'd grown more fretful now, as if the words were a
command, a deeply encoded order, and I was expected to know the
cipher to the code. "My name! My name!"

"I don't know what you want, Daddy."

"My name. My name. My name." It became a flattened chant, a
strange, mystifying song.

I decided simply to listen. And soon, after eight or ten repetitions, the
chant changed tone, timbre, and tune, and he seemed to be speaking

whole sentences, then paragraphs, but using only those two short words. *My name my name my name my name*, it went—questions, answers, declarations, pauses, all the parts of an extended monologue. *My name? My name! My name my name my name. My name. My name my name? My-y-y-y NAME! My nam-m-m-e, MY name.*

As suddenly as it began, it stopped. He went silent. His eyes closed, and he collapsed in on himself, as if exhausted. His face slackened, and his breathing slowed, and he seemed to have fallen peacefully asleep. I touched both his cheeks, his forehead, and his lips, and then touched my own cheeks, forehead, and lips.

And that was the end of it. I left the hospital with Mother. According to the death certificate he died within an hour of our departure.

IN THE DAYS that followed, I moved into my old room, now the guest room, though I did not unpack my duffel. I helped Mother with the funeral arrangements and worked behind the scenes, advising her on her dealings with the accountants and lawyers, and helped her go through Daddy's papers and files. The *New York Times* and the *Boston Globe* each gave him a half-page obituary with a photograph from the early 1970s of Daddy marching arm in arm with the Berrigan brothers in Washington at the march that earned him two whole paragraphs in Norman Mailer's book *Armies of the Night*, a point that had been of considerable pride for him. Both obituaries mentioned his daughter, Hannah, naturally, a member of the Weather Underground, "indicted in Chicago in 1969 and a fugitive still at large."

I stayed completely out of public view and even at home lay low and spoke to no one on the phone. I instructed Mother to say, only if asked, that as far as she knew Hannah was still in Africa and unable to return to the U.S., and to tell Eleanor that I was Mother's niece from Ottawa and my name was Dawn Carrington. It wasn't exactly deep cover; it was more like being in the FBI's Witness Protection Program.

We argued over that. Mother insisted that I ask one of Daddy's famous lawyers to negotiate my surrender in exchange for a suspended sentence, as so many other Weathermen and -women had done; I insisted that no Reagan-appointed federal prosecutor, especially in an election year, would agree to letting me off without jail time. "And there's no way, Mother, that I'm going to jail for two or three or more years. Not now, not ever, not after all this time on the run. And not with a husband and three children who expect me to come straight back to them as soon as President Doe gives the word."

"I just don't understand all that," she said. It was the day of the funeral. Eleanor had gone ahead early to prepare the post-burial reception at Saint Tim's. A public memorial service at Riverside Church in New York City would be held later in the summer, when most of the people who would want to memorialize Daddy would have returned from the Hamptons, the Vineyard, and Maine. The funeral itself had been advertised as a private service for family and close friends, but Mother had extended her personal invitation to well over a hundred people, friends and acquaintances and colleagues alike, and most of them had said they'd be there. They'd be there for her, she kept saying. "Ruth and Roy Pelmas, sweet things, they said of *course* they'll come, they'll come out of love for Daddy and for me. So many of our friends know how hard it's going to be for me with Daddy gone. Perhaps you could make a list of everyone who comes to the funeral. And get the names of those who send flowers. So I'll know who to write my thank-yous to."

"No, Mother, I can't. I'm not going to be at the funeral."

"*What?* And why not, may I ask? Your own father's funeral!"

For what must have been the tenth time since my homecoming, I described the risk I ran just being in the country, let alone sleeping in my parents' house, which, for all I knew, was still under surveillance. "And Daddy's funeral is definitely going to have a team of FBI agents attending, Mother. You know that. What are you trying to do, set me up for a bust?"

"How can you say such a thing!" she cried.

"Just kidding, Mother."

"How can you even *think* it?" she continued. "After all I've done for your father. And for you, too, young lady. Your political views were never mine, you know, and many of your father's weren't either."

"I was kidding."

"But even so, I stood by you. Year in and out. I made sacrifices, Hannah. *Real* sacrifices." Her eyes narrowed, and her mouth tightened, as muddled anger cleared, rose, and spilled over. We had moved into Daddy's study and had been shuffling through his files in search of a life-insurance policy whose premiums she was sure he had been paying for years. Mother had never paid a monthly bill herself, not even Eleanor's paycheck, or balanced a checkbook or reconciled a bank statement. She had no idea how little or how much money she now controlled, no notion of whom Daddy owed money to or who owed money to him. She hadn't so much been widowed as orphaned. And she was angry at Daddy for that. And angry at me, who had apparently not been similarly orphaned. And angry at everyone who, in offering their condolences, praised Daddy and not her, remembered his wise and witty sayings and not hers, expressed gratitude for his many public services and good deeds and none for hers. She was angry at dear old Reverend Bill Coffin, who was supervising the funeral service at Saint Timothy's Episcopal Church and presiding over the burial, mad at him for knowing which music by Bach and which by Charles Mingus and Judy Collins Daddy would want played and which passages from the Bible he'd want read over his casket. She was angry that Daddy's death was his and not hers.

You must think I'm being unkind, remembering her this way. But it was the first time that I had seen and understood my mother so clearly, and I felt a terrible, sad pity for her. In the midst of my own grieving, I saw that she was unable to grieve, which made her loss that much greater than mine. In the midst of my swelling gratitude for my father's love, I saw that she felt only resentment and bitterness towards him. It was if I had loved, and been loved by, a man whom she had never even met.

I placed my hand over hers and said, "I know you made sacrifices,

Mother. You sacrificed a lot. For both me and Daddy. And you deserve recognition for that. I'm sorry that we both had to ask so much of you. I truly am," I said, and meant it.

Her eyes filled and tears spilled across her cheeks, and she buried her face against my shoulder and sobbed for several moments, like a child who had been lost and now was found.

Eleanor came back from the church in time to drive Mother to the funeral in Daddy's Buick. I waved goodbye to her, then walked into Daddy's study and flopped down in his red-leather chair. His throne, he used to call it, where he read, listened to music, drank his dry martinis, and held court. As a child and later as a teenager, I had loved sitting on the carpet beside his chair, and I read there, and sometimes he talked to me about things that I knew he rarely, if ever, spoke of with Mother. Music, science, politics, religion—he talked to me of these things as if I were an adult. And now, probably for the first time, I was seated in his chair, and I was an adult. *The king is dead. Long live the queen.*

After a few moments, I got up and went to his wide mahogany desk, opened the stationery drawer, and took out a sheet of letterhead paper and an envelope. I sat down and began to write.

> *Mother, I want to make things easier for you, and the only way I can do that is to go away and stay away. I'll be fine, so you mustn't worry about me. And you'll be fine, too. Someday I'll be able to come back and be with you in a natural, normal way that won't ask any sacrifices from you or from me. But that's impossible now. When I'm settled again, I'll contact you. Until then, please know that I love you, just as I know that you love me.*

And signed it with my initial. I folded the letter and sealed it in the envelope, wrote "Iris Musgrave, Personal" on the outside, and carried it into the kitchen, where I placed it under the sugar bowl on the break-fast table.

I went upstairs and grabbed my duffel and took a last look around at my old room—it wasn't my room anymore; it hadn't been mine for a lifetime, it seemed. It was truly a guest room now. I lugged my duffel out to the garage and tossed it into the trunk of Mother's Toyota, a red, five-year-old, woman's car. Perfectly anonymous. And drove away.

At the cemetery, I parked a short way downhill from the Musgrave family plot, where I could see the grave site and my ancestors' head-stones and not be seen myself. I sat in the car and smoked. Good old Marlboros. At the urging of Woodrow, who said he hated to see a woman with a cigarette in her hand, I'd stopped smoking. After seven years, I'd picked up the habit again.

I sat there under a blue, cloudless sky in a kind of reverie, inhaling tobacco smoke mingled with the smell of newly mown grass, listening to birdsong and the distant thrum of a lawn mower, adjusting slowly to the peace of resolution. Shortly, the funeral cortege began to arrive—the long, black hearse with the casket and baskets of cut flowers; the trailing line of mourners' cars; a pair of Cambridge police cruisers to escort the cortege; a van from one of the Boston TV stations; and two nondescript sedans with two nondescript middle-aged men in each—FBI agents, I assumed—who remained inside their cars when the others got out and walked across the grass to the grave. Fifty or more cars were parked along the lane that passed the Musgrave family plot, and a crowd of nearly a hundred mourners had gathered at the grave, most of them well-dressed, elderly white people, all of whom looked vaguely familiar to me, as if as a girl I'd seen them at my parents' cock-tail parties and hadn't seen them since. There were no pallbearers. Two men from the funeral home transferred the casket from the hearse to the grave on a wheeled, stretcherlike dolly, rolled it onto a platform, and lowered it efficiently, smoothly, into the ground.

Reverend Coffin, in ministerial robes, read from his Book of Com-mon Prayer; my mother in black, her face covered by a veil, visibly wept; a man standing behind her passed his handkerchief to her. At the back of the crowd a black teenage boy with a trumpet stood forward, raised the trumpet to his lips, and began to play a slow, stately piece that I rec-ognized at once. It was from Daddy's favorite composition by Charles

Ives, "The Unanswered Question," a strange, haunted, and haunting tune, like a long, unspoken cry from the other side of this life. It was more a warning from the dead than a welcome. When I was a child and adolescent, I'd listened to my father listening to it a hundred times, but until now had never heard it myself. It was my father's true voice, the one I knew and loved best. The music floated down to me from the grave, spectral, implacable, and disjointed. The tempo increased, the music built, and I pictured my father rising from his leather chair, his mournful expression fading, and he beginning to dance a syncopated waltz, turning and stepping elegantly around the book-lined room, not quite happy, not quite manic, but a little of both. He lifted me in his arms and danced with me, my feet dangling far above the carpet, until gradually he seemed to tire, and he let me down and released me. The music grew heavier, slower, lower, and my father sat back down into his chair. The music reached the furthest extension of its mystery and longing, and at last ended in permanent silence. My father placed his hands on his knees, looked down at me seated on the floor beside him, and closed his eyes.

THE CROWD BEGAN to break apart, and people headed for their cars. I started the Toyota, backed and turned it around, and made for the exit ahead of them. I don't think anyone noticed my presence or saw me leave. It was by then late afternoon, and the leafy streets of Cambridge were golden in the sunlight. College boys and girls lounged and read and flirted with one another on the green banks of the Charles River, while sculls skimmed across its surface like elongated water bugs. I took the Massachusetts Avenue Bridge into Boston and passed through Copley Square, made my way across the newly gentrified South End, and just ahead of rush-hour traffic picked up I-95, in the southbound lane.

At the time, there seemed nowhere else to go, so I drove to New Bedford. And no one else to turn to, so I turned to Carol. I wanted to erase as much of the last seven years of my life as possible. I wanted to be like one of those husbands who leaves the house for a loaf of bread and disappears for seven years and then one day shows up again on the doorstep and is welcomed back into the family, as if he'd never left it.

It was late when I pulled up in front, nearly ten o'clock, and there was no one on the street. The house was the same sad, sorry triple-decker in need of repairs and paint, with laundry drying on clotheslines out back, uncollected trash at the curb, and a pair of beat-up old cars on cinder blocks in the driveway. Empty beer cans and soda bottles and fast-food wrappers cluttered the stoop. The tenants who'd earlier sat out there drinking and socializing, now that their sweltering apartments were habitable again, had retreated to their TVs and bedrooms, leaving their refuse behind.

The tag under the third-floor mail slot still had Carol's name on it—and mine, too: D. Harrington. I pushed open the door and stepped into the dark, musty hallway and reached automatically for the wall switch next to the door. I flipped on the low-wattage lights and followed them up two flights of bare stairs to the landing at the top, inhaling the familiar smell of moldy old linoleum, corned beef and cabbage, and stale cigarette smoke.

I knocked lightly at first. No answer. Maybe she's asleep. I knocked again, more forcefully. Someone, a woman in high heels, approached from inside. That's not Carol, I thought. A barefoot gal, Carol never wore shoes at home, let alone high heels. Someone's replaced me, someone kinder than I, someone who, late at night, tells her the truth about herself.

A familiar, lilting voice called, "Who's there?" It *was* Carol.

"It's me. Dawn."

"*Don?* Oh, my God! *Don!*" The door swung open, and she came rushing towards me. We flung our arms around each other and kissed on the lips, and then stepped back and looked at each other, grinned shyly like kids, and hugged again. "I can't believe it!" she said. "Wow! Don! You look the exact same as you used to. Except your hair's a lot longer." She lifted my hair off my shoulders and hefted it in both hands, framing my face.

"It's gotten pretty gray," I said, and felt oddly conscious of my looks. "In this light you just can't see it."

Laughing, she pulled me into the apartment and locked the door. In high heels, she was as tall as I. Her hair had grown out, too, a mass of dark curls that she wore loose over her shoulders like a shawl, and she was wearing makeup, elegantly applied eye shadow and rouge, which was new, and a simple black dress with spaghetti straps. Very chic. I touched the tattoo of a rose on her bare shoulder. "I remember that," I said softly. "Look at you. How beautiful you are. You must be just going out. Or just coming in?"

"These are my work clothes," she said brightly.

"Oh."

She saw my expression and hurried to explain that she was still working at the same restaurant, the old Clam Shack. She'd been promoted from waiting tables to assistant manager and hostess. "But it's a kind of like a fern bar now, called The Pequod. I'll tell you everything," she said. "There's so much news. And I can't wait to hear all about you. I'm sure *you've* got news. I've even heard a little of it already," she said and walked down the hall ahead of me.

"What? Who from?"

"You'll see," she answered and disappeared into the living room. I could hear the television, the chatter and buzz of a baseball game. "Guess who's here," she sang. *Bettina must be about nine now,* I thought.

But no child was there. The person slumped in the couch watching television was Zack. My one-time comrade-in-arms, my fugitive traveling companion. *Impossible,* I thought. *I'm dreaming.* But no, it was he, all right, the grand deceiver and unapologetic schemer, just as shocked to see me standing in the doorway off the hall as I was to see him slouched on Carol's couch in front of the TV, a big blue can of Foster's lager in one mitt, a bunch of pretzels in the other.

"Well, well, well," he said. "The gang's all here." He smiled broadly, flashing those fabulous teeth and glittery blue eyes, then stood up and wrapped me in his long arms. He was unshaven and had put on weight and developed an early paunch, which made him seem not merely a very tall man, but a very large man.

Carol beamed like a proud parent. Zack aimed the remote at the TV and snapped off the sound. "So, babe, what brings you to our fair city?" He lighted a cigarette, sat back down, stretched out his long legs and crossed them at the ankles. He wore khakis and a tee shirt and sneakers, and looked like a factory worker after a long day on the line.

"I should be asking that of you," I said.

"*Me?* I live here. Welcome to our humble abode," he said, and then added, "Missus Sundiata."

Mrs. Sundiata? I laughed, as if he'd been uncannily witty, and quickly asked Carol, "Where's Bettina? How old is she now?"

"Nine and a half, in fourth grade. Amazing, huh? She's at my mom's. She stays there 'cause we both work nights on Fridays and Saturdays. Me at The Pequod and Zack in his cab. We only just came in ahead of you," she said. "You hungry? We were gonna order in Chinese."

I said sure, and Carol kicked off her shoes and headed for the kitchen, and I followed. Zack hit the remote and went back to his game.

As soon as we were out of his hearing, I said, "So he's actually *living* here? With you and Bettina?"

"Yeah. It's kind of weird, I guess. But we're okay together. For now, anyway. What do you want, fish or meat or what?" She pulled a Chinese restaurant flyer from a stack of take-out menus on the table by the phone. The kitchen smelled of fresh paint and looked clean and well kept. More so, certainly, than when I lived here.

"I don't care. Anything. You know me."

"Yeah," she said. "I know you."

She dialed and ordered, and when she hung up the phone I asked her how long she and Zack had been together. "As a couple, I mean."

"Only about six weeks. Since he got out."

"Out?"

"I'll let Zack tell you the whole story. It's pretty complicated. But he was in prison over in Plymouth, the federal prison, sort of a minimum-security place."

"Prison?"

"He'll tell you. Six months was all. Anyhow, one day out of the blue he calls me up, and we talked, and then I started going out there to visit him. He didn't have anyone else to visit him, and I felt sorry for him. Even though him and you ran out on me like you did. But he explained all that. I got over it."

"I . . . I'm sorry about that, Carol. At the time—"

"Yeah, it's okay. I'm over it. Anyhow, we started writing letters and all, and before you know it we'd gotten real close and all. So when he was released, it seemed sort of natural for him to move in with me. He's been real sweet. He helped fix up the apartment and everything. He even got his old job back driving a cab. Different company, of course. The other company went out of business, so nobody remembered how he ran out on them. When you and him went to Africa back then."

I put my hand on her shoulder. "You do know Zack lied to me about that. We never really had to leave, or at least I didn't. But I thought—"

Zack suddenly appeared beside me. "Fucking Yankees," he said and grabbed a fresh can of beer from the refrigerator. "You filling in the details for 'Dawn'?" he asked Carol.

"You tell me your story, Zack, and I'll tell you mine," I said.

He sat down at the table. "You'll show me yours if I show you mine? Sounds fair. Except I already know yours."

"C'mon, Zack, be straight with me." I sat across from him and gave him a hard stare. Carol stood behind me with a friendly hand on my shoulder. "How do you know my story?" I asked him.

"A guy I met knows you."

"And who might that be?"

"Okay, babe, I'll tell you everything," he said. He had done very well in Accra buying and selling Ghanaian arts and antiquities. He'd bought himself a house, set up two galleries and a warehouse for selling work wholesale to galleries in the U.S. and Europe. A year ago he'd come across a private collection of very old gold and bronze masks and plaques and other artifacts from Benin owned by a retired British army colonel who had stayed on in Ghana after independence. The colonel had died, and his widow had asked Zack to sell the collection abroad. For his trouble he was to receive a third of the selling price. "This was a major collection, man. Museum-quality stuff. Off the scale. Probably worth two, two point five million at auction. But you'd have to show provenance, pay the auction house a fat commission, pay New York and federal taxes, all that. By the time I got my piece, it'd be a small piece. Besides," he said, "I didn't have an export license and couldn't move the stuff out of the country my-self without a Ghanaian partner, who'd probably want half of whatever I got. So I guess I had what you'd call a *Maltese Falcon* moment."

He had painted over the gold and bronze artifacts—masks, wall hangings, statuary, and pendants—with gray, latex-based housepaint that could be removed without damaging the objects. He carried the objects to the States in his luggage and a beat-up cardboard box tied with heavy twine. Claiming that the lot was made up of cheap sou-venirs not to be resold, he declared its value at six hundred dollars, and thought he'd made it, until the customs officer pulled out a pocketknife and scraped the paint off the chin of one of the gold masks. Zack's family had refused to help him or even see him, and since all his prop-erty and cash were in Accra, he couldn't raise bail and spent a month in jail in Charlestown awaiting trial. He had to accept a public defender and got sent to Plymouth for six months. "If I'd had a decent lawyer, I'd have gotten a suspended sentence."

"If you hadn't been greedy, you'd never have been arrested," I said.

The doorbell rang, and Carol hurried off to meet the delivery man at the bottom of the stairs. "End of story," Zack said. "It could've been worse. It was mostly white guys convicted of white-collar crimes, short-termers in for tax evasion, kiting checks, insurance fraud. Small fish, most of them. People were catching up on their reading and taking mail-order courses in art appreciation."

"What about Carol?" I asked.

"What about her? She's been great, man. My port in a storm. She came out to see me every week, when no one in my family would bother making the trip. When I got out, she picked me up and brought me here and said I could stay with her and Bettina till I got back on my feet. The rest is history, man."

"You started sleeping together, I suppose."

"First thing, man. You're not jealous, are you?"

"A little. Yeah."

Carol returned with the food and spread it out on the table, and the three of us ate and drank beer. After a few moments, I asked Zack again how he knew my story. I wasn't convinced he did know it. When I left Accra I'd not told a soul where I was headed. I'd never written from Monrovia to him or any of his friends or mine and didn't believe that anyone who knew me in Liberia also knew him.

"Actually, I figured you'd gone back to the States. A-mer-i-ka. But then I met an old friend of yours," he said. "In Plymouth. One of the inmates. He claims to know you and your husband well. Very well."

"Who? What's his name?"

"Charlie. But he hates being called that. Charles is his name. I used to call him Chuck, just to piss him off."

"Charles?"

"Charles Taylor," he said. "Remember him? He got sent up about a month before I got out, so we weren't exactly buddies. But I pegged him right away for an African, and I thought maybe he's from Ghana. You can always tell an African black guy from an American black guy, even without hearing him. They walk differently. Turns out he's Liberian. And turns out he knows your old man very well. And knows you pretty good, too. You ever sleep with him?"

"No! For Christ's sake, Zack!"

"Too bad. He lied. African guys, man, they want you to think they've fucked every white woman they ever said hello to. Anyhow, he told me a whole lot of other stuff, which I assume *is* true. Stuff about you and your kids and all, and about your husband, Woodrow, who Charlie thinks dropped a dime on him so he'd get nailed by the feds when he got to JFK. True?"

"It's more complicated than that," I said. "More pathetic, actually."

Carol said, "I think it's great you have kids, Don. I bet you're a terrific mother."

"Not so terrific," I said.

"You know, you are a damned attractive woman," Zack said suddenly, as if it had just that second occurred to him. "You both are," he continued. "Two incredible-looking women!"

I looked at Carol. He was right about her, at least. She smiled, as if agreeing with Zack—about me, anyhow. A cascade of memories washed over me, memories of Carol when we first found solace and simple pleasure in each other's arms. In different ways, even though most of my injuries had been internal and self-inflicted, we'd both in a sense been battered women. She'd been victimized by men generally; I'd been victimized by ideology. In each other, we'd both for the first time found someone we could trust. More than anything else, simple tenderness and intimacy were what we wanted then. We were too weak and shaken to be alone, and too wounded and confused to be with another person. Especially with a man. I'd invalidated and tried to overthrow all the old forms of tenderness and intimacy between men and women—missionary-position sexual relations, monogamy, fidelity, state-recognized and -regulated marital roles and responsibilities, even childcare—and afterwards found myself with nothing to replace those forms. I'd deliberately set out to shatter in mere months a social structure that had taken fifty thousand years to harden. It was like jumping from a ship that was in no danger of sinking and finding myself alone in a tiny rowboat in the middle of the ocean.

I'd chosen to abandon that ship, but Carol had been tossed off hers. The captain and crew had left her on a desert island, a castaway. One night I rowed solemnly, hopelessly, to shore, and there we were, the two of us, marooned together. I figured her for a working girl right off, barely twenty, heavy eye makeup, miniskirt, and fishnet stockings—the whole uniform. She stood at the end of the bar nursing a drink made with grenadine, trying to look exotic and available for a reasonable price to the crowd of half-drunk construction workers and fishermen bonding beneath the TV screens and around the pool table. A blow job in the parking lot, a quickie in the men's room with the door locked, or an hour in a motel out on Route 28—it's all the same to her, I figured, merely a way, the only way available, to pay the rent and buy food for herself and her kid and maybe get high enough to ignore for another day the way she makes her living. Until, of course, the drugs turn on her, and the way she makes her living becomes the only way she can get the money to get high. I could see by her stoned gaze, her flattened, self-amused affect, that she was on the verge of that turnaround. *In six months,* I thought, *she'll be doing tricks strictly to get high.*

It was nine o'clock. I offered her twenty dollars to come back to my apartment with me, and she said, "Sure, why not?" At the apartment, we drank a bottle of cheap red wine and quickly found ourselves talking like friends from high school, and never got around to having sex that night. She was bright and funny and warm, and at a time when I hated myself for having failed to save the world, she made me feel that I could at least save her.

Her daughter was at a sister's place, she said, and was okay till midnight, when the sister, who worked the night shift at the clam cannery, went to work. At eleven-thirty, I invited Carol to move in and share my apartment, take the larger of the two bedrooms for herself and her daughter. I'd carry the rent and cover food and other costs until she got herself cleaned up and found a job. She accepted, and shortly after midnight she and Bettina moved in. Two nights later, Carol and I were lovers. In a week, she had a part-time job as a waitress that after a month became full-time.

And look at her now, I thought, *a free and independent woman who's saving someone else. She's become what I tried to be and couldn't.*

Carol, Zack, and I sat up late drinking beer, smoking pot, and elaborately talking around the difficult question of who was going to end up in bed with Carol. We played an old Neil Young tape over and over, seventies ballads and hymns that celebrated reckless abandon, which didn't help change the unstated subject. We wandered back and forth between the kitchen and the living room, feigning interest in how Carol had redecorated the place. The walls and woodwork had all been repainted in new colors like mauve and taupe and lapis. My old room was now Bettina's. The Che Guevara and John Brown posters had been replaced by New Kids on the Block and Paul McCartney in a band called Wings.

Finally, we three found ourselves standing together at the door to the bedroom Carol shared with Zack. The double bed was unmade, and a harried working mother's clothes draped from chairs and the dresser.

"Sorry about the mess," Carol said. "Zack's such a neatnik and takes care of most of the place, but he refuses to pick up after me in the bedroom. It's the one thing we fight about."

Zack crossed in front of us and flopped down in the middle of the bed. "C'mere, you," he said.

"Who?" Carol asked.

"Both of you."

"Zack," I said. "I'm not your type, remember? And you're not mine." Carol walked over, and sat down on the edge of the bed. Zack began to stroke her bare arm.

"Yeah, but you're Carol's type," he said. "And she's yours."

Carol and I looked at each other. When the object of your past desire is placed in front of you like that, sexual nostalgia can be very powerful. There are so many vague, lingering memories of having once been satisfied and so few specific details that you want to revisit the source.

Zack reached over to the bedside table and lighted a chunky blue candle. I hit the wall switch, and he said, "That's better. Now, c'mon over here with us."

I stayed put by the door. "Is a threesome what you're after?"

"I wouldn't mind. But if you're not into that, it's okay by me. There's other possibilities."

"What about you, Carol?"

She shrugged. Zack slowly unzipped the back of her dress, and she looked down and smiled coyly.

"Maybe you'd like to watch me and Carol," Zack said. "Or maybe you'd like me to watch you and Carol. Like I said, there's other possibilities. I've never seen two women make love before. In real life, I mean."

"Real life," I said. "Is this real life?"

"It's not a movie, man," he said. "Come on over here. You know you want to."

I took one step, then two, and then I was standing beside Carol on the bed. Zack slid over to make room. I sat down, my ears buzzing like a teenager's, and placed one hand over hers. With my other hand, I brushed her hair off her shoulder and touched her throat. She turned to face me, closed her eyes, and kissed me on the lips.

And the rest? Well, you know the rest.

No, that's not true. You don't know the rest. You don't know that Zack and I both made love to Carol. You don't know that while he fucked her I leaned back against the headboard and watched them and touched myself and for the first time in my life was swallowed whole by sexual pleasure. I left my body behind and merged with theirs and had no thoughts, no awareness of my mind or body. You don't know that afterwards I felt deep, nearly inexplicable gratitude to Zack and Carol, as if they had gone through a terrible, mind- and body-searing ordeal solely for me, so that I would not have to endure it myself. Though, of course, unlike me, all they had done was take their pleasure.

*   *   *

THE NEXT MORNING, after a breakfast as casual and companionable as if we had been sharing the kitchen for months, Carol drove over to her mother's apartment in the East End to pick up Bettina, leaving me and Zack for the first time alone in the apartment. I was washing the dishes from breakfast and the night before; he sat at the table smoking a cigarette and reading the sports section of the morning paper. He seemed content. He knew that what happened last night was going to continue for a while, at least until something unforeseen, a factor outside the equation, stopped it. Instead of waiting for Carol and me to betray him in secret and then, after a period of deception, displace him, Zack had right away made me a player in his sexual relations with her. I hadn't seen that coming. He liked having me watch them make love. It put him in control of the sexual aspect of my relationship with Carol, which was the only part of it that had threatened him.

Zack looked up from the paper and smiled. "So, babe, do you think you'll go back to Liberia?"

"I have three sons and a husband there."

"That doesn't mean you'll go back, though."

"No. But I will, as soon as it's allowed."

"By whom?"

"The president, Samuel Doe." I gave him the short version of the events leading up to my departure from Liberia, including the reasons for Charles's flight and Woodrow's brief arrest. Mention of Charles brought a wide grin to Zack.

"So my man Charlie is very cool after all," he said.

"What do you mean?"

"It's true, he skimmed over a million bucks from some fund over there? Him and your husband?"

"Yes."

"That bastard. I thought he was lying to me. I thought it was all a con."

"What was?"

"He told me he's willing to turn a million bucks over to anyone who can spring him from prison and get him out of the country. He's a very political guy, you know, a guy with large freedom-fighter ideas and big ambitions."

"No, I don't know."

"Yeah, well, he is. A genuine comrade. I was telling him about our years in SDS and Weather, which was naturally of great interest to him. And at some point I told him how Weather had sprung Timothy Leary out of a California prison and got him all the way to Algeria, and Charlie goes nuts for it."

"Goes nuts for what?" I leaned against the sink and faced him. I wasn't sure where this was leading, but the conversation made me anxious. I was reasonably certain that Charles was smarter than Zack and probably more cynical, too.

"For having Weather break him out. Doing a Tim Leary. I tell him Weather doesn't even exist anymore, it's just a few people still more or less underground, like you, and that's it. Then he says he's got a million bucks U.S. stashed in an offshore bank that he'll turn over to anyone who successfully gets him out of prison and out of the country. He's got some kind of deal with Ghaddafi, but he's got to get to Libya, where there's all these training camps for African freedom fighters looking to liberate their homelands." Zack looked past me and out the kitchen window to the cloudless, morning sky. "You know, we can do this, babe. You and me."

"Forget it, Zack."

"Just hear me out, man. I can't do it alone, I'm an ex-con and still on parole and can't get inside to talk to Charles personally and privately. You know, to coordinate things. But you can, Miss Dawn Carrington. Or Musgrave. Or Sundiata. Whoever you are these days. I assume you still know how to cook up a phony passport that would get Charles out of the States."

I laughed. "Yeah. I can. But tell me why I should do this, Zack. It's high risk. And for what?"

"For the dough. But also because this guy is the real thing, babe. A Third-World freedom fighter. And he's got plans for your man, Doe. Big plans. And besides, seems to me you've got some interests back there in Liberia that would make you want to get Charles Taylor the hell out of an American prison and back in action in Africa. You've got to talk to this guy, man. He's been *through* it. He's the kind of revolutionary we were, only we were in the wrong place at the wrong time. This cat is *heavy*. If we can help him get back to Africa, then he'll be in the right place at the right time. Otherwise, I'm telling you, man, with Charles Taylor in jail here and Samuel Doe in power over there, you may never see your husband and kids again."

"You don't understand, Zack. Charles thinks Woodrow flipped him to save his own neck."

"Not true, babe! He told me Woodrow was cool. Actually, the way I read it, Charlie probably flipped Woodrow and feels bad about it. He didn't say that exactly, but I got the picture. The bad guy in this is Doe. He's the one your husband's got to worry about."

"I can't, Zack. I don't even know what I'm doing here. With you and Carol, I mean. In New Bedford."

"Just talk to Charles, man. Go out and visit him in Plymouth. It's real easy. The place is minimum security. All you'll need is an ID, which you've got, and a home address. You can use this address. Just talk to the guy. Then decide. Okay?"

I didn't answer. Then, after a few seconds, I heard myself say, "Okay. I'll talk to Charles. Once."

"That's all I'm asking."

"No, it's not, Zack," I said and grabbed his empty coffee cup and overflowing ashtray. "You're also asking me to wash your dirty dishes."

"Hey, no way, babe!" He took the cup and ashtray back. "Here, let me do that."

*   *   *

IT MAY SEEM STRANGE to you, but something about prisons, jails, cages comforts me. All my life I've run from confinement and tried to keep others, even animals, from being imprisoned. Yet whenever I come close to an actual place of confinement, whenever I'm physically in its proximity, something inside me clicks off and something else clicks on. Dread gets replaced by complacent, almost grateful acceptance. When with hundreds of other demonstrators I was arrested and jailed in Mississippi and Louisiana and later in Washington and Chicago and spent a night or two in a cell awaiting bail and quick release, while the others rattled their cages and chanted in continuing protest and sang "We Shall Overcome" and "Amazing Grace," I sat quietly cross-legged on the floor in a corner of the cell and gave myself over to the logic and clarity of imprisonment, as if, having relinquished my physical freedom, I was somehow free in a new and more satisfying way. In later years, driving past the high, razor-wired walls of state or federal prisons or catching a passing glimpse of the barred windows of a county jail, after the first flush of fear and anxiety passed, a certain restfulness came over me, and an ease that was almost a longing took my mind. In zoos I gazed into the cages and pens with an edge of envy. When I cared for the chimps all those years, partly it was so that I could vicariously join them in their iron-barred boxes. It still goes on. Today, at my farm in Keene Valley, even though I'm ideologically committed to providing my livestock and birds, all my animals, with as much free range as possible, I confess that I regularly have to argue away a desire to set Anthea and the girls to work building fences, pens, and cages for them. The freedom of the dogs to roam the woods, to abandon the farm any time they wish and race through the forest in pursuit of deer, threatens me. Something low in me wants to lock them in the barn, keep them on leashes tied to the porch railing, or just keep the beasts locked inside the house.

I know, of course, that it's what I want done to me, not to my poor dogs. Not to my sheep and ducks and geese and my hens. Not to my dreamers. And not to Charles Taylor. Though when I visited him that day in federal prison in Plymouth, I did think, as I parked my mother's car in the lot and saw the stately, brick, Victorian residence of the superintendent, the barracks that housed the security personnel, the neatly trimmed, sun-splashed lawns and spreading oak trees, and the sprawling complex of what looked like the dormitories of a small, slightly impoverished state college, and the high chain-link fence topped with strands of barbed wire that surrounded the prison, I did think, *Charles must be very happy here.*

He was not happy. He was furious. Even before he sat down at the table in the visiting room, he was talking full speed, practically spitting the words in that loud, high-dramatic mode that West African men use in response to perceived insult and impersonal injustice taken personally. "This a bad t'ing they done t' me, all of 'em! Doe, him an' the U.S. gov'ment them, an' your sweet li'l husband, Woodrow, too, especially him, Hannah!" He scraped his chair up to the table and glowered at me.

"Dawn," I said in a low voice. "Dawn Carrington." The room was a low-ceilinged hall half the size of a high school cafeteria with a dozen square tables placed so as to be in plain view of a guard, who monitored the room from behind a desk on an elevated stage at the front. A row of food- and drink-vending machines were posted along one wall. Seated at several of the other tables a half-dozen inmates with their lawyers, wives, and girlfriends engaged in quiet conversation, domestic problems mixed with legal and financial strategies.

"How's that?" Charles lifted his eyebrows in puzzlement.

"My name. It's Dawn. Here."

"Oh, okay." He smiled knowingly. "Okay by me. Who tol' you where I was? Who sent you here?" He looked healthy and strong, as if he'd been lifting weights. He wore a tight, white tee shirt and loose-fitting dungarees and sneakers. I'd never seen him without a tailored suit and tie or the occasional pressed and starched guayabera shirt. Charles was strikingly handsome back then. His smooth, round face shone with health and vigor and self-confidence, and he looked like a professional athlete. His hair was cut tight to his skull like a glistening black cap, and his skin was the color of polished old mahogany.

"Zack Procter said you might like to see me."

Charles smiled broadly. "Oh, yeah. Zack." He laughed. "Zack! When he tol' me all about you, I didn' believe the man at first. But then I put two an' two together an' come out four." He paused and examined my face as if looking for a scar. "You always been a mystery woman to me, y' know. Especially bein' married to Woodrow an' all. It always seem t' me you could be fryin' bigger fish, if you know what I mean. Your man Zack, he thinks he a big-time freedom fighter an' all that," he said and laughed. "What about you? You a freedom fighter too? *Dawn.* What your last name now?"

"Carrington. Actually, no, I'm not. Not anymore."

"What are you, then? *Who* are you?" He laughed again.

"Good question," I said and laughed with him. I liked Charles and for a long time had been sexually attracted to him. His large, open face and intelligent eyes, his easy smile, his immense physical energy pleased and relaxed me and, for the moment at least, distracted me from the confused jumble of my emotions. Grief, guilt, fear, and anger: different feelings aimed at different people. Grief over my father's death; guilt for having abandoned my children and now my mother, too; fear of being arrested and sent to jail; and anger at Woodrow and Samuel Doe for sending me out of the country. Yet, at the same time, in a brand new way, I was grateful to them all: to my father for having let me see him diminished and dying, a mere mortal at last; to my children and my mother, who I had to say were probably better off without me; to the FBI who, with their warrant for my arrest, had driven me back underground, returning me to Zack and Carol, giving me the chance now to conduct an operation that might redeem me for long years of political passivity and cowardice. I was grateful even to Woodrow and Samuel Doe for breaking me out of my Liberian cocoon. Charles distracted me from that muddle of emotions, he energized me, creating for me a context that for the first time in many years let me feel like a woman of principle. A woman capable of acting on her principles.

I said to him, "Zack says you have a plan."

"Of *course* I have a plan! I always have a plan. Ever since the day that monkey Doe stole my country an' now has stole everyt'ing in it I've had a plan. Why you t'ink that monkey an' his CIA friends put me in this cage? They scairt of me, y' know. An' for good reason. I got friends in high places all over Africa who would like nothin' better than to see that monkey's head on a stick an' the Americans gone home an' the people of Liberia rulin' themselves for the first time in history." On the day of Doe's coup, he said, he'd decided to overthrow him by any means necessary and give the country back to the people. *All* the people, he emphasized, not to the Americos and their white American overseers who had run it like their plantation for a hundred and fifty years. And not to the Russians and the Chinese either. He would establish a socialist democracy, he said, the kind of localized, tribe-based socialism that lay at the heart of every African tradition. Speaking rapidly and building steam as he went on, Charles declared that, if given a chance, this could be accomplished in Liberia, he was sure of it. Because of Liberia's peculiar history, it could happen. Even though he knew that similar attempts to create a democratic socialist "third way" had failed elsewhere; in Kenya and Ghana and Jamaica and Cuba and Chile, they had failed because the U.S. and other capitalist countries had sabotaged leftist governments and leaders even before they'd had a chance to consolidate their power. I had never heard Charles or any other Liberian talk this way before. The only people I had ever heard say these things were white American intellectuals, fantasists, neo-Marxist theoreticians whose idea of Africa was based on the Black Power movement of the sixties and seventies and Stokely Carmichael in a dashiki and Huey Newton in leather and black beret posing with his automatic rifle in a high-backed bamboo chair. It took a decade for us to admit it, but the dream of a truly democratic socialist revolution in America or anywhere else in the so-called developed world had died shortly after 1969, probably in Chicago at the end of a police club in a cloud of tear gas. In small, mostly agrarian countries like Cuba and Vietnam, and for a while in Jamaica, the dream had lingered on a few years longer, before it got appropriated by strongmen and their party chieftains or undermined by coups and assassinations engineered by the old colonial powers. But as Charles continued to describe his vision of a Liberia that was free and democratic and economically self-sufficient, a small country quietly going about its own business of providing its own food and shelter and health care and education, trading its agricultural products with the rest of the world for the technology and manufactured goods it would require and no more than what it required—no luxury goods, he said, no Mercedes limos or Rolex watches, no private jets, nothing imported that did not advance the people as a whole—I began to believe that it could be done. It could happen, and very possibly Charles Taylor was the man who could make it happen.

He asked me if I had some cash on me.

"What? What do you mean?"

He pointed to the row of vending machines lined up like sentries along the wall. "I want a Coke," he said.

We got up from the table and walked to the cold-drink machine. "You do it," he said and indicated a line painted on the floor a few feet out from the machine. "Can't cross that line. You can, but not me. Don't ask why," he said. "Prisons is all about rules."

I bought us each a Coke. We returned to the table and he resumed talking. The guard at the front of the room occasionally looked up from the magazine he was reading to survey his charges, but otherwise we were unobserved, ignored, unheard, as Charles unfolded to me his grand plan, and I took it in and with reckless ease and alacrity believed in its feasibility and, by the end of our meeting, its necessity.

Hearing this, you must think that I was unforgivably naive, that I had learned nothing about people or the world outside a university classroom, that I had been asleep for ten or more years, as if in my early twenties my mind and heart had been put into suspended animation. You must think that my slow, sheepish withdrawal from Weatherman and the Movement, where I had been positioned only at the margins anyhow, that my flight to Ghana with Zack, the years I lived in Liberia with Woodrow, bearing his children and raising them and taking care of Woodrow's home for him, *the years I spent being other people*, had displaced, erased, obliterated the girl I had been in my early twenties. The idealistic girl who was passionate about justice, especially for people of color, the girl who was convinced that in the fight for justice her life and sacrifice would count for something. The girl who, in the interests of justice and equality for all people everywhere, was perfectly willing to break as many laws as seemed necessary. The girl who found moral clarity in the phrase *by any means necessary*.

You would be right, of course, for that girl had indeed been replaced by another. But also wrong. Caught as I was that morning in a descending whirl of conflicting needs and desires, unable to grasp onto anything or anyone solid, with no plan of my own, no place or person or ideal to cleave to, suddenly there was Charles. And Charles seemed more solid and inescapably *present and accounted for* than anyone else in my life, more real to me than Zack or Carol or my mother, my children or my husband. And Charles had a plan, he wanted to break out of prison, make his way to Libya, raise a guerrilla army there and return to Liberia and overthrow Samuel Doe; and he had a place, Liberia, that I had come to know better than any other place; and he had a dream: to establish in his country and, as I was beginning to think of it, mine, a socialist democracy that could by its very existence renew the dream of my youth. At that moment, it was for me a way, perhaps the only way, not to descend into cynicism or despair. It was a way to avoid utter collapse, a total nervous breakdown, hospitalization, drugs, and (why not?) suicide. When I walked through the gates of the prison, passed the security checks, and entered the visitors' hall and sat down at my assigned table to wait for Charles to arrive from his cell, I had not known this, I could not even have imagined it, but as soon as he sat down opposite me and began to talk, I knew that, wherever he led, I would follow.

It would not be difficult for him to break out of here, he said. The inmates had considerable freedom of movement. He explained that the left field of the baseball field backed up to the section of the chain-link fence that was farthest from the watchtowers. The fence was ten feet high, with six strings of barbed wire at the top. Beyond the fence was a thicket of trees, and beyond the trees Route 1, the old coastal highway, which led south towards Cape Cod and north to Boston. Every Monday, Wednesday, and Friday morning, beginning at ten o'clock, there was a baseball game between the two main cell blocks, A and B. Charles was the regular left fielder for the A team. There were always plenty of arguments and now and then a bench-clearing brawl that ended the game and got the players and the inmates watching the game sent back to their cells.

Charles would arrange to have his team's pitcher deliberately, flagrantly hit a batter and initiate a brawl, and while everyone, including the watchtower guards, was distracted, he would scale the fence. It would be at least half a day before his absence would even be noticed, he said. "They don't check every cell till nine o'clock at night, an' by then I be long gone."

"Where will you go?"

"I'll be on my way to Libya," he said. "If you does your job right." He wanted me to wait in a car out on Route 1, parked at the side of the road, headed north. He wanted Zack with me. "White woman alone with a black man attracts attention. Nobody notices a white couple with their black friend in the back seat." I was to provide Charles with a U.S. passport, a thing Zack had told him I was skilled at forging, a small carry-on suitcase and change of clothes, five hundred dollars in cash, and a plane ticket to Cairo. Once Charles got to Cairo, he'd simply present himself at the Libyan embassy, and the next day he'd be in Tripoli, a guest of Mohamar Ghaddafi. At a coastal training camp east of Tripoli, half a thousand armed Liberian fighters were waiting for him to arrive and take command. "In twelve months' time, we'll be back in Liberia. In eighteen months, we'll be in Monrovia, an' Samuel Doe will be a dead man."

I said, "I understand why you want me to help you. But why bring Zack in? Any white man would do, right? Zack's only willing to do this for the money. Which he says you promised him. The money you and Woodrow stole from the people of Liberia," I added.

"Stole it from Samuel Doe, you mean. He the one stole it from the people. And now it's circulatin' back to 'em, since it's gonna help pay for weapons an' transport an' such, whatever Ghaddafi don't wanna give us. As for our friend Zack, the freedom fighter," he said, smiling, "I tol' him I'd turn the money over to him if he helped break me outa this place. But that was before you come around. So now, if I don't use him in the breakout and he finds out before it's done an' I'm outa the country, he'll be mad enough to screw us both up. Zack's a main-chance man, y' know? Very opportunistic."

"So you don't intend to give him the money? Even if he helps you escape?"

Charles looked at me as if I were stupid. "Hannah, please. That money belongs to the people of the Republic of Liberia."

"Dawn."

"Right."

I pushed my chair back and stood. "I'll come back as soon as I know when everything will be in place. The passport is the hard part, but it shouldn't take more than a few weeks at most."

"Can do it any Monday, Wednesday, or Friday morning. When the prisoners play the all-American game of baseball."

He stood and put his arms around me and kissed me on both cheeks. I liked his smell. It may have been the first time in my life that a man had smelled right to me. No, not the first time. My father always smelled right to me. No other man. Until Charles. And none since.

* * *

TWO WEEKS LATER on an overcast Friday morning, Zack and I drove out from New Bedford on Route 1 in my mother's car. I pulled over and parked on the gravel shoulder of the northbound lane. It was late August, unseasonably cool and threatening to rain, the trailing edge of a New England summer passing through. The leaves of the roadside oak and maple trees in the copse beyond had turned their dry undersides up, shifting the late summer morning light from pale green to silver. It was a little after nine.

Zack lighted a cigarette and looked nervously back and forth along the highway. Morning traffic was thin; Cape Cod weekenders from the Boston suburbs hadn't started their pilgrimage to the sea yet. On the floor of the backseat was a small nylon carry-on bag. Inside the bag was a tan, tropical-weight suit, size forty-two, and a dress shirt and tie from Filene's Basement. Inside the breast pocket of the suit jacket was an envelope with five one-hundred-dollar bills and a one-way Egypt Air ticket for the 1:05 p.m. flight from Boston to Cairo—everything drawn from my going-away gift from Samuel Doe, an irony that was not lost on me.

Also inside the jacket pocket was a U.S. passport in the name of Charles Davis. The photo was of a round-faced black man who resembled Charles only slightly, but close enough that a white man would think it was an exact likeness. This took place some fifteen years ago, remember, when it was safe to assume that Charles's face and passport photo would not be examined by a black man in uniform until he got to Egypt. Also, back then, before Americans started seeing anyone whose skin wasn't pink as a potential suicide bomber, security was light and the technology of surveillance was slow and unreliable.

Getting a passport for Charles had been a simple matter. I'd driven Carol to the Federal Building in Boston, where for the first time in her life she applied for her passport. Ten days later it arrived in the mail, and that evening I doctored it with Whiteout and a photo-booth head-shot of one of the cooks at The Pequod, a handsome black man named

Dick Stephens, divorced and lonely, Carol said. I'd pretended to have a crush on him, had spent a day in Provincetown with him, and had asked for a picture for my wallet, so I could memorialize the lovely day and had promised with lowered eyes future payment for the favor. We snapped four pictures each; I gave him mine, and he gave me his.

Carol had been uneasy with what Zack and I were up to, especially after I assumed ownership of her brand new passport, which represented to her in tangible form the power and authority of the United States government. But by then she and Zack were once again sleeping together without me, and I had assumed the leadership position among the three of us and had made my mission the only important one. Zack happily complied. He believed that when I completed my mission, he would assume ownership of at least half, possibly more, of Charles's million-dollar cache in some secret Caribbean bank account. According to Zack, well before we saw Charles off at Logan Airport, we'd stop at a Shawmut Bank branch in the suburbs, where Charles would arrange the transfer of the funds from his account to Zack's little checking account at the New Bedford branch.

I asked him how he could be sure Charles would be willing and able to do that.

"No way Charlie won't deliver the goods. Until he walks into the Libyan embassy in Cairo, we can always get him busted by the feds."

"Not without busting ourselves."

"We can drop a dime on him, and the feds'll greet him when he lands. He's connected to Ghaddafi and the fucking Libyans, man. He's an escapee from an American prison. The Egyptians'd give him up in a minute."

"Zack, you do that, and I swear I'll kill you."

He laughed. "Yeah. Sure. Suddenly you're Weather Underground again. A revolutionary. A true believer. C'mon, you just want to fuck the guy."

"Zack, I'm doing this to save my country."

"*Your* country? What, Liberia?"

"Yes. My country. And my sons' and my husband's country. And their lives, I'm doing this to save their lives," I said, and meant it, too. Believed it.

It had started to rain. Zack checked his watch. "Ten twenty-five. Shit. Where the fuck is he?" Southbound traffic was building into a steady stream. Inevitably, a trooper cruising for speeders would spot us and pull in behind the Toyota, ask us for IDs, and run the plates. My driver's license, like my passport, was phony and long expired anyhow, and I was driving a car registered in my mother's name.

"Maybe he fucked up getting over the fence," Zack said. "I know that fence, and it's not all that easy to climb. Maybe we oughta book."

"No. We'll wait."

"How long? Some cop comes along, we're in deep shit."

"I won't abandon him, Zack."

"Yeah. Sure. C'mon, don't go all high church on me. You're in this for the money as much as I am," he said.

"No. For maybe the first time in fifteen years, I'm acting on principle."

"Those days, when it made some kind of sense to act on principle, are long gone, babe. Now the only people acting on principle are right-wing born-again Christians, and I'm not so sure about them. These are the eighties, babe."

"Charles Taylor is acting on principle."

"Yeah, right," he said and turned to roll down the window and toss his cigarette, and there was Charles, standing in the rain beside the car, looking in at us with a broad smile on his wet face.

"Can you give a man a lift?" he asked and pulled open the rear door and got in.

DRIVING NORTH TOWARDS Boston we said little to one another. Charles exchanged his prison garb for the clothes I'd brought, and examined the ticket and cash and his new passport.

"Who's this a picture of? This black man s'posed to look like *me*? Hell, I'm much prettier than this guy."

"It's the best I could do," I said.

We were outside Natick, barely a half-hour from the airport. I felt strangely calm and clearheaded, as if I were merely dropping a friend off and didn't have to go much out of my way to do it. Twice we passed a police car, and I had to remind myself to keep to the speed limit, for God's sake, I'm helping a man break out of a federal prison, I'm a fugitive myself with a forged passport and driver's license, my partner in crime seated next to me is a parolee, and if we're stopped and caught, he'll cut a deal in a minute, he'll say anything, and will betray both me and Charles to keep from going back to prison.

Without turning, Zack said, "Charlie, maybe we should talk about our little agreement."

"Eh? How's that?"

"Well, as you no doubt recall, there was to be a certain payment for the services. You no doubt recall our earlier conversations on the subject. And now here we are, man. Almost home."

In the rearview mirror I watched Charles nod and look out at the passing suburbs and smile as if to himself. He was silent for several long minutes.

Zack said, "Well? What about it? We gonna transfer those funds from your account in Switzerland or the Caymans or wherever the hell they are over to my account in New Bedford or . . ."

"Or what?"

"Or not. Because if not, then we've got a problem."

"Really? Is that true, Hannah? I mean 'Dawn,' of course. Is that true? If I don't pass Zack the money that Samuel Doe say I stole wit' your husband, then we have a problem, you an' me?"

"No," I said. "This is strictly between you and Zack."

"Good girl," he said. "You a good girl. You a true Liberian patriot. But my friend Zack here, I dunno, man. Seems like he in this for the money. An' once I give him the way to get it into his pocket, him don't need me for nothin' no more an' can fuck up my travel plans real easy, if he want to. I think I'll wait till I get me a boarding pass an' they call my row to board the plane, before I give you what you want. You understand, Zack."

"Yeah. I understand."

Charles asked for a piece of paper and a pen. My mother's list-making pad and ballpoint pen were clipped to a plastic holder stuck to the dashboard, and I handed him both. Charles wrote for a few seconds, tore off the top piece of notepaper, and returned the pen and pad. He folded the notepaper once and put it into his shirt pocket.

"This here," he said and patted his pocket, "is a telephone number and a man's name. When I board my plane for Cairo, I'll give this paper to you. Then all you got to do is say your name to the person who answers and tell him the man whose name I wrote down gave you permission to arrange for the transfer of Charles Taylor's funds. This telephone is in Washington, D.C. It's a secret contact number only I know about, and the name on the paper is a name only I use. My code name. No one else knows both these things. Whoever answers at that particular telephone number and hears that particular name, he'll know the instructions are comin' straight from me. He'll know to give you what you want, no matter what it is, no questions asked."

"Why can't we stop at a pay phone and make that call now?"

"Not enough time, Zack. Don't want to miss my flight. Only one a day, y'know."

"Sounds a little funny to me," Zack said. "Can I trust you?"

"'Course you can trust me, man. It's what I owe you."

We reached the airport at 11:45. I parked the car in the first empty space I saw, which put us on the third level of the parking garage, and the three of us raced down the stairs and into the international terminal, Charles loping along ahead of us as if he'd made this run many times before. When we arrived at the gate for Egypt Air, they had already begun the boarding procedure. A knot of first-class passengers, men in business suits with briefcases, an old lady in a wheelchair, and two couples with small children were already passing into the access way. Charles handed his ticket and passport across the counter to the young woman attendant, who hurriedly punched out his boarding pass and went back to calling out the rows. Charles turned around and faced me and Zack.

"Well, my fellow freedom fighters, we at a parting of the ways." He reached for me and kissed me firmly on the lips, more a promise than a thank you. He released me slowly, then stepped away in the direction of the passengers lined up to board.

"Wait a minute!" Zack said sharply. "That little piece of paper in your pocket is mine, I believe."

"Oh, sure, almost forgot," Charles said and handed the paper over. "All the excitement of departure, I guess." He smiled again, then quickly moved into line and walked through the gate and disappeared from sight.

Zack stared down at the piece of notepaper.

"Is it what you wanted?" I asked.

"I hope the fuck it is. It'd better be."

"What'll you do if it isn't? What if the money never left Monrovia? It's possible Samuel Doe has it by now, you know. It's even possible the U.S. government has it."

"Charlie knows I can still get to him, man. He won't fuck me over. I know people, man. *African* people."

"Oh, Zack." I started walking back towards the main terminal. Quickly Zack caught up and touched my elbow and asked if he could have five dollars. I gave it to him, and he crossed to a newsstand and made change while I waited.

He stopped at the bank of phones just inside the main terminal. I moved next to him and stood there while he fumbled with the quarters and dialed. I glanced over my shoulder and saw a uniformed cop watching us. On a bench next to him two men with briefcases read newspapers as if they wanted to be seen reading newspapers. A maintenance man with a dustbin and push broom came to a meaningless stop twenty feet away and looked straight at me.

"Zack, I'll be outside," I said and walked with careful nonchalance through the door into the parking garage. No one appeared to follow me. The elevator crawled to the third level, and as soon as I was free of it, I ran for the car. I jumped in and started the motor and raced, tires squealing, for the exit, down the ramp to the second level—still no one following in the rearview mirror—and on down to the first level, and there was Zack crossing into the garage from the terminal, looking for me. He saw the car and ran towards it, his face angrily bunched, and I jammed on the brakes and stopped. He got in and slammed the door hard, and I hit the gas and exited the garage, stopping barely long enough to pay the parking fee, then drove full bore towards the tunnel under the bay and downtown Boston beyond.

Zack said, "I thought you'd pulled out on me, man. Why the hell would you want to do that?"

"I was just bringing the car down to meet you."

"Oh," he said, glum and downcast. He still held the piece of paper in his lap and studied it as if it carried a message difficult to read.

"Well? What happened?" I glanced at him. He looked like a child ready to cry putting on a big man's face to hide it.

"You're right about me," he said.

"How?"

"I'm an asshole," he said. "I fucking hate myself." He turned away from me and toward the window so I couldn't see his face.

"Was it a working number?"

"Oh, yeah."

"And . . . ?"

"It was the number of the Liberian embassy in Washington, for Christ's sake."

"Oh, dear," I said, not very surprised. "So you just hung up?"

"No, I didn't," he said. "I didn't just hang up. I should have. But I followed instructions. I told the guy, who had this fucking British accent, I told him my name and gave him the name of the guy that Charles wrote down. I said this guy was supposed to transfer the money being held for Charles Taylor into an account that I had the number for."

"What did he say?"

"Nothing at first. Then he asked my name again, and I told him. And then he laughed like hell. And hung up."

We were silent for a few seconds. It had stopped raining, and the clouds were breaking up, and patches of blue sky behind them skidded south ahead of us. I asked Zack, "What was the name of the man who was supposed to do this, transfer the money into your account?"

"Sam Clement," he said. "Who the fuck's Sam Clement? You ever heard of him?"

"No," I said. "I never heard of him."

WHEN ZACK DECIDED to move out of the apartment we weren't disappointed. His presence had become confusing and burdensome to Carol, who preferred my authority to his, although I don't think it mattered to her which of us she slept with. In a strange way, Carol was never less present and accounted for than in bed; she was merely accommodating there, blandly accepting other people's needs as if they were her own. Carol's mentality was that of a permanent servant, ingrown and generations old, and what she liked and needed most, what she understood best in the world and in all her personal relationships, was authority. My apparently principled control of Charles's breakout and flight and Zack's humiliation by Charles's million-dollar promissory note had deflated Zack's ego and made his male bluster sufficiently defensive and obnoxious to put me in charge of our little family.

We live in packs as much as dogs or wolves, it sometimes seems, and like them need to be clear at all times about who's the alpha dog. It's a practical matter. For Carol, as long as I was in the pack, Zack's ongoing presence only confused the question of authority. He didn't announce his departure or even discuss it with us and didn't leave a note behind to explain or say goodbye. Simply, one morning, a week after Charles's breakout, Zack and his few possessions and clothes were gone.

"I guess he felt crowded here," Carol said and shrugged. That same night I moved from the living room sofa to Carol's bedroom, and the next morning at breakfast, Bettina said to me, "I like it better now, with you and Mommy together and him gone." Bettina had learned early, practically from infancy, to be scared of men. It had always been men who took her mother from her, stuck her with her aunt or her grandmother while her mother behind closed doors did mysterious, private business with the men. Or if, like Zack, the men stuck around, they talked too much and treated her as if she were an inconvenience. They were too large, had rough cheeks and hands, loud voices, and were often drunk or high on drugs. Even Zack, who to his credit did try on occasion to pay attention to Bettina, because she was diffident as a cat and withdrawn around him, grew quickly bored and turned his attention elsewhere. With me she was only slightly less suspicious and distant, but I warmed to it; I knew it was merely a self-protective affect that probably resembled mine. Our innate shyness had a hostile edge to it, and she seemed to recognize and like the similarity as much as I, and soon we were like a favorite aunt and favored niece. I was still living off the money Samuel Doe had slipped me for leaving children, husband, and home with minimal fuss, so I didn't need a job yet and was usually at the apartment when Bettina came home from school and took care of her nights when Carol was at The Pequod.

In the mornings before leaving for school, Bettina sat silently at the table and ate her Cheerios, while I, also silent, braided her long, pale hair into pigtails like mine, and Carol slept in. At night, before Bettina went to bed, I brushed her hair out again. Grooming. Before long, my days and nights were organized around Bettina's, which helped me avoid thinking about what I was doing living here with this child and her mother and what I would do when my money ran out. It helped me avoid thinking about Liberia and Charles's promise to give the country back to its people and what that might mean to Woodrow and our sons and to me, which meant that I didn't have to ask myself if the promise Charles had made to me was as empty as the promise he'd made to poor, gullible Zack. And it helped me avoid thinking about the children I had left behind in Monrovia, my three African sons and their father, and the life I had, after a fashion, led there. Then one Friday late in September, Carol borrowed my car—my mother's car—and she and Bettina and Carol's mother drove to the White Mountains of New Hampshire to view the technicolor fall foliage, an annual rite for them, apparently, but for me little more than an occasion for making intelligence-deprived declarations about the beauty of nature. Not my cup of tea. I declined the invitation to join them, and for the first time since my return to America was alone for two whole days and nights. In the gray silence of the empty apartment—once I had vacuumed and dusted every room, finished the laundry, mopped the kitchen floors, and scrubbed the refrigerator down, once I was unable to come up with anything else to do that was in the slightest way necessary or merely useful to me or anyone else—my thoughts turned helplessly to my home in Monrovia. I sat down at the kitchen table with Bettina's school tablet in front of me, opened it, and began a letter to my husband.

> Dear Woodrow,
>
> It feels strange to be writing to you like this, as if we're on different planets. In spite of everything, however, you are still my husband and I'm still the mother of our three sons. Yet from this distance and for a variety of reasons which I'll not trouble you with, I feel like an unnatural wife and mother and have no idea of how you and the boys feel towards me. Do you hate me? Are you glad that I am so far from you? I sometimes think that my absence has freed you to live a more natural life, a normal life, something that my presence made nearly impossible for you.

I wondered if now I was living a more natural life, too, if this was *my* normal life, or if I even had one. What were other women like me, my social peers and contemporaries, doing now? I wondered. They were white, American baby boomers born to privilege and trained to sustain that privilege and pass it on to their children. They'd had their taste of political activism in the sixties, "experimented" with drugs and sex, and after a year or two of graduate school had chosen mates with the same degree of ease and confidence with which, thanks to the women's liberation movement, they'd slid into professions. By now they'd had two-point-three babies, at least one short-lived love affair, and seen a shrink once a week for a year or two to deal with guilt, marital strife, and early-onset depression generated by the failure of the women's liberation movement to make them feel liberated. Most of them had resolved the conflict between child-rearing and career by temporarily shelving the career, and half of them had gone through a divorce, or would as soon as the children became teenagers and went off to boarding school. They were worried about their weight and their husbands' eye for younger women. They were becoming their mothers. But what about me? What had I done all those years? Who was I becoming?

> *I don't want to burden you with my feelings. They haven't been of much use or interest to you in the past and are probably even less so now. I'm writing so that you and the boys (if you choose to relay this information to them) will know where I am and that I still love you. Though it has been very painful for me to have been exiled like this, I do not blame you for it. I know that you (and I) had no choice in the matter. I also know that someday this separation will be over and we will be together as a family again. Perhaps you have worried about me since I left Monrovia three months ago. Perhaps you haven't. I have no way of knowing. Surely the boys have wondered how and where I was? I think of them all the time, especially at night when I am alone, and I can hardly keep from crying. I'm living with an old friend who has taken me in and I'll soon be working as a volunteer at the school that my friend's daughter attends. I'll be the school librarian and will be with children all day long. My friend's daughter is a lovely child and we've grown close, but it only makes me miss my own children all the more. Please tell me how they are faring without me. Naturally I hope that they are doing so well and are so happy that they barely notice my absence. At the same time I want to think that they miss me as much as I miss them.*

It wasn't true that I could hardly keep from crying at night. Nights, after I put Bettina to bed, I sat up reading paperbacks of nineteenth-century English novels—Dickens, mostly—waiting for Carol to come home from work. She got back to the apartment shortly before ten, and on Fridays and weekends came in around midnight. Our routine varied little. We'd smoke a joint together, watch a half-hour of television, and go to bed, and once a week or so, seduced more by the pot than each other's bodies, we'd make slow, languorous love to one another. It was more a form of mutual masturbation than actual love-making, and afterwards I slept deeply and without dreams.

> There is some sad news—sad to me, at least. Within days of my return to the States, my father passed away. I know you always thought of me as something of an orphan, a woman without a family, but I'm not. I loved my father very much, although from afar, and always hoped that you and the boys and my parents would come to know one another. Now that's impossible—at least with regard to my father. Perhaps someday you will know my mother, however, even though I myself find her very difficult to be with, for reasons I'm sure you would never understand or respect. But that's all right. I've grown used to the deep differences between you and me and accept them and do not mind them. I hope you can feel the same way.

A week earlier, I'd suddenly found myself worrying about my mother's health and telephoned her in Emerson. Relieved when she didn't pick up, I left a message on her answering machine "It's Hannah. I'm staying with friends. If you need to reach me in an emergency, call The Pequod Restaurant in New Bedford and ask for Carol. She'll know how to reach me. But call only if it's an emergency. And don't worry about your car. I'll return it as soon as I have one of my own. 'Bye."

That night I said to Carol, "If anyone ever calls you at work and wants to send a message to someone named Hannah, it's okay. That's me."

"Who is?"

"Hannah. It's not really me. It's what my mother calls me."

"Don, that's weird."

"It's just a family nickname."

"No, weird that you never talk about her."

"Who?"

"Your mother."

"I know."

"That's weird, Don."

"I know."

You can write to me (if you wish to) at this address as I expect to be here until I'm able to return to Monrovia without endangering you or the boys in any way. From this distance it's hard for me to believe that you are in danger, yet I know it's true. There is no news here of Liberia, and I have no Liberian contacts except through the embassy in Washington and the consulate in New York, and I'm afraid to get in touch with anyone there, for reasons I'm sure you understand all too well. I don't know how private this letter is, so there are certain personal matters I won't go into here, for obvious reasons. We are still husband and wife, after all, and I still have many wifely thoughts that are meant for your eyes and ears only. You were never much for writing letters, unless on official ministry business, but I do hope you'll write back to me and tell me as much as you can of your and the boys' circumstances. I'll understand if you have to be circumspect. These days one can't be too careful. But surely the boys can write to me? And I to them? We haven't been forbidden that, have we? Well, I'll know the answer to that if this letter goes unanswered by you and I do not hear from my sons. I don't know if I could bear that, Woodrow. But I don't know what I can do about it. My life as a wife and mother is not in my hands anymore. Perhaps yours, as a husband, is not in your hands anymore either. I don't mean to sound overly dramatic, but I need you to tell me what I am to do with my life. I have very few options, and they are somewhat extreme. What I want is to come home

to Monrovia (yes, it is my home, I have no other). I want to come home
to my husband and my three sons.

Love,

Your Hannah

My options *were* extreme. And few. I thought of following Charles to Libya and imagined myself in fatigues and a black beret and an M-16, a latter-day Patty Hearst without the Stockholm syndrome to cloud my mind and divide my heart. A guerrilla fighter. A liberator with a nom de guerre, Nonnie, after the famous female chieftain who led the escaped Jamaican slaves in the Maroon wars. And when Charles's war of liberation was won, I would have a role in the new revolutionary government and would be able to protect my husband from the victors' execution squads and would be reunited with my Liberian sons. And then I thought of moving back in with my mother in Emerson and taking care of her in her old age, becoming one of those faithful maiden daughters who, forsaking marriage and children, dedicates her life to the care and feeding of an aged, demanding parent. And to the end of her days my mother would be truly grateful to me, making my mind and heart clear and undivided, and when she died, I would inherit the house on Maple Street and my father's fortune, which I would use to start a home for abused children from the inner city. And I thought of staying in New Bedford with Carol and Bettina until . . . until Carol fell in love with a man, as I knew she would, and I would no longer be a suitable housemate or fantasy aunt for her daughter and would have to move on, to where I did not know. I was forty years old and had nowhere forward I could go and no permanent place to stay. All I could do was go back. Back to Africa.

Hannah darling,

I read your letter with great pleasure and have conveyed your words
of motherly love to the boys. It pleased them very much. They are fine and
in good health. Jeannine has taken excellent care of them.

There is little news to report. Things here are very much the same as when you left, politically and otherwise. I have spoken about your situation to our American friend, who seems to have some influence with the president. He tells me that he can arrange a meeting between the president and the U.S. ambassador, Mr. Wycliffe, on the matter of your return. Our friend tells me that in exchange for certain favors, which he did not divulge, it may soon be possible for us to be a reunited family. This would be wonderful for all.

I am sorry to learn of your father's passing. I too regret that I never met him, but I'm sure he was a fine gentleman and doctor of medicine. Please give my condolences to your mother.

I have enclosed several Polaroid pictures of the boys. Also, Jeannine has asked me to include herein letters from the boys to you that I think you will find quite charming indeed. Jeannine has been learning to read and write in a class taught in town by one of the Peace Corps volunteers. She tells me that she will write to you herself when she has graduated from her class. She is very proud of her newly acquired skills but is not yet ready to expose them to you, whom she greatly admires.

When I first arrived in Monrovia and through Woodrow came to know Sam Clement, I carefully avoided him. The cultural attaché at the American embassy, he was present at any official gathering that was deemed insufficiently high level for the U.S. ambassador to attend in person, but I was almost always able to slip out of the receiving line and head for the ladies' room before he got close enough to shake the hands of the minister of health and his American wife. Then for a few years he was no longer there. Woodrow mentioned that he'd heard Sam had gone to work in Zimbabwe for the new national telephone company that the Americans were setting up. In 1980, after Samuel Doe and his cohort butchered President Tolbert and his cabinet and took over the government, Sam returned to Monrovia, once again as the cultural attaché. By this time I had become accepted in what passed for high society in Monrovia and had grown more secure in my identity as the white, foreign-born wife of the minister of health and no longer avoided Sam. He became Woodrow's and my American friend. He loaned me books and newspapers and magazines from the embassy library. He once drank too much gin at a dinner party at our house and followed me onto the terrace and tried to kiss me, and when I gently declined, he apologized profusely and seemed genuinely embarrassed and sorry. I wasn't at all offended. Mostly surprised. I had thought he was homosexual.

> *I will write to you again as soon as there is news. If you can, would you please send a first-quality video camera and VCR to me? They are very expensive here and only a few poor brands are available. Sony is the best. You should have it shipped to me at the ministry. Thanks in advance.*
>
> > *Your loving husband,*
> > *Woodrow Sundiata*

The brief letters from the boys were in pencil on lined tablet paper a lot like the paper I had torn from Bettina's tablet for my letter to Woodrow. I quickly read the letters and put them into my backpack and then looked at the four Polaroid photos, splotchy and already fading, as if the Liberian heat and humidity had partially spoiled the film. I merely glanced at them—one photo was of Dillon, Paul, and Willy standing together on the lawn stiffly at attention, unsmiling in their Sunday school suits, with the huge, red bougainvillea behind them; the other three were of each boy in the same spot alone. I put them into my backpack with the letters. Which is how I still have them in my possession today.

> *Dear Mammi,*
> *School is very fun. My new teacher is Mrs. Mbeko and she is very fat, but I like her. She makes jokes all the time. Pappi bought two new dogs. They are named Bruno and Muhammad Ali. They are mastiffs and are both brothers, but not twins like Willy and Paulie. Bruno is bigger than Muhammad Ali. He weighs 125 lbs. Pappi won't let us play with*

them yet because they are to be watchdogs and should not become friends with anyone, even the people they are watching. Jeannine is the one who feeds them. Bruno killed a cobra in the garden. I miss you. I hope you will come home soon. Love,

Dillon

Jeannine. Always Jeannine. My shadow self. It was probably she who stood in front of the boys with the camera and snapped the pictures. It was probably she who urged them to write to their Mammi, then gave the letters and pictures to Woodrow one evening and suggested that he send them to me. She was better at being me than I was.

Dear Mammi,

How are you? I am fine. We went to the beach. School is nice now. It rained every day so far. Our new dog Bruno ate a spitting cobra. It was six feet long. Love,

Paulie

Spitting cobras lurk in every flower garden. They aim their poison at the eyes of man or beast and can hit their target from ten feet away. A large, courageous watchdog can kill it, but may die itself as a result. Everything that lives in Liberia and that you kill will eventually kill you for it. Something rots beneath the soil and taints the air above it.

Dear Mammi,

How are you? We miss you a lot. What is America like? Pappi showed on a map where you live now. Is it nice there? I hope it's not too cold! I have to go now. Goodbye! Love,

Willy

The leaves had fallen to the ground, and autumn was becoming winter. I had forgotten how unjust and autocratic the approach of a northern winter seems. I said to Bettina that the bare branches of the trees in the small park that she and I crossed every day on the walk to and from her school looked like the scrawny arms of beggars.

"Yeah, right," Bettina said.

"They do. And they're asking the sky for the return of light and warmth. They're begging for the simple kindness of the sun. But it's abandoned them for the tropics."

She shook her head and said, "You are such a bummer, Don. You sound like winter is something to feel good about. But what you're *really* saying is a total bring-down."

"Yeah, right."

Dear Woodrow,

Your letter and the photos and the letters from the boys arrived today. Thank you for doing that. They made me very happy and also very sad, as I'm sure you can understand. I've put the photos in little frames and keep them on my dresser where they are the first thing I see in the morning and the last thing I see at night.

I am glad to hear that our American friend is trying to be of help. I do want badly to come home and will do anything that President Doe requires of me. At the same time I don't want to do anything that puts you or the boys in danger, even if it means we must continue to live apart like this.

Thank you for your kind words about my father. I am sure that, had you two met, you would have been friends. You are alike in many ways and would have understood one another. I have shipped a Sony VCR and video camera to you at the ministry. I hope you'll use the camera to make videos of the boys, so that someday when I return I can watch them. Perhaps you could make videos and send them to me now, and I could watch them here. You could set the camera in front of the boys and let them talk to me directly, right into the camera. They might like that better than writing letters to me. Woodrow, I want you to know that if the president will allow me to return to my family, I will be his loyal supporter and will do everything in my power to help him and the people of Liberia. Please convey these exact words to him. It can't hurt to do that, and it might help. Please give my love to the boys and my thanks to Jeannine for taking such

*good care of them in my absence. I am writing to them myself and will
mail the letters to them separately so they'll each have the pleasure of opening their own mail sent all the way from the United States. (And what's
this about the new dog killing a cobra in the garden?)*

> *Your loving wife,*
> *Hannah*

I tried several times to write an answer to Dillon, Paul, and Willy,
but could not do it. I couldn't locate the right voice, a voice as natural
and easy as theirs. In correspondence as much as conversation, one
takes on the tone of one's correspondent. That's how it has always been
for me, anyhow, and is probably why I am reluctant to open a conversation. He who writes or speaks first gets to set the tone. And my sons
had written first. I kept putting off the moment when I would finally
have to write back to them, until days became weeks and it was almost
too late to answer without having a plausible excuse for the delay. And
then came the letter from Woodrow.

My dear wife,

*I received your most recent letter yesterday and last night conveyed to
President Doe your assurances stated therein. To my amazement he
expressed a sincere desire to have you return to Liberia. He also
apologized for what he said must have been a misunderstanding on our
part. He claims never to have wished for you to be separated from your
husband and children. He is a man who often changes his mind and
policy, but I believe he is sincere in this matter and does indeed want to
welcome you back, as he said, "into the official family of Liberia." No
doubt the American ambassador, Mr. Wycliffe, was helpful in changing
the president's mind.*

*It may be too late by the time you receive this letter, but if possible,
could you be home for Christmas? It would be very nice for all of us if you
could. It would especially please the boys.*

By the way, this morning I stopped by the American embassy and spoke with our friend there. I wanted to confirm that your return would in no way trouble the U.S. authorities. He assured me that you are free to travel anywhere in the world and that he very much looked forward to seeing you here again.

Your loving husband,
Woodrow Sundiata

It was the last letter that I would ever receive from him, although I did not suspect it at the time, of course. I read it and immediately packed my clothes into my backpack and began to compose what I would say to Bettina when she got home from soccer practice and noticed my pack by the door and asked where I was going, and what I would tell Carol that night when she got home from work. I would tell them both the same thing, the essential truth, that I was leaving them in order to join my family and to prepare for the liberation of my country from a cruel dictator. It would make no sense to either of them, but they both would accept it as natural and inevitable. I had come into their lives like a pale ghost, and now I was leaving like one.

IV

I FLEW FROM BOSTON to New York in an early January snowstorm that delayed the flight three hours, then sat on the runway at JFK for another three hours before taking off, and landed in Robertsfield the next morning in bright sunshine with a sparkling blue sky above and palm-lined, white sandy beaches below. As the wheels touched down, the passengers, most of them Liberians returning from the States, suddenly bloomed with applause, and I happily joined in. We were safely home again. We'd come to where we knew we belonged.

Woodrow and the boys and Jeannine and Satterthwaite were gathered together to greet me at the terminal—my African family, which from that moment and for the coming years I regarded as my only family. My true family. My best family. For all its tensions, disconnections, divisions, and conflicts of interest, this little tribe was my claque and cohort. I hadn't realized it at the time, but on the day I helped break Charles out of prison, I had cast my lot, not just with him, but with them as well. And I could do this, of course, nowhere but at my home in Monrovia. So when Samuel Doe, for reasons then unknown to me, offered me the chance to return to Liberia, I had no choice but to accept it.

I'd made up my mind long before the plane landed at Robertsfield, however, that things would not be the same as they had been. A consequence of my having tied my fate to my little household's fate was that I now felt empowered to make demands and take on responsibilities that I had never made or taken before. And I planned to set a few wrong things right very quickly.

After the hugs and kisses inside the sweltering, crowded terminal, we piled into the Mercedes, set the air conditioner to blowing, and headed for Monrovia, Satterthwaite driving and Jeannine beside him in front, Woodrow, the boys, and me crowded into the back. We rode in a pleasant, well-behaved silence that I found both amusing and peculiar, as if everyone were waiting for me to do exactly what I fully intended to do—take charge. As if, for reasons both known to me and unknown, they each individually felt guilty, and in the months of my exile, to the degree that they had been collectively weakened by guilt, I had been strengthened.

I was not imperious, merely firm and clear. "Satterthwaite," I said to him. "I'll no longer need you to drive me and the boys. I'll be doing my own driving from now on," I announced. "And if for some reason I need someone else to drive the car, I'll arrange it through the ministry or hire someone from town myself."

"Yes, m'am," Satterthwaite said and did not turn or even glance at me in the rearview mirror.

Woodrow noisily cleared his throat. "Are you sure, Hannah darling? Satterthwaite's quite—"

"I'm sure," I said, cutting him off. "I'm an excellent driver. Requisition another car for your own use, if you want. I'll keep this one strictly for household needs. I'll need it all day every day, anyhow. For taking the boys to school and picking them up and for shopping. And for my work," I added.

"Your work?"

"Yes. And, Jeannine, I won't be needing you to help me with the boys. I'll look after their meals myself. It's quite enough if you'll just do the housekeeping. Especially since you should be going to school now yourself. I'll pay you an hourly wage and will pay all your school expenses. But I'll have to ask you to find another place to live."

"'Nother place to live?" she asked, incredulous.

"I'll need your room for my office. I'm sure Woodrow can find you a place to live in town."

Woodrow quietly said, "Really, Hannah."

"And, boys, from now on you won't have Jeannine or me following you around, picking up your clothes and cleaning up your messes and treating you like little princes anymore. You are little princes, of course, but you're going to learn how to be good men, too, and the first step is learning not to expect women to do all your housework for you. That includes cooking and washing dishes and making your own beds and, as soon as you're able, doing your own laundry."

Woodrow said, "Men don't do laundry, Hannah."

"In my house, Woodrow, everyone washes his own clothes. Even you."

"Missus," Jeannine said. She did not turn around. "Can't I stay inside the garden house? I can put a cot in wit' the yardman's t'ings."

"No, you can't. I'm sorry, but I'm no longer going to tolerate what went on before," I said and looked straight at Woodrow, who turned away and stared out the window at the passing scenery.

"Mammi," Dillon said, "is this the way American boys do? Do they have to wash their own clothes and cook and stuff?" In the six months I'd been away, Dillon had added half a foot in height and fifteen pounds of muscle. The twins, too, had outgrown their little boys' bodies.

"Not always. But when they don't, who do you think does it for them?"

"Their mammies."

"Right. But lots of American mammies have jobs they go to every day. So, who does it then?"

"The boys do, I guess."

"Right."

"Well, I think it's okay then. We can be like American boys. So, are you going to have a job, too? Like American mammies?"

"Yes, I am."

Willie said, "Me and Paulie think it's okay, too. We want to be like American boys."

Woodrow said, "You're going to have a *job?*"

Ignoring him, I said to my sons, "You're going to have to be even better than American boys. They grow up to be American men. But you're going to grow up to be Liberian men, the kind of men this country will be proud of. And I'm going to help you."

"Thanks, Mammi," Dillon said, and the twins said it, too. "Thanks, Mammi."

Still gazing out the window, Woodrow in a morose, resigned tone said, "Tell me about this job. And why you want Jeannine's room for an office. There's no need for the wife of a minister in the government to work outside, you know. It will make me look bad, Hannah."

"Everyone in this country who can should go to work. And I can, so I will, yes."

"Will you work for an American company? Or at the embassy?" he asked hopefully.

"I've got plans. I'm going to do something that's never been done in this country before."

"And what is that?"

"I'm going to build a sanctuary for chimpanzees. For the chimpanzees that have been abandoned by the lab, if any of them is still alive. And I'm going to buy up and save as many chimps as I can find, those pets on chains and in cages that are sold in the markets and in back alleys. And the chimps that people try to smuggle out of the country to be sold as pets or used in experiments in Europe and America. I'm going to restore them to health and sanity, if I can, and eventually I'll return them to the jungle, where they belong."

Woodrow looked at me, as if checking to be sure I was the same woman who had left his home barely six months ago."That's . . . insane," he declared,

"Can we help with the chimpanzees, Mammi?" Dillon asked.

"Yes," I said. "And so can you, Woodrow."

"How? No one cares about dumb animals. Not even the lab. That whole monkey program is dead. Been dead for years."

"I want you to tell President Doe that I have an offer to make that he'll not be able to refuse."

"Why?"

"Because I do."

"Indeed," he said.

And then I saw that we had arrived at Duport Road, home, with the two huge, drooling mastiffs behind the gate. They were staring cold eyed at a white man in a rumpled white suit and Panama hat who stood in the street a safe distance from the gate, Sam Clement. When the dogs saw the car, they backed off and wagged their thick tails and smiled as Satterthwaite got out and unlocked and swung open the gate. He patted the dogs on their bony heads and told Sam to come on into the yard, then returned to the car and drove it up the driveway. Sam waved at us as we passed him, and by the time we arrived at the door, he was standing at the top of the steps to greet us.

WHEN I FIRST cared for the dreamers, back when the lab was still functioning, I saw them as creatures less evolved than we, as weaker, as deprived of essential and powerful abilities to reason and communicate. Later, when I knew them better, and they knew me, I saw, not that the dreamers in amazing ways closely resembled humans, but that we in equally amazing ways closely resembled them. As a result, I revised those early assumptions and came to believe that I could empathize with the dreamers.

But then, during the months that I was away from my little colony of apes, I began to see the built-in limitations of empathy. Perhaps because of my relationship with Carol and the rivalry with Zack, and because I am a woman, I came for the first time to believe that even the best-intentioned man, one who truly does empathize with women, is nonetheless incapable of knowing how the relations between men and women *feel* to a woman. Mainly, he is incapable of knowing how he is perceived by her. And therefore she, despite her likeness to him, remains opaque to him, unknowable.

This doesn't mean that conflict between them is inevitable or inescapable. But there are useful parallels in the relations between men and women, between whites and blacks, between people without disabilities and disabled people, and between human primates and non-human primates. We who have more power in the world, like men with good intentions, try to empathize with those who have less. We try to experience racism as if I who am white were black, to see the world as if I who am sighted were blind, and to reason and communicate as if I who am human were non-human.

And thus I dealt with my chimpanzees as if I were one myself. And what was wrong with this? What was ethically and even practically wrong with having empathy towards the other? For a long time, I answered, *Nothing.* Nothing at all. It's good politics. I see a blind man about to cross a street and think, *He can't see the whizzing traffic, he needs me to see it for him, to take his arm and escort him over to where he clearly wishes to go.* Operating on the assumption that, if I were blind, I'd need me to help me, I grab the man's arm and pull him panic-stricken into the traffic, terrifying and endangering him. Because I am sighted, I have relied and insisted on using a guidance system that utilizes sight as its main source of data. But the blind man has his own system for crossing the street. The blind man hears what I merely see, isolates bits of information that are lost on me, and coordinates and remembers data that I've not even registered.

I'm talking here about the difference between *empathy* and *sympathy*, between feeling *for* the other and feeling *with* the other. The distinction came to matter to me. It still does. When you abandon and betray those with whom you empathize, you're not abandoning or betraying anyone or anything that's as real as yourself. Taken to its extreme, perhaps even pathological, form, empathy is narcissism.

WOODROW DECLARED that he could not do without the car, promising that I would have a car of my own in a few days. I couldn't wait, however, and the morning after my arrival home, as soon as Satterthwaite had driven the boys to school, I pedaled my bicycle out to the old lab, knowing fairly well what I'd find there. In my backpack I carried as many fruits and vegetables as I could stuff into it, along with my lunch and the video camera that I had shipped back from the States. Woodrow had assured me that in my absence the dreamers had been fed and their cages kept clean by Elizabeth and Benji, but I knew how casually and carelessly they would have done their work. I feared the worst.

The lab was a wreck. The office had been looted of nearly everything that remained—every stick of furniture, the filing cabinets and most of their contents, the remnants of medical equipment, all of it either gone or smashed to pieces. Plumbing fixtures and electric lights had been ripped out. The doors to the three cabins swung open, and the window frames had been pulled out and were probably way across town by now, installed in a permanently unfinished cinder-block hut. In those days half of Monrovia had been vandalized to build the other half, and work on the other half had unaccountably ceased. A strange sort of stasis had settled over the city.

I smelled the dreamers before I saw them. From halfway across the yard, the stench enveloped me—rotted fruit and urine. The old, rusted Quonset hut was silent as I approached. The padlock was gone, and the door hung half-open on one hinge, as if someone had tried to rip it off and had given up. Thus the stench, I thought, but I would have smelled it even if the door had been shut and locked. It was overpowering, putrid, like nothing I had smelled before, and though in subsequent years I became almost familiar with that odor, I knew at once that it was the smell of dead bodies, if not human bodies then enough like human to smell the same, to repel and frighten me in the same primal way and fill my throat and mouth with the soured contents of my stomach.

I untied my head scarf and covered my nose and mouth and swung the door back, reached blindly into the darkness and found the switch. Miraculously, the fixtures and fluorescent tubes were still in place and working, protected against theft no doubt by the awful smell of death. The pale, flickering light drove the thick darkness from the building. I could almost hear the darkness flee. But the stink remained. There was no movement in the cages. Brown and black lumps of hair were all that remained of my dreamers. I staggered along the row of cages and one by one said their names, as if taking a macabre roll, and as I passed, first one of the lumps of hair, then another, came slowly to life, rolled its head into view, showed me its flattened, expressionless gaze. They were shrunk to half the size they had been when I'd last made this walk from cage to cage and called their names and they'd leapt to the front of the cages to greet me with glad hoots and hollers. Now they barely stirred at my passing. They lay in their feces and urine and the rotted remains of their last feeding, which from the looks of it had taken place weeks ago. Some of them did not move at all. Others turned their faces to me, but did not open their eyes.

Of the twelve dreamers I'd left behind six months ago, only eight survived. Four cages had a dead body locked inside: Ginko's, Mano's, Wassail's, and Edna's. I flipped the switch of the video camera and slowly, back and forth in front of the cages, from one foul end of the Quonset hut to the other, I shot close-ups of the dreamers' flaccid faces, their emaciated, scab-covered bodies, their sores and self-inflicted abrasions and wounds, and I took lingering footage of the dead. Then I stepped to the center of the hut and panned the length of it, filming a slow, sweeping medium shot of the rack of cages. Doc lifted his huge head, and when he looked at me, I switched to zoom and closed on his blank gaze and held it for a full minute.

I brought water to those that still lived and distributed the food I had carried in my backpack, and afterwards hurried to the nearest market and brought back a large sack of fufu leaves and cabbages. I stayed with the dreamers for hours, coaxing them to eat and drink. It was mid-afternoon before I had managed to remove the bodies of Ginko, Mano, Wassail, and Edna from their cages and drag them outside to the yard, and by dusk I had buried them together, side by side, in a small plot of bare ground at the rear of the Quonset hut. The last thing I did was make a circle of rocks around the grave. Then I returned home to my family of humans.

A DAY LATER I had my own car, and after dropping the boys off at school, drove myself straight to the Executive Mansion and once again marched up the long, wide staircase as if on a mission from the American ambassador himself and presented myself at the office of the president. Samuel Doe welcomed me with a warm smile and a familial hug. I shrugged out of it and stood away from him.

"It is a wonderful t'ing that you have returned to us," he began and sat slowly behind his vast desk.

"Yes, well, I have something for you." I pulled the video cassette from my purse and set it on his desk before him.

He pursed his lips in surprise and curiosity, then gave me a lecherous grin. "Aha! An American movie! You know my taste in movies?"

"This is a Liberian movie, Mister President," I said. "Let's watch it together, you and I." I looked around the room for the television set and VCR that I knew would be close at hand, for, indeed, I did know of his taste in movies. His addiction to pornography was a nationwide joke. In the corner was a cart with a TV and VCR ready to go. I walked over and snapped them on and inserted the cassette, then came and stood next to the president.

Together, in silence, we watched the film. A ghastly study of pain and cruelty, it ran for about fifteen minutes. Neither of us spoke for the entire time. Yes, it was only a video of some apes in their cages, dead and dying of hunger and thirst and neglect, but flattened out on the screen like that in unedited documentary mode with no sound-track, it was as shocking and indicting as footage of the hold of a slave ship.

The film ended, and I rewound and retrieved it. The president said, "These them chimps from out at the old American blood-testing place?"

"Yes."

"Why you showin' them to me?" he asked, genuinely puzzled. "I was expectin' some other kind of movie," he said. "You know the kind."

"I have a proposal to make to you, Mister President," I said. I began to lay out my plan in very simple, straightforward language. I told him that, with his help and protection, I would establish a permanent sanctuary for the chimpanzees someplace not far from Monrovia. I would need a building and a secure open space for them and enough funding to care for and feed them and to pay a small staff. I would need money to purchase, whenever possible, chimps that were being sold illegally for pets. I explained that I intended to develop a national program designed to protect this internationally protected species. It would provide him and his administration with good public relations worldwide, especially among the Americans, and people would come from all over the world to visit the sanctuary. The Americans would make films of the project to show on American television, and Liberia would finally become known as something other than a place to register foreign oil tankers.

He lighted a cigarette and waved me to the chair nearest his own. "Sit down. Would you like a drink with me? Not too early, is it?"

"That depends on your answer to my proposal."

"My answer." He smiled and smacked his lips with his red tongue. "I like them chimps, y' know."

"Yes, I know."

He laughed. "I mean not just for eatin'. I like 'em. I t'ink this a very good idea. Good for the chimps, an' good for me. Good for Liberia. So I'm gonna say yes to your proposal, to this sanctuary idea."

"Then it's not too early for me to drink with you, Mister President."

He laughed again and pulled a bottle of Johnny Walker and two glasses from the drawer at his knee and set them before us on the desk and poured three fingers of scotch in each. Raising his glass, he said, "To the chimps, then."

"To the chimps," I said and did the same.

Before I left the room, Samuel Doe by phone had ordered his chief of staff to turn over an old, unused military prison located in Toby, five miles east of Monrovia. He knew the place well, he said, because he had once been stationed there. It had twenty cells and an exercise yard surrounded by a high electrified fence. It was in decent repair and could be modified for the chimps easily and cheaply. From the desk drawer where his whiskey had been stashed, he pulled handfuls of American currency, hundred-dollar bills, and counted out one hundred of them, ten thousand dollars, as if counting out playing cards. He wrapped the bills with an elastic band, handed the wad to me, and said, "You on the unofficial presidential payroll now. An' when you need some more money for your sanctuary, come straight to me. Don' go no place else. An' when the place ready and open for business, we'll make us a big ceremony out there at Toby. Lots of press people. Television. All the foreign ambassadors. 'Specially the Africans! I want them peoples to see what us Liberians doin' here for the poor endangered species of Africa!"

"Thank you, Mister President," I said.

He refilled our glasses and raised his again. "To the chimps!" he said and drained it.

"Yes. To the chimps."

AND SO BEGAN my life as keeper of the chimps, as their rescuer and champion of their cause in Liberia. All right, as their surrogate mother.

My human children seemed to require little of me. Perhaps because they were boys and because of my inescapable peculiarities—I don't want to say my neuroses or personal deformities—but from the beginning, my sons were more Woodrow's than mine, more African than American, more black than white. I looked after them, of course, made sure they were properly fed and clothed and bathed, drove them to school and picked them up, oversaw their education and social lives in town, but did it in a general, distant way, and left the details to others. Left them to Woodrow, mainly, who guided their religious training, encouraged them to become sportsmen, and, increasingly, took them to visit their grandparents and the rest of the Sundiata clan in Fuama, where they were being prepared for initiation into the Poro society, which, of course, would distance them even farther from me. They were good boys, well behaved, obedient, smart, and only occasionally mischievous or troublesome, and it was not difficult for us, despite our daily proximity, to grow distant from one another. They seemed to welcome and utilize that distance as much as I. Certainly neither they nor I complained of it.

Was I altogether without a maternal instinct? Let's say I was ignorant of it, that in me it was deflected early on. It was an instinct not so much repressed as stunted, bent, deformed, so that I could not engage and express it in the normal way. In my twenties, in Weatherman, I so severely attacked what we think of as natural instincts, so pruned and cropped them, cutting them back to their roots and in a few cases pulling up the roots as well, that in my thirties and forties I was nearly incapable of cultivating them. My youthful radicalism of necessity masculinized me. To feel regret for having thwarted so many of my so-called natural instincts I would have had to feel regret for my youthful radicalism and the idealism that drove it, and I could not do that. I still can't.

I was a bad mother, yes, but not a neglectful one. And I was an inattentive, detached wife, but not a cruel or malicious one. And though I was a solitary, self-absorbed woman, I was nonetheless socially compliant and friendly to all, just as I am today with Anthea and the girls who work at my farm and with my neighbors here in the valley. I was as devoted then, and am still today, to certain abstract values like justice and equality as I was in my early years, and if the price I paid in my early years for that devotion was anger and violence against those who were unjust and oppressive, then in my later years the price was cool detachment from those who loved me and whom I claimed to love. Over the years, as I grew older, the dark shadow I cast slowly paled and turned white.

AN ADULT MALE CHIMP can weigh over two hundred fifty pounds and is strong enough to overturn a car or hurl an adult male human across a large room. Adult female chimps are considerably smaller and more pliant, although they can be and often are fiercely protective of their young. Both male and female adolescents are like human adolescents—awash with hormones, amorous, quarrelsome, competitive, energetically testing themselves against one another and adult authority, and capable of fond attachments that seem nearly homoerotic. It's the babies and youngsters, of course, that we know from circuses and kiddie shows on television. It's the babies that get captured and sold as pets, after their mothers and other protective adults have been gunned down and sold for food or consumed by the killers on the spot.

All species are in danger of being killed by humans, even the human species, but only a few are as endangered as the one that most resembles us. Like us, they have no tails; like us, they have fingernails and toenails and not claws. They have elbows and knees. They have necks thick and thin, and soft, round bellies when they grow old. They have reproductive systems and endocrine systems and interior organs—heart, liver, kidneys, lungs, and intestines—that are located and shaped like ours. Though they cannot speak, they communicate with one another and with other species with subtlety and ease and efficiency. They have eyes located at the front of their head and open ears attached to the sides of the skull, and they vary in the same degree as humans in complexion and pigmentation and hair color and facial features from one to the other. Because of the extra Y chromosome carried by the males and the number of specific genes attached to it, a male chimpanzee is genetically closer to a male human than to a female chimpanzee, and a female human is closer to a female chimpanzee than to a male human. They are not our distant ancestors; they are our close cousins.

If humans, like the rest of the animals, could not speak, we would all live together in peace, devouring one another solely out of necessity and instinct, our positions in the food chain nicely balanced by need and numbers. If we were as speechless as my collies on the farm or the hens and sheep and the geese, if we barked or baa'd or clucked or if like the chimps we could only hoot and holler and otherwise had to depend on body language, we would not kill one another or any other animal solely for the pleasure of it. The power of speech is the speech of power. Vows of silence are pledges to peaceableness. Silence is indeed golden, and a golden age would be silent.

FOR A FEW YEARS, then, and for the first time in my life, I not only had a cause, but was able to pursue it with measurable success. There were few to witness my success, few who mattered to me. My father was dead; my mother was thousands of miles away and wouldn't get it anyhow; and everyone from the Movement from the top to the bottom was scattered and lost to me, many of them gone over to the other side. Those who remained on the Left, from what I gleaned from occasional newspaper and magazine accounts, were more interested in designing holistic lifestyles than in working for radical social and political change. The very idea of revolution, which in the late sixties and early seventies had seemed ready for immanence, had been turned into a comic metaphor for self-indulgent self-delusion. Not for me, however. Not in those later years in Liberia, where, while I awaited the return of Charles

Taylor at the head of a rebel army, imagining him as a latter-day African Fidel Castro, I busied myself with saving a little troop of chimpanzees in a renovated prison a few miles east of Monrovia, tirelessly working to keep them from being exploited or killed, as if they were my disadvantaged neighbors and I, by accident of birth, had the power and privilege and the right to do so.

People called me "Monkey Lady," and sometimes "Madame Sundiata of the Chimps," and several times I heard myself referred to as "Queen of the Apes," like a female Tarzan. The first time I heard that one it came from Sam Clement, not long after I finished the renovation of the prison and had completed transferring the dreamers from the Quonset hut, a job that required considerable help from a crew of four strong men, a flatbed truck, and a four-foot-by-four-foot, specially constructed cage on wheels that we used for transporting the adults and larger adolescents. The cage had a sliding door that we opened and placed next to the door of the old Quonset hut cage. We slid both doors open, and one by one, sometimes with the younger chimps two by two, they entered the larger, wheeled cage; then we slid the doors closed, locked and wheeled the cage to the truck and loaded it and drove it out to Toby, where we repeated the operation, releasing the chimps into the cells that in the Tolbert years had been built to hold humans, but which were five or six times larger than the Quonset hut cages. The chimps entered their vast, new space, where I had placed fresh water and food to welcome them and had suspended tires from ropes and built racks of iron pipe for climbing and swinging and cocoa-leaf mats for sleeping nests, and made themselves at home. It wasn't exactly a minimum-security prison, but it was an enormous improvement over their previous conditions of confinement.

The last to be transferred to his new prison cell—I can't call it his *home*—was Doc, who must have felt, as he saw his troop diminished one by one, that we were executing them one by one, for as each left the Quonset hut, he grew sadder and more downcast, until at the end, when we came for him, he lay curled in a corner of his cage, a huge, dark hill of depression, as if prepared for burial. But at Toby, as soon as we removed the wheeled cage from the truck and pushed it up to the open door of the cell that was to be his, which was located at the command center of the block and from which all the other cells were visible, he stood and looked out at his troop—his subordinate males and his female consorts and his children and their playmates and companions—and grasping the bars of the cell, he shook them with spectacular delight and display, as if he himself had arranged all this and it had gone precisely according to plan.

I was feeding the dreamers, passing large chunks of watermelon through the bars, when I heard a voice behind me. "So you're the Queen of the Apes now. And this is your palace." I turned. It was Sam Clement. Our American friend. It wasn't the first time since my return that I'd seen him; he had been at our doorstep to greet me on my first arrival and had visited the house for dinner once since. But it was the first time that we'd been alone with no other humans present.

Sam smiled and stood next to me and for a moment studied Doc, who studied him back. "That's a big fella," he drawled. "What's his name? I expect you've given them names."

"Doc. Yes, they have names. Though I don't know what they call one another. Kind of an interesting question, don't you think? Whether animals have names for one another."

He laughed. "I suppose they grunt, 'Hey, you,' with various inflections and tones and get answered, 'You talkin' to *me*?' Hey, show me around, will you?"

I walked him through the prison, and he admired, or pretended to admire, the way I'd recycled the cells and the exercise yard and had converted the old interrogation rooms into storage and had made what had once been a windowless room, probably used for torture or solitary confinement, into a nursery for the babies. As we walked we touched delicately on the subject of his role in facilitating my return to Liberia and the aid and comfort I was now receiving from President Doe.

"Sam, were you keeping track of me through Woodrow while I was in the States?" I asked him. "Or were there other, more official sources of information?"

"Oh, Woodrow kept me posted well enough. Our paths crossed at the embassy every now and then. Say, is it possible to get close and actually touch these beauties?" he asked and took a step towards the cell where Tina and her daughter Belle were happily sharing half a watermelon. From his cage Doc saw him and raised an ear-splitting protest, and Sam backed off. "Whoa! Steady there, big fella."

"He sees you as competition," I warned. "He thinks you want his wives."

"They aren't my type, believe me."

"I haven't really thanked you, Sam," I said. "For speaking for me. With Doe, I mean. I assume it was you who brought him around."

"Yes, sort of, but he didn't need much convincing. The guy he's pissed at, and damned afraid of, too, is Charles Taylor."

"Oh," I said and changed the subject. "Actually, if you want, you can play with the babies. In the nursery. I'll bring them in for you. They're still a little frail, but quite gentle and sweet."

"No, thanks. Not for me. I'm a people person, if you know what I mean."

We'd ended the tour at the front of the sanctuary, where I'd taken over the prison chief's office. It was a large, bright, freshly whitewashed room furnished with a desk and filing cabinet, where I'd started combining as much of the data left over from the old lab with the data that I was now accumulating, birth, medical, and behavioral information, along with a rapidly swelling file of correspondence from primate sanctuaries in other countries, mostly African, but also a few located in the United States, in Ohio, Georgia, and South Carolina, and one in Canada. I was finding allies and teachers everywhere.

"Well, m'love, I ought to be getting back to the office," Sam said. Out the window I saw his Land Rover with the U.S. seal on the side. His driver was chatting with several of the men I had hired to help me move my dreamers to their new home. "You heard about Taylor, didn't you?" Sam said.

"Heard about him? No. What?"

"He escaped from prison. In the States."

"He was in prison?"

Sam smiled, that warm, Virginia, white man's smile reserved especially for silly women. "Yes, Hannah. He was in prison. A federal prison in Massachusetts. Not too far from where you grew up, Hannah."

"And he escaped?"

"It wasn't but minimum security, so he didn't need a hacksaw blade in a cake. I guess he just sort of walked off the place."

"Where . . . where is he now?"

He opened the door and stepped into the glare of the yard. "Who knows?"

IN THOSE DAYS, rumors passed through Liberia like weather systems, one following hard upon the other. To me it seemed unlikely if not impossible, but Charles was supposed to have fled the United States for Mexico, not Libya. And from there to Cuba, where Fidel Castro was providing him with military training and sanctuary. Then we heard he was in jail in Ghana for plotting to overthrow the government of President Rawley. Or he'd recently been seen in Abidjan trying to raise money to finance an invasion of Liberia from Côte d'Ivoire. Or he was up in Freetown, in Sierra Leone, making arrangements to invade Liberia by sea. The next week he was in a training camp outside Tripoli, building an alliance between Samuel Doe's old Americo enemies in exile, a cadre of ex–Black Panthers, and a battalion of young pan-African communist revolutionaries. It went on like that, month after month, year after year. He was said to have gotten married. He was getting divorced. He was said to have become a Baptist. For a month we heard he was in the pay of the CIA. A month later the CIA was trying to assassinate him. And so on, until the only way for me to process the rumors was to discount them altogether, to go about my daily rounds at home and at Toby, and wait.

Meanwhile, as the boys approached puberty—and they were close enough in age to arrive there more or less together—Woodrow started taking them to Fuama with increasing frequency and for longer and longer stays. They made these trips without me, as I was unwilling to leave my dreamers in the care of others for longer than a day. At least that's what I told Woodrow and the boys, until they stopped inviting me to join them—happily, it seemed, almost with relief, as if my presence out there embarrassed them. The bamboo wall that separated me from Woodrow's family and village was cultural and linguistic, not racial or even economic, and I should have been able to scale it and join them on the other side, but I was unwilling, perhaps unable, to do fieldwork on my own family. Woodrow's people and their world, especially as the boys became increasingly comfortable and knowledgeable there, frightened and threatened me. Consequently, I coped with my ignorance and feelings of exclusion by backing away from that wall, instead of learning how to climb over it, and only increased the distance between me and Woodrow's people, between me and Woodrow himself, and between me and my sons.

This allowed us to keep deep and wide secrets from one another. Of Woodrow's village life, whether he had one wife in Fuama or many wives or none, whether he had fathered children there with other women or, except for my three sons, was childless, I knew nothing and did not ask. And of my sons' tribal initiation, of the secret Poro rites that moved them out of childhood and taught them the ancient ways of becoming men among their father's people, I knew only that these rites had taken place in the bush and at night and that women were not permitted to inquire about them, a restriction I complied with easily. And though during those years I was no one's lover or mistress and certainly no one's wife but Woodrow's and underwent no ritual initiation or life-changing religious experience, public or private, I had secrets, too. Mine were the secrets of my past: deviancies, as Woodrow surely would have viewed my relationship with Carol and earlier with other women; and brief and furtive sexual dalliances, as with Satterthwaite; and a certain long-held dream of violence against people and institutions and governments that exploited the poor and the weak—a dream that over the years had faded and nearly been forgotten, but that had been called back vividly into service by Charles Taylor. It was my biggest secret. Once again I was caught up in that old fantasy of the imminent arrival of justice. Though I appeared to be a dutiful mother and spouse and the successful manager of a locally famous primate sanctuary, I was underground, again.

FOR A LONG TIME, we heard no more rumors concerning Charles, and I began to fear that something bad had happened to him, that he had indeed been jailed or possibly even assassinated. But then one morning in early December 1989, news came of a formal armed assault against the government of Samuel Doe. It had been launched along the border in Nimba County by a small force calling itself the National Patriotic Front of Liberia and led by Charles Taylor. The second in command was a "strange man" named Prince Johnson, but there was little else known about the group. No one seemed to take the incursion seriously, since it had occurred in the jungle far to the east, some two hundred miles from Monrovia, and this National Patriotic Front of Liberia, the so-called NPFL, was said to number no more than a few dozen poorly armed men.

On December 26, we got word of a second raid in Nimba, this one conducted by a much larger force augmented by men and boys recruited from Butua and Karnplay, the Gio villages out there, Charles Taylor's mother's tribespeople. In the papers and on the radio the men and boys of the NPFL were being referred to now as rebels. But the fighting was still taking place in remote villages, and with no reliable firsthand reports available, no one, except for me, took the incursions seriously. Finally, in late February, Doe sent a battalion of his soldiers to

Nimba County with orders to drive the NPFL back into Côte d'Ivoire and claimed a few days later to have gone to the front himself to assess the seriousness of the situation. Upon his return, he assured the nation by radio and TV that there was no cause for alarm, for the Armed Forces of Liberia had everything under control, and the rebels were in disarray, fleeing for the border. Within a few days rumors came that Doe had never made it to the front, that halfway there he'd abruptly turned back, trailed by persistent claims that Taylor's men were protected by special powers, juju charms and magic waters, that the fighters were "gun proof," and that often in the midst of battle they became invisible.

By April, the rebels had captured Ganta. Around this time, the AFL, Doe's frightened and disorganized army—in a vain attempt to terrorize the villagers and keep them from providing recruits, food, and shelter to Charles's rapidly growing force—had started committing atrocities in the distant villages. The rebels advanced with an ease and speed that surprised everyone. Everyone except me. Things were unfolding just as I'd expected. Just as I'd dreamed. By May the rebels had reached Buchanan, and by June they were in the Bong Mines region. Doe kept showing up on television to assure us that his army had suffered no casualties, that Charles Taylor had lost three hundred fifty men in Kakata, his second-in-command Prince Johnson had lost a hundred fifty fighters in Careysburg, and both were in retreat. Which to us meant only that Charles Taylor had advanced as far as Kakata, barely thirty miles from Monrovia, and Prince Johnson was in Careysburg, eighteen miles from the capital.

I did not know what Charles Taylor would become and what he and the thousands of men and boys who followed him would do to the people of Liberia and to my family and to my dreamers. I could not have imagined it. I believed not so much in him as in his rhetoric, which I had welded to the remnants of my youthful ideology and disappointed idealism. And when I ask myself now what I should have done, once I had made it possible for Charles to escape the cage he'd been put in and I had been granted permission by Samuel Doe to return to my husband and sons, to my home, and to the dreamers, I have no answer other than what in fact I did: I came, like John the Baptist, I thought, to prepare the way; or like Mary Magdalen, to welcome him at the gate, and until he came, to do good works: keeping house.

I wasn't alone in this. As the season wore on, it began to look as though the rebels might actually succeed in overthrowing Samuel Doe. Support for Charles Taylor quietly spread across the country. It didn't hurt that in July he broke with Prince Johnson, supposedly over depredations and atrocities committed by Johnson and his followers in villages around the Bong Mines near Kakata. Members of Doe's government, his press secretary, the minister of transport, and some members of the legislature fled the country. There were demonstrations in Monrovia and Buchanan, led by prominent churchmen, calling for Doe's resignation. All the while, from a portable radio station somewhere in the jungle, Charles was telling us of his progress and intentions, explaining his principled break with Prince Johnson, condemning Johnson and Doe as if the two were in cahoots together, and we all, Woodrow, too, secretly listened and silently cheered him on.

Doe fought back, of course. Many of his more outspoken critics—journalists, academics, churchmen, and even a few government officials—were brutally murdered by death squads, non-uniformed thugs who came out from under rocks at night and left the mutilated bodies of Doe's enemies on the streets and door stoops to be found in the morning. Violence begat more violence. Single incidents of murder, disfigurement, and torture quickly justified massacres, villagewide amputations of limbs, gang rape, and the forced recruitment of children. Tribal war erupted. Doe's Krahn soldiers started imprisoning and executing Gios and Manos, and in the countryside Charles Taylor's and Prince Johnson's men started killing Krahns, Doe's tribe, and Mandingos, a tribe that in legal and extralegal commercial matters had long been favored by him. One of Doe's death squads massacred hundreds of civilians huddled for safety in a Lutheran Church. Another raided a hospital and singled out Gio and Mano tribespeople and slew them in their beds.

Now the whole of West Africa was threatened by the conflict. Entire villages, towns, and cities from Senegal in the north to Nigeria in the south and inland east of Guinea were made up of Mandingos, Krahns, Gios, and Manos. Consequently, in mid-August, a fourth army, one made up mostly of Ghanaians and Nigerians, entered the war. Ill equipped and barely trained, they were sent into Liberia by the Economic Community of West African States. The new army was called ECOMOG, or the Economic Community Monitoring Group, and it was supposed to keep the warring parties apart and somehow broker a peace settlement. It did nothing of the sort. The Ghanaians and Nigerians simply joined the fray, and soon they, too, were brutally murdering civilians and being murdered back. Unbelievable tales of massacres committed by all four armies, bizarre accounts of ritual killings, random executions, rape, cannibalism, and pillage accumulated and became believable, and people who could leave Liberia for safe havens in the U.S. or other West African countries packed up and fled. Those who could not or would not leave—among them Woodrow for his reasons and I for mine—kept inside their houses and prayed that the war would soon be over and the horror would stop.

ONE AFTERNOON late in August, the rain was falling like drapery, and Sam strolled into my office, only the second time he had come there, which meant he had a purpose. Even under a big black umbrella in a heavy downpour, he never seemed to hurry or stride along: he sauntered like a boulevardier, as if he had no place special to go and all the time in the world to get there. Which in those months was unusual, especially for a white man, when everyone in Liberia, even the locals, either hurried from one place to another or else slunk from door to door and, if you looked away and back again, was gone from sight. Sam folded his umbrella and perched on a corner of my desk and glanced at the logbook open before me.

I put down my pen and closed the book and said hello.

"Secrets?"

"You interested in the ovulation cycles of female chimpanzees?"

"Not really." He whistled a tuneless tune through his teeth for half a minute while I waited in silence. We'd reached that point in our relationship where we could be both present and absent and not take it personally. Not exactly intimacy, but on its way there.

The rain drummed against the tin roof. Finally, Sam sighed and, without looking at me, said, "Things are going badly for Doe, you know. Very badly."

"Yes. I know."

"We've started advising American citizens to get the hell out of here while they still can. The country's a house of cards, Hannah. Doe's going to fall any day, and when he does, things will get savage for a spell. Between Johnson and Taylor and ECOMOG, there won't be much wiggle room. It's time for you and your boys to leave, Hannah."

"I can't leave. I've got the chimps. And the boys, they're not Americans anyhow. They're Liberians. Where would we go?"

"Please. Don't play dumb with me. I've got exit visas for them and for you and Woodrow, too, in case Doe's people give you shit at the airport. I've also got you entry visas for the U.S. All non-essential embassy personnel are flying out tomorrow. After that, getting out will be dicey at best. C'mon, Hannah, go home and pack."

"Woodrow won't leave. Not as long as Samuel Doe is president. He's still a faithful member of the cabinet. And if he can't go, neither can I or the boys. We'll be all right. Besides, like I said, who'll take care of the chimps?" I smiled up at him.

There was a break in the rain, and suddenly the room was very quiet. Sam walked to the window and peered out. "Doe's a sinking ship, and all the rats who can are jumping off. Including Woodrow. And Doe knows it. He's going nuts over there. Jesus, I hate this time of year," he said suddenly and laughed. "I feel like Noah, collecting Americans for the ark, two by two." He was silent for a moment, then said, "You've got five seats on the eleven o'clock to JFK tomorrow. If you're not at Robertsfield by ten to claim them, there's a whole bunch of gringos who will have been waiting all night, and they'll happily take your place. It's not the last flight out, but damned near it."

"Have you spoken to Woodrow? Does he know about this?" I heard low hoots from Doris and Betty and then Doc down the hall, advising me that it was feeding time. In a moment the others would take up the call.

"Yesterday. I went by the ministry."

"Yesterday? He never mentioned it."

"I didn't think he would. He said you wouldn't leave your 'dreamers,' but mainly he still thinks Doe can pull it off as long as Johnson and Taylor are fighting each other. Doe thinks the Marines are gonna land and save his sorry ass. He's wrong, of course. And ECOMOG's not gonna save his ass either. All they'll do is pick up the pieces after he's gone and keep as many of them as they can for themselves. No, Woodrow's deluded by Doe, who's self-deluded. Your husband's been in government too long. It was useless talking to him. That's why I came by to talk to you. Woodrow said he planned to ship the boys out to his village, Fuama. But that won't do you or him any good. And when he goes down, it won't do the boys any good either. Or anyone else connected to Woodrow, so long as Woodrow stays connected to Doe. That's going to be a death sentence, Hannah. Even for you." He grabbed his umbrella and opened the door. Without turning, he said, "If Woodrow insists on sticking it out till the end, let him. But you and the boys, you get out, Hannah. In a few months things'll be back to normal again, believe me. Charles Taylor will be sitting in the Executive Mansion, and Prince Johnson will either be dead or, if he's lucky, in a cell, maybe right here alongside your 'dreamers,'" he said and laughed lightly.

"You know that," I said.

"I know that," he answered and stepped outside and closed the door behind him. Seconds later, the rain resumed pounding on the roof. Then the chimps raised their voices in unison, hollering for their meal, each trying to outdo the others in volume and intensity. What began as a mild signal to their keeper rose to screeching rage, accompanied by the steady, rhythmic drumming of the rain.

WOODROW'S CAR PASSED through the gate and up the driveway at the usual time, five o'clock. He drove himself, however, which was not usual. I stepped from the kitchen, where I had started preparing supper, to the terrace and said, "No Satterthwaite?"

"No. Where are the boys?" He came rapidly towards me, ignoring the dogs, who looked after him with downcast but still expectant faces. Woodrow always arrived home with a small bag of meat purchased at a roadside stand and made a big show of feeding it to the dogs. But not today, evidently. Disappointed, they flopped in the shade at the rear of the car.

"In their room, I suppose. I've been in the kitchen. Why? What's the matter?"

"Can't you hear that?" he said and brushed past me.

Yes, I heard it, I'd been hearing it for weeks, the chatter of gunfire in the distance coming from the other side of the river in Logan Town, beyond Bushrod Island. We'd been hearing it off and on and had grown almost used to it, as if it were not the sound of men and boys shooting to kill people, but some mild form of celebration in a neighborhood we seldom visited and where we knew no one. When, after the first few days, it no longer seemed to be coming closer to our part of the city, I'd more or less tuned it out, and since my daily route to the boys' school and the sanctuary in Toby and Woodrow's route to the ministry were all in the opposite direction of Logan Town, the scattered bursts of gunfire we heard in the evening and during the night, seldom in the morning, came to us as if broadcast over the radio from some other part of the country. Despite the war, we'd managed to maintain so much of our normal daily life and routines that we felt not just protected from the war, but as if it were taking place somewhere beyond the border, in Guinea or Sierra Leone. You can do that in a war for a long time when you have enough money and your family and friends are still able to cling to power.

I followed Woodrow into the boys' bedroom. Dillon lay on his bed, huge, eyes closed, lost in his Walkman, a muscular, barefoot giant of a boy in his green Boston Celtics tee shirt and gym shorts. The other two sat facing each other cross-legged on the floor. They were practicing their newly acquired skill in sign language, learned from a chart I'd brought them after having tried and failed to teach a few basic signs to my dreamers, the signs for *yes, no, mother, father, baby,* and *My name is. . . .* William and Paul had quickly mastered the signs and now could carry on lengthy, utterly silent conversations with each other without our knowing a word of what they were saying.

"Come, come, boys, pay attention!" Woodrow snapped.

Dillon opened his eyes and removed the earphones. He sat up slowly, as if waking from a nap. The twins' hands went silent.

"Hi, Papa," William said and sweetly smiled.

"What's the matter, Papa?" Paul asked in a small voice. He looked to me as if for an answer.

Woodrow stepped over the clutter of the small room and went into the closet, where he rummaged through its contents for a moment before emerging with my old duffel bag, unused for nearly four years, except to store temporarily the boys' outgrown clothes before donating them to the church. He emptied the bag on the floor and tossed it to Dillon. I suddenly noticed that Woodrow was sweating and smelled of anxiety and fear. His movements were abrupt and ill coordinated, as if he'd been drinking. He turned to me and said, "Get them packed," and I smelled the whiskey.

"Packed? What for?"

"I'm taking them to Fuama," he said and roughly pushed Dillon on the shoulder and the twins by the back of their heads. "Hurry up! We goin' now."

"What about the checkpoints? Prince Johnson controls the road to Fuama, doesn't he?"

"We'll get through. I got money. It ain't Johnson I'm worried about anyhow."

"Who, then? Not Charles. Charles is our friend," I said. "Remember?"

He ignored me and set about helping the boys, tossing random articles of clothing, sneakers, and a few books into the duffel. "Hurry, hurry, hurry!" he said. "For God's sake, hurry up! Hannah!" he shouted and abruptly turned to me. "Go wrap some food, as much as you can. Rice, tinned beef, beans, anything. Hurry!"

I did as instructed, and by the time I'd put together a large string sack of provisions, Woodrow appeared in the kitchen, ready to go, the boys coming along behind him, bewildered and frightened.

"Hurry up," Woodrow ordered. "You comin' wit' us," he said to me.

"I'm not staying in Fuama," I said. "What on earth are you running for anyhow? Who are you running *from*? Look at the boys, you've got them terrified. *I'm* terrified, Woodrow."

He grabbed me by the wrist and pulled me towards the door. "You go where I say you go. Don't vex me now, woman," he warned. "Wit' you in the car, them soldier boys'll let us pass the checkpoints."

"No! I'm not leaving this house, I have to be here for my dreamers. And you can't take the boys until you tell me what's happening."

He looked me coldly in the face, as if at that moment he despised me and wished he'd never married me. "Sam Clement seen you at Toby today, didn' he?"

"Yes, he came out for a few minutes."

"An' you think Doe don't know that?"

"What if he does?"

He shook his head sadly. He no longer despised me; he pitied me. "This man Doe is crazy, but crazy like a fox. Look, he knows the Americans got their hand in this war from the beginnin'. He knows they been secretly backin' Charles. He knows you an American, missus! An' 'cause of that old business 'bout me an' Charles, Doe been puttin' two an' two together. He sent two of his soldier boys aroun' for me this afternoon, but I knew it was a trick, so I sent Satterthwaite across to the Barclay Barracks where Doe and his top boys all holed up, tol' him to say I be right along, an' when Satterthwaite didn' come back, I know what Doe got in his head for me." He passed me at the door and scooted the boys outside. "Get in the car," he ordered.

"What about Bruno and Muhammad Ali?" Paul asked.

"Never mind them dogs, they'll guard the house. Jus' get in the car. Jeannine or Kuyo or somebody'll take care of 'em." He turned and grabbed my wrist again and yanked me outside.

"Let me get the food," I said, and he released me, and I returned to the kitchen.

"Wait a minute, Papa," Dillon said. "I forgot something, too." He followed me into the house and jogged into the living room, and when he returned he carried the camera bag and video camera. Except for the video I made for Samuel Doe, no one but Dillon had ever used it. He had become fairly proficient and had accumulated a small collection of home movies, mostly of his friends and sports events, but a few family events as well, which we usually watched once after they were shot and not again.

"Might be something interesting out there to tape," he said, as together we passed out of the house. I locked the door and walked to the car, where Woodrow waited impatiently. Dillon got in back with the twins, and I walked to the gate, while Woodrow backed the car down the driveway and out to the street, where he stopped and waited for me to lock the gate. It was our routine.

This is how it happened. As I turned to clip the padlock onto the gate, I saw them waiting for us, Satterthwaite with three men I didn't know, civilians in sweat-stained sleeveless shirts and caps and sneakers, street kids, the kind of feral young men without jobs or family whom

I'd gotten used to seeing hanging out on corners and stalking the alleys in Monrovia over the last few years. Satterthwaite moved on me, his face expressionless; the others, carrying machetes, went for the car. Satterthwaite lifted his shirt and showed me a pistol against his bare belly. "Go back inside," he said and pushed me through the gate, then quickly closed and locked it. The dogs, sensing my alarm, barked once; then, having recognized Satterthwaite, stopped.

"Woodrow, go!" I screamed. "Drive! *Drive*, for God's sake!"

He didn't move. Several seconds passed as the men walked to the car, two of them on Woodrow's side, the other on the passenger's side. Satterthwaite leaned his back against the gate and watched the car. Woodrow, round faced, wide eyed, looked over at me, a prisoner locked in our yard behind the iron-barred gate, and the boys did the same. They stared at me as if I were standing on the deck of a departing ship and were waving goodbye to them.

"*Leave*, Woodrow! Go!" I yelled.

It seemed they had done this many times. The men moved slowly and methodically to the sides of the car. The one on the far side opened the rear door and pointed his machete at the boys and said something to them. Another opened the driver's-side door, and the third reached in and grabbed Woodrow by the arm and pulled him from the car to the street. It happened in an instant. While the first man stood by the open rear door and kept the boys inside, the other two forced Woodrow to his hands and knees. One of them pulled Woodrow's head back, forcing the small of his back down and his narrow shoulders up, and the other flashed his machete on a deadly path parallel to Woodrow's back and shoulders towards his head, then lifted the machete, and with a single blow separated my husband's head from his body.

There was no sound, not a word or a cry from any of us, no screams, no weeping. Nothing. The dogs remained silent. There was only the sound of the birds and the cicadas and the frogs and the evening breeze in the trees. Woodrow's body collapsed onto the street and poured blood into the dirt. The boys, as motionless as a photograph, stared out the car window at their father's body. The man with the machete looked at the other, who held Woodrow's head in his hands. He pointed at the head with the tip of his machete and laughed, an odd, high-pitched, silly laugh, and the other tossed the head across the street into the gutter like a rotten melon.

Satterthwaite turned to me and brought his face close to the bars between us. I remember his yellowed eyes, his handsome broad nose, his thin moustache and sharply defined lips. I remember his loathing. In a low, cold voice, he said, "Take your boys now, an' go home to America wit' 'em." Then he joined the others, and the four nonchalantly walked down the street together and were gone.

The boys were still inside the car, peering out cautiously as if at a forbidden movie. I shouted, "Stay there! Don't leave the car! I'll be right there for you! I have to fetch another key for the gate!" I cried and ran for the house, cursing myself for not having kept a duplicate on the ring with the house key. I found it in Woodrow's desk drawer and raced back outside and, fumbling with thick fingers, managed to get the padlock open and off the hasp and pushed the gate back. I stepped quickly past Woodrow's body without looking at it and flung open the rear door of the car.

The car was empty. My sons were gone.

I REMEMBER DRIVING through the city like a madwoman chasing ghosts. There was very little traffic—a few military vehicles was all, trucks and jeeps carrying soldiers who handed open bottles to one another, laughing and, when they passed by, ignored me as if I were invisible. A pack of teenage boys in looted clothing ran from an electronics store lugging stereos and armloads of CDs, the Indian shopkeeper gazing mournfully from the doorway. A few cars with household possessions lashed to the roof were headed inland to some imagined place of safety. It was not quite dark, and plumes of black smoke rose ominously in the south from the vicinity of the airport, where Charles

Taylor's forces were rumored to be dug in, battling the remnants of Doe's ragtag army. From Mamba Point the sea was glazed red by the setting sun. Across the harbor there was more smoke rising. Prince Johnson's bands of marauders were advancing towards the city, looting, burning homes, killing and raping women and girls as they came. A large crowd of people was gathered outside the closed gate of the American embassy, shouting to be let inside. Behind the gate a pair of stone-faced Marines with automatic weapons stood ready to fire if the crowd tried to climb the wall or rush the gate to get inside, where they imagined entry visas to the U.S. were there for the grabbing. People shook their fists, held up their babies, and waved their hands pleadingly as if for alms. I recognized some of the faces of my neighbors and several people we knew from the government agencies and ministries, a judge, a doctor and his wife with whom Woodrow and I had occasionally played bridge, the man who owned the big appliance store on Broad Street, a teacher from Saint Catherine's. Still I drove, left and left and left, in a gradually widening circle, like a rat seeking its way out of a maze. Out by the hospital, when I came to a barrier of burning tires, I stopped, reversed, and started turning right and right and right, until I got held at a checkpoint by a half-dozen soldiers and was forced to turn back. My sons had disappeared, that's all I knew. I didn't think they'd been marched off at gunpoint by their father's murderers or by Doe's soldiers. I hadn't left them alone in the car long enough for them to have been captured and taken away. But how long were they alone? How much time passed when I ran into the house and got the key to unlock the gate? I didn't know. It could have been sixty seconds, it could have been five minutes or even ten. But what good would it do anyone to imprison the three sons of Woodrow Sundiata, now that Woodrow was dead? It was Doe who had him killed, I knew that. Probably from the beginning Satterthwaite had been working for Doe and not Woodrow. Until the end, because of what Satterthwaite reported back to him, Doe believed he had nothing to fear from the small man who ran the Ministry of Public Health. But now, with Charles closing in from the south and Prince Johnson from the east and north, with his army abandoning him in droves, and then with the Americans stepping stealthily away from him and Sam Clement visiting first Woodrow and later me, suddenly Woodrow must have seemed dangerous or, at the least, disloyal. But in this chaos, no one was loyal. Alliances were made and broken hourly. Betrayal was standard operating procedure for everyone.

It was dark now, and I couldn't get out of the city. I heard the hard clatter of gunfire from the port where the Nigerians were stationed and the boom of artillery and the occasional shriek and explosion of a rocket grenade coming from the direction of the Barclay Barracks. It was useless, driving in circles around the city like this. My sons, wherever they were, did not want me to find them. I drove slowly past the homes of their schoolmates, the few whom I knew. The city was entirely in the dark. No streetlights, no house lights. Even the hotels and restaurants were without electricity. Candlelight and kerosene lanterns danced behind windows, and now and then, crossing ahead of me, the headlights of prowling military vehicles. I drove past the several houses where I knew the families, people whose children at one time or another had played with my children, houses where Dillon or the twins had once stayed overnight, but I could not bring myself to leave the safety of the locked car and walk to the darkened door and knock and ask, *Have you seen Dillon, William, and Paul? I looked away for a moment, and suddenly they were gone. They watched their father being murdered, and I had to leave them alone for a few seconds, and when I returned, they had disappeared.* I couldn't imagine saying that to anyone.

Finally, hours later, I found myself parked in an alleyway outside the narrow, wood-frame shack where Jeannine had gone to live with her aunt and uncle and their children. I got out of the car and walked up the rickety steps and knocked quietly on the door. There were no lights inside, not even a candle. After a moment, I heard Jeannine's voice, little more than a whisper. "Who that?"

"It's me. Hannah."

The door opened a crack, then a little wider, and I made out Jeannine's round, brown face in the gloom. I sensed others behind her, as if the room were crowded and I had interrupted a meeting of conspirators. Jeannine said, "What you want here?"

"I . . . need you. I need you to help me. I've lost the boys. I don't know where the boys are, Jeannine."

"No," she said. "The boys not here." She started to close the door, and I held it back with my hand.

"Wait. Woodrow . . . he's been killed. Woodrow's dead, Jeannine."

She looked at me blankly, as if I'd said my telephone wasn't working. "Plenty-plenty people dead. Go 'way, *missus*."

"Please, Jeannine. I need you. I can't find my sons."

"You don' need me for nuthin'. *Missus*."

We looked at each other in silence for a moment. We had been servant and mistress, then she the teacher and I the student, then friends. We had shared my husband, and then, at my doing, had become servant and mistress again. Now we were enemies. The truth of our relationship had finally become its reality.

"Will you come back to the house with me, Jeannine?"

She did not answer. She pushed the door closed on me, left me standing on the little porch alone in the darkness.

Slowly I drove down Duport Road towards our house and realized that I would have to pass Woodrow's body and would somehow have to bring it into the yard and wrap it and bury it. I would have to search in the gutter in the dark for his head and carry it, too, into the yard and bury it with his body. I didn't know if I was capable of performing this grisly task alone, now, in the middle of the night, but decided that I had no choice, I had to do it for the boys. For Woodrow. For myself. I was not going to leave my husband's body lying in the street for the rats and wild dogs and the buzzards.

I steeled myself and slowed the car and pulled up before the closed gate. I didn't remember closing the gate, but must have, to keep the dogs inside the yard. But had I locked it? I wondered, for I saw in the headlights that the padlock had been hooked into the hasp and was snapped shut.

I got out of the car and walked to where Woodrow had been murdered. There was a splash of moonlight through the trees on the ground where he'd been forced to kneel and a pool of blood where he'd fallen. But his body was gone. I crossed to the gutter where his head had been tossed like garbage and grimaced as if I were already looking at it in the muck and refuse. But it was not there. Someone, something, had taken my husband's decapitated body and his head, his *remains*. Someone had taken first my children and now the remains of my murdered husband.

I stumbled back to the car, and as I got inside, looked up and saw that the gate was swung wide open, and standing behind it in the driveway was Sam Clement. He waved me forward, and I drove the car in from the street. As I stepped from the car, Sam clanked the gate shut again and locked it.

"You left the key in the lock," he said. "Not a good idea. It's lucky I came by before anyone else did, or you wouldn't have much to come home to."

My entire body was shaking, and I started to cry. Sam put his arms around me and held me until I could finally speak. "Woodrow . . . he's dead, Sam. They killed him. And the boys, my sons, they're gone. I don't know where they are! I've been driving around all night trying to find them. Can you help me, Sam? I don't know what to do anymore."

"C'mon inside," he said in a low voice. "I know about . . . Woodrow. I saw his body when I got here."

"His *body!* They cut off his head, Sam. It was Satterthwaite, him and three other men. They weren't soldiers, but I know Doe sent them."

"Probably, yes. He's gone all paranoid and wiggy and is sending out all kinds of headhunters. They're doing their dirty work all over the city. C'mon, I'll get you a drink. I found some candles inside and Woodrow's whiskey. Hope you don't mind," he added as we crossed the terrace and went inside.

"But the boys, Sam? Doe wouldn't take my sons, would he?"

"Can't imagine he'd bother," he said and in the flickering candlelight stepped quickly to the liquor cabinet and half filled a glass with scotch. "Besides, they're Americans."

"What?"

"Well, half and half." He handed me the drink, took up his own, and sat in Woodrow's easy chair.

I fell back into the chair opposite, suddenly exhausted. The whiskey burned my throat, but it calmed my shaking limbs and brought my thoughts more or less back into focus. I realized that I hadn't heard or seen the dogs. "Where are the dogs?"

Sam exhaled heavily. "Yes, well, the dogs. When I got here, with Woodrow's body out in the street and the car gone and the house dark and silent, I was afraid something equally bad had happened to you and the boys. I had to get inside. I unlocked the gate easily enough, due to your leaving the key in it, but the dogs wouldn't let me pass. I'm sorry, Hannah. I had to shoot them. There was no other way to get inside the house."

"Oh, God, you shot our dogs?" I put down my glass. "Sam, you carry a gun?"

"I do." He touched the breast pocket of his suit jacket.

"Christ," I said. After a few seconds of silence, I asked him again about the boys. "I'm terrified. They're my babies, Sam." I started to cry again. "Damn it, I hate my fucking crying!" I yelled, and stopped immediately.

Sam asked if the boys had seen Woodrow killed.

"Yes. They watched from the car. Satterthwaite and three others pulled him out of the car and made him get down on his hands and knees. And then one of them cut off Woodrow's head, Sam. It was . . . awful. He did it with a machete. And the boys . . . they watched it happen."

He stood and refilled his glass at the bar. With his back to me, he asked, "Did they know it was Doe who had Woodrow killed?"

"Dillon, I think Dillon knew. Woodrow came home afraid and

crazed and insisted on driving to Fuama with the boys tonight. He said Doe had turned on him. I'm sure that registered with Dillon and very likely with the twins, too. They're fourteen and thirteen, Sam. They don't miss much."

"So they know," he said, still with his back to me.

"Yes."

He turned and sat back down in Woodrow's chair. "That's too bad, then."

"Why? I don't understand."

"Yes, you do," he said quietly. "You just don't want to admit it to yourself. You probably knew it the second you realized they were gone."

For a long moment neither of us said anything. Distant gunfire rattled the windows. Otherwise, silence. Finally, I said, "You're right. I've been driving all over the city tonight as if I were looking for my sons. But I knew the whole time I wouldn't find them."

"So you understand that by now they're either with one of Prince Johnson's outfits on the other side of the river or else with one of Charles Taylor's."

"Yes."

"More likely Prince Johnson's. Charles's people are still pretty much locked down at Robertsfield for the time being. Johnson's just over the bridge."

I nodded. I understood what was happening, I was living inside it; it was my life, but I couldn't quite believe that it was real. I asked Sam if he had moved Woodrow's body.

"Yes. I dug a shallow grave out there in back of the house. It's in the flower garden. When this is over, you can put together a proper funeral for him. I'll show you later where I buried him."

"You found . . . the head, too?"

"Yes, I'm afraid so."

"Thank you."

"You're welcome."

"Sam, what am I going to do? What *can* I do?"

He took a swallow from his drink. "Only one thing you can do now."

"What?"

"Get the hell out of Africa."

BUT I DIDN'T LEAVE. For a while I was able to continue searching for my sons and caring for my dreamers. There was murder and mayhem all around me during those weeks, but strangely very little of it touched me directly. At least at the time it seemed strange. Later, I understood.

Every morning I drove through the nearly deserted streets of Monrovia, passing bodies, many of them mutilated and half devoured by dogs and other scavengers during the night, with smoke rising from the outskirts where fighting continued between Doe's dwindling forces and Prince Johnson's bands of men and boys in the eastern suburbs. Charles Taylor's forces were approaching from the south. Rumors of Doe's imminent collapse and surrender floated through the city like errant breezes. There were hourly radio broadcasts and declarations of victory by all three parties to the war, each of them in turn denying the claims of the other two, until it became impossible to gauge the direction or flow of the conflict. Because I seemed to be immune to its effects, of so little value or threat to any of the warring parties that I was able to pass through the checkpoints more or less at will, I was able to ignore the daily advances and retreats and dealt with the war as if its outcome would have nothing to do with me or my sons or my dreamers. I was too numb with fear and grief, too horrified and shocked by the killing of Woodrow and my sons' disappearance, to worry about the larger effects of the war.

And so I moved more or less freely throughout the city, while the war raged around me. There were checkpoints all over now, run by boys not much older than Dillon, heavily armed and wearing looted clothing and gear, bizarre combinations of women's clothes, formal wear, and shirts and shorts plastered with the logos of American sports teams. They wore juju amulets that were supposed to make the boys bulletproof and heavy gold chains and medallions that made them look like deracinated rap singers. Regardless of the time of day or night, they were high on drugs and raw alcohol, their minds deranged by what they had seen and done in the war. At every stop they demanded money from me, and as soon as I gave them a few dollars, they let me pass. Every time I saw a new group of boys coming towards my car with their guns cocked and their hands already out for money, I asked them if they knew the whereabouts of the sons of Woodrow Sundiata, and usually they cackled and laughed at my question, as if I'd asked if they knew the whereabouts of Michael Jackson, or they ignored my question altogether, took my money, and waved for me to go on.

Finally, I gave up searching the city for my sons, and decided to risk driving to Fuama, where I half believed they might have gone, although I couldn't imagine why. I left Kuyo in charge of the dreamers. He had grown to love them and they him. A few times the soldiers, Doe's men, had come by the sanctuary to see if I had left yet, and when they saw that I was still in charge of the place, they departed, shrugging and smiling over my foolishness. Except for the bodies of the dreamers themselves, bush meat, there wasn't much to interest them at the sanctuary, nothing of value to loot or destroy. Estelle, Woodrow's sixteen-year-old cousin, a sweet country girl who'd come to the city to work for me at the sanctuary, was as loyal as Kuyo to me and the dreamers and had stayed on at Toby long past the time when she should have fled back to her village. When she first arrived from the backcountry, I'd given her an unused room at the sanctuary, an old storage shed, that she had made her home, and I'd begun teaching her to read. She was a pretty, shy girl, not as bright as I might have liked, but kind and eager to please.

For a long time, she and Kuyo and the dreamers had been my only companions, and because I seemed almost magically protected against the depredations of the soldiers, Kuyo and Estelle had come to think of me as their protector, and thus both had stayed on longer than they should have. Everyone in Monrovia had a tribal village they could flee to, but no one knew for sure if it was safe there. Tribes thought to be loyal to Taylor, like the Gio, were viewed by Doe's men and Johnson's as the enemy and were therefore legitimate targets of opportunity, even though they were unarmed civilians. Tribes thought to be loyal to Doe or Johnson because of lineage, were slaughtered by the soldiers of one or the other or both of the others, the women and girls raped, their villages razed and rice and cassava and garden stores looted or burned. All over the country, people were in confused flight from one or the other of the three forces, and sometimes from all three. When the fighting had been mostly in the bush, people had fled into Monrovia; but now it had come to the outskirts of the city, and everyone who could had fled back into the bush. Monrovia seemed like the still center of a swirling, countrywide storm, with all its inhabitants waiting, heads lowered, hands tied behind their backs, for the three armies to converge there.

THE ROAD TO FUAMA was littered with abandoned cars and pickup trucks, tires stripped, hoods and trunks open, some of the vehicles still smouldering. The rubber plantations and plowed fields were empty of workers and overgrown, neglected for months now, since Charles's band of rebels had crossed into Liberia from Guinea at Nimba and Johnson had come in from the north. The villages all seemed to have been abandoned by the inhabitants, and most of the buildings had been burned. Desolation lay all around.

At the river I was met by a group of four boys, two of them carrying AK-47s and bandoliers of ammunition draped over their bony shoulders. They wore do-rags on their heads and cheap wraparound sunglasses that made them look like spindly insects. When they approached the car, I opened the window and said that I wanted to cross the river to Fuama.

They didn't answer. One boy held out his hand, palm up, and I put a dollar in it. The others did the same, and I put a dollar in each hand and said again that I wanted to cross the river to my husband's village. I noticed a man, also in sunglasses and wearing a do-rag, camo shirt, cargo pants, and Timberland boots, lounging by a cotton tree nearby, smoking a cigarette and barely watching the boys under his apparent command. Though I had many times over the years made this journey to Fuama with Woodrow and had come to know most of the inhabitants of the settlement, at least their faces, these boys and their commander were strangers to me. Many of Woodrow's people did not speak English, or spoke it only a little. *Perhaps they don't understand me*, I thought.

The man got up slowly and strolled towards the car. I said to him, "My husband is Woodrow Sundiata. His father is headman of Fuama. My sons—"

The man cut me off. "Go home now," he said. He waved the barrel of his gun in the direction I had come. "Turn and go home."

Something in his voice was familiar. "Do I know you?" I asked. "What's your name?"

"You know me." He took off his sunglasses, and I recognized him at once. It was Albert, Woodrow's nephew, who had guided me into the village years ago, on my first visit to Fuama, when I'd been left behind, a teenage boy who was in missionary school and hoped to follow Woodrow's example in life. And indeed he had, or so I believed. He had finished high school in Liberia and, at Woodrow's expense, had attended business school in Baltimore for two years and had returned to Liberia, where he had taken a job in Loma, up near the border of Sierra Leone, with an American-owned sand-and-gravel company.

"Albert!" I cried. "I'm so relieved it's you." His eyes were red rimmed and his expression was cold, utterly without feeling. "You're a soldier," I said.

"Everybody makin' war now. You g'wan home now, missus," he said and put his sunglasses back on.

"Albert, my sons . . . are they here? In Fuama? Do you know where they are?"

For a moment he said nothing. He turned to the boys with him and spoke rapidly in Kpelle. They answered with slow shakes of their heads. Then Albert said, "Mus' be them dead. Most everybody from the family dead now. On account of Woodrow an' Doe."

"Woodrow is dead, Albert."

"I know that."

"He's your uncle. Don't you care?"

"I care, yes. But now everybody in the family, the whole village almost, they dead, too. On account of Woodrow bein' for Doe an' against Taylor."

"It was Doe's men who killed Woodrow," I said. "Not Taylor's."

"Don't matter who kill him."

"No, you don't understand!"

He started to walk away at that, but I got out of the car and followed him down to the edge of the river, where he stood looking across to the landing on the other side. The river was high from the rains and dark red with runoff from the highlands. "The raft is gone," I said. "How do you get over to the village?"

"The village gone, too. The soldiers, them come an' mash it all up. Burn all the houses, kill all the peoples inside an' shoot the ones who run out."

"What soldiers? Doe's?"

"Charles Taylor's soldiers. He come here with them and help to kill all the people himself. Then he goes on the radio an' says it a great victory over Samuel Doe's army boys. But there ain't none of them here. Never was. Only old men an' women an' little babies here. When I hear Charles Taylor on the radio I came very fast from Loma to see what happened. Only these little boys left. Them an' me, we been buryin' all the dead peoples."

"Where did you and these boys get the guns?" I asked him.

"Prince Johnson. He got plenty-plenty guns for people who wants to go against Charles Taylor while Prince an' his soldiers goes against Samuel Doe in the city."

We stood side by side in silence. He was a small, frail-boned, young man—like Woodrow a decade ago, before alcohol and middle age thickened him. "Albert, what will you do now?"

"Can't say. 'Cept to keep killin' peoples. Till Taylor an' Doe both dead or run out of the country. Prince Johnson give us plenty protection. Nothin' can hurt us. No bullets, no machete, nothin'. He promise me a good job after the war an' a house in the city. My war name ain't Albert, y' know," he said. "No more Albert Sundiata," he said with pride. "My war name is Sweet Dreams Gladiator. Pretty cool, eh?" He smiled broadly, boyishly. Then, still smiling, he said to me, "I need your car. Woodrow's car."

"My car? No!"

"We need to take your car. This Benz belongs to Prince Johnson now and no more to Samuel Doe."

I argued, I protested, I begged, but it did no good. He'd gone stony on me. The boys had crowded into the car, ready to travel, pushing and punching one another playfully, as if headed out for a day at the beach.

Albert said, "Gimme the keys."

"No! If you take the car, how will I get back?"

"Not my problem. Gimme the keys now."

We stood there arguing a moment longer, when one of the boys walked over with the keys dangling from his fingertips. I'd left them in the ignition. He handed them to Albert, Sweet Dreams Gladiator, and that was the end of our argument. Albert headed for the car, and I said, "You're not leaving me here," and ran for the passenger's side, flung open the door, and yanked the boy sitting there out of the car and took his place. "There! Now get in back with the others if you want to ride," I said to him and locked the door.

Albert laughed and got behind the wheel, while the sour-faced boy fought for a place in back, where the others were jammed together with their guns and ammunition. They were little more than children, twelve and thirteen years old, one minute killers, the next playful and innocent-seeming as puppies. Albert said to them, "Better do what Mammi say, before she put the eye on you."

*　　　*　　　*

WE PASSED THROUGH the town of Millsburg to the far side of a
cinder-block school, where several troop carriers and seventy-five or a
hundred men and boys and a small number of women and girls loi-
tered around campfires. It was nearly dark. I smelled food cooking—
palm oil, rice, and meat. Albert parked the Mercedes next to a vehicle I
recognized, a white Land Rover with the seal of the U.S. government
on the door and U.S. embassy plates.

Immediately, a gang of fighters surrounded the Mercedes, admiring
it and praising Albert for having brought it in. He turned and said to
me, "Maybe I can get you a ride back to town." He nodded in the direction of the Land Rover, then got out of the car. "Wait here. I'll bring
Prince to decide things," he said and walked into the school with most
of the crowd in tow.

A few moments later they returned, with Albert still at the center
but walking a few feet behind a tall, very dark man in a proper military
uniform, Prince Johnson, evidently, and striding along beside him, Sam
Clement, his face barely concealing a sly smile.

I got out of the car and stood by the door, waiting. Johnson had
the look of a successful preacher, a crowd-pleasing, handsome, back-
slapper happiest when surrounded by admirers and impossible to
imagine alone and in a reflective mood. He came straight to me and
took my hand in both his huge hands and said, "I mus' tell you how sad
I am for the cruel an' untimely death of your husband. I only jus' now
heard about it from my good friend, Mister Sam Clement. Please
accept my heartfelt condolences, missus."

I stammered a thank you and glanced at Sam, whose expression
told me nothing at all. Johnson continued to talk. His English was very
good, and he thanked me on behalf of his people and all the people of
Liberia for the gift of the Mercedes, which had been bought and paid
for by the poor people of Liberia and was now being returned to them,
its rightful owners, and I could be sure that when this war was over

there would be a proper public tribute to me, full government honors and privileges to be granted to me before all the citizens of Liberia. "We Liberians love the Americans," he declared. "An' we remember all their many generosities." Then he moved close to the car and swung open the driver's door and leaned in, examining it with obvious pleasure.

Sam came up to me and took my arm and in a low voice said, "Get in my car, I'll take you back to town." He walked me around to the passenger's side of the Land Rover and opened the door. I climbed inside and waited while he exchanged a few words with Johnson, who now sat proudly behind the wheel of the Mercedes. Then Sam was beside me in the Land Rover, and we were driving very fast out of town, heading towards Monrovia.

For a long while neither of us spoke. Finally I said, "What were you doing there?"

"More to the point, darlin', what were *you* doing there?"

"I had no choice. They wanted the car."

"I mean, what were you doing way out here in the bush, for heaven's sake?"

"My sons, Sam! My . . . lost boys. I thought maybe someone in Fuama would know . . . and would help me. Would help me find them and bring them home."

"Ridiculous. All the Kpelle have scattered into the jungle or headed for the border. Except the ones who've signed on with Johnson. Like your young friend there. One of Woodrow's people, no?"

"Yes. Albert. All he wants to do now is kill people loyal to Doe or Taylor."

"He's got reason."

"Yes. I know."

"Hannah, give it up," he said. "Don't go looking any further for your sons."

"I have to, Sam."

"They don't want to be found. Believe me, I've asked around. The sons of Woodrow Sundiata, they're well known, Hannah, and they're either under the protection of that crazy sorry-ass Johnson, or Taylor, who isn't much better."

"They could have been back there, back at Johnson's camp?"

"Exactly. And if they wanted you to find them, darlin', you'd find them without looking. They know where *you* are, m'dear." He was silent for a moment. "If you won't leave the country, Hannah, and I can't force you to leave, then for God's sake stay at your house. I'll make sure it's secure. We've hired some locals to protect certain properties from looting and certain individuals from harm. But if things keep getting worse, we'll have to close down the embassy completely, and if we do, I won't be able to help you, Hannah. You'll be on your own here. A white woman all alone in hell."

"Who do you think will win the war, Sam?"

He didn't hesitate. "Taylor. This guy Johnson is nutty as a fruitcake, a real piece of work. But Taylor, him we can deal with."

"I'll be all right then."

Our route back to town passed near Toby, and I asked Sam to let me stop at the sanctuary for a moment to check on my dreamers. With things falling apart so fast, I couldn't be sure of Kuyo's and Estelle's willingness or ability to cover for me. When we pulled up in front of the office, the place was dark, and no one came out of the building to greet us. The headlights of Sam's Land Rover flooded the small yard, and long, fluttering shadows from the cotton tree in the center of the yard flashed across the gravel. While Sam waited in the car, I walked quickly to Estelle's cabin and knocked on the door and called, "Estelle? You there?"

No answer. Returning to the car, I said to Sam, "You go on. I've got to feed and water the chimps. I think my helpers have run off."

"How'll you get home?"

"I'll camp here. I've got a couch in the office. It's okay. I've done it before."

He passed me a flashlight. "Here. You'll need this. Looks like the power's off all over the city."

He drove away, and I snapped on the flashlight and headed for the office, when suddenly the door opened, and there was Kuyo, and in the shadows behind him, Estelle, both of them wide eyed, frightened. "Why didn't you come out before, for heaven's sake?" I demanded. "If I'd known you were here, I'd have gone home with Mister Clement."

"We didn' know it was you," Kuyo said solemnly. "Might be the soldiers comin' back."

I entered the office and lit a kerosene lamp, filling the room with a dull orange glow. "They were here again? Doe's soldiers?"

He said he didn't think so. Not Doe's soldiers. Not this time. "Maybe from Prince Johnson. Real wild boys," he said. They had gone through the place and emptied the petty cash box and had taken the radio and my old manual typewriter. They'd noted the eleven chimps, pointedly counting them, Kuyo said, and they'd told him that as soon as they got themselves a truck, they were coming back.

"Them gonna make plenty-plenty bush meat, Miz Sundiata," Estelle said and started to whimper. "Them men are terrible peoples!" she cried.

"Then we'll have to move the chimps," I said.

And we did move them. It took the entire night, but the three of us managed to transport all eleven dreamers from the sanctuary out to Boniface Island, a small, mangrove-covered islet in the middle of the broad estuary. Chimpanzees cannot swim and are afraid of open water, which made the island, though more of a sanctuary, as much a place of confinement as the renovated prison at Toby had been. In pairs and with the larger adults one by one, we moved the dreamers in the same large, wheeled cage that we had used to bring them to Toby from the blood lab in the first place. The river bank was only a few hundred yards down a narrow lane from the sanctuary, and luckily Kuyo had a friend with an old, leaky Boston Whaler with an outboard motor that hadn't been stolen by the soldiers yet. For fifty dollars, Kuyo's friend agreed to let us use the boat for the night. We flattened the bottom of the hull by laying a sheet of plywood into it and used another for a ramp to load and off-load the chimps. Seven times we rolled the cage onto the boat and kept it steady during the three-mile voyage out to Boniface, where we rolled the cage from the boat onto the short, dark beach and released the chimps, strangers suddenly freed in a strange land. Until they discovered, of course, that the land was very small, not much larger than their communal space at Toby, and was surrounded by water.

With genuine interest and curiosity, the dreamers watched us work. All night long, sweating and grunting from the effort, we bumped and scraped our knuckles and shins against the cage and the gunwales as we fought to keep the cage steady during the crossing. Estelle and Kuyo were both very strong, much stronger than I, and even they were exhausted from the work, but neither complained or held back or asked to rest. Once we had our plan and technique in place, we worked in silence, except to comfort and reassure the dreamers, who seemed somehow to recognize that we were all in great danger and were trying to save their lives. None of them panicked or cried out.

We moved Doc first, the largest and strongest of the dreamers, their leader. His compliance and trust instructed the others to do likewise. When we released him from the cage and quickly pulled the cage back onto the boat and let the boat drift a few feet out from the beach, I cast the beam of my flashlight onto him. He was crouched on the short beach, peering around at the low mangroves, sniffing the air, taking the measure of the space that surrounded him. He scooted in a quick circle over the island and returned to the beach. He looked out at the boat, then looked aside and down, as if pondering a deep question: *Why am I here instead of someplace else?*

"Doc scared, but don't want nobody to know it," Kuyo whispered.

I flicked off the flashlight. "Me, too."

By the time we'd moved all eleven of the dreamers, it was nearly dawn, the safest part of the day in Monrovia, when the only people out and about were women and children scouring the city for food and water and kerosene for cooking, stepping over fresh bodies, the night's kill, and heading quickly back to their huts and shanties to hole up in darkness for the rest of the day and night, avoiding as much as possible being caught alone and unarmed by one of the roaming gangs of men and boys sky high on drugs, palm wine, and murder and lusting for blood and sex and loot. But it felt safe enough for me to walk the few miles from Toby back to Duport Road. I had no other place to go now anyhow and couldn't stay at the sanctuary waiting for the soldiers to return. Kuyo wanted to leave at once for his village in Lofa, to be with his wife and children, who had fled the city a few weeks ago, but he agreed to pack up my records and logbooks and bring them to Duport Road for safekeeping as soon as he got a few hours' sleep. Estelle had already locked herself inside her shed to hide and sleep. She had a vague plan of waiting till nightfall and trying then to slip past the checkpoints north of the city. She'd heard that her village was under the control of Prince Johnson and there was no longer any fighting. The looting and rape, for the time being, at least, had been completed out there, and something resembling civil order had returned. These loosely controlled armies roared through the villages like hurricanes, and it was usually safest after one of them had passed on and another had not yet arrived, when they were killing people elsewhere over food, pillage, women, and territory. Right now, all three armies were converging on the city, Monrovia, closing in on it like three hungry lions trying to take down a wounded bull and keep the other two at bay.

I had no provincial village to return to, no family or tribe to hide or protect me until this war was over. My dreamers were for the time being safe on their island, stocked with enough food to last them a week or so, when I planned to bring over a fresh supply of fruits, vegetables, and leafy greens. But beyond that, I had no plan, except to wait out the war and hope that it would end quickly, possibly in the next few weeks, with Charles Taylor vanquishing Samuel Doe and Prince Johnson alike. I still nurtured the belief that once Charles had removed Doe from power and kept Johnson from coming to power, he'd quickly pacify the rest of the country with the help of ECOMOG and the other regional forces, and in short order he would establish a constitutional assembly and hold elections, redistribute land, create social and economic equality, and bring about a socialist democracy in this little corner of West Africa that would shine across the continent like an alabaster city on a hill. My sons would return to me then. Together we would bury their father properly in the cemetery of the church he so loved. They would heal from their terrible ordeal, and the four of us, mother and sons, would build a coherent, useful life together in the new Liberia.

It was a flimsy excuse for a vision, a sorry patchwork made of scraps of fantasy, but it had not been willed into being or chosen from among others, for I had no alternative vision available to me then, no plan, no option, no blueprint for action that did not lead me to flee this place, abandoning my missing sons, my murdered husband's body buried among the flowers behind our house, my dreamers marooned on an island. That tattered vision was my life, the only life I had now.

YOU MAY REMEMBER my telling early on how the soldiers, returning to the sanctuary, mutilated and killed poor Kuyo—while I drank myself to sleep on half a bottle of warm gin back at the house on Duport Road. You may remember my telling how Estelle and I started to gather the rain-soaked, muddied records I'd taken years to accumulate, when I grew suddenly despondent beyond repair or relief, and instead of saving those records and logbooks, I burned them there in the yard of the sanctuary. And when Estelle asked me, "Why you doin' that, Miz Sundiata! After we work so hard to collect 'em!" I said, "I don't know, Estelle. I don't know why I'm burning the papers. I just don't. There is no sanctuary here now, Estelle," I said to her. "It's gone. Like Woodrow. Like my sons. Like Kuyo. Like the chimps. Gone. And if you don't go home and stay there, you'll be gone, too," I told her, and she obeyed me, and I never saw the girl again.

That same night Sam Clement found me at the sanctuary. He arrived in the backseat of a Humvee driven by a helmeted U.S. Marine with a second, heavily armed Marine in the passenger's seat, big, pink-skinned southern boys with necks like tree trunks, crisp, camo'd uniforms, their weapons and boots oiled and glistening, so different from the rusting weaponry and motley uniforms of Doe's soldiers or the bizarre costumes worn by the rebels. For weeks, Marine helicopters had been airlifting embassy personnel and U.S. and other foreign civilians from the U.S. embassy grounds to four destroyers stationed a few miles offshore, there to receive and ferry people north to Freetown, in Sierra Leone, where there were commercial flights to London and charter planes to the States.

Rain poured down on us in the middle of the muddy yard. We stood in the beam of the headlights, while the Marines stood guard beside it, as if expecting to be attacked. Sam grabbed me by the shoulder. "For Christ's sake, Hannah, come to the embassy *now!* You'll be dead or worse by morning if you don't. Doe's dead. This place is turning into a goddamned killing field."

"Doe's dead?"

"Where the hell you been, girl? Prince Johnson and his boys got him."

"Home," I said. "I've been at home. And here."

He was disgusted. "I'm surprised you're still alive," he said and pulled me towards the Humvee. "Get in."

We rode in silence, until halfway back to town I said to Sam, "I've got to go by the house first. I need my passport and some papers and a few clothes, Sam. And some money."

He didn't answer at first, then said to the driver, "Sergeant, we'll make a stop back at Duport Road."

"Yes, sir. Same place we was watchin', I suppose," the Marine drawled.

"Yes."

When we pulled up to the house, I got out and unlocked the gate and swung it back. The driver drew the Humvee up to the terrace and parked, and Sam and I went inside the darkened house. I lit a kerosene lamp on a table by the door and started for the living room.

Sam said, "You out of fuel for the generator? Smells like you haven't had the air-conditioner on for weeks."

"I guess there's fuel. I just haven't used it. I've been going to bed early, I guess, and making do with candlelight and kerosene lamps."

He told me to wait while he got the generator started and left me alone in the living room. He was right; the house smelled amphibian. I looked around the room as if I hadn't seen it in weeks, as if I'd been in another country. Mildew and mold had darkened the walls and ceiling, and the cloth on the furniture and the rugs had started to rot. For weeks I had sleepwalked through my days and dreamlessly slept through my nights and had barely noticed the rapid disintegration of my home. Now, as I lit candles and lamps and walked from living room to dining room to the boys' bedroom and mine and Woodrow's, I saw that the house and everything in it and all the memories that it contained were dying before my eyes.

Returning to the living room, I heard the generator rumble to life, and suddenly the lights came on, and the air-conditioner fluttered and whirred. Sam came inside looking pleased with himself. "Let there be light!" he said. He hadn't shaved in several days and looked very tired. His rumpled suit was spotted with mud and coffee stains and sweat and looked like he'd been wearing it for weeks. But he was oddly attractive all the same. Fatigue and anxiety became him. They undercut his Tidewater arrogance, his genteel self-assurance, and gave him a more humble mien and manner. He shot me a crooked smile and said, "Too bad we don't have some time to kill. We could throw us a little party."

I looked up at him. "In all these years, Sam, you've only hit on me once, when you tried to kiss me out there on the terrace. Remember?"

"Yes. That was an accident. I was a little drunk, I'm afraid. But I don't mean that the way it sounds. You are an extremely attractive woman, I can say that. It's just that I don't make a habit of coming on to married women."

"I never thought of you as especially scrupulous, Sam."

He laughed lightly. "I'm not."

"What about widows?"

"Yes, well, that would alter things a tad, wouldn't it, now? But this is not a good time, Miz Sundiata, for you to be coming on to me. If that is what you're doing."

"I don't know what I'm doing anymore. Maybe I'm just curious."

"Curious, eh? The truth is, sometimes after I've been out here in this goddamn heart of darkness I get horny for white people, that's all. I suppose you do, too. I expect that's a little of what's going on with you right now," he said.

I exhaled slowly and sat down on the sofa. "No. I'm lonely. And I'm confused. And I'm frightened. And terribly sad, Sam. I'm sad. And suddenly, in this light and in this room, you are a very attractive man to me, and if it would make my loneliness and confusion and fear and my sadness go away for a few moments, I'd like you to make love to me. That's all."

He furrowed his brow and looked steadily at me, as if he suspected a trap was being set for him. "That's all, eh? I was under the impression that you preferred women," he said.

"Oh, really? And what gave you that impression?"

He laughed. "A boy can tell. Especially one that prefers men. C'mon, m'dear, pack your bag. We can continue this discussion later." He reached out for my hand and took it and drew me slowly to my feet. The rain pounded against the roof and splashed against the terrace and walkways outside. I thought of Woodrow buried in his shallow grave at the side of the house and my sons' empty cots, their clothes and books and games still lying scattered around their bedroom.

"I can't leave," I said to Sam.

His face stiffened. "I'm under orders to bring you to the embassy, Hannah, and get you the hell out of the country."

"I have to be here for when my sons come back."

"No, you don't."

"I can't find them. And I can accept that for now. But I have to make it so they can find me. You don't know, because you don't have children. You're not a mother," I said. "This is what mothers do, Sam. I know. I'm a mother. They wait for their children to come back home. Like my mother did with me."

"I was afraid of this," he mumbled and walked to the TV and turned it on. Nothing came up except snow, both television stations having been captured by the rebels days before and all the broadcast equipment mindlessly looted or smashed. "You got anything to drink?" he asked. "You're gonna need one, and I'd like one, too."

I pulled a bottle of Woodrow's whiskey and two glasses from the liquor cabinet and poured us each a drink. I noticed that Sam had a videotape in his hand.

"Sit down, Hannah. I want you to watch this."

I sat in Woodrow's overstuffed armchair opposite the TV, and Sam put the tape into the VCR. He stood aside with the remote in one hand and his drink in the other and fast forwarded past footage of what looked like bands of rebel troops. Then suddenly I was looking at the face of Samuel Doe. He was seated on the floor of a brightly lit room with several men in rebel military uniforms standing over and around him. He was naked, except for a pair of blood-spotted underpants. He was fat, big bellied, his spindly legs splayed before him, his thin arms bound tightly behind him. The camera is shaky and moves erratically off Doe to the others and back again. Two of the men stroke his head, which has red abrasions and cuts and appears to have been roughly shaved with a knife or a dull razor. Doe looks mournfully up at his captors and says, "I want to say something, if you will just listen to me." I recognize one of the two men stroking Doe's head. It's Albert—it's Sweet Dreams Gladiator. He has a small smile on his face that looks almost gentle. Doe says to him, "You untie my hands, and I will talk. I never ordered anybody's execution." The camera swings away from him, blurs past the others in the room, some in uniform, some not, and there is Prince Johnson seated at a large desk. Hanging from the wall behind him is a pink and pale blue Sunday-school portrait of Christ carrying a lamb on his shoulders. I can read the legend below Christ: *Look at me and be saved.* Prince Johnson says, "I'm a humanitarian." He sniffs and coughs lightly, as if from cigarette smoke. "Cut off one ear," he says. The camera drifts back to Doe. Someone has a long knife in his hand, but the camera wobbles on Doe, who is pushed over on his back, and I can't see who is sawing at his ear with the knife. Doe shrieks, and when the man steps away, I see that he is not a man, he is a boy. It is Dillon, my eldest son. Doe thrashes and flips his head wildly from side to side. He manages to sit up and begins blowing on his bare chest, as if to put out a fire. He ceases blowing and looks off camera at his tormentors. "I beg you . . ." he says. A hand shoves his head back and pushes him onto the floor again, and the knife goes to work on his other ear. He screams, a wail of pain and helpless fury. Then there is a quick swerve of the camera back to Prince Johnson, still at his desk, dangling a human ear above his open mouth, lowering the ear slowly. Chewing. Now Doe is in a garden, entirely naked, his face puffed and bloody, his ears reduced to pulpy stumps. There is a small group of men and boys hovering around him, among them Dillon and William, looking bored and half asleep, as if they've just been roused and told to get ready for school but would rather have stayed in bed a while longer. Doe moans and says to someone off camera, "Varney, I'm dying." A man's voice says, "We are asking you in a polite manner now. What did you do with the Liberian people's money?" He speaks slowly in good English, as if for an American audience. Doe shakes his head and then is shown the knife, and he cries, "My penis! No, please, not my penis!" The camera jiggles and moves at a tilt, changing point of view as it gets passed over to William who turns its gaze on the previous cameraman, who is Paul, unsmiling, unafraid, almost blasé-looking. A man off camera says to Doe, "Repeat after me. 'I, Samuel Kenyon Doe, declare that the government is overthrown. I'm therefore asking the armed forces to surrender to Field Marshal Prince Johnson.'" Doe complies, his voice thin and weak. Off camera, someone says, "Fuck." Doe whimpers, "I want to talk. I need to pee." The screen fades to white, then black.

Sam and I remained silent for a long moment. Finally, I said, "Where . . . how did you get this?"

"Friends in high places," he said and popped the video from the VCR and slid it into his jacket pocket. He refilled his glass and then mine, leisurely, as if we had all the time in the world. "No, it's a bootleg copy. Half the foreign journalists in West Africa have seen it by now." He sat down on the sofa and stretched his long legs out and crossed them at the ankles the way Zack used to. "Hannah, we're shutting down the embassy tomorrow. I'm leaving the country tonight, and you are, too."

"I can't."

"You haven't much of a choice. It's simple suicide for you to stay here now. In a week, Monrovia, the whole country, will belong to Taylor. And he'll come after you, Hannah. Believe me."

"Charles? I'm in no danger from Charles," I said. "Since we're both truth-telling, Sam, I'll tell you this: I helped Charles. In the States. I was the one who helped him break out of jail."

He smiled, cold and knowing. "I'm well aware of that."

"You are?" I said, and then suddenly all the lights went out. "Shit! That's the end of the fuel for the generator, I guess." I couldn't see a thing, as if I were blindfolded. I started to get up and search in the dark for a candle or kerosene lantern, but my body wouldn't obey, as if my arms and legs were bound. Into the darkness I said, "Oh, Sam, what is going on? What do you mean, you're well aware that I helped Charles escape?"

His voice came out of the darkness. "Back then, the last place we wanted Charles Taylor was in a cell in Massachusetts. We wanted him here in Liberia. Our man in Africa."

"'We'?"

"We didn't quite count on Prince Johnson showing up at the party, of course. But we more or less got what we wanted. At least

Doe's out of the picture. But Charles Taylor ain't your friend, Hannah."

"I don't understand." The rain had let up, and in the sudden silence our voices seemed amplified, as if we were miked. I heard Sam loudly sigh. I said, "What are you telling me? That you somehow arranged Charles's escape from prison? That's impossible. No one knew I was there. No one out here knew, certainly."

"Some of it was dumb luck, I admit. We were going to use your friend, Zack, who wasn't all that steady a hand. But then you turned up, and ol' Zack was happy to step aside, long as he thought he'd still get him a sizeable payday out of it."

"And I suppose he did."

"Yeah, eventually. We all got what we wanted out of it. Zack wanted a big payday, and you wanted to help Charles turn Liberia into a social-ist democracy, which he might yet do, but don't count on it. And we wanted Charles to get rid of Samuel Doe. We just didn't get what we wanted in the form we'd imagined or planned. But that's history. Zack's happily back in business in Accra, buying and selling artworks, nicely protected and properly licensed. The man must be a millionaire ten times over by now. And I expect Charles will be an improvement on Doe. He's a whole lot smarter than Doe and nowhere near as crazy, but he ain't Nelson Mandela. Hell, even Nelson Mandela's no Nelson Mandela."

"I was working for you, then. The Americans. The CIA."

"Let's just say you were a protected asset. Still are. Which is why, Miz Sundiata, it's time to get your ass out of Africa. You know too much for Charles to let you stay here alive."

"Such as?"

"Such as how he got out of an American prison. First thing he'll do when he takes Monrovia is send some of his nastier boys over here to Duport Road looking for you. Then he's going after Prince Johnson and everyone else in that video. He's probably got his own copy and watches it every night, making his hit list. Charles definitely did not want Doe dead. He wanted a televised show trial that would establish his own legitimacy and right to run the country."

I heard Sam get up and grope his way from the room out to the terrace, where he called to the Marines and asked for a flashlight. A moment later he returned with the circle of light dancing in front of him. "C'mon, girlfriend, pack your bag. We got us a helicopter waiting out there on the basketball court at the embassy. You'll be home in Emerson, Massachusetts, by tomorrow night," he said. "I assume that's where you'll want to go."

Home? Whose home? Not Hannah Musgrave's. And not Dawn Carrington's. And not Mrs. Woodrow Sundiata's home. All the women I have been disappeared from the planet that night. "I don't want to go to jail, Sam," I said. "If I go back, I stand a good chance of being arrested. I'm still a fugitive, Sam."

"You won't be arrested. You still got that old fake passport, don't you?"

"Yes."

"It'll do. You haven't been underground anyhow. Not for a long time. We got those old Chicago bail-jumping charges against you dropped before you went back in eighty-three. You've been clean as a whistle for years, Hannah. Practically a virgin."

"Sam, I hate this."

"Yeah, well, that's about the size of it, Hannah." He took both my hands in his and pulled me to my feet. "C'mon. It's time to turn this war and this damned country over to the Africans again."

"As soon as the war is over, I'm coming back. This is my home, Sam."

"Maybe so, darlin', but I've got a feeling that by the time this war's truly over you're going to be an old lady."

Sam's dour prediction was not far off. More than a decade passed before I felt able to return and face the aftermath of that last night in Monrovia, and I was fifty-eight by then. Not an old lady, exactly, not by today's standards, but pretty much gone in the face and body. Most people in the village view me as old and sexually irrelevant, and here at the farm even Frieda and Nan and Cat and Anthea, though they work alongside me day in and out, treat me as an old lady, which is to say, they treat me as if I were of a slightly different species than they, and there is a certain amount of truth in that. I'm a husk of what I was twelve years ago. As we age we become a different animal. Women, especially. And when we've become an animal that's no longer sexually viable, the young, because they think they'll never be old themselves, treat us as if we're another kind of primate than they. As if one of us were a chimpanzee and the other human.

Because of my age, I have many notable incapacities and limitations that the girls don't have, and they know it and show it, for they are as competitive with one another and me as men are with men. For example, I can't lift as much as they. Cat, so delicate and precise in her movements, can lug more firewood and can load a truck with apples faster than I. And I have less stamina than they. Frieda and Nan are athletes and, regardless of their seasonal debauches, can work all day behind a rototiller in rocky Adirondack soil and have enough energy to drink and dance till closing time at one of the local roadhouses and then go home with a college boy working summers as a waiter at the Ausable Club and screw him blue till sunrise and still show up at the farm at seven ready for work. Anthea, after a lifetime of hard physical labor, has a strong man's upper-body strength. Though she's in her early forties, she can climb a ladder with a fifty-pound bundle of shingles on her shoulder, shear a dozen sheep without a break, and dig post holes from dawn to dusk without complaint, except of boredom. I can't do any of that. Nor can I attract the erotic gaze of a man or woman anymore. Only low curiosity comes my way now.

But for every incapacity and limitation of age there is a compensatory gift and attribute. So while the girls flirt and gossip, I lay out their day's work. I leave the rototilling to Nan and Frieda, but when we plow the riverfront fields in spring and in August cut hay in the high meadows, I drive the tractor; and when we go to market, I drive the truck, and Cat loads and unloads it, and the stock boys all come running to help her. I do the bookkeeping and select and purchase our seed and fertilizer and livestock and, inasmuch as it can be done selectively, control the breeding of the animals and fowl. Though I haven't a quarter of Anthea's experience and have no more natural intelligence than the girls, who are all very smart people, mine is the mental faculty of the farm. In this little troop, I am the rational one, the one who anticipates and prepares for catastrophe and crisis and the breakdown of machinery, the one who watches for capricious weather, sudden price fluctuations, illness in the livestock, and blight on the crops. The others merely go about their appointed daily rounds. I am the one who holds her tongue. The others are forever talking. I am the one with secrets untold, the one whose life's meaning is shaped by her memories and not by her ambitions or desires. I am the serious one.

And I am the one with the money. Let us not forget that. The farm is not a democracy or a socialist experiment, so the girls and I are as different as two separate species for that, too. Money and the power that comes with it distinguish between us as sharply as our differences in age. I own the farm and finance its operation and pay the girls' salaries with the money from the crops, but mostly run it with the money I inherited from my father by way of my mother. The sheep and goats are mine; the chickens and geese, the orchards and the fields and everything that grows on this land are mine; the house and outbuildings and vehicles and farm machinery and all the tools are mine, and the land and the forests on it and the river that runs through it. Even the dogs, Baylor and Winnie, who like all Border collies seem to belong to no one but themselves, they, too, are mine.

Thanks to my father and mother, I own a great deal now. In 1990, when I fled Monrovia, I owned nothing but a change of clothes—a pair of jeans, a sweatshirt, socks, and underwear—and a packet of old letters and a few photographs of my sons and Woodrow, grabbed almost as an afterthought when Sam and I ran from the house like terrorists who'd planted a bomb inside it. When I showed up at my mother's house in Emerson, I had nothing—no money, no property, no future. Only a past, and that shattered.

Who's the poet who said home is the place that when you have to go there they have to take you in? My mother took me in. She housed and fed and clothed me as if I were a child again, an errant teenager come reluctantly back to the nest, unwilling and unable to say where she had been, what she had seen and done, unable to tell anyone, even herself, what had gone terribly wrong out there in the wide world.

But my mother was by then very old, nearly eighty, and had grown feeble with Parkinson's disease, and soon, a few months later, I was taking care of her. For the first time since I left my dreamers on their island and the night I gave my sons up for lost, I felt useful again and necessary to another person's welfare. I fed her and clothed her and kept house for her as if she were a small child and I were her mother. The months passed, and she retreated from childhood to babyhood all the way to infancy, until she could no longer feed herself and then could no longer speak and was like a newborn animal and became incontinent. And then one night, without a sound, while I lay sleeping in the cot beside her bed, she simply stopped breathing, and when I awoke, I was all alone in the house that I had been raised in and had fled at the first opportunity and, when I had no place else to go, had returned to and was taken in.

My mother lies buried beside my father. There is no room there for me, even if I wanted it. In life as in death, for me and everyone else, there was no room beside or between my parents. In our family drama they were the only players. Standing off to the side all by myself, I was the chorus and sometimes played a messenger with news from the front, but more often was merely an extra, an onlooker. My small fate in the larger family fate was to be for my father an example, his Exhibit A, and for my mother a looking glass that told her she was the fairest of them all.

I sold my parents' house and everything in it. I packed into my Daddy's old Buick my few personal belongings, barely enough to fill the trunk, and drove to where for a few weeks each summer I had been a happy, contented child among other happy, contented children. I wanted to see the place again and try to remember what it was I felt back then during those five summers when my parents sent me away to live with other children and a few supervising adults on a lake in the forest. It was before I turned myself into the girl named Scout and the only time I felt as autonomous and free and authentic as an animal must feel all its life. I thought that if I could bring back the memory, I could bring back the feeling, and I would know for the first time what I truly wanted for myself, and then I would go and find it. That was my plan. But memories are always of things lost and gone and never returning. On a rainy, cold April morning, I sat in my car at the side of the road and wept bitterly. Saranac Lake Work and Arts Camp no longer existed. It had been sold to a private developer, who had torn down the bunkhouses and arts and crafts shops and cut the land into ten-acre lakeside lots for summer homes for suburbanite dot-com millionaires from Westchester County and Connecticut. The Adirondacks had become fashionable.

I thought of Alaska, of the far Northwest, of the Canadian Maritimes, but before leaving the Adirondacks for any one of those places, I stopped first at the Noonmark Diner here in Keene Valley. While waiting for my omelet to arrive I leafed idly through a brochure listing local real estate for sale and saw an ad for a property called Shadowbrook Farm, one hundred twenty acres with Ausable River frontage, meadows, open fields, a seven-room, hundred-year-old farmhouse with fireplace, outbuildings, farm equipment, and all furnishings included. It was listed for $130,000 with Adirondack Realty, whose office was conveniently located next to the diner, and by noon I had signed a contract to buy it. A month later I closed on the farm, hired Anthea and moved in, and commenced the life I have now.

It's a life eleven years on, and the first ten passed very quickly, like a dreamless sleep, until the end of August morning when Anthea and I finished butchering the chickens, and I saw that I could not live out the remainder of my days here on the farm unless I returned to Liberia and learned what had happened to my dreamers and my three sons and over his grave made a private peace with my husband. But I no more knew what I would find there than I did on the day I first arrived from Ghana a quarter-century ago. Liberia is a permanently haunted land filled with vengeful ghosts, and I had committed many sins there.

I made my way first to Boniface Island, where I had abandoned my dreamers. When the fisherman who carried me across the bay in his pirogue left me alone among the buried bones of my dreamers, I thought that I, too, had been abandoned on an island. Terrified and sick from hunger and thirst and the brain-boiling heat of the equatorial sun, I fell down before the ghosts of my dreamers and accepted their bewildered rage. I was ready, almost eager, for them to devour me. Their curses rained down on me, and my long remorse and secret shame were replaced that day by the permanent mournfulness that has given rise to the telling of this story.

I told none of this to Anthea or the other girls later, or else, once started, I would have had to tell them everything, as I have you. They asked, of course, but not until I'd been home again at Shadowbrook for weeks. There was so much else to preoccupy and frighten us then, with the world seeming suddenly to have turned murderous for everyone and anyone, even for four young women and an old lady ensconced on a farm in upstate New York, that my quick trip to a place in West Africa that they could not have located on a map did not count for much. It could wait, and has, until now. And when finally one evening in early October Anthea shyly asked me if my trip back to Liberia had been "successful," for that was how she put it, I said only that I had learned what I needed to know and that someday I would tell her everything.

I won't, of course. I can't. Eventually, however, as winter came on, because I like and trust Anthea more than the others and because she is a few years older than they, I told her some of it. She genuinely wanted to know what had happened and to give me sympathy and comfort if I needed them. Nan and Frieda merely thought it was cool that I had gone to Africa alone, but weren't at all curious as to why I'd gone or what I had learned there, and with them I was glad to let it go. Cat asked only if I'd seen a lot of people dying of AIDS, and I said no, which was the truth.

At Boniface Island I was rescued by the fisherman returning to the island with a jug of water. He paddled me back to the mainland and put me ashore below Mamba Point, where I made my way on foot up the hill and over the peninsula and through the town towards Duport Road. The city of Monrovia was a burnt-out shell of what it once had been. The long civil war and pandemic corruption and the abandonment of Liberia by the Americans had nearly killed it. The walls and houses along the way were splashed with bizarre graffiti, the names, claims, and mottos of madmen, and people on the street stared at me when I walked by, as if I were from a distant planet and my odd resemblance to them were more striking than my difference.

I crossed Tubman Boulevard, and when I passed the old Western Union office, I glanced through the broken window into the dim room and saw in the shadows a man I had once known. His name was Reuben Kanomae, whom I remembered as a spectacled, pipe-smoking fellow proud of his small skill and use to the foreigners and expats in town. A gregarious man in his late sixties, he cultivated warm relations with anyone he thought might need to wire money abroad, including me, although I myself had never required his services. Still, I enjoyed his easy banter and his habit of giving the boys candy when they were with me and had made his shop a regular stop whenever I went downtown. He sat in a corner of his dingy, unlit office slumped on a broken-backed chair beside a huge, no-longer-functioning air-conditioner, poking through an old, torn copy of *Sports Illustrated*. His iron-rimmed spectacles were gone, his eyes were dead, his gaze flat and without expression. I wondered what, if anything, he saw on the pages of the magazine.

I took a small step into the shop. He heard me and looked up slowly, then recognized me. "Miz Sundiata? You back? When you come back?"

"A day ago."

He put the magazine on the floor. "Why?"

"To look for my sons," I said.

He shook his head slowly as if he didn't quite understand.

I said, "You remember them, don't you? My three boys?"

He nodded slowly, as if calling them back to mind one by one.

"I saw you still had your shop, and because you send messages for people, I thought you might have heard or seen . . ."

"I don't got no more shop. All them boys gone now!" he blurted. "Gone!"

"Where?"

"Don't know. Can't say."

I asked him when was the last time he saw them.

His gaze came back into focus. "Long-long time ago," he said. It was after President Doe got killed by Prince Johnson and before Charles Taylor drove Prince Johnson out of the capital. "Them boys, your sons, they got famous for a while. They had famous names, too," he added.

"Peoples all over was very-very scared of them. Scared of all them crazy boys with the guns and the bad names. Still are."

I asked him to tell me their names, and he did. He said that because their father had been a minister in the government of Samuel Doe and their mother was an American white woman, everyone remembered those three. "The big one, the oldest, he call himself Worse-than-Death. The twin boys named Fly and Demonology. Last time I seen 'em, I was hidin' from the soldiers," he said. He wasn't sure whose soldiers they were, but they had smashed up his shop, and he had fled to the roof of the building, where he had a clear view of the body-strewn street below. "There was dead peoples everywhere for a long-long time. That's when I seen 'em." He told me that the two younger boys wore women's nightgowns over their trousers, and the older boy had on orange coveralls and no shirt. All three were carrying guns, all three were wild eyed and grinning, filthy, running from store to store and screaming bloody murder. Until they stopped over the crumpled body of a man. Reuben said they kicked it a few times to be sure the body was dead, then rummaged through the pockets. When they came up empty, the older boy, Worse-than-Death, stripped a watch off the man's wrist and tried in vain to pry off his wedding ring. One of the twins, Fly or Demonology, he wasn't able to tell, reached under his nightgown and pulled a bayonet from his belt and sliced off the ring finger, jammed the bloody end into his mouth and sucked the ring from the finger. Then the boy stuck out his tongue and showed the ring to the others, and when the older brother reached for it, the twin swallowed it and laughed and started running again. The other two followed, and the brothers darted across the deserted street and disappeared from sight.

Slowly I backed from the shop to the street, my sneakers crunching against broken window glass. "After that," Reuben said, his voice rising, "they was just gone! No one saw them boys again, Miz Sundiata!" he called after me. "No one!"

When I got to Duport Road, the gate to our house was open, and there were four young children at play in the yard, white children, three

little girls and a boy of about eight, and they were speaking American English with a southern accent. I told them that I was Hannah Sundiata and
that I had lived in this house a long time ago. The children led me to
their parents inside, a serious, blond couple in their mid-thirties named
Janice and Keith Crown, Evangelical Christians from Ashville, North
Carolina. Janice and Keith were intensely polite and eager to talk with
an American visitor. When I told them who I was, they said that they
knew of me and had heard of my chimpanzee sanctuary at Toby and that
it had been destroyed in the war. The Crowns had been in Liberia and
living in the house, which their church had leased from the government,
for nearly two years. Previously they had worked in Haiti, they said.
After the war ended and Charles Taylor was elected president, their
church had established, with President Taylor's permission and help, a
series of small missionary outposts in the backcountry. Keith, who had
a pilot's license and a single-engine plane, kept the missions supplied
with medical equipment, medicines, schoolbooks, hymnals, mail from
America for the missionaries and Bibles for the natives. Keith and Janice and their children liked the house on Duport Road very much, they
said, and on Sundays Keith conducted religious services for the local
people right here in the living room, although Keith confessed that it was
easier to bring God's word to the natives in the backcountry than here
in Monrovia. In the city, he explained, people had been severely traumatized by the horrors of the war, and many of them had reverted to
Islam and ancient forms of animism. "But people in the bush are very
open to Christ's healing spirit," he said, and Janice agreed.

They asked me if I was a Christian, had I been saved, and I said no,
which seemed not so much to disappoint as to surprise them. This part
of the story I told to Anthea, who like me is not a Christian and has not
been saved but, unlike me, probably doesn't need it. It was the end of
October, and I was at my desk paying the monthly bills. Anthea came
into my office off the kitchen for her pay and, apropos of nothing, at-
tempting perhaps to fill in a blank that I had placed in an earlier version
of my story, asked me what became of my house in Africa. I thought

that she would find the presence of the Crowns in my old home and their Christian missionary zeal ironic and faintly amusing, which she did. But when she asked if the Crowns knew anything about my sons, since I had already mentioned that the couple knew who I was and had heard about my sanctuary, I lied and said no and wrote out her check and gave it to her.

The Crowns hadn't been in the country long, but they had friends in high places, as Sam Clement used to say, among them President Taylor himself, whom they claimed to have personally introduced to Jesus Christ, causing the president to be born again, they told me, adding that I should not believe the ugly rumors of barbarism, corruption, and decadence sown by his enemies here and abroad. Charles Taylor had many enemies, they explained, especially among tribal leaders who did not want him bringing Jesus to this benighted land.

When I asked them if the president considered me one of his enemies, they looked away, for it was difficult for them to lie. Keith said that the president knew that in the war my sons had supported Prince Johnson, who was his enemy and was hiding in Guinea and still plotting to overthrow him. Janice added that the president also knew about my husband and that he had supported Samuel Doe, and he knew, of course, that in the war, when the fighting reached Monrovia, I had left for America alone.

"What are you telling me?"

Keith walked to the door and told the children to go back outside and play. Janice was silent for a moment. "We're not apologizing for Charles Taylor," she said. "It was a brutal war, people on all sides did terrible things. Both during the war and afterwards. And we're not judging you, Missus Sundiata. Only God can do that."

Keith took his wife's hand in his and in a soothing tone said to me, "In this house we often pray for you. And we pray for the souls of your sons and your husband. Surely, Jesus has forgiven them. Just as He will forgive you, if only you ask. Seek, and you shall find salvation, Missus Sundiata."

I tried to explain that my husband had been murdered by Samuel Doe's men, one of whom was known to us, and that my sons and I had witnessed it, and that my sons had joined Prince Johnson solely to avenge their father's murder, not to oppose Charles Taylor. But that was my story, my truth, not Charles Taylor's, and although they did not contradict me or call me a liar, the Crowns would have none of it. They nodded and looked at me with pity and a craven hunger to save me from myself.

It was a hunger that I would not let them satisfy. Without warning I told them that my husband's body was buried in their flower garden, which surprised and confused them. "And I would like to be alone there for a few moments," I said. I told them that my husband was a Christian, and they could put a little cross over his grave there and continue praying for his soul, if they wished. "I'd also like to see my boys' bedroom, if that's all right. And then I'll leave."

There is not much more to tell. It was September 10, 2001, and one dark era was about to end and another, darker era to begin, one in which my story could never have happened, my life not possibly been lived. I stood at the edge of the garden at the side of the house where Sam claimed to have buried Woodrow's body and waited for my husband's ghost to rise from the flowers and punish me, as the ghosts of my dreamers had done. But he was no longer there. I was alone in the garden. In spite of the Crowns' prayers for the salvation of his soul, Woodrow had gone to be with his ancestors in Fuama.

And when I went back inside the house and stood in my boys' bedroom, I was alone there, too. Their spirits had long since disappeared from the room, replaced by the bright spirits of the four children who slept there now. My sons were with their father and their African ancestors. And it made me glad. They were with their people, the people who, living and dead, were loving them in death as I had never been able to love them in life.

I came back to the living room and prepared to leave. The Crowns asked me to stay the night with them, for it was dark by then and dangerous on the streets of Monrovia. I accepted their offer, and later, during dinner, Keith mentioned in passing that the next morning he had to fly supplies from the small in-town airport to their mission outpost in Ganta, close to the border of Côte d'Ivoire. I asked if he would take me there with him, so that I could cross out of the country and return to the States from Abidjan, the way I had come in. This was perfectly agreeable to him, he said, but why not fly out from Robertsfield? I explained that I had entered Liberia illegally without a visa and did not want to alert the authorities, especially the president, to my presence in the country. I said that I was, indeed, Charles Taylor's enemy. And that is how I got to Abidjan, where I boarded a Ghana Airways flight to New York and made my way home to a nation terrorized and grieving on a scale that no American had imagined before, a nation whose entire history was being rapidly rewritten. In the months that followed, I saw that the story of my life could have no significance in the larger world. In the new history of America, mine was merely the story of an American darling, and had been from the beginning.

ACKNOWLEDGMENTS

SPECIAL THANKS are owed to my assistant, Nancy Wilson, for her help with much of the research; to my agent, Ellen Levine, whose support and friendship have sustained me for, lo, these many years; and to my editor and friend, Dan Halpern, whose tact, intelligence, and trust guided me throughout the writing of this book.

Also, heartfelt thanks to Bela Amarasekaran of the Tacagama Chimpanzee Sanctuary, Freetown, Sierra Leone; Sally Boysen at Ohio State University, Columbus, Ohio; Gloria Grow of the Fauna Foundation, Chambly, Quebec; and the many other individuals around the world who have dedicated their lives to saving chimpanzees from medical experimentation, abuse as entertainers and pets, and outright extermination.

BOOKS BY RUSSELL BANKS

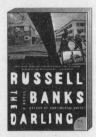

THE DARLING
A Novel
ISBN 0-06-095735-2 (paperback)
ISBN 0-694-52423-9 (unabridged CD)
A political/historical thriller of terrorism,
political violence, race, and cultures.

CONTINENTAL DRIFT
ISBN 0-06-095673-9 (paperback)
A story of love and sex, racism and poverty,
and the failures of the American dream.

THE SWEET HEREAFTER
A Novel
ISBN 0-06-092324-5 (paperback)
A small-town morality play that asks: When
the worst thing happens, who do you blame?

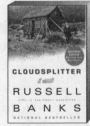

CLOUDSPLITTER
A Novel
ISBN 0-06-093086-1 (paperback)
A dazzling re-creation of the political and
social landscape before the Civil War.

THE ANGEL ON THE ROOF
The Stories of Russell Banks
ISBN 0-06-093125-6 (paperback)
Thirty years of Banks's best short fiction,
including eight new stories.

RULE OF THE BONE
A Novel
ISBN 0-06-092724-0 (paperback)
A journey of self-discovery through a world
of magic, violence, betrayal, and redemption.

AFFLICTION
ISBN 0-06-092007-6 (paperback)
Spellbinding and inexorable as a fuse
burning its way to a stick of dynamite.

FAMILY LIFE
ISBN 0-06-097704-3 (paperback)
Transforms the dramas of domesticity into
the story of a royal family in a mythical
contemporary kingdom.

HAMILTON STARK
ISBN 0-06-097705-1 (paperback)
A thoroughly engaging story of life on the
cold edge of New England.

THE RELATION OF
MY IMPRISONMENT
ISBN 0-06-097680-2 (paperback)
A work of fiction utilizing a form invented
in the seventeenth century by imprisoned
Puritan divines.

SUCCESS STORIES
ISBN 0-06-092719-4 (paperback)
Explores the ethos of rampant materialism in
a group of contemporary moral fables.

TRAILERPARK
ISBN 0-06-097706-X (paperback)
A portrait of New England life that is at
once dark, witty, and revealing.

THE BOOK OF JAMAICA
ISBN 0-06-097707-8 (paperback)
"A compelling novel....Banks achieves effects
at once beautiful and brutal. A virtuoso
performance." —*Publishers Weekly*